Confessions

of the Meek

and the Valiant

By

Steven R. Porter

Confessions of the Meek and the Valiant
by Steven R. Porter

Print Edition
2011

Books and other works created by Steven R. Porter can be obtained either through the author's official website: http://www.stevenporter.com or through superior retailers.

Published by the author.
ISBN-10: 1-46354-200-3
ISBN-13: 978-1-46354-200-9

Cover design by Dawn M. Porter and Steven R. Porter.

To Dawn:

without whom I and this book are incomplete

May 19, 2011

PROLOGUE

There are 1,225 inmates in the overcrowded maximum security wing of the cold, gray Souza-Baranowski Correctional Center, representing 1,225 tales of terror, woe, heartbreak and dread; tales of wrongful arrest, mistaken identity, legal incompetence, misunderstanding, and morality tales of misdirected revenge.

There are also 1,225 tear-jerking sagas from the 1,225 mothers of those inmates who swear their boys were all good boys, altar boys, friendly, smart and full of life -- all with loving friends and caring families. And each with a set of clueless neighbors who make tired statements to reporters like, "he seemed like such a nice boy" or "I never thought he would have done such a thing -- there must be some mistake."

This is the story of the 1,225th inmate -- a likable and friendly fellow named Riley Lynch who drove his sedan over the head of a notorious underworld kingpin squishing it like a vandalized Halloween pumpkin, killing him stone dead, and who then felt mighty good about it.

O N E

Riley Lynch awoke to the shuffling of a little girl's sensible patent leather shoes along the gritty sidewalk outside his second floor apartment window. At first annoyed by the interruption of the first good sleep he had enjoyed in a year, he smiled and a warm wave of contentment enveloped him. Other children were gathering outside his window, too, tittering and chattering, no doubt waiting for the arrival of the morning school bus.

Riley's roommate, Mikeé, was not as sentimental. Also rustled by the noise, he groaned, rolled over, and muttered unintelligible obscenities to himself.

Riley had just enjoyed his first night outside of Massachusetts's maximum security Souza-Baranowski Correctional Center, or SBCC. His unexpected release caught everyone by surprise -- he had been sentenced to 35 years to life for the murder of a business associate and didn't even have a parole hearing listed on the prison docket. He was hustled to the prison administrative offices late in the afternoon, told to sign some papers, and was whisked out the prison's rear gate in a private car before he had a chance to absorb what was happening. It wasn't until last evening when he checked into the room with Mikeé at St. Peter's Center (sort of a halfway house to house recent parolees waiting for a permanent residence) that the veracity of his unexpected freedom began to sink in.

The colder than normal November air gushed into the room when he opened the dirty window to watch the kids at the bus stop. The air, rich with car exhaust and a bitter urban dust, filled his mouth and lungs with purpose, and he welcomed the frosty twinge deep in his chest. There were a few surprise snow flurries in the air as one of those cruel Alberta clipper cold fronts was pushing through New England, reminding everyone of the harsh winter that was assembling its legions just over the western horizon. The kids didn't seem to be bothered by the cold air or biting wind one bit, and

1

wrestled through it like a litter of cavorting puppies. All their moms huddled together clutching Styrofoam coffee cups, each one wrapped and bundled with more vigor than the next, and had they brought along their Sherpa guides, they would have been prepared to survive any Himalayan expedition. They hopped up and down together like players in a choreographed amateur community ballet. To the moms' relief and gratitude no doubt, a yellow bus appeared and approached them from the corner.

"What the hell are you doin'? Close the damn window! I am freezing to death over here," Mikeé exclaimed.

"Oh stop your whining, this is a glorious day. A great day to be alive."

Mikeé Evans was a beast of a man, over six and a half feet tall and appeared to many to also be six and a half feet wide. He made the cheap cot he spent the night sleeping on look like it belonged stashed away in a little girl's doll house. The sight of the top of his big, bald, black head protruding from beneath the epic mound of his snow white blanket created a frightening sight, as if a coroner had thrown a body blanket over a dead giant. A stranger might find it hard to believe there was just one person inside the mound. Riley and Mikeé had become good friends as part of the morning kitchen crew in the prison cafeteria. They were both clever enough to figure out on their own that volunteering for the unpopular, pre-sunrise work shift in the kitchen meant they had access to the prison's food supply when it was still fresh off the supply trucks, offering a chance to enjoy the not so spoiled parts, and before the first shift guards took all the blueberry muffins. It was by sheer coincidence that they were paroled and assigned to St. Peter's at the same time.

"Come on and get up, Mikeé... I smell breakfast and we're not cooking."

"Oh that does smell somethin' sweet now, don't it?"

Never known to be late for any meal, Mikeé glided downstairs first, and joined a rag tag collection of a dozen other recent parolees for breakfast in a community room that served as the St. Peter' Center's place to watch TV, play cards and enjoy a meal. A large, new, widescreen HD-TV sat in the corner and babbled on about traffic, stocks and the unseasonably cold weather. Mrs. Cavanaugh was St. Peter's house mother and program supervisor, a spry elderly woman in her mid seventies so full of energy she outpaced women half her age. Her "boys" (as she preferred to call them) huddled around a breakfast table too small for half of them, and the sight of the arrival of Mikeé and his girth caused a collective groan. Mikeé took his seat between two of them, and with one purposeful deep breath, spread his elbows, and moved all twelve men at the same time. Mikeé's sheer size, giant white teeth, bulging white eyes, and ear to ear grin, were the only things preventing a fresh, new murder.

Mikeé enjoyed an evil chuckle, "*Heh... heh... heh.*"

"Oh, my," Mrs. Cavanaugh said, "*what a big boy you are!*" And from behind, Mrs. C put her head on Mikeé's shoulder and gave him a wide, creepy bear hug. Her pale, wrinkled arms didn't reach all the way around him. Mikeé's back stiffened and he scrunched-up his face. He endured an eerie feeling of discomfort as her hands slid down his thick arms and massaged his biceps. The tone of his chuckle had changed.

"*Heh... heh... heh?*"

One of the men noticed Riley on the stairs, and all waxed silent as Riley descended. A few of the men stood up.

"Good morning, Mr. Lynch."

"How are you, Mr. Lynch?"

"Here, take my seat, Mr. Lynch.

"A pleasure to see you, sir."

Riley was used to the attention. Before he could complete the act of sitting he was handed a plate overflowing with eggs and hash browns from one direction and an extra large mug of hot, steaming coffee from another. Mrs. C offered him a nervous yet reassuring pat on the shoulder.

"You just let me know what you need, my boy. I'll take care of everything."

"Thank you, ma'am."

All eyes were on Riley as he savored his first home-cooked bite of non-prison food in months. Mrs. C was an exceptional cook, and the rich flavor of the buttery hash browns and fluffy yellow eggs distracted him. The cons continued their polite and silent vigil until Riley opened his eyes and looked up from his plate. He glanced with precision to the right, then glanced with precision to the left, and then with the flair of a 17th century monarch, he instructed the table with a brief expressionless nod that he was satisfied with the offering and it was now acceptable to continue the meal. And as if someone had fired a starter's pistol, the men sprinted into their breakfast.

No sooner had the normalcy of chaos been restored, then the room once again fell into an uneasy silence.

...and now breaking news from Boston's Channel 9 News Center. I'm Marcia Small. Channel 9 has learned that mob boss and convicted murderer Riley Angus Lynch has been released from the Souza-Baranowski Correctional Center. Lynch was convicted in the grisly killing of well-known mob associate and Los Angeles restaurateur Giovanni "The Chef" Marcellino. The Attorney General's office will be holding a press conference later this afternoon. We will be bringing you that press conference live. Stay tuned to News Center 9 for continuing updates as we...

"Your middle name is *Angus?*" Mikeé inquired. "*Heh... heh... heh.*" Riley smiled and said nothing. No one else dared laugh.

Mikeé was not as intimidated by Riley's presence as the other parolees. Although they had met and become friends in the prison kitchen, Mikeé knew all about Riley through his own connections in the New England and New York criminal underworld. Mikeé had served just two years of a seven year sentence for racketeering after being caught running a very lucrative gambling enterprise on behalf of a New York strip club owner. (Mikeé insisted he was framed.) He knew Riley's name from the scuttlebutt on the street but didn't meet him until they were both assigned to slice bread one morning at SBCC. Mikeé was never one for watching much television or reading newspapers, so he had missed most of the sensationalized trial that made Riley Lynch a local, and notorious, celebrity. And although friends, both men were intelligent enough not to trust the other.

Following the news report, Mrs. C wasted no time leaving the room, zipping about the three story house closing windows and securing the door latches. She knew what would happen next. It wouldn't take long for the reporters to figure out where Riley was staying, and she assumed that at least one of the fine, upstanding young men at her breakfast table would no doubt already be dialing their cell phone.

"What do you think, Mr. Lynch? What are they going to say?" One of the men inquired.

"Don't know... don't care," he responded, with a terse and unemotional demeanor. "The AG never did get much right anyway. It's just more grandstanding. He's going to explain how it's possible that a convicted murderer gets released and it's not his fault."

"So whose fault is it?"

"It's not anybody's fault. But that is one hell of a good question."

Riley's brief early morning moment of contentment was gone, replaced by the sudden anxiety of notoriety. He never wanted to be famous, never mind infamous. He had started to accept the permanence of his life behind bars and didn't expect to ever see true freedom again. Hope, in all forms, had been abandoned. And these mood swings were now exhausting him.

"Oh dear, oh dear!" Mrs. C whispered peering into the street from the front door, wringing her cupped hands high on her chest. Three black Lincoln Town Cars had appeared along the curb at the front of the Center. Two large men with the letters FBI emblazoned on their sweatshirts hustled toward the building and glided through the Center's doorway, dusting by Mrs. C as if she was cloaked in invisibility.

"Mr. Lynch, come with us." One of the agents demanded.

"Am I being arrested? I'm not going anywhere without my lawyer."

"I am Agent Manning, This is agent Wills. You are not under arrest, but it would be in your best interest to come with us now. Mr. Ward will be waiting for you when we arrive."

From the moment he was notified of his impending release, Riley had been trying to reach his defense attorney, Malcolm Ward, but could only get through to his answering service. Riley surmised Ward was off on some Jamaican holiday with a sassy new office paralegal -- again -- and wouldn't be heard from for a long while. Ward had represented Riley in the murder trial, and although he lost the case -- with intense public scrutiny -- his willingness to be perceived as a brash mob lawyer, along with his flowing white hair and a dark, mysterious avant-garde look, guaranteed his future professional, and financial success.

"You've heard from Malcolm? Where are you taking me?"

"That's classified, sir. We'll tell you when we get there."

The rhythmic purr of a news helicopter could be heard near the Center, it was getting louder, and was the only encouragement Riley required to go along with the agents. Outside, a gathering storm of vehicles in all shapes and sizes were assembling along the boulevard including a limousine, several police cruisers and then a second deafening helicopter. A news truck with a satellite dish mounted on the roof, so large it wanted to capsize, drove up onto the sidewalk, scattering bewildered pedestrians and the leftover bus stop moms. With one hand, Agent Wills grabbed Riley by the back of his pants and tossed him into the back seat of the Town Car like a sack of dirty laundry. Through the frenzy of blowing snow flurries, lying on the back seat, Riley could see what looked like a police sniper stationed on top of the factory across the block.

"Like vultures circling over a fresh kill," Mikeé muttered as chattering reporters with microphones popped up like April tulips all along the sidewalk. Mrs. C had bolted the door, but the others struggled to peer through whatever grimy window they could find. One of the men unbuckled his pants, pirouetted, and mooned the TV cameras from the dining room window, and was able to watch his pale, pimpled bottom across the room on the new widescreen TV, in high definition.

"Looks like Mr. Lynch gonna have a busy day. Heh... heh... heh." Mikeé declared.

The three black Town Cars sped away.

T W O

Throughout his life, Riley Lynch was never the type of person who ever chose to make a scene or even wanted to be noticed for that matter, and being physically average in every way, he was content to blend unnoticed into any group. Riley was smart, or scary smart as an elementary teacher once described him in a news interview following his arrest, and what he lacked in social grace he made up for in intelligence and cunning ingenuity.

It wouldn't be until much later in life that he appreciated how badly people would always need him.

Way back in eighth grade at South Boston Middle School, he developed a mad but secret crush on a pretty classmate named Tammy Meeks. She was shy, petite, well-dressed, soft and quiet, and on the rare occasion when she would look his direction, her big brown eyes would drown him, and he would look away as if he had glanced into the piercing rays of the sun. Riley was careful to never sit in front of her in class, and though it was rare for her to utter a word to anyone, he didn't mind and took innocent pleasure in the simple rhythm of her breathing as it soothed and warmed him. When a teacher would call on her to answer a question, she would blush on cue -- and he would blush right along with her bearing witness to both their acute social anxieties -- and would cheer and celebrate in silence when she answered the question right. Once she missed school for an entire week, and Riley's overactive imagination concocted an array of off-beat fantasies explaining her absence. Maybe she had been kidnapped, or perhaps was lying in a ditch somewhere bleeding to death. (It turned out that she had gone on a surprise Vermont ski vacation with her family). If the teacher assigned Tammy a male partner for some sort of class project, the rush of jealousy would cause his teeth to clench and his fists to stiffen. And on those days when the teacher droned on, and the

7

weather was warm, and an enticing spring breeze whirled through the classroom, he would stare from behind at the gentle curve of her cheek and imagine the two of them walking together on the spongy carpet of needles in the old pine forest behind the city park. Here, he would share his innermost thoughts, and she would always be smiling and laughing. And in his daydream, he wouldn't dare look away but would instead stare with power and confidence into her cavernous brown eyes. She would always smile, close her eyes and lay her sweet head upon his chest.

Though he wasn't sure if she knew his name.

It was unimaginable to Riley that anyone could find any flaw with Tammy whatsoever -- in his mind, she was perfect in every way. But Tammy's innocent childhood had been pillaged by the evil Yvonne Tannen -- a bully of epic proportions even by eighth grade middle school standards. Yvonne was tall, blonde, and wore a faded army jacket that up close smelled of mildew, cigarettes, sloth and decay, and who sported big, bony shoulders wider than those of most boys her age. The sane, observant children knew to stay out of her way, but it didn't stop her from preying upon the weak and defenseless just the same. And that year in eighth grade, poor sweet Tammy, as innocent as a grazing gazelle on the savannah, became tasty fresh meat for the school's most dominant and hungry lioness.

It all began with juvenile nasty name calling, such as: "Hey, loser..." "Hey, pig..." "Hey, slut..." and worse, and the negative attention escalated every day. Each time Yvonne, with chest pumped out and shoulders back, would strut past Tammy's desk, Tammy's books would be victimized and fall, and loose papers would flutter down to her feet. Yvonne would grin and circle, but Tammy never looked up, instead, she would blush, the corners of her lips would turn down and with steadfast determination, she would stare at her desk waiting for the torment of the moment to end. All eyes in the room would fix on the two, including Riley's, whose gaze was firm and whose head was bursting with heat and fire. He swore he could feel and see the waves of fear emanate from Tammy's body, and he wanted to absorb them for her like a telepathic sponge. Riley fantasized about making a chivalrous charge and pounding the snot out of Yvonne in front of everyone, slaying the dragon, but Riley had never struck anyone in anger, and wasn't sure how to go about it. And he had to accept that Yvonne was much more powerful than he was, and the mere thought of the humiliation that would ensue from being beaten-up by a girl was more than anything he could endure. So day after day, Tammy would absorb the punishment and pain alone, and Riley, too immature, too much of a coward and too ill-equipped to help would watch within his own self-imposed torture chamber from across the room.

Yet despite his own fear, he felt compelled to do something, there was no one else, so Riley appointed himself Tammy's secret, private sentinel. He stalked Yvonne and studied her tendencies, memorized her class schedule, remembered where she liked to hang out, the amount of time it took to get to her locker, the amount of time she spent in the lavatory, and the length of time it took to eat her lunch. He wrote ample remarks, filled a notebook with observations, and discovered that Yvonne would terrorize Tammy eighty percent of the time during three critical moments of the school day -- at second lunch, then during Mrs. Beckmeir's anarchic honors English class, and finally at dismissal, when the girls walked past the rows of buses on their way home. Riley then went about creating diversions as each of these key moments would come up. As the girls reached the buses on Monday, Riley pushed his buddy Donnie into a bus monitor sending the monitor's hot coffee spewing across both Yvonne and Tammy, resulting in an innocent and befuddled Donnie getting one day's detention. On Tuesday, when Yvonne started to approach Tammy in English class, he persuaded his friend Anthony to belch the first few lines of Hamlet's famous Act 3 soliloquy, which annoyed Mrs. Beckmeir but was guaranteed to keep her attention:

"To be or not to be, that is the question. Whether tis nobler in the mind to suffer the slings and arrows of outrageous fortune... blaaaaaatch."

And then on Wednesday, Riley saw Yvonne heading for Tammy at lunch and read on her face an intense and rabid determination. He was in the process of paying for several ice cream sandwiches from Agnes the lunch lady and was going to give them away free to create a scene, guaranteed to attract Yvonne, but Agnes interfered.

"Sorry Mr. Lynch, you are allowed to have just one ice cream sandwich per day." Agnes said.

"But these aren't for me, they're for my friends."

"Then let your friends come up and buy them themselves. The school nutrition policy says you can have one. It's not healthy. You will get fat."

Now short on time, Riley paid for one and headed for the girls, but realized he wouldn't make it. To his right on the wall was the red school fire alarm and before he could think about what he was doing, he pulled it and ran. The deafening alarm screamed through the lunchroom, and everyone jumped up, stuffed a last bite of sandwich in their mouths, and headed for the exit doors as they had been drilled so many times before. For Riley, it was a pure, selfless act of love and bravery well out of his character. Following the fire drill, after the fine men of the Boston Fire Department had declared the building safe and drove away in their bright red trucks, every known troublemaker in the school was called down to Principal Leonard's office one at a time. Mild-mannered Riley was not included on the guest list, and it became evident that no one in the school suspected him. Riley never knew it, but Yvonne had been called to the office first, claimed to be an eyewitness, and fingered Riley as the culprit. Principal Leonard laughed. Riley? Not likely. The principal's inquest was a complete failure. The interrogation netted no suspect. No one was ever accused or punished for pulling the false alarm that day. Tammy was saved from the bully's wrath one more time.

Riley was never late to class, or ever missed a day of school -- except once. His mother had brought him to the dentist that morning, and then hopped the bus to the mall to run a few quick errands where they enjoyed a rare one-on-one lunch together without interference from his six brothers and sisters. Riley's mom, Sarah Lynch, worked two jobs and raised her seven children by herself, her husband Seamus Lynch had disappeared from family life before Riley was born. Riley walked into class feeling pretty special that day, and couldn't wait to tell his friends about his morning and all the wonderful reasons why he was late.

Mrs. Wanda Beckmeir was South Boston Middle School's grouchy old, polyester-clad English teacher. Her classroom was disheveled and always too hot, forever warmed by the collective trapped exhales of hundreds of bored pre-teens, but always accented with a subtle whiff from whatever packaged, high calorie snack food was hidden in the top drawer of her desk that day. Decades old posters covered the walls of her classroom, many torn or falling, and

10

all were yellowed and faded. The room was always loud and discipline non-existent. Students learned it was a lot like recess, except it was right before recess.

When he marched with confidence through the classroom door that day, he stopped cold in paralyzed terror.

The class of twenty or so boys and girls of Mrs. Beckmeir's English class stood in a circle, chanting, "*Hit her again harder, hit her again* (clap) (clap)... *Hit her again harder, hit her again* (clap, clap)."

Riley realized he had not been there that morning to protect Tammy.

Tammy lay on her back on the floor with Yvonne sitting on her chest; Yvonne's knees were holding down Tammy's arms and Yvonne was pounding her with a right fist, then a left fist across her bloodied face. Tammy was screaming in horror, and her legs were kicking in all directions sending one of her black patent leather shoes high in the air and toward the door. Riley found he had forgotten how to breathe or speak, and his legs wouldn't move. The beating lasted seconds though for Riley and Tammy, time had stopped dead making it feel like hours. From out of nowhere two teachers charged into the room. Mrs. Beckmeir had felt overwhelmed when the fight started, and darted out to get Mr. Aronson from the math class across the hall to provide reinforcement. Mr. Aronson, who also served as the assistant football coach, utilized the efficiency of his burly frame and grabbed Yvonne by the back of her grubby, stinking army jacket, lifting the big girl up with one hand and dragging her out of the room, arms flailing. Yvonne swore like a midshipman as she passed through the door and disappeared up the hall.

Mrs. Beckmeir cradled Tammy's bludgeoned face in her arms. A gory design of blood, snot, spit and tears painted the front of the teacher's yellow cardigan and overstuffed blue polyester pants, and Tammy gasped for air and wailed. The once unruly flash mob of eighth grade cowards now stood silent. A shrill Mrs. Beckmeir barked at them.

"Everyone, get to your seats! Immediately! Now! Oh my dear Tammy, let's get you down to the nurse and get you cleaned up, honey."

The minute Tammy and Mrs. Beckmeir left, the class burst into loud conversation all at once as everyone started chattering on cue.

11

"Holy shit, Riley, did you see that? Where the hell were you? You almost missed it, that was un-freakin'-believable." Anthony said as if it was the most exciting moment he had ever witnessed.

"I had a dentist appointment," Riley explained, heart racing, still trying to catch his breath and trying not to cry or vomit. "My mom just dropped me off. Does anyone know how it started?"

"Tammy got destroyed!" Donnie chimed in, "I'm glad Yvonne likes me, she is friggin insane. Tammy is a whack-job anyway, I'm guessing she deserved it. I don't know what she did to Yvonne, but it must have been something good. Tammy just sits there and never says anything to anybody; I wonder what she's hiding? She's just weird."

"Yea, Tammy's weird and gross," Riley said to his own astonishment. He had failed to protect her, his guilt ran deep, and he knew that because of the great impenetrable and immature caste system of middle school society, he could never admit fondness for someone now so ugly, unfeminine and humiliated. Tammy was now beneath him. It was an unwritten rule that to retain one's stature at the top, one must look down upon the dirty, strange outcasts below and work hard to keep them there.

When the bell rang and the classroom emptied, Riley fell back and was the last to leave. He retrieved Tammy's missing shoe placing it on her desk with both hands like the laying of a wreath on a fallen serviceman's open grave.

The very next day, Yvonne was back in class being the same rotten, evil kid she had always been as if the fight never happened, bullying others at random, auditioning new, fresh victims. Outside the classroom window, Riley caught a brief glimpse of the Meeks' family van with Tammy strapped in the front seat, arriving on school grounds. Within the hour, the van was gone. Riley and his friends surmised that there were some intense meetings happening with Principal Leonard and Tammy's mom and dad at that very moment. They were right. Part of Riley never wanted to see her again and hoped she would just disappear, while in his heart, he craved her presence, her essence, her being, and her every breath.

Riley stayed after school that day along with Anthony and Donnie to attend the middle school baseball game against cross town rival Roxbury. The three boys didn't care much for baseball, but it was an excuse to hang out and fool around and avoid homework --

plus Mr. Aronson always gave extra credit to athletic boosters. The fight between Yvonne and Tammy was already fading from the collective memories of most of the class, replaced by new fights and melodrama, and was taking its place among the great stories of middle school lore, but not for Riley. Riley stood at his locker depressed and teeming in anger. He was angry at himself for not being there; he was angry at the evil creature Yvonne for the senseless violence she had unleashed; he was angry at Tammy for not saying anything or fighting back; but most of all, he was angry at Tammy for shattering all the fanciful daydreams and fantasies that gave him hope for true love.

From his locker, he could hear Mr. Aronson and Principal Leonard talking through the thin walls of the English room.

"We need to separate the Tannen girl from the Meeks girl," Principal Leonard began.

"That crazy Tannen kid is NOT coming into my room," Aronson shot back. "I already have my hands full with the other two animals you sent me last month. I don't have to take her. And I'm not taking the Meeks kid either. I am too crowded."

"Look Bob, we can't leave them together. If anything else happens, it's my ass. I spent an hour with the Meeks' lawyer this morning. We have to keep this girl safe."

"Why don't you just tell Wanda to control her own damn class? We have watched Yvonne bully Tammy all month. Wanda is afraid of Yvonne's fucked-up parents; you know that -- so she won't even look at her never mind reprimand her. That's where the real problem is. We have all watched Tammy get abused. It's Wanda's responsibility to do her job, why is it always mine to do it for her?" And Mr. Aronson stormed past Riley and back across the hall.

A cold wave of realization came over Riley.

They knew.

They knew all along. They knew Tammy was being victimized, dissected like a jigsaw puzzle piece by piece, and they watched from their selfish perches as those pieces were shredded and cast into the wind, each along with a little piece of Tammy's soul lost forever. They knew what Yvonne was doing to her every step of the way -- and they didn't care... not one bit. They watched and let it happen. It didn't matter to any of them. The *bastards*.

13

By the end of the week, Tammy returned to sit in her usual seat, her face still swollen, her once soft pink cheeks replaced by lifeless gray bruises from Yvonne's vicious assault, on display for all the world to see. Yvonne sat in the back of the room. Riley tried not to look at either of the girls again.

After eighth grade, Riley and his classmates graduated on to South Boston High School, though not Tammy. That summer, the Meeks family moved away. He would never be able to forget her.

THREE

The Lynch family existed in an old, cramped, three bedroom apartment on East Broadway, just above Murphy's Used Bookshop, in an Irish Catholic lower middle class neighborhood a few miles south of downtown Boston. One of Riley's favorite pastimes was to browse through the musty boxes of new arrivals in the back of the bookshop before old Mr. Murphy had a chance to sort them out. It was here where he learned all of life's lessons in the absence of his father -- from Asimov, Pohl, Heinlein and Wells, or from Christie, Conan-Doyle, Poe and Wolfe; or from Orwell, Huxley, Verne and Thoreau. And he learned all he needed to know about girls and sex from Anais Nin and D.H. Lawrence, or so he thought. Mr. Murphy let the family borrow as much as they liked for free, and in a family with little discretionary income, it was popular entertainment. Riley's apartment was a favorite hangout for his friends, too, as there was always some activity going on, and if things got boring, the boys would slip down to the bookshop for impromptu browsing, hoping to discover a discarded *Playboy* or *Penthouse* magazine buried among the great pyramids of paperbacks, *Readers Digest*, and *National Geographic*.

Riley was lucky to be the youngest of seven and to have three older brothers and three older sisters to care for and fuss over him when his mother was at work. His mother Sarah worked two different menial jobs to make ends meet -- one as a part-time secretary to a local real estate developer, and the other as a cashier at the Blue Hills Wal-Mart.

Sarah Lynch was an absolute wonder of a woman, thin, plain and mousy but with a bottomless store of energy -- Riley never remembered her ever being tired. (Many years later at her funeral, Riley commented to his sister Meghan that she looked all wrong, as it was the first time he had seen her lying down.) Sarah could work two jobs, clean house, prepare gourmet meals for eight, pay bills, shuttle the kids to school for activities, and still have time to volunteer at church, read romance novels, crochet, and chat on the phone for what seemed like hours with her nosy sister Eileen. Sarah would be hovering about the apartment whistling show tunes when Riley woke in the morning, and would still be humming when he went to sleep at night. He assumed she never turned cross, and did not sleep.

Riley never met his father Seamus who ran off a few days before he was born. Only his eldest brothers and sisters remembered their father much at all, and those memories were fading. Seamus Lynch was a dark and mysterious man, a licensed plumber by trade, and was a true son of a bitch (as his Aunt Eileen called him) who would turn up every year or so in a conciliatory mood, bearing money and exotic gifts for the kids, and who would stay just long enough to impregnate Sarah then disappear again. Sarah claimed she never knew where he went, though she was able to figure it out sometimes from the papers the sheriffs served or from the questions from the police detectives' periodic visits. No one would have blamed Sarah if she had divorced dashing Seamus the bum years earlier, and many encouraged it, but she found the concept morally offensive and wouldn't hear of it -- she never considered it to be an option. Seamus Lynch had not been heard from in the many years since Riley's birth, and though no one would admit it aloud, they assumed he was no longer alive.

When Riley was 13, his brothers (Sean, Ryan and Liam) were 19, 17 and 14, while his sisters (Erin, Meghan and Siobhan were 21, 15 and 14) respectively -- Siobhan and Liam were twins. Mr. Murphy called the children the "Irish Septuplets" with great affection. And though Erin and Sean were both adults, they still lived at home and tried to contribute to the family well-being as much as they could.

Both Seamus' and Sarah's families traced their roots in the old neighborhood back over 150 years, having arrived with the immigrants from Ireland in the 1820's. They came to the new world to sweat and toil in the old textile mill which still stands refurbished now as an artists' colony a few blocks away. East Broadway was the heart and soul of the Irish community both then and now, populated by row upon row of tightly constructed three-story, flat-topped red brick buildings, most with identical faded green awnings and frilly white curtains. The lower level of most buildings serve as some sort of shop or restaurant, each owned and operated by an Irish merchant whose family's roots in the community were well established. (Except for Theodora's Greek Restaurant on the corner who, as Mr. Murphy used to say was allowed to stay because, "the Irish can't make good pizza... and Mr. Theodora wasn't Italian.") Pride in the neighborhood kept the streets safe and clean, and would only became disorderly on weekend evenings when the pubs would fill with drunken suburbanites creating trouble to excite their dull, meaningless lives.

Many of the pubs had private backrooms where local and trusted men could still hang out, visit and play cribbage, nine card don or penny ante poker. Sarah lived in constant fear of these rooms. During her childhood, the notorious Winter Hill Gang would meet in the Dog Rose Pub below her parents' apartment, and she would talk about how her father would stay awake nights listening for any sign of disagreement, terrified that misdirected bullets would launch up through the floor killing his family in their sleep.

In the Sixties and Seventies, the FBI had pretty much wiped out the murderous old street gangs and chased the organized criminals out of town, ending a dark and brutal era in the neighborhood. But the street legends and lore remained, and the men would still gather in the pubs to share stories of life in the neighborhood when men were men, the world was right, the community was one, and the Southies ruled New England.

And it was the mythology and legend that Sarah feared most -- that Riley, Sean, Ryan or Liam, would become attracted to these patriotic war stories and would join all the other young mob wannabes who were caught up in the romance and intrigue of the past. Even though he was just 19 and not yet of legal drinking age, Riley's oldest brother Sean was already hanging around the dank pub backrooms, drinking with the boys, and not coming home until the wee hours smelling of beer and exhale.

Sarah prayed to God for her children's safety, well-being and mortal soul every day. She and Eileen built a small but elegant altar in a spare closet in the family's already cramped apartment, complete with statues, candles, chalices and ornate holy relics, to save busy Sarah the time of walking all the way down the block to St. Finian's for her daily worship and prayer. It wasn't uncommon for older, pious neighbors to drop in unannounced from time to time, often during spats of bad weather, for an opportunity to pray, and gossip. Sarah would almost always share a Hail Mary with them. The Catholic faith

17

was an essential part of all their lives, it fueled Sarah's every breath, and she would demand respect and allegiance to their faith from each of her children at all times.

Sarah's proudest moment would occur many years later when Ryan was ordained a priest and had she lived to see it; her darkest would have been Riley's arrest and subsequent imprisonment for the mob related murder of Giovanni Marcellino. Ironic it is that both these paths began in St. Finian's CCD classes on Spring Street.

St. Finian's, a glorious, gothic, white marble church was home to the neighborhood Catholic community, served as a place of worship, and was the area's largest soup kitchen, meeting hall and parochial school to the neighborhood. The church was created over 100 years earlier from the sweat and inspiration of the neighborhood's Irish immigrants who constructed pointed spires so tall Riley assumed they reached through the clouds to the heavens themselves; its ceilings high and proud, and its large windows stained and intimidating to the impure soul. It was obvious to all who entered that oh yes, God did in fact live here. And despite Sarah's profound faith, devotion and impeccable service to Father O'Connell and the parish, she just couldn't afford the tuition to send her brood to the church school. So the kids took the yellow public school bus with all the heathens to South Boston Elementary and Middle Schools, and three nights a week, the children would be schooled in their Catholic faith by deacons at the free CCD classes at St. Finian's.

Riley thought of CCD classes as "guilt classes." The boys would be separated from the girls, and then sorted by age. Father O'Connell and the deacons would drill the teens in the immorality of sex, infidelity, masturbation, abortion, contraception and a colorful array of other perversions that Riley hadn't even heard of never mind understood. Deacon Sabol, an old, sweet Lithuanian man who also ran the church soup kitchen, was responsible for Riley's group. Once a month, old man Sabol would invite each of the boys to meet with him in private to counsel them on whatever was on their minds and explore their faith. Each time it was Riley's turn to go, he would become apprehensive and his spine would tingle -- an inexplicable internal radar alert warning him of impending danger. Riley almost always found an excuse to avoid Deacon Sabol, often with Liam's pre-planned interference. (He learned from his brothers to avoid "the funny deacons.") At the end of each class, all the devout, God-fearing young students would rifle through the desks of the day students stealing pens and other items to sell at public school the next day, or to trade with the other CCD students on the walk back home.

"What did you get?"

"Just a few pencils and a notebook."

"I got a pencil sharpener this week, and a sticker book.

"I got a Hershey Bar."

"Whoa.... you made out, man! Trade me! I'll give you the pencils and the baseball cards I got last week for the Hershey Bar."

"Oh, no friggin' way! You'll have to do better than that. It's white chocolate with almonds."

Riley despised CCD classes. At the ripe old age of 13, he was questioning his faith. Why wouldn't God let his devout mother divorce his loser of a father and re-marry a nice man like Mr. Murphy? Why did the kids who steal the most things from the school always get to be the altar boys on Sunday? Why was he afraid of such a nice man like Deacon Sabol? Why would he get punished by God for wanting to hug and kiss Tammy Meeks, but God wouldn't punish the psychotic Yvonne Tannen and make her end her reign of terror? He did not understand, and CCD was not giving him the answers his mother promised it would. Liam said he used his brain too much.

While Riley traded hot Catholic school contraband with his friends, Ryan often stayed back to worship and study with Father O'Connell in the rectory. Ryan was working on a full-boat scholarship to Sacred Heart University, in Fairfield Connecticut to study theology (Father O'Connell was pulling a few strings). No one in either Seamus' or Sarah's prodigious clans had even set foot on a college campus, never mind attending class.

Sarah would never be more proud of her boys.

Riley was never more confused.

Sarah's bubbling pride with her four handsome boys (Riley smart and inquisitive, Ryan pious and driven; Sean responsible and practical; Liam devoted and helpful) didn't match her boundless disappointment with her three distressed girls -- Erin, Meghan and Siobhan.

Erin, who was the eldest at 21, was short, dumpy, drank heavily and pursued her life in a constant foul mood. Sarah believed that had it not been for her daily morning prayer to St. Thomas Aquinas, the patron saint of students, Erin would never have graduated high school. She had many friends but each was a more negative influence than the next, and many an evening's family dinner ended in a shouting match between Sarah and her cranky eldest daughter over Erin's irresponsible use of her burgeoning independence. Erin worked as a waitress across town at the 24-hour Howard Johnson's several nights a week, and though she would make a modest contribution to the household finances, more times than not she would drink away her tip money with her friends at one of the local pubs on her way back to the apartment.

Meghan was 15 and tantalizingly pretty. Her long, luscious red hair, soft smile and deep blue eyes turned many an adolescent head, and she knew how to use all of it. Meghan seemed to have a new boyfriend every other day, whose longevity depended upon their devotion and ability to acquire and shower lavish gifts upon her. And once the hapless new boy's wallet had been drained, a cheerful Meghan would bat her red silky eyelashes and move on.

Siobhan was 14, quiet and withdrawn. She was born 10 minutes after her stronger, bigger twin brother Liam, and being so small and underdeveloped, was given less than a 50 percent chance of survival. It was only through the miracles of science that the doctors at Massachusetts General Hospital on Fruit Street were able to save the poor girl (or, as Sarah would explain, the miracle of prayer) and Siobhan was expected to live a long and normal life. Though older than Riley by a year, Siobhan was small and skinny and assumed by outsiders to be the baby of the family.

Whenever thinking about his crazy brothers and sisters, Riley always recalled one especially unforgettable and infamous Christmas from his childhood.

Each Christmas Eve, as is the long observed Irish tradition, a single red candle would be lit in the front window as a symbol welcoming Joseph and Mary to their home if they might happen by. It was Riley's responsibility, as the family's youngest, to light that candle each year, and even at age 13, it was still an honor. The family gathered round the well-decorated window and Riley lit the candle as his family sang a heartwarming rendition of *Silent Night*.

Mr. Murphy had kept the bookshop downstairs open late to capture the last few procrastinating Christmas shoppers, then he joined the Lynch family upstairs for dinner. Mark Murphy was a widower, who lived alone in the suburbs, but loved the old neighborhood and loved books. His only child, a grown daughter named Mary, lived and worked as a translator in China for a pharmaceutical company, so he was often alone and adopted by the Lynch clan each holiday, serving as a de facto "dad" to the kids -- a role he, and the kids, accepted with enthusiasm.

The Lynch apartment was filled with the intoxicating aroma of mince meat, cinnamon and spiced beef. Sarah was at her culinary best, and had somehow whipped up an authentic Irish Christmas feast complete with an amazing Christmas dessert pudding, with rum sauce and raisins, that was legendary in the neighborhood, while still clocking extra hours at Wal-Mart and getting all the present-wrapping finished well in advance. And there was another dinner to prepare and serve the next day when Aunt Eileen and her family came to visit in the afternoon.

At around 11:30, led by a triumphant Riley, they all started the trek up the hill to St. Finian's for midnight mass. East Broadway was calm and breathtaking, with twinkling lights and garland in the window of every storefront and apartment, and other families were coming out to join the Lynch's on their short pilgrimage. The loudspeakers above the patio of Theodora's Restaurant broadcast *Good King Wencelas*, and light fluffy snowflakes fell and nestled together on the sidewalk on the crisp, windless night.

"Looks like St. Stephen must be plucking his Christmas goose a little late this year," Mr. Murphy told them gazing up at the moonless, flake-filled sky.

"Mom," Erin began, "do we have to go to mass tomorrow morning since we are going tonight?"

"I don't want to go either," Meghan interrupted, "my new boyfriend Aiden wants me to go to his house in the morning."

"Yes, ladies, you will be attending mass in the morning, too. We haven't missed a Christmas Day mass since your father and I were married."

"Isn't that redundant? To go tonight, and then tomorrow?" Erin asked.

"No, Erin. Mind yourself."

"I am an adult. You can't make me go, you know."

"And I don't have to feed you either," Sarah replied in jest, sensing Erin was trying to pick a fight. Riley sensed a battle brewing, and fell to the rear. Meghan thought it safe not to repeat her request.

"I'm not going in the morning," Erin volleyed, "and there isn't anything you can do about it."

Sean had heard enough. "Erin, zip it. We're going to church in the morning like we always do. Relax."

"Don't tell me what to do. I do not need to relax."

"Come on Erin, not tonight. Don't do this tonight," Ryan chimed in.

"We stick together as a family, "said Sean.

"If we are a family, then where's Dad? I'll bet he's not at Christmas mass tonight or tomorrow," Erin said.

Sarah's heart sunk. It was the only thing her kids could say that could chip the enamel of her spirit. No matter how hard she worked at it, she could not replace Seamus' presence in the family. The older kids still missed him.

"Your father..." Sarah paused, swallowed, paused again, and then resumed. "...is a very special man. We all miss him, I know you all do. I do dearly. But I know that God watches over him wherever he is, and he is with us at church tonight because his presence is strong and in my heart now. He is with me, with us, tonight... on Christmas Eve, right now. I feel him." Mr. Murphy put his arm around Sarah and gave her a reassuring, tender squeeze.

There was silence among the group as the kids recognized the serious and dangerous turn of their mother's voice. "Your father gave me seven of the most precious gifts ever -- each one of you. As God gave his only son Jesus to us, your father gave all of you to me. I am truly.., truly blessed by God."

Tiny, little Siobhan had not said anything all evening -- always the first to enter a room, and the last to leave, and always the last to say anything to anyone. Siobhan's eyes watered, her mouth turned down, and she looked at Sarah, with affection and love.

"Mommy, I am blessed by God, too."

"Yes dear, you are... we all are blessed. Each one of us."

"No Mommy, I'm pregnant."

FOUR

Riley graduated from South Boston High School first in his class, a proud valedictorian, but his fear of crowds was so acute he had considered flunking his senior year history final just so someone else had to deliver the stupid speech. His mother sat in the audience, center of the front row, eyes wide with a smile that appeared permanent across her face. The only thing that would have made Sarah's moment any more perfect would be if Riley's four-year old nephew, little Brian Seamus Lynch-Lopez wasn't climbing her like a garden fence.

Minutes before the ceremony, Riley threw up. His friend Donnie was unlucky enough to be in the bathroom with him to witness the colorful ugliness of the Chinese buffet Riley had rented for lunch.

"I can't do this, Donnie, I'm going to puke on that stage."

"Well I'm not doin' it for you. I graduated third in the class. You get to hear from first, and even second, but nobody gives a shit about third."

"I'll give you one million dollars if you switch with me."

"You don't have a million dollars."

"Ok... what do you want? Name your price."

"You can't afford me."

The call went out for the graduates to assemble for their distinguished march to the stage. The lights in the auditorium blinked, announcing that the show was about to begin, and the late arriving audience scrambled like mice to find their seats. Riley's whole family was there, including Aunt Eileen and even Mr. Murphy who had given him a 1980 Encyclopedia Britannica and a new boxed Oxford English Dictionary, unabridged of course, as a graduation present. Notably absent was Sean.

Riley stared at his shoes from the opening remarks through the National Anthem and right through Father O'Connell's dull and long-winded invocation. He did all he could to breathe deeply and quiet his nerves, and then following the remarks of an endless line of unimpressive school dignitaries, his name was announced to thunderous applause. Donnie smirked in evil anticipation, having bet Anthony five bucks Riley wouldn't make it through to the end without somehow humiliating himself.

He walked to the podium clutching his speech in one hand and his lower intestine in the other. He cleared his throat and began to deliver the antiseptic, pre-approved speech his English teacher had drafted with him.

Ladies and gentlemen, graduates, distinguished faculty, friends and honored guests.., today marks not the end, but the beginning. The graduates seated here on this stage represent the result of a great journey, a journey that began four years ago full of spirit and wonder and ends today, ready to partake in the next stage of their lives...

Riley was amazed that it was going so well. The audience was silent and hanging on his every word. His endless hours of practice had paid off. He continued.

... and as we look to our futures, bright and wondrous as they may be, we cannot forget those who have helped us and guided us on our journey...

He shot a quick glance at his mother, then across his brothers' and sisters' faces. He thought of all the late night projects and term papers, or of his mother's proof reading, or of borrowing his sisters' old notebooks. He felt their pride warm him, and wondered again why Sean had not made it to the ceremony which was most unlike him -- the family always stuck together.

...and as Mark Twain once said, "Twenty years from now you will be more disappointed by the things that you didn't do than by the ones you did do. So throw off the bowlines. Sail away from the safe harbor. Catch the trade winds in your sails. Explore. Dream. Discover...

He noticed little Brian had escaped his mother's grasp and was now crawling beneath the rows of chairs like an infantryman, startling random attendees which caused them to shriek as he grabbed at their unsuspecting ankles.

...with great hope for our future. Thank You.

The crowd stood and applauded, none louder than his brothers and sisters. Sarah wept with joy. Riley had finished his speech without vomiting or soiling himself, and had it not been for the taught, poorly placed microphone cord he overlooked on his triumphant walk back to his seat, Anthony would have won his bet with Donnie.

"Well that sucks," Anthony said, handing over his financial obligation.

Riley had fallen flat on his face at Father O'Connell's feet, mortar board sliding across the stage like a hockey puck, and was helped right up and given a reassuring hug. The crowd never stopped applauding, and clapped a little harder when Riley reached his feet in full blush.

Outside the auditorium, a spectacular spring day was drawing to a close, and the sweet fragrance of freshly cut grass complimented the warm sunshine and the rows of rhododendron spackled with large pink blooms. Having now graduated seven siblings from South Boston High, Sarah was as much of a celebrity among the teachers and parents as Riley, who stood aside and endured the obligatory hugs from his classmates and teachers but felt uneasy. Sarah held court with all the other veteran moms.

"So where is Sean? It's not like him." Riley asked his mother.

Sarah sighed, "Oh I don't know. He's been acting strange lately, and he's not answering his cell phone. I'll be giving him a good piece of my mind later on."

"Good luck at Columbia, Riley! A petite and pretty blonde graduate shouted from the passing crowd.

"*Oooooh*, who's she?" inquired Liam, head spinning. "Damn, I thought I knew everybody."

Riley had been accepted at Columbia University, which would be paid in full by an academic scholarship he was awarded from the Sons of Dublin Foundation. He would leave by train in August to live in New York City, which would mark the first time he had ever been away from home for more than a night or two. His much celebrated older brother Ryan had already graduated with a degree in theology from Sacred Heart University, was studying at the Our Lady of Providence Seminary in Rhode Island, and was sprung from the joint for the week to attend Riley's graduation. Ryan offered Riley a wonder of advice about college, dorm life, and living alone, but was met with disinterest. Riley couldn't accept the fact he would be leaving his family and neighborhood behind and refused to accept even the advice of hope and adventure from his own speech. It just didn't seem real.

"I think I want to walk back, it's a beautiful night," Riley announced as the family was loading into their cars.

"That's fine," Sarah replied. "That will give me a head start getting dinner on the table for everyone. I made all your favorites tonight -- lamb stew, potato farls and even a big rhubarb pie. I just have to pop it all in the oven." Riley would have been just as happy with a pepperoni and mushroom pizza from Theodora's, but such a suggestion on one of his mother's big days would have been sacrilegious, and potentially fatal.

"Mind if I walk along with you?" Ryan asked.

"I guess so," he responded with reluctance.

Ryan and Riley started the mile and a half walk through the old neighborhood back to the homestead on East Broadway. There was no doubt it was dinner time in the village. Renegade whiffs of garlic and spices floated through the air, catching their attention and reminding their neglected stomachs it was well past the supper hour. Ryan fancied himself the family historian and along the way, Ryan after being quiet for some time, began a comprehensive historical commentary on the neighborhood, neighbors and sites.

"Gerry Finn lived on that corner," Ryan began. "I graduated with his sister. Gerry was the most violent man I have ever heard of. Nasty. He got involved with the mob and though he was convicted of only one murder, they say he pulled off about a dozen of them. I bet the bodies are buried right between the lilacs and the arborvitae on the front lawn. He was executed in Texas a few years ago. And over there is where the old South Boston Bowlarama used to be. Do you remember it? When I was little, you were just a baby, Mom took me and my friends there for my birthday party. It was the most pathetic excuse for a bowling alley you ever saw -- it had four lanes and none of them were flat, so the soles of your bowling shoes would stick to

26

the floor. Then we went across the street for ice cream at the Dairy Queen, but that's gone now, too. And see that used car lot over there? It used to be a duplex where Montgomery Meeks lived. He was the neighborhood's one honest lawyer. His son Benjamin was in my gym class, I think he had a sister..."

"Tammy?"

"Maybe. It was Tammy or Pammy, or Kimmy or something like that. Very strange but cute little girl, I recall. Anyway, they moved away just before I went off to Sacred Heart then the landlord bulldozed the whole lot. It was a disgusting rundown building, with rats and trash everywhere. You'd think a lawyer could afford a better place than that dump. All I remember about Benjamin Meeks was that he smelled rotten -- his locker stunk up the whole gym. Did you know the girl?"

"Just a little. She was in my class." Riley thought about Tammy all the time. In his mind's eye, she was still thirteen, still smart, still sweet, still pure. Then the realization hit that she was seventeen or eighteen now, graduating somewhere just like him and preparing to go off to college and an exciting new life. He wondered what a seventeen year-old Tammy would look like. He wondered and hoped she was happy.

"Boy, I miss this old neighborhood. Once you leave, you just can't come back. I should tell you something..," and Ryan paused for an uncomfortable moment. "After my ordination, I volunteered to be assigned to a church school in Nicaragua. Father O'Connell knows a bishop down there -- *please* don't tell Mom yet, I don't want her to freak out. It's a very depressed area, lots of unrest and crime, and quite violent. And there is a real need for good priests to spread the word of God. The whole idea scares the crap out of me. I'll tell you, Riley, I don't see myself back here visiting with the family for a long time."

"Ryan, I don't think I want to go to college. I think I want to stay here."

Ryan was taken back. "Are you crazy? You're the smartest one of the bunch of us. If anyone has a realistic chance of making it outside this neighborhood, it's you. And what do you think you'll do here? Hang around in the bookshop your whole life, or make a career out of waiting tables at Ho Jo's like Erin? "

"I don't know. Maybe Mr. Murphy will give me a job."

27

"Don't be stupid. That old bookstore is barely staying afloat as it is. The big chain bookstores they opened near the mall are killing it. I don't know why Mr. Murphy thinks he can afford to stay open anyway -- he must be losing a ton of cash on that old dump."

"So you want me to be more like you? You say you miss this place, but then you say you're going to Nicaragua? What the hell, Ryan?"

"I miss my old neighborhood, not this place, not what it has become. All the places I remember when I grew up have either been bulldozed or eroded away. Real estate is way too valuable around here now. They knock down all the old buildings and put up condos for rich people, along with a dozen Starbucks and The Gap. They are starting on South Street and moving their way up the block. They will kick Mom out of our place too you know, one of these days. And Mr. Murphy. It's a just matter of time. Anyway, I wanted to talk to you about Mom. I'm getting worried, did you notice..."

"Hey, what the hell is that!"

The two brothers turned the corner together in lock step pace toward their building, looked ahead, and gasped. Two police cars were parked parallel on the sidewalk in front of the bookshop, their lights flashing in sync. The boys ran toward them, Riley's maroon graduation gown fluttering in his wake behind him. They stormed up through the door and up the staircase to the apartment tripping over each other every rickety wooden step of the way. They tumbled through the door and startled the four police officers holding court around the living room. One panicked and drew his weapon.

"No!" Sarah shouted. The two boys froze.

"What's wrong, is everyone OK? Ryan asked, heart pounding and still hyperventilating from the rapid climb and sudden excitement.

"Sean?" Are either of you boys Sean Lynch?" The first officer asked.

"No! No!" Sarah exclaimed," flailing her arms. "This is Ryan and Riley!"

"Sit back down, ma'am." Sarah acted as if she did not hear the request. "Do you boys know where we can find Sean?"

"No sir, I don't know," Riley responded, "he was supposed to be at graduation with us this afternoon but he didn't show up."

"OK gentlemen, let's see some I.D."

As they fumbled in their pockets for wallets, Meghan whispered in Riley's ear, "They think Sean robbed some place. They don't know where he is."

Riley looked around the room. One officer was gazing across Sarah's desk heaped with unpaid bills, Ladies Home Journals, and assorted junk mail; another had just emerged from Sarah's closet shrine both surprised and intimidated; and a third was looking over a wall of framed photographs of all the kids at different stages of their childhood -- the Christmas snapshots, the St. Patrick's Day Parade, the birthdays and the graduations. Liam, Erin, Meghan and Siobhan sat silent and respectful on the sofa like overstuffed pillows. Little Brian ran and screamed, oblivious to the drama surrounding them all. Sarah was distressed and pacing, worried about the whereabouts of her oldest son. But still in perfect and unflappable Sarah Lynch form, she removed the rhubarb pie from the oven seconds before the oven timer sounded.

"Oh, poor Sean. This isn't possible. He's a good boy. He doesn't get involved in these things. This is not like him."

"Sorry, ma'am, but he was named by two different witnesses as involved in this incident, and we need to speak with him."

"Where is your husband?" the officer inquired. "Do you live alone?"

No one responded.

According to the officers and subsequent news reports, several homes and new condominiums had been burglarized along South Street, in the most affluent and growing section of town, relieving the upscale squatters of their personal computers, televisions and fancy new home furnishings. The break-ins had become chronic over the past several months and the police and upwardly mobile new residents were growing impatient, pressing the politicians to demand the police take action. An anonymous tip led them to a rundown pawn shop next door to Gulliver's Pub (one of Sean's favorite hangouts) a few blocks from the Lynch's apartment. The police surmised that a young, organized gang of low class hoodlums who had been meeting in the pub's backroom planning the break-ins were responsible for fencing the stolen goods through the unassuming pawnshop -- just like they used to in the old mob days. (At least that's what the richer condominium owners kept insisting.) Earlier that morning, the police raided Gulliver's to round-up the slovenly group and they scattered -- Sean and a few others slipping through a stockroom door into the alley just before being apprehended. Those that were arrested swore their innocence, and wasted no time eschewing their loyalty and giving up the names of their missing mates.

"Ma'am, please call us as soon as you hear from your son, Sean. It is imperative we speak to him immediately."

Moments after the police left and their squad cars disappeared around the end of the block, an uncomfortable spring night finished blanketing the neighborhood. Riley folded up his mortar board and gown, along with his crisp new diploma in its leather holder, and brought them to his bedroom while the rest of the family zipped around the apartment like butterflies, each with a cell phone and slice of rhubarb pie, trying to track down a neighbor, friend or old classmate who might be able to help find where Sean had gone off to. Sarah's eyes were bloodshot and moist and she invested most of her time at her private closet altar in silent prayer. After at least two dozen *Hail Marys* and almost as many *Our Fathers*, Sean either aided by magic, or through divine intervention at Sarah's request, appeared standing in the doorway.

"Sean!" Sarah leaped across the living room with arms outstretched, landing on Sean's chest rapt with joy. "Oh my, thank God you are OK! Thank God!"

While Sarah wept and hugged her tall, oldest prodigal son, the family took turns firing random questions at him.

"What happened?"

"Where were you?"

"Where have you been?"

"Where did you go?"

"Do you want some pie?"

"Is everything OK?"

Sarah grabbed his shirt at his chest with both fists, "Now you listen to me, mister, you march down to that police station and tell them what you know. Tell them what happened. Sean, I am scared to death. They think you robbed somebody, or stole something. You have to go straighten this out now."

"It will be alright Mom, really," Sean tried to reassure her. "I didn't do anything wrong -- I swear to God."

"Then go tell them that."

"We will, Mom, we will. I want you to meet somebody."

In her exuberance to welcome Sean back under her wing, Sarah didn't notice a man standing in the hallway just outside the door. He was small, frail and thin and in his thirties but could pass for sixty standing hunched in the shadows. His flowing white hair cascaded across the shoulders of his black leather jacket, and his hands were adorned with several large gold rings. His arms were crossed and he clutched an ornate tan leather briefcase that hung to his knees.

"Mrs. Lynch, my name is Malcolm Ward. I am an attorney and will be representing your son and his friends. It is my distinct pleasure to meet you and your family. However, I am sorry to make your acquaintance under such unfortunate circumstances."

Malcolm was short and odd looking, but smooth spoken and charming, much like a well-dressed elf. The crotch of his oversized trousers hung down to his knees, reminiscent of Charlie Chaplin's mischievous tramp, and the stiff scent of an expensive cologne hung in elegance around him.

"Ma'am, we will be heading down to the precinct in a moment, I assure you."

"Riley, come here kid," Sean began, talking fast, "I am so sorry I missed the graduation this afternoon. You have no idea how bad I feel about that. There was nothing I could do. We were playing cards at Gulliver's and without any warning the door exploded and all these men ran in and started grabbing and tackling people. We didn't know what was going on -- I had no idea they were police officers at first. Everybody scattered in different directions, and I made it out the back of the stockroom with a couple of other guys..."

"It's best not to discuss the details right now," Malcolm advised.

"I told you not to hang around that place," Sarah interjected, wagging her index finger in Ryan's face. "Now look what's happened."

"And I am sorry, Riley. I love you, kid. Congratulations." Sean draped his arm over his shoulder.

"So why are you here, shouldn't you both be at the police station right now?" Riley asked.

"There was a rumor about rhubarb pie. My client and I were hungry," Malcolm answered.

F I V E

The summer train from Boston's South Station to Penn Station in New York City takes about four hours and makes several frustrating stops along the northeast corridor to pick up commuters, and it is unfortunately, not a scenic excursion. Passengers with nothing to keep them occupied are sentenced to gaze through dusty oversized windows at the back of old factories, junk car lots and the occasional tent of a vagabond. It was as if the Amtrak construction detail went out of their way to avoid and hide all the lush, visual majesty that New England offered and created a sightseeing tour of the bile and rust of urban decay. The other problem with the trains is the frequent breakdowns that wreak havoc on busy commuters' schedules. The first train breakdown for Riley's epic trip to New York occurred at a station near Attleboro, Massachusetts only a half hour out of Boston. From his window, he enjoyed an enchanting half-hour view of overstuffed mall dumpsters, stacks of broken wooden pallets, and an abandoned set of aluminum retail fixtures stored so long outdoors that milkweed and goldenrod grew several feet high through them. The next breakdown occurred outside New Haven, Connecticut, where he gazed upon a grandiose vista of three bombed out automobiles that had recently been burned, tires, engines and useful pieces long removed, with a creeping rust overtaking each of them. And the final breakdown happened near Stamford, close to the New York state line, where Riley was provided a breathtaking view of a hill at the back of an apartment building. The hill was littered with the most disconnected array of trash imaginable, including a bleach bottle, a child's bicycle, several truck tires, a lawn chair, an umbrella, a gas grill, a roll of chicken wire, and a colorful collection of newspapers, fast food containers, candy wrappers and wet, moldy, corrugated cardboard. He wondered if any of this trash was related to each other, and

32

imagined archaeologists centuries into the future excavating all this crap trying to make sense of it. *"Eureka Gustav! They must have hunted prey by bicycle and cooked it in the rain."* He pitied the residents of the neighborhood and their profound and depressing lack of pride.

Right on time about ninety minutes late, Riley's train pulled into Penn Station. The bulk of his luggage had been sent ahead to Columbia a few days before, and would be waiting for him when he got there -- he hoped. He gathered up his shoulder bags and marched headlong through the train doors materializing on a platform surrounded by a maddening maze of signs, stairs and escalators. He shuffled along through the station following the person in front of him, not sure where to go, becoming absorbed into a large crowd. He thought it ironic that he could feel so alone with so many people around.

He had been to New York City once before to visit Columbia with his mother the previous year, and with his sister Meghan who came along because she was recovering from her most recent relationship break-up and said she needed a change of scenery. Opportunities to be alone with his mother were rare, and he hated Meghan for elbowing her way into the trip. *"Of course, poor Meghan, you can come too. I'll just sleep on the floor."* Riley was incensed, but said nothing.

On that trip, despite the prevalence of Yankee fans at every turn, Riley fell in love with New York. Had he loathed the city the way he expected to (there was no way a full-blooded Boston kid was going to love the foreign culture of Manhattan Island) there would have been zero chance that he would have accepted his scholarship. But he found the pace and sights of the city intoxicating, and his intellectual curiosity piqued as he sampled the history, museums and never-ending nightlife with his mother and sister that weekend. When they arrived at Columbia for their pre-arranged private tour, he stood in awe at the large, marble library and imagined himself immersed in its collection for hours, thrilled to learn his student residence brownstone on Amsterdam Avenue would be nearby. Sarah was thrilled to discover that St. Paul's Chapel would be smack between the two, and after pointing the fact out to Riley multiple times until he acknowledged it, she was content that her participation on the trip had been purposeful.

Although terrified, a spark of adventure had been struck somewhere within him that weekend. He tried his best to suppress it.

On the hot, dry August day before he left home forever, Sarah and Mr. Murphy threw Riley a going away party. Many of his friends including Anthony and Donnie and all his family were there. And Sarah shocked everyone by not cooking, and ordered a tall stack of pizzas from Theodora's down the block.

"My God, the Earth must have stopped rotating on its axis," Sean exclaimed.

Riley spent most of the evening playing video games with and talking to Donnie who would be living at home and attending Boston University in the fall.

"You can come to New York anytime you want to, bring friends." Riley said.

"Oh, I will, count on it. The Sox play at Yankee Stadium at the end of September this year, we have to be there."

"Bring some of this pizza with you."

"I'm going to miss you sooooo much," Siobhan hugged Riley from behind, startling him a bit. "I don't know what we will do around here without you."

Mr. Murphy approached from the corner with an envelope. "If you can drag yourself away from killing those zombies for a minute, I want to give something to you. Take this. It's the name and address of an Italian restaurant on the upper west side called Americo's. It's run by an old friend of mine, Carmine Mantano. You're going to need to find a job pretty quick once you get to Columbia. The cash you have isn't going to last you more than a few months -- New York is an expensive place to live. Mr. Mantano has offered you a job in his restaurant waiting tables as a special favor to me. Now he says the restaurant is very nice, and it's near a busy theater, the clientele is upscale and the tips on Friday and Saturday nights are excellent. He says he always has room for a smart, hard-working college kid."

"Thank you, Mr. Murphy, that's awesome. I was worried about finding something. I didn't know where I was going to look first.

"Oh Mark, that was so sweet of you," Sarah interrupted.

"Good luck, Riley, we are all rooting for you," Mr. Murphy said.

Everyone at the party took turns hugging him, wishing him well, each offering some tidbit of obscure advice. Sean told him to stay out of trouble and gave him Malcolm Ward's business card. Liam had done some Internet research and gave him a list of the ten best places to meet girls in the city, and two five-star escort services. Erin gave him a cookbook, written with the single college student in mind, and reminded him that he needed to call home to check in every few days. Meghan gave him a book of movie passes and reminded him not to waste too much time studying. Siobhan offered no advice, but would reach up and hug him every few minutes with true, heartfelt emotion. Riley swore he could feel it tingling in her arms.

"We are all going to miss you, Riley," Siobhan repeated.

"I will miss all of you, too." Riley kissed her tenderly on the forehead.

Riley went to the kitchen for another slice of pizza, startling his mother who was sitting in a chair, head leaned against the family's kitschy, magnet-filled refrigerator.

"You OK, Mom?

"I am fine dear, just a little bushed. Getting old isn't what it's cracked up to be."

"You'll never get old, you just get better!" Riley said, acting as if nothing was wrong.

"Now you listen to me mister, you will not worry about me. You take care of yourself. I'm proud of every one of my children -- even when they get in trouble -- because I know they are good kids, that God loves them, and that they are on earth for a reason. You too, Riley, I am more proud of you than anyone in the family, I know God put you here for a wonderful reason -- he told me so. You are destined for something great. You will change the world, somehow. God put me here to make sure you achieve your purpose and fulfill your destiny."

"I love you, Mom."

As Riley emerged from the kitchen a little emotional and shaken, Sean pulled him aside. His solemn look concerned Riley even more. He spoke in a whisper. "Kid, listen... if you get in any trouble at all, call me first, OK? Don't call Mom. I'm sure you have noticed that Mom is slowing down. All the things that have happened the last few years have taken a lot out of her, and she just doesn't have the energy any more. Ryan and I pulled her aside a few months ago and tried to get her to see a specialist, but she wouldn't hear of it. She thinks... no she believes she can pray her way out of this. She says

35

she is fine, but I'm worried about her. Mr. Murphy and I are still working on getting her to the doctor, but if anything bad happens..."

"Sean, nothing bad is going to happen to me, I swear. I know it almost killed her not to make dinner for us all tonight and I know she hasn't been feeling great. Keep an eye on her, Sean. I told Ryan I didn't want to go to New York anymore, I wanted to stay and look after her like she looked after us all these years. Ryan thought I was crazy."

"You have to go. Mom wants you to graduate college more than life itself."

"I know that, I am going. I have to go. And I want to go now."

"And promise you will call me first if..."

"OK, OK I promise."

Sarah raised her arms and called her family to attention.

"Alright, everybody, we all know Ryan couldn't be here tonight because that mean, old bishop wouldn't let him out of the seminary, but he didn't forget us, he sent a gift for Riley."

Sarah handed Riley a small, box wrapped in silver with a large yellow ribbon. Riley opened it revealing a small, sparkling gold crucifix.

"Ryan told me the Bishop had it blessed by the Pope just for you, Riley. It's very special."

As Riley walked across Penn Station to find the local subway line to Columbia University, he thought about all the little things his family said to him the evening before. His mind was a minefield of dangerous and conflicting emotions that he struggled to control -- fear, excitement, loneliness, anticipation -- just to name a few. He tried to stay focused on the task at hand which was to make it by subway across town, find his dorm, locate all his luggage, and then call home to alert them he had arrived. (And he knew his mother was pacing the living room, telephone in hand.) If he could accomplish this by five o'clock, he thought, he would deem the day a roaring success. Tomorrow, he would worry about everything else. He was arriving early, by almost two weeks which required special permission of the school, so he could better acclimate himself to his new living arrangements and alien surroundings. (His mother thought it best.) His roommate, a young man from California named Alvin Foster, wouldn't arrive for some time so he would have the room to himself for a while.

Riley took the Broadway 7th Avenue Local train north toward school, and disembarked as planned at West 116th Street. The day was hot and stifling, the air soupy and difficult to breath, and his shoulders were starting to chafe from his sweat and repeated rubbing from the leather straps of his bags, which seemed to be getting heavier. Two stunning hand-carved marble obelisks announced the welcoming tree-lined entrance to the university grounds, like a doorway to another dimension, and just in front was a hot dog truck and an empty park bench. Had he not known better, he would have suspected his mother arranged the truck and bench to be there at just that ideal moment. He approached the truck and placed an order for a chili dog, half expecting to see rhubarb pie on the truck's billboard menu.

After enjoying his hotdog and a lukewarm bottle of water, checking in at his dorm (yes, his luggage had arrived safe) and making his obligatory phone call, Riley spent the lazy summer afternoon wandering the campus quadrangle and exploring his new Morningside Heights neighborhood. There was more activity than he expected for a late August afternoon as co-eds with books and backpacks darted back and forth around him. He prepared a mental map for himself so he could better find his way around, and as promised, his first stop was the St. Paul Chapel. Surprised to find the front door unlocked, he entered and allowed his eyes to wash over the long rows of aligned wooden chairs, the tall stained glass windows, and the copper-colored and stately brick dome. He felt satisfied that God lived here too, paid his most humble and sincere respects, and let God know not to worry as he did not intend to be back for a very long while.

A cooling twilight had arrived and was settling over the steamy city. Riley was still too wired to sleep and didn't want to be alone just yet. He pulled out the crumpled paper that Liam gave him at the party about the best places to meet girls and third on the list was a place called the Cafe Marie Anne a few blocks north on Amsterdam. The article said that not only were the beverages "rich and delicious" and the scones "fresh, sweet and out of this world" but the prices were reasonable for New York. The article also pointed out that it was across the street from the only women's health and fitness club in the village. Riley ordered a black cup of coffee and a cheese scone, then plugged-in and booted-up his laptop and sat at a corner table in a curious attempt to be both seen and blend in at the same time.

Riley came to several quick conclusions about the Cafe Marie Anne and typed them up on his computer to appear busy to the rest of the patrons. First, he noted that the coffee was awful, too bitter even for a Bostonian. Second, the scones were dry and a little stale, and he would have preferred some authentic Irish soda bread with raisins from the bakery in the old neighborhood. And third, the twenty-something girls who lined up at the counter both before and after their workouts were perky, lithe and pretty, spectacular by anyone's standards. Liam's list did not disappoint. He then ran his hands across the soft sponginess of his stomach and decided he would also take up jogging.

Riley then set to type up a "to do" list for his second day in New York. First, he would go jogging. Second, he would hurry back to Cafe Marie Anne for a leisurely breakfast. Third, he would go back to his dorm to unpack his belongings and get his room in order. Fourth, he would hurry back to Cafe Marie Anne for lunch. In between typing each sentence, he would pause to scan the room for new arrivals. A young, petite blonde girl at the back of the line caught his eye, and she caught his and smiled back, and he felt himself awash in a warm blush. He put his head down and continued typing. Fifth, he wrote, he would take the subway down to the Theater District and the West End, and see if he could locate Mr. Mantano at Americo's Restaurant.

It was not surprising that Mr. Murphy knew people in the Hell's Kitchen West End neighborhood of Manhattan. Mr. Murphy came of age like Riley did on East Broadway in South Boston. However in the 60's and 70's, the infamous Irish Southie street gangs were on the rise, creating havoc and exerting their influence on everything and everyone. Mr. Murphy often would be heard denouncing and condemning the violence and organized crime of that era, but Riley accepted that it wasn't possible to live in that neighborhood and be able to divorce oneself from the culture. The Southies of Boston would often communicate with and share resources with the Irish Westies in New York City, centered in and around the city's West End. The Westies had a well-documented pact with the Italian mob, and Riley would later learn, that the Italian restaurant Americo's was allowed to open in the Irish West End as a thank you for a difficult but well-executed mob hit. The crime sprees in both Boston and New

York had been cleaned-up by the 80's and 90's, however the violent memories, and Americo's, remained.

Americo's was easy to find, across the street from the famed Six Star Theatre just as Mr. Murphy had described. The front of the establishment was unremarkable with the only announcement of its location being a small, red neon sign and bright red awning hung above a large black door. Riley was apprehensive about working as a waiter -- he had no experience whatsoever. Other than two Christmas season's schlepping merchandise around the bookshop, he had never held a real job (Sarah had always discouraged it, preferring he spend more time on his studies.) In fact, he had barely even eaten in a restaurant much more sophisticated than Howard Johnson's or Denny's, as restaurant outings were a rare treat for such a large and under-financed family.

The interior of Americo's was lavish. Bronze drapes covered most of the walls, punctuated with original oil paintings of Italian landscapes, each opulent painting highlighted by a single small, bright spotlight. There were about two dozen tables in the restaurant, each set with blood red tablecloths and lacy white linen napkins. Every chair was upholstered in fine black leather, and a single candle, vase and red rose adorned the center of each table. Classical violin music danced in the background. Against the back wall of the restaurant, in very dim light, were four small enclosed booths, each with tall red drapes, perfect for more intimate dining or to meet with an important associate and not be overheard.

"Can I help you, sir?" A small, but stocky old man had emerged from the kitchen wearing an apron, rubbing his gray stubbled chin with one hand and carrying a spatula in the other.

"Yes, please. I am looking for Mr. Carmine Mantano."

"And who is askin'?"

"My name is Riley Lynch. Mr. Mark Murphy sent me.

"Oh! Oh my! Come here, come here... I didn't expect you for a few more weeks. Come over and sit, sit down and rest. Do you want something from the bar?"

"Umm, no sir. Thank you sir." Riley focused on being polite. Carmine grabbed his hand with a tight grip and wouldn't stop shaking it.

"It is so good to meet you. Murph told me a lot about you. He says you are very smart, and you love your mother. I told him,

'Murph, that's all I need to know.' That tells me you are a good boy... a loyal boy. I says, 'Murph, you tell that boy to come see me when he gets into the city. I'll keep an eye on him for you. I'll take care of him."

"Thank you sir. I very much appreciate this job. I am looking forward to working here."

"Well, I have to warn you... it's hard work, but it's honest work. You will be kept running a lot. My customers are very demanding. They expect the best service in the neighborhood, and it's your job to give it to them. So, how long have you been in town?"

"I just got here yesterday afternoon. I wanted to make sure I came by to meet you right away."

"Good, good. Murph was right, a very loyal boy. Very loyal... I like that. But I gotta tell you, I don't need you for a few weeks just yet. A new play opens at the theater at the end of September -- it'll be great for business. Here, then, let me get you something." Carmine walked around to the back of the bar, unlocked a draw and rummaged through it.

"Here, boy here, take this." Carmine handed Riley a stack of twenty dollar bills, about a half-inch think. "There should be about $400 there. You're gonna need some spending money in this city, it's an expensive place."

"For me? That's not necessary... "

"No, no I insist. You take it, it's like an advance. You do good things with it. Maybe take your girl out to a nice dinner some night, eh? You find a New York girlfriend here yet?"

"No sir, I've only been here twenty-four hours." Carmine threw his hands in the air.

"*Oh my, Madonna...* what's wrong with a nice boy like you. When I first come to New York I have three girlfriends my first night. Lots of pretty girls in New York." Riley smiled and looked to the rear of the restaurant where a beautiful young twenty something girl was standing in a summery flowered dress, long flowing curly black hair, and the deepest, richest eyes he had ever seen, seeming to pose as if the great Raphael himself had painted her into the restaurant's decor. Carmine turned to see what had captured Riley's attention.

"Oh, no, no, no..... ha, ha, ha..... no, no, no, that's just Mici. Come here Mici and meet Riley. Riley, this is Mici my granddaughter."

"Hi," Mici reached out her small, pale hand, and Riley accepted it with both of his. "It's nice to meet you."

"Riley's gonna work here, waiting on the tables. He is a nice boy." Carmine paused and leaned toward Mici, speaking in a whisper. "He's from Boston. *He's Irish.*"

"That's very nice," Mici responded to Riley with a slight smile, a little embarrassed. "I look forward to working with you."

"As do I," Riley said with a more confident smile than he expected to muster considering the circumstances.

"So how is that boy Murph? He was a good boy too. He worked for me for a bunch of summers many years ago. He would come with his father who worked in construction, he worked steel on the skyscrapers, and they would come to the city every summer. His father wanted him working a job, not hanging around getting into trouble. There were problems back then in the West End. Big problems. Kids Murph's age would get caught up in the most terrible things -- terrible. Murph did a good job here, and you'll be doing the same things he did. After he left the restaurant, Murph never forgot to send me a birthday card and Christmas card every time, never forgot. Very polite. He was a good boy."

"Mr. Murphy is doing well. He owns a bookshop on East Broadway in South Boston in the same building where my family lives."

"Books? Ah, who has time to read books? He's gonna go broke. He should have opened a restaurant like I told him. Not everybody has time to read, but everybody has to eat."

After leaving Americo's, Riley elected to forego the rest of his Cafe Marie Anne prepared list for the afternoon, and chose to skip the subway ride and take a self-indulgent tourist-like stroll back through the city's more famous sites. First he walked from Americo's over toward Time Square where he stopped to absorb the hustle and bustle, then headed down toward Rockefeller Center, skipping in and out of all sorts of eclectic gift shops along the way. After walking around Radio City Music Hall, he followed Sixth Avenue to Central Park where he stopped and sat for a time in front of the world famous Carousel, and watched as dozens of excited little kids, and pigeons, zigzagged about at his feet. The balance of the afternoon was spent in strolling within the cooling shade of Central Park, as Riley, exhausted from the whirlwind of an eventful and stressful week, started to

41

become comfortable within his own skin. For the first time in months -- perhaps in his whole life -- he felt like he belonged and had a purpose. He knew what he needed to do, where to go and how to act. Independence suited him. His mother told him he was destined for greatness, and though he wasn't sure what that meant and chalked it up to his mom just being his mom, he too felt that something big was brewing and that he was destined for something exciting. He also needed to learn to deal with another foreign emotion: optimism. Oh there were millions of questions and anxieties at every turn, but he felt empowered and ready to conquer the world -- or at least ready to figure out his little part of it.

S I X

Years later wasting away in his lonely cell at SBCC, resigned to the fact that the fruitful part of his life had ended, Riley would fixate on those early months in New York as the most carefree and enjoyable of his life. The weather was always better than Boston's, the food selection more diverse, the friends more inquisitive, the girls far more interesting and worldly, and the real life complications far more tame.

And then there was Alvin Foster.

Alvin was Riley's pre-assigned college roommate for all four of his years at Columbia. It wasn't that Alvin was a bad person, or even an unpleasant one, in fact he was always upbeat and positive, it's just that Alvin was as clever as New York falafel. The two roomies were nearly evicted from their dorm during their first week together, when after Riley added a hot plate to the room to cook up a few midnight snacks, Alvin wasn't content to just take over the project and burn dinner, but instead he ignited and incinerated the cookbook Erin gave Riley at his going away party. So at three a.m., the fire alarm screamed through the halls of the dorm, fire trucks roared up to the Ivy covered entrance, and all the coeds were herded and corralled onto the dorm's front green where they huddled in the chilly air. The boys were later lashed with a stern, obscenity-laced warning by the residence hall coordinators -- and received a lifetime of pissed-off looks from the rest of the pajama-clad, sleepy-eyed residents.

Alvin was a tall, blonde and muscular figure far more attuned to riding a Del Mar surf board than attending class at an upscale Ivy League university. His arms were thick and muscular, with small blonde curls that Alvin's multiple, nameless girlfriends loved to play with and try to straighten while giggling, which drove a studying Riley to consider homicide. And though Alvin's physique was solid and

43

well-sculpted, he was lazy and had never invested a single moment lifting weights, running or working out in his life. Alvin had led a soft and sheltered upbringing in his parent's renovated San Diego hacienda, and they decided it best to send him away to school as far from the warm, laid-back California lifestyle as possible. It didn't take Riley long to understand why. Conversations with Alvin never ran too long or deep.

"Hey Alvin, it's 37 degrees out there, please tell me you don't plan to wear those sandals again, do you?"

"Yeah, why not?"

"Because it's cold as hell. Do you even own a pair of socks?"

"Of course. I have two pair. Do you want to borrow them?"

"Never mind, Alvin."

"Hey Riley, have you seen my blue shorts?"

"You don't own a pair of blue shorts."

"Are you sure?"

"Yes, Alvin, I'm pretty sure. I did all our laundry this week. And I've never seen you wear blue shorts."

"You know what? I think you're right. Hey Riley, do you know where I can buy a pair of blue shorts?"

"It's winter. Maybe you should buy a pair of blue *jeans* instead."

"That's a great idea, Riley."

"Thanks, Alvin."

"And could you help me cut the legs off them when I get home?"

"Sure, Alvin, right after you help me cut my jugular vein."

"OK, you got it buddy."

Riley and Alvin were once invited by a favorite English professor to an exclusive party at an up-and-coming artist's private loft in SoHo. Tired of waiting for Alvin to finish getting ready, and growing anxious that he would miss the best part of the party, Riley left the directions scribbled on a note on the coffee table and headed out alone. (Waiting for Alvin to finish primping in the bathroom was not unlike waiting for one of Riley's sisters, or sometimes Riley thought, all of them.) Riley arrived in SoHo right on time, and he mingled and enjoyed the party for a while, often checking his watch and keeping an eye on the door, feeling a little guilty that he left Alvin behind. Riley's cell phone started vibrating, and he struggled to hear a confused Alvin over the energetic crowd in the undersized loft.

"Riley, where are you?"

"I'm at the party, where are you?"

"At the airport."

"Why are you at the airport, is something wrong?"

"I think I'm lost. I gave the directions you left me to the cab driver, and he brought me to the airport."

"Holy crap, Alvin, those directions said to come to the upstairs loft of the art gallery on the corner of LaGuardia Place and Houston Street."

"Oh... that explains what happened. The cab driver took me to LaGuardia Airport for a flight to Houston, Texas. That's not the same thing, is it? You now, I was thinking to myself, 'something doesn't look right.' "

Despite Riley's growing and understandable frustration, it was obvious to him that Alvin needed a guardian angel, a personal life guide -- someone to watch over him and protect him from the snake oil salesmen and con artists from the darker, seedy underbelly of the city. And to also be there to protect Alvin from Alvin, before he whistled and skipped, shorts, sandals and girlfriend in tow, over the jagged cliff at the end of his flat and carefree planet Earth.

Friday, September 27th had been circled on the calendar for several weeks -- it was to be Riley's first day of work at Americo's. Alvin was off somewhere with his anonymous, giggling girlfriend of the day, and Riley had the dorm room alone for a change to primp himself and get ready. From his dresser, Riley took the crucifix and chain that Ryan had given him before he left, and placed it over his head and around his neck -- he was embarrassed to realize he had almost forgotten he had it. For good luck, he thought, he would wear it tonight. Outside, a heavy driving rain was assaulting the city, and had been in full rage all day. He had been soaked to the bone at least four times attempting to traverse the campus to and from class that morning. And although drainage in and around his residence hall was good, once he got out on Amsterdam Avenue to hail a cab for his trip to the West End, he had to wade through what felt like Hudson River itself. He thought he had done the smart thing by avoiding the walk over to the subway station and instead hailing one of the frequent cabs that sped by, but now that it was raining, the cabs were off hiding somewhere dry no doubt, nowhere to be found. By the time he arrived at Americo's and made it through the impressive waterfall streaming off the red awning in front of the great, black front door, he looked like a skinny half-drowned river rat. Carmine, having lost the disheveled look Riley remembered, now sporting a dashing crisp tuxedo and red bowtie, met him at the host's stand.

"Ahh, Riley, good to see you boy. Looks like you got a little wet. Didn't somebody tell you it was raining? Go in back and clean yourself up." Riley's shoes squished and squeaked with each step.

"Oh no, look at you!" Mici laughed. Come with me and I'll help." Riley tried very hard to ignore that Mici looked stunning -- black hair, soft pale complexion, and bright red lipstick, and she smelled like a bed of spring flowers. Riley's first day of work was off to an auspicious start.

Once Riley's shoulders were toweled off, his hair combed and he had been more or less put back together by Mici, Carmine gathered the staff together for a quick meeting. "Riley, this is Lorenzo and this is Armand. They are the other two waiters here at Americo's. Now you listen to them and do what they do. They are very good and very nice to the customers."

Lorenzo was tall and gaunt with olive Sicilian skin and dark curly hair. His thick bushy eyebrows met at a point above his nose giving him an intimidating stare. Armand was a shorter, heavier, quieter version of Lorenzo who knew his place and said very little.

"Yes, sir, I will. And it's nice to meet you both," Riley said as he extended his hand in friendship. Lorenzo ignored it, and Armand taking his cue from Lorenzo, looked away and stepped back.

"What the fuck, Carmine? We don't need another waiter. Business has sucked for the last three months, why do we need another waiter? All this means is that we have to share the customers and split the tips three ways. This is bullshit," Lorenzo said.

"Hey... I know this business," Carmine replied, waving his finger. "That new play opening across the street is a big deal. We're gonna be busy. Very busy. I know it. You will see."

"So we get busy, that's good. But Armand and I can handle it just fine. We don't need this guy, what's his name.... Riley? Riley? What is he a friggin Westie? Holy crap, Carmine hired us a friggin Irish Westie."

"Hey, watch your language or I'll smack you upside the head," scolded Carmine. "Riley here comes to us recommended by a very dear friend of mine in Boston. He's a good kid, a smart kid."

"From Boston? Oh Jesus Christ, this just keeps getting friggin better. I suppose now you're gonna tell me he has no experience and hasn't worked in a restaurant before."

"No, I haven't... I'm sorry, I don't want to be any trouble. I'm just looking to make a few dollars while I'm going to Columbia. I just want to do a good job." Riley jumped in and humbled himself, hoping to calm Lorenzo's resentment. Armand cringed, and Lorenzo's eyes bulged and rolled upward. Both shook their heads.

"And you're going to school? Columbia? Since when do they let Irish into Columbia... or idiots from Boston for that matter?"

"That's enough, Lorenzo, knock it off. Riley is going to follow you around tonight, like a shadow, so he can learn the ropes. And here..." Carmine held out a small bag and dumped out a set of gold name tags on the table. "Everybody take a nametag."

"Nametags? What is this now, a friggin Taco Bell? Carmine, I think you lost your friggin mind this time." Lorenzo steamed.

"OK," Carmine began, "Everyone put your nametags on, we open for dinner in a few minutes. We got a new guy here, and I want our regulars to remember his name. Now.... let's go over Chef's specials and menu for tonight...."

Shaken up and becoming angry, Riley watched Lorenzo and Armand head into the kitchen after Carmine's briefing. Mici pulled Riley aside. "Hey, don't worry about Lorenzo, at all, he can be very nasty sometimes but he is very nice once you get to know him. He just doesn't like things to change. He's been here a long time and the regulars do love him, and he gets amazing tips. They ask for him by name every night. You'd be smart to learn from him. He could make you a lot of money."

"Thanks, Mici for the pep talk. I'm the type of person who gets along with everybody. I don't make enemies. I'm sure it will all workout great." Riley took a deep breath and walked with confidence through the kitchen doors and into the kitchen itself, shoes still waterlogged, and crashed head first into Americo's sous chef sending a platter of salads and fresh leafy greens swirling overhead, then falling with a thunderous crash across the stove, floor and Armand. The expected barrage of sharp and angry voices followed.

"You think this is going to work out?" Carmine asked Mici.

Mici tilted her head to one side and smiled, but she didn't answer.

The rest of the evening was busy and uneventful. From the moment the first customers walked in the door, Lorenzo transformed into the most courteous, helpful and diligent waiter in the city. His ability to anticipate, charm and serve each guest with a flourish of personal service was impressive. Riley did, in fact, learn a lot from Lorenzo and Armand. He also learned a lot from Americo's rich and elite clientele, many of whom were visiting from Italian suburbs throughout New York and New Jersey. They would come to the city for the weekend, catch a play, and dine in elegance at Americo's. Carmine said they had been entertaining themselves this way for many years, and they were not afraid to tip well, many times in excess of $100 each, for elite, personal service. Carmine knew everyone who came in the door by name, and would greet each of them with enthusiasm, with arms outspread as if they were a long, lost favorite cousin. While Armand, Lorenzo and Riley looked after the patrons, Carmine would mind the host's stand and tend bar. Mici served as the restaurant's busboy, and would cover her grandfather's back if he was occupied or things got a little busy. Riley spent part of his first evening helping her clean up tables.

"You watch where you put those hands, Southie," Lorenzo warned. "I see the way you're looking at Mici. Don't go getting any crazy ideas."

"She is gorgeous, but I don't plan to lay a hand on her. I swear." Riley said.

"You'd better not. Old man Mantano will break your legs. He's pretty well connected if you haven't figured that out yet. You don't think I haven't thought about putting it to that young, little thing? The old man would have my dick cut off if he knew I was even thinking about it. Mici gets lots of attention from the customers, and she is real good at flirting with all the dirty old men, but it's all an act, kid. Part of the job here is theater -- making these people happy, making them believe they are the richest most important SOB's on the friggin' planet, and kissing their fat, white asses. The other part of the job is keeping an eye on Mici and making sure she don't get into any trouble. Some of these old farts don't get it and take it too far."

Riley took Lorenzo's advice. He could accept the role of protector for Mici -- a role with which he was becoming all too familiar. And he didn't want to bring any sort of shame upon Mr. Murphy back home either. He would mind his own business and work hard and continue to admire Mici from afar. Riley figured that a girl that beautiful was taken anyway, with a large assortment of dashing rich suitors at her beck and call. Riley did not categorize himself worthy of such a prize. She was way out of his league.

"Nice job, boys, nice job," Carmine said. "Very busy tonight. I think the rain drove them and kept them here longer, they bought lots of drinks. Riley, you did a nice job. See Lorenzo... I told you Riley would do a good job."

Riley fought falling asleep on the subway ride back to campus. Waiting tables was much more tiring and harder work than he expected it to be, and his arms and back ached. It was well after two in the morning, and even the usual colorful assortment of vagrants, gangbangers and drunks on the subway didn't interfere with his advancing drowsiness. He staggered out of the station and started to walk through campus, wondering how he could find the energy to go back to Americo's Saturday night. The torrential rain had ended and the September air, fueled by a steady north wind, was crisp, perhaps signaling an early autumn. Riley was damp and chilled and couldn't wait to crawl into bed, warm up, and pass out.

The door to Riley's dorm room was ajar when he arrived, and he could hear both the rhythmic beat rumbling from his stereo speakers, and the rubbery voice of an infomercial blaring from the television. A cautious Riley entered and flipped on the lights. The first thing he noticed was a pair of killer knee-high black suede women's boots sitting on top of the coffee table with a pair of pink cotton panties laid across the top. The room was littered with all manner of clothing, beer bottles and two empty pizza boxes. Beneath the noise from the stereo and TV, he could hear the distinct sound of a steady snore, a female snore, and snuggled up asleep in Alvin's undersized bed was Alvin and someone who Riley assumed to be Alvin's date for the evening, heads, arms and legs sticking in so many directions he wasn't sure which body part belonged to who. But what was more concerning to Riley was that his own bed across the room was also occupied. Riley approached his bed, feeling like a burglar in his own room, trying to decide if he should rouse the sleeping stranger or flip the whole damn bed in anger and send the inconsiderate bastard sprawling. Riley chose the former.

"Hello? Excuse me?" Riley jostled the stranger, staying quiet. Up close he could tell the mummy-like stranger was female from the long wet blonde hair draped across his pillow, and from the unquestionable shape of two large, rounded breasts jutting out from the stranger's blanket-wrapped chest. He jostled the mummy again.

"Hey there, hello?" The stranger awoke and turned, and opened her eyes half-way, in a dreamy and welcoming manner.

"Are you Riley?' She answered, mumbling, not yet awake. "Alvin said you'd be mad. I'm sorry. My friend over there fell asleep so I took a shower. I think I drank too much." She yawned and her eyes closed. "Do you want me to leave?"

"No, no that's OK, stay there," the ever-polite Riley responded. Her eyes opened half way again, and she smiled.

"Hey... I know you. You're that cute guy who always sits in the back of the cafe." Riley couldn't remember the last time he had been called cute by someone other than his mother, and was shocked anyone would recognize him from his table at the Cafe Marie Anne. He scanned the room trying to figure out where he was going to sleep.

"You look cold, come here and let me warm you up," the strange girl said, extending her arms. Her moist lips curled into a very sweet and seductive smile. Riley was taken by surprise and was unprepared for the moment. Not sure what else to do, Riley accepted her invitation, flipped off his shoes, and laid stiff, fully clothed and wet next to her on the bed.

"Oh, you are cold, you poor thing," and the girl unwrapped herself and crawled up on top of his fully clothed body.

Riley's arms wrapped around her back, and he realized she was naked. His hands washed down the warm arch of her spine to her bottom, which was small, round and firm. He cupped each of her cheeks in his hands. The girl smelled of an unpleasant mix of beer and shampoo, and she purred as she buried her face into the curve of Riley's neck and started to kiss him.

His mind raced. He had options. He could push her away -- it was wrong to take advantage of someone who was so drunk. But wasn't it the other way around? Wasn't she taking advantage of him? After all, it was she who had climbed into his bed, and this was all her idea. But he didn't know her. And where would he sleep? The chairs in the room were uncomfortable to just sit in, never mind sleep in. He could sleep on the floor somewhere, too. Or, he could just succumb to his most guttural instinct, his now profound horniness and his increasing exhaustion, and make love to the girl. At that moment she bit him on the right ear, and like a Victorian vampire, she sucked the will power clean out of him. He never stood a chance. He stripped off his clothes with urgency and the two made love. Neither of them took long to climax, and in a matter of minutes, both were slotted somewhere between sleep and unconsciousness

Riley was not a virgin, but wasn't experienced either. He had enjoyed two other sex partners in his life. His first was named Holly, who took his virginity after the Junior Prom on the cold and windy Savin Hill Beach behind the Dorchester Yacht Club. Riley had asked her to the dance because of her reputation for being easy, and his shallowness that evening paid off in spades. The two had sex a few other times before they broke up the relationship, when, which should not have been a surprise, Riley discovered she was cheating on him. His second sex partner was a prostitute that frequented a corner on East Broadway. For twenty bucks, she would take him (or any one of his friends) behind a dumpster in the alley next to Gulliver's Pub, raise her skirt, turn around, spread her legs, and let him have at it. She was old and dirty, but the sex was exciting and dangerous. Riley was surprised that as gross and unfulfilling as it was, he still had to resist a powerful, animalistic urge to go back and do it again.

Riley was the last to awaken the next morning. The sunshine seared through the blinds across the window and felt as if it were burning a hole into Riley's forehead. Alvin and the girls had been up and about for a while as all were dressed. Alvin's date was finishing cleaning the hotplate, and Alvin was eating something that looked like eggs. Riley's first thought was that he was grateful the girls didn't let him cook breakfast alone.

"Goodbye, Riley!" Before he could respond, the blonde grabbed her handbag, pecked him on the forehead and the two girls hand-in-hand shuffled together out the door. Riley was surprised to see that his date wasn't as sexy and enticing as she had been the night before.

"Nice girls." Alvin said, with bits of crumbled scrambled egg falling from the corners of his mouth. "The blonde one had huge tits."

"Hey Alvin.., about that girl, what was her name?" Riley asked, still trying to rouse himself from the drowsiness.

51

"What girl?"

"The blonde one. What is her name? She didn't tell me."

"Oh... I don't know."

"You don't know? How do you not know!?"

"Hey don't get all pissy at me, dude, I'm not the one who slept with her."

"So what was the other girl's name?"

"What other girl?"

"Your girl... your date? What is her name?"

"Umm, let me think. It'll come to me in a second."

The boys' attention, and another opportunity for homicide, was averted by the sudden ringing of the telephone. Alvin answered.

"Hello?....Uh huh, ummmm. Hey Riley, do you know some chick named Sarah?"

"Holy crap, dude, that's my mom!" Riley sprung to his feet and raced across the room wearing nothing except the pillow he held over his crotch and yanked the receiver out of Alvin's hands. Alvin threw up his hands and looked at him as if he was insane.

"Mom? Mom? Hi! It's Riley"

"Oh my dear, it's so good to hear your voice. I miss you so much. How are you?"

"I'm great, Mom, just great! Everything is great!" He looked down at his pillow and was overtaken by a rush of old-fashioned, South Boston Irish Catholic guilt. She couldn't know, could she?

"I haven't heard from you in a few weeks, I was starting to worry."

Riley rambled. "I know, I'm sorry. I have been so busy with school and studying, and... oh I started work last night at Americo's. Tell Mr. Murphy it's working out great. Carmine says... he's the boss.... said..."

"Hold on for a minute Riley, I want to hear all about it. But first I have some wonderful news. It's about Sean. Mr. Ward came by on Friday and said the police would be dropping all charges against Sean and his friends, they just didn't have the evidence. Our prayers have been answered. Isn't that wonderful!"

SEVEN

Attorney Malcolm Ward had successfully defended Sean and his friends, forcing prosecutors to drop charges of racketeering, delivering stolen goods and evading arrest. The affluent residents of the City Point neighborhood condos were furious. In their minds, the crime waves and unrest of the past were re-emerging, like a Phoenix from the ashes, threatening their expensive new homesteads and lifestyles. Malcolm Ward was public enemy number one in their eyes, corrupt, paying off prosecutors and judges, and backed by the deep, evil pockets of organized crime. It wasn't even a little bit true, but Ward realized he could gain easier access to information and get through doors if people *believed* he was a mob lawyer. Reporters were the most gullible, though many knew he wasn't corrupt, but often went along with the story anyway to build ratings and readership. In fact, Malcolm discovered he would be offered better seats in restaurants, too, even in Boston's Italian North End. When asked, Ward would neither confirm nor deny his involvement in organized crime stating with a good dose of arrogance that it was a ridiculous and irrelevant question.

Now free of the charges, Sean moved out of the family apartment, took a low paying maintenance job at a local manufacturing plant, and moved in with his long-time girlfriend. He promised Sarah they would be getting married soon to avoid the whole "living in sin" drama, and though she knew better, Sarah pretended to believe him and didn't put up much of a fight. He still enjoyed playing cards with his buddies on weekends in the pub, thumbing his nose in defiance of his entanglements of the past. With Riley off at school in New York, and Ryan in Rhode Island approaching graduation from the seminary and preparing to ship off to Nicaragua, Liam remained the only male left in the Lynch household. Even Mr. Murphy, who had all but moved in with the Lynch clan, made the painful and heart-wrenching

53

decision to accept fate and close his beloved bookshop. He couldn't afford to continue hemorrhaging so much money. He liquidated all his merchandise, cleaned out his personal belongings, and posted a black and red "for lease" sign in the front window. His visits to the neighborhood became less frequent as time moved on. Sarah, too, was showing her age and slowing down. Having Siobhan's spoiled brat of a child running around in the house was almost too much for her. Erin, Meghan and Siobhan, now young women, each worked an assortment of menial jobs to help make ends meet, but caught up in their own selfish dramas, loathsome boyfriends and endless bickering, left it to a weakening Sarah to continue to work her two jobs and still manage everyone else's daily needs.

At the end of his first year at Columbia, Riley made the difficult decision not to return home for the summer. Mr. Mantano had offered to expand his schedule to a six night-per-week assignment once school got out because, as it turned out, old Carmine was right -- Americo's was doing well, and Riley was making very good money and still loving New York City. The decision was difficult not because he didn't want to stay, but because he feared it would break his mother's weakening heart. He had gone home for the Christmas holidays and remembered what Ryan had told him during their stroll down East Broadway; the neighborhood wasn't his neighborhood anymore. Thomas Wolfe was dead right -- *You Can't Go Home Again.* Hanging around the old East Broadway apartment was depressing, sharing his old room with immature Liam demeaning, and he was appalled at how little his sisters would help their mother tend the apartment. The annual family holiday feast was as magnificent as always, and the mass at St. Finian's exactly as he remembered, beautiful hymn complimenting beautiful hymn, but it wasn't the same. He had only been away a short time, but everything had changed. He had changed.

More surprising to Riley than anyone else, the biggest change in his life was that he had established a relationship with a real live, warm-blooded breathing girl -- someone he was often heard to introduce to people as his girlfriend. Her name was Magnolia Fair (or just plain Maggie when he spoke of her with his family and friends back home) and as the refined product of two late-Sixties hippie parents, she was as aloof, spontaneous and unpredictable as the "we decade" itself. And the refined, conservative, intellectual Riley was surprised to discover he liked the impulsiveness. After their eventful introduction in Riley's bed, Riley spent the better part of three weeks trying to just figure out her name. Alvin was, as usual, no help whatsoever, so he began his quest with the one reliable clue she had given him -- she liked to visit the Cafe Marie Anne.

At first, Riley had no intention of falling in love -- he just wanted to know her name (it was killing him.) His initial motivation was to avoid an embarrassing future meeting as it was inevitable that he would see her somewhere on campus, and then there was pure human curiosity mixed in, punctuated by the raging horniness of the American collegiate male. So he began his investigation lurking around the shrubbery between the cafe and the fitness center, stalking at different times of day and night and keeping careful notes on the traffic patterns of each business, until he could catch a glimpse of her happening by and follow her home or to a class, since he assumed she was a student. The strategy handed Riley a couple of problems. First, he wasn't sure if he was going to recognize her. He saw her for just a tantalizing moment that night, and after a couple of weeks, his memory of her face was fading. Twice he followed girls who looked something like her, but he couldn't get close enough to confirm if it was her or not. And then one morning he saw her for sure, ducked behind a shrubbery to avoid being discovered, and lost her among a crowd of tourists disembarking from a bus. A week later when he saw her again, she was walking with a friend into the fitness club. Eureka. He followed her up to the glass door careful to not be discovered, and watched her sign-in on a clipboard at the main desk, then slip through a door and into a backroom to begin her workout. With all the panache of Sherlock Holmes or Charlie Chan, Riley waited for the attendant to leave for a moment, charged into the facility, and stole the clipboard.

The entry on the clipboard was clear: Magnolia Fair, Emerson Hall, and a phone number.

Magnolia? Interesting name, he thought.

Tracking her down after that was easy. He called and invited her to meet for coffee at Cafe Marie Anne. To his surprise, she accepted with enthusiasm.

Magnolia ordered a standard cup of Earl Grey Tea, then added cream, milk, honey, sugar and lemon to create her own unique brew, blended by the artistry and energetic stirring of a disposable plastic knife.

"Is it still tea," he inquired, "after you put all that stuff in it?"

"Oh, I'm not going to drink it." And from her purse she produced two wrapped chocolate chip cookies and a banana wrapped with great care. Magnolia peeled the banana and unwrapped the cookies, sliced the banana with the plastic knife, then squished it between the cookies to create some sort of anomalous sandwich, which was then broken in half and dipped with care into the tea.

"You know, Riley, I was surprised you called. I didn't expect to hear from you again. Most guys wouldn't have gone to the trouble. How did you find me?" Magnolia said as she slurped a bite of her breakfast.

"I got lucky, I guess," Riley lied.

Magnolia smiled. "I'm so glad you did. I wasn't even sure if that rock head of a roommate of yours would remember my name. Stupid guys are such a drag, though he does have a great ass. This needs shredded coconut. Do you think they have any coconut? In fact, most other guys would have just invited me back to their room to see if they could get me back in bed."

Riley abandoned his plans to invite her back to his room. "Oh, no, I wouldn't do something like that."

"I know you wouldn't, I can tell, you treat people with respect. I could tell by the way you held me, like you didn't want to damage me, like I was special like a piece of crystal.., before I passed out." Magnolia responded, stuffing napkins and sugar packets into her purse. "You have class. That's what turns me on." Magnolia looked like something of a Gypsy fortune teller. Her large gold hoop earrings, purple shawl, and a flowered kerchief stood out among the mostly yuppie-dressed cafe crowd, and her insistence on stealing condiments was not going unnoticed by the snooty patrons at the next table. Magnolia sensed Riley was becoming uncomfortable with her actions.

"Oh don't worry, I just need to stock up the pantry at home. I do this all the time. They don't mind. The guy that owns this place... I went out with his son once. I think the kid is gay. I am pretty sure I was the only female date the poor kid ever had. His father was thrilled. They are from Iraq and they execute people for being gay

56

over there. Oh, remind me before we leave, I need to get a roll of toilet paper out of the bathroom. Did you want a bite of this?"

They talked for a long while. Riley was fascinated by the sharp, unexpected twists and turns of her conversation, and while she wasn't the prettiest girl in the world, her eyes were full of energy and her face round, radiant and full of life. She viewed the most mundane of daily activities as an adventure, and perilous adventures as drab and mundane. He also learned that she was a good listener, and without thinking about what he was doing or saying, he unloaded both barrels on her. Until he started talking -- about his brothers and sisters, his idiot roommate, his job at Americo's, his worries about a big research paper, and even his mother's failing health -- he didn't realize how lonely he had become and how he needed someone to talk to and to just be there for him. To just listen. She finished her breakfast focused on his stories, hanging on his every word.

Business at Americo's had boomed all winter, and Riley had become a very important and valuable employee to Carmine. His life was now split between class and spending time with Magnolia, but he never missed a shift waiting tables, and as his service skills improved, so did his tips. Business was good enough that Lorenzo couldn't complain about his daily tip allotment, and left Riley to himself. Riley even felt comfortable enough to start making suggestions to Carmine on how to improve the way the business was running. His suggestions were simple at first, little issues of efficiency about where Mici could stack her trays, or how to reorganize the bar so they could get at the wine glasses without knocking the beer bottles over. After each suggestion, Carmine would sigh, wrinkle up his face, rub his chin, pause, then nod his approval. When Riley arrived early one night to help the chef unload a produce shipment, Riley happened to notice the invoice didn't match up to the truck's manifest. Riley and Carmine spent a few hours in the office tracing through yellowed stacks of old orders, and were horrified to realize that the produce company had been skimming from them for a long time -- and no one had noticed. Carmine threw a cabbage at the wall and screamed at the chef, then grabbed a phone and unleashed a torrent of Italian obscenities into the receiver for what seemed like an eternity. The next day, Americo's had a new, more honest produce vendor. Riley's success was paid with interest when Mici gave him an unexpected and affectionate hug and planted a big wet kiss on his right cheek. "*Nonno* is very proud of you."

While in class, Riley had never been more productive. Even with the roaring successes in his personal life, it was immersed in study where he was most comfortable and could relax and be himself. The jumbles of numbers and formulas demanded order and solution, and it soothed his soul to oblige and conquer them. After careful thought and discussions with his professors, he elected to shift his major to international finance hoping to hook up with a big Wall Street company so he could reside in the city after graduation. His advanced skill in mathematics, and a particular talent with accounting, put him in a favorable position for future, gainful employment.

"Oh my God that is boring. But that's *sooooo* cute!" Magnolia commented.

Professor Friedman recommended Riley to the department honors program, and he soon became a department favorite. Friedman recognized in Riley many of the same qualities that both Carmine and his mother valued -- commitment, intelligence, and loyalty -- attributes that could take Riley far. And Friedman was always on the lookout for candidates who could be tailored to make fine representatives of the university community.

At Americo's, Riley continued to immerse himself deeper into the financial details of the business. He showed Carmine several techniques he could use to save money and operate a more efficient operation, and he spent more and more time in the office and off the floor, to Lorenzo's continual whining annoyance.

Late one evening, three individuals wandered into the restaurant without reservations and asked for Riley by name. A concerned Carmine rushed in back to get him.

"Riley, do you know any of these people?" Carmine asked. It was Alvin and Magnolia with his old friend Donnie from South Boston in tow.

"Donnie!" Riley charged across the room and the two old friends embraced. He had not seen his friend Donnie in a year, and was shocked he could be here in New York. He hugged and shook him. "How did you get here?"

"Took the train, stupid." Donnie responded. "Classes ended yesterday at BU, and I was looking for someplace to burn off steam and have a good time. I called the other day and Alvin told me where to find you. I just got in a couple of hours ago. How are you, man? How are you!"

Alvin, why didn't you tell me?" Riley inquired.

"Sorry, Riley, I forgot."

"And you're in on this, too?" Riley asked, hugging Magnolia and kissing her on top of the head.

"Alvin tried calling your cell phone and dialed me by mistake, so I came along. I thought it would be fun to keep it a secret. Sorry!" Magnolia answered with a shy but evil smile.

The realization struck Riley that the group looked crass, and out of place for such an exclusive restaurant. Patrons wasted little time shooting disapproving glances their direction. And even Lorenzo and Armand were becoming annoyed at the distraction, no doubt concerned for their take of the evening's tips. Magnolia had chosen some fine skin-tight black leather with a white scarf tied around her neck for her ever-changeable wardrobe of the evening, as if parodying a fifties harlot. Alvin was wearing his trademark black tee, paisley shorts and sandals. Only Donnie looked close to normal in blue jeans and a light windbreaker. Yet none of them came close to meeting the restaurant's rigid dress code. Carmine could read the concern building on Riley's face, and stepped in.

"All of you come here and sit, come and sit. If you are friends of Riley, you are friends of mine."

"Mr. Mantano, they can go. It's OK. I didn't know they were coming in. I'm sorry."

"That's crazy talk, Riley. They should sit and eat... as my personal guests. And you sit down with them." Riley was uncomfortable with the arrangement, but he didn't want to argue with everybody.

Carmine passed around menus to the group.

"So what have you been doing, Donnie, my God, what is new?" Riley asked.

"First of all, your Mom says hello. I stopped by East Broadway to pick-up a few things. Man, it looks depressing with old man Murphy's bookstore gone. The weeds out front are already three feet high. Some idiot threw a rock through the front window yesterday, and made a huge mess of broken glass. Liam and I taped over the hole with cardboard last night. It's hard seeing the whole block fall

59

apart like that. But other than that, college life has been good to me. I'm studying hard, working hard, not much changes in my life."

"How about a girlfriend. Meet anyone?

"Not me man, I plan to stay single forever and play the field." Alvin lifted his water glass and nodded, to signal his approval of Donnie's philosophy.

"What about Anthony? He doesn't return my calls anymore. What's he up to?" Riley inquired.

"He's got it tough, dude. Don't be too hard on him. He knocked up his girlfriend and his parents freaked out on him. The baby was born a few weeks ago. He dropped out of school and is working around the clock at a shoe store at the mall in Braintree to make it all good. He doesn't have a moment to himself. Sad story." Donnie said.

"Do they have sushi here? I'm in the mood for sushi. And pudding." Magnolia chimed in.

"Hey Magnolia, this menu doesn't make sense. Which one says cheeseburger?" Alvin asked.

Riley re-focused and saw where this impromptu dinner party was heading, and saw its growing potential to end ugly. "Are you sure you don't want to eat somewhere else?"

"Nonsense, I'll take care of everything." Carmine chimed in from behind. "Here's what I'll do. I'll bring out something for everybody. You will all like it. You all sit and relax and have a drink." Carmine set a carafe of red wine and four glasses on the table. The four underage patrons wasted no time pouring themselves a sampling.

Within minutes, the chef had whipped-up a delectable, world-class sampling and filled the table with all the best Americo's had to offer -- calamari, escargot, fois gras, oysters, steak tartare, smoked salmon, and enough pasta and sauce (or "gravy" as many call it in New York) to feed a whole dorm of inadequately dressed starving students. The gang chatted and attacked ravenously.

"Kid," Donnie said as he raised his wine glass in a toast, mouth overstuffed with calamari as if the squid was trying to escape, "this is incredible. What could be better than this? To my good friend Riley!" Both Magnolia and Alvin raised their glasses together.

"To Riley!"

Magnolia went back to work coiling each strand of pasta into her oyster shells, and topping them with a dash of sugar and grated cheese. Red tomato sauce adorned her cheeks, earlobe to earlobe, as her silverware and napkin sat accessible but undisturbed. Without warning, the kitchen doors swung open and Mici appeared, wearing a flowing red dress, as radiant and scintillating as ever, maybe even more so. She floated up behind Riley and with a warm smile, placed her hands on his shoulders with a polished elegance, yet startling him. "I just heard your friends were here, Oh, Riley, please introduce me to your friends."

"Of course! Everybody, this is Mici Mantano. She is Mr. Mantano's granddaughter. Mici, this is Donnie my old friend from Boston, this is Alvin my roommate, and this is Magnolia."

"Hello! It is so nice to meet you all. I've heard so much about each of you. And Oh, Magnolia -- such a beautiful name." Mici smiled in Magnolia's direction. Both boys sat up straight and widened their eyes, sucking in their stomachs and puffing out their chests. Magnolia, however, looked like she had encountered a poltergeist. Her eyes were fixed on Mici's hands on Riley's shoulders, and Riley could sense something was wrong, but wasn't sure what it was. Then in an instant Magnolia and Mici's eyes met. Magnolia's cheeks bulged like a squirrel's full of fresh bread and pasta, and to Magnolia's consternation, Mici never ceased smiling. Magnolia tried to swallow with grace without choking, hoping no one would notice. Then she reached for her napkin intending to remove the renegade sauce from her face like a gunfighter might reach for a revolver at a poker game gone wrong.

"It was so nice to meet you all, but I must go back to work. There is much to do. *Mangiare Bene!*" And Mici slipped back into the kitchen.

"Hey, what was her name again?" Alvin asked.

"Remember what I said about staying single? That was all bullshit. I lied." Donnie cracked. "I am in love. She is gorgeous, dude!" Alvin raised his glass again in support.

"You didn't tell me Mici was pretty," Magnolia added, embarrassed and boiling with jealousy. "Not that it matters, I guess." The boys could almost see the steam rising from her leather-clad body. An uncomfortable pause met them all, and Riley was at a loss for what to say or do next. Alvin, ignorant in all things except the filthy business of women and love, knew what to do and put his arm around Magnolia and drew her body to him.

61

"You, my dear, are the prettiest lady in this restaurant tonight. Listen to me... Riley tells me every day how pretty you are and how lucky he is to have you. You are nothing compared to that girl, whatever her name is." Alvin released her, and Riley, having never, ever said any such thing to Alvin or anyone else, and having used Alvin's delay to think up a variety of responses, drew Magnolia toward his direction and kissed her on her red sauce splattered cheek. He chose a direct and simple response.

"I love you, no one else." Riley told her. Magnolia smiled.

"You two are sweet," she said. The compliments had diffused her fury for the moment, and the group directed their attention back to the real business at hand -- devouring Americo's prodigious samplings. Magnolia stayed subdued and wounded for the rest of the evening. But before leaving, she found her inner self and slipped the salt and pepper shakers along with a few napkin-wrapped stuffed mushrooms into her purse.

Mr. Mantano gave Riley the rest of the evening off, and the four walked out onto the busy sidewalk. The hustle and bustle of the city was in full swing, as cabs and pedestrians darted in all directions. Riley and Donnie walked out ahead.

"So Donnie, what part of the city do you want to see first?"

"To be honest with you kid, I am beat. It has been a long day. I have a reservation at the Marriott in Times Square. I'm thinking I should go back and crash. Besides, I think you have some work to do." Donnie gazed back at Magnolia who was dragging her feet and pouting, several paces behind.

"Hey Riley, I'll call you in the morning. I plan to stay around a few days. It's good to see you, kid." Alvin overheard the conversation and excused himself, too.

"It's still early, and there's something I want to do. I'll catch up to you two love birds later," Alvin said.

Riley and Magnolia watched their two dinner guests jog off in different directions. The evening was warm and breezy and doused in a hazy moonlight, perfect for a romantic midnight stroll. They walked for a while in an uncomfortable silence.

"Can I ask you something, Riley?" Magnolia began.

"Of course."

"Do you think Mici is pretty?"

It was one of those questions that every girlfriend asks, and every boyfriend loathes, and Riley knew that any answer would be the wrong one. He elected to remain honest, at least for the time being.

"Yes, she is pretty. She is a very pretty girl. But there are lots of pretty girls in New York and in the world, that doesn't mean anything. You're my girlfriend. You're the girl I like to look at and be with."

"Can I ask you another question?

"OK?"

"If she asked you to sleep with her, would you do it? With her?"

"No, absolutely not. That's silly. I would stay loyal to you."

"Do you think I'm being silly?"

"No... no. I guess I can understand why you might ask. She is pretty and most guys wouldn't consider turning her away. I'm just not like that. Plus she's not like that, she's very respectful. In fact, I bet you'd like her once you got to know her. I wouldn't want to hurt you. I love you."

"Can I ask you another question?"

"Then when you introduced me to her... why didn't you introduce me as your girlfriend?"

Riley paused. Didn't he? He thought he did. Maybe he didn't. He wasn't sure.

"Oh, I thought I did. Sure I did."

"No. You said.... *'and this is Magnolia'* like I was your pet gerbil or something."

"Oh, no. I didn't mean that."

"Is that all I am to you? A pet? Am I some kind of trinket or little toy to show off and play with when you get bored? Or am I just here so you can get your rocks off once in a while?"

"Oh, come on. That's not fair."

"So what is fair? That I went out and spent three hundred bucks on this leather outfit and spiked heels to turn you on tonight, just for you, and you never said a word -- not one. Then I get to watch the three of you perverts drool all over yourselves when *she* walks in the room, and then I have to sit there and watch as that Italian slut moved in on you. And then you tell me *she* is very pretty. Which part of any of that is fair?!"

Magnolia frowned and her eyes were welling with tears. Riley had never seen her as anything but confident and independent before now. Her insecurity unnerved him, and his heart ached with hers. He had not meant to hurt her.

"I'm sorry, Magnolia. I am. I guess I wasn't thinking. I don't want to hurt you. I would never hurt you. Maybe it's because you, Alvin and Donnie caught me by surprise when you showed up tonight."

"Look Riley, I know I'm not that pretty. I see the same face you do when I wake up every morning, OK? I know I don't weigh 98 pounds. But if I am going to fall in love with you, I need to know you love me too. I have been hurt before. I can't... I won't go through that again."

"I swear, Magnolia, I do think I am in love with you." Riley stopped and placed his hands on either side of her face and stared into her weepy eyes. Listen to me, I think you're pretty. Very pretty. I can't tell you where our relationship is going to lead, I don't know because I've never been in this position before. This is all new to me, but I do like what is happening. You make me feel alive. It's a feeling I had never experienced before I met you." Beneath a streetlight on the corner of Broadway and West 52nd Street, among dozens of theater goers and late-night tourists, in the glow of a large neon sign and spring moon, Riley wrapped his arms around Magnolia and let her weep into his chest.

The couple took a slow stroll and Magnolia talked. She talked about her family's large farm in upstate New York where her mom and dad grow garlic. She talked about her youth as an only child and the long hours her parents devoted to keep the farm out of bankruptcy. She talked about the deep and painful loneliness she endured every day, and how it led her to an extended sexual relationship, or what the police might call statutory rape, with a fifty year-old neighbor when she was just 14. She talked about the hour after endless hour staring out her bedroom window, summer after summer, at the fields of garlic stalks that would sway at the whim of the breeze, and how she would cut herself, scream and bleed and how no one would notice, but how the searing pain would make her smile and feel better. She talked about being the outcast at school -- the weird kid, the strange kid -- having no friends, and having other kids' parents go out of their way to make sure their precious, little darlings didn't ever come into contact with her for fear she would contaminate them. She talked about crying herself to sleep, night after night.

They reached Magnolia's dorm room hours later and it was late. Magnolia lived alone as the parents of her pre-assigned roommate needed only to visit once to be convinced their daughter needed to be relocated to preserve her sanity. Her room was a disorganized mess, strewn with wardrobe remnants representing every imaginable geometric shape and color of the rainbow. Dirty dishes and empty takeout boxes were stacked on the counter of her kitchenette, and the room smelled of a confusing mix of rotting food, vanilla and patchouli. Above her bed was a four foot tall gravestone rubbing of some other poor girl named Magnolia who had died over a hundred years earlier. It caused her bed to resemble a shallow grave. Magnolia said having a gravestone mounted above her as she slept made her feel safe and relevant.

Magnolia flopped her overstuffed handbag onto the floor and sighed at the embarrassing mess in her room. Riley pretended to not notice, and walked up behind her and placed a hand on each of her shoulders and squeezed. He noticed her hair was soft and smelled sweet, and told her so. Riley caressed her shoulders and arms and allowed the side of his face to brush up against hers. Magnolia smiled and arched her head back, exposing her neck knowing that Riley would kiss it. He kissed her beneath her ear, then again and again on her exposed neck and shoulder. Magnolia could feel he was aroused, and he was pressing against her.

"It's about time you noticed me." she whispered.

He reached around her and unzipped the front of her black leather top -- she wore nothing underneath. Her breasts were large and firm and fell into the room. He took one breast in each hand and squeezed, and circled each of her soft little nipples as if ordering them to harden at his command. Without warning he pinched them, causing her to lurch and gasp for air in a wicked moment of painful pleasure. Magnolia turned to him letting her top fall to the floor, pressing her bare chest against his and kissing him. Riley felt her tongue darting around deep in his mouth, and his jaw opened and ached to take her all in.

Magnolia stepped back and slithered out of her outfit, and paused to allow Riley's eyes to paint over the young curves of her body. He stepped forward and kissed each of her breasts, one at a time, pausing at each nipple to suckle. She liked his hot breath on her chest. Then he dropped to his knees before her, rubbing his face

65

across the pale, sweaty skin of her soft belly, scratching her with his day-old beard. With both hands she pushed his head down lower and thrust her hips forward, and his lips slid into the warm curly blonde triangle between her thighs where he outlined her with his playful tongue. She gasped and moaned again, then fell back on her disheveled bed opening her legs wide, offering herself to his every whim.

Riley stood before her and undressed, and she could see he was rock hard and looked ready to burst. Their eyes met as he fell upon her and kissed her again, and he slid into her in a spasm of pain and delight. Riley found her wet, inviting and very tight, and she found that his size both filled and startled her. She had not remembered him this large before. Magnolia felt him grow inside her even more with every thrust, and felt his large, tight balls slap against her as each stroke drove deeper. Riley could feel her heart beat increasing deep within her. Magnolia squeezed Riley so tight that neither of them could draw a breath, and she bit into his shoulder, pulled his hair and groaned again as they came, together.

They cuddled in each other's arms for a while, and said nothing. Then Riley could see through the maple trees outside Magnolia's window that the sun was beginning to rise.

"I'm going to go," he told her.

"No, stay here with me. We can nap and cuddle all day."

"Donnie is in town. He's going to be looking for me soon."

"Hey Riley, tonight was nice."

"Yes it was. Very nice." Riley leaned over and kissed her.

"Next time... you, know, it would be OK if you want to slap me around a little."

The city was coming alive bit by bit as Riley staggered back to his residence hall, trying to absorb some energy and inspiration from the early morning joggers and taxi cab horns which were on the increase. Large dark clouds in the east gave the eerie illusion that the sun was rising in the west, as the sky was brightening backwards in anticipation of a new day. Riley was exhausted again. It had been a long, eventful night without sleep and he looked forward to a two or three hour catnap before he heard from Donnie. He anticipated Donnie would sleep late, too, as even in the old days he wasn't ever an early riser and was always late. He had missed his good friend and looked forward to spending the day with him, seeing the sights and raising hell, but he was supposed to be at Americo's by four to get ready for the Saturday night dinner crowd. Riley wasn't sure how he would survive the day, but a nap, shower and sandwich seemed to be what a good doctor would prescribe at the moment.

He thought a lot about what Magnolia had said the night before. He did love her, he was mostly sure he did, but not having been in love before gave him no point of reference. How much did he love her? Could he quantify it? He tried working it out in his mind like a calculus problem, which of course, couldn't work. Then he tried a geometric theorem which left too much to interpretation. He also wondered how much she really loved him. He knew she said she loved him, and wanted to be with him, and offered her physical self to him upon his demand. But did she love him, or just need him, or use him? Maybe he was using her, too? Maybe that *was* love? Riley found no answers, but as long as Magnolia was there for him, he would be there for her.

Riley opened the door to his room relieved that he had arrived and rest was moments away. He was surprised to see Alvin sitting up in bed wrapped from the waist down in blankets, sipping a steaming cup of what appeared to be coffee.

"Hey Alvin, you're up early. And on a Saturday morning, too?"

"I haven't been to sleep yet." Alvin winked and laughed, and Riley gazed at the bathroom door which was closed. Alvin's most recent acquisition was taking a shower. "I'm thinking of sleeping all afternoon to catch up. And hey, where have you been all night?"

"I've been at Magnolia's place. I want to try to get a couple hours sleep before Donnie calls if it's OK with you....Alvin? Are you drinking coffee?"

"Yes, why do you ask? Want some?"

"You made that yourself... without burning down the building?"

"Oh, no..." and Alvin smiled and glanced at the bathroom door.

"Oh she made it. That makes more sense, whatever. I'm going to sl...."

The bathroom door swung open and standing before the two boys was an attractive naked girl, dripping wet, toweling her long dark curly hair.

"Mici!"

"Riley?"

67

"Oh that's right, I forgot you two know each other," Alvin added with a dash of misplaced exuberance.

Mici tore back into the bathroom and slammed the door.

"Oh my God, oh my God, oh my God..." Riley was pacing and hyperventilating in a visible panic.

"What's wrong, dude? Relax. She's an awesome girl. We had a great time last night. Thanks for introducing us."

"Mici? With Mici? You screwed Mici? In my room? Oh my God, oh my God..."

Mici opened the door and emerged from the bathroom, this time wrapped in a large white bath towel. Her hair was still wet and it cascaded down her bony shoulders and dripped on the long, skinny toes of her bare feet. She spoke first.

"Riley, I am so sorry. I didn't want you to see me here. I was hoping to get ready and leave before you got back."

"That's fine. This all took me by surprise. You were the last person I expected to see come through that door." Riley's emotions were percolating and in his exhausted physical state, it was all he could do to not lash out -- at either of them. He also wanted to cry, but didn't understand why.

"Oh Riley, you are so sweet." And Mici smiled.

"Carmine...., umm your grandfather is going to kill us if he finds out." Riley reminded her.

"Oh no! Please... don't tell him. Please don't tell *Nonno.* He would be furious, he would kill all three of us. He thinks I never date, that I don't like boys, he is so sweet and protective and treats me like I'm still six years-old. It would break his heart. Please don't tell him I was here."

"I won't, I swear Mici, I won't tell anyone." A stunned Riley sat on the corner of his bed, arms crossed, as if he had been violated. He couldn't bear to look at her.

"Oh thank you, thank you. I'm going to get dressed." Riley recognized her beautiful dress from the night before rolled in a ball at his feet, and realized his left foot was resting on her black bra, then feeling awkward, handed it to her. Mici smiled and scooped up all her clothes then returned to the bathroom to dress.

Careful to keep his voice down, Riley scolded Alvin. "How could you do this, you asshole! How could you do this to me!

"I think you're confused. I didn't do anything to you, I did it to her."

"You screwed her and me both."

"She's an energetic little thing, always wiggling around when you're on top of her..."

"I DO NOT want to hear this!"

"Oh come on, dude, listen to yourself. Nobody's going to tell her grandfather. He won't find out. She just wanted some fun. It's all good. It's all between us."

"No. You disrespected her and me. You went back to Americo's, where I work, after we left to seduce her so I wouldn't find out about it. That old man, her grandfather, has been nothing but nice to me -- like my own father -- since the day I met him. I'm responsible for keeping an eye on her, making sure no one messes with her, keeping her safe. If something happens to her, I'll lose my job, and my family will be humiliated. Mr. Mantano would probably break my knee caps, too."

"Who made you responsible for her actions?"

"Well, I did. I decided that...."

"You're insane. And you know what, I think you're jealous."

"That's ridiculous."

"You spend the night doing *whatever* to Magnolia and now you're jealous of me and Mici. Amazing. What if Magnolia heard this conversation right now? What do you think she would do? After the way she was pouting last night at the restaurant, I figure she'd yank Mici's eyeballs out -- and yours too, if you were lucky."

"You leave Magnolia out of this. This has nothing to do with her."

"I think that gravestone over her bed fell on your head, that's what I think."

"That gravestone is on paper you idiot, it's a rubbing -- it's not real."

Riley paused. The room fell silent except for the sporadic gurgle of the coffee pot. Riley asked his next question with his eyes closed, and with slow, deliberate care.

"Alvin.., how is it you know that there is a gravestone over Magnolia's bed?"

"Thank you, boys!" Mici had returned from the bathroom dressed and eager to leave. "I'll see you tonight at work, Riley." Mici winked at Alvin, and as the door clicked closed behind her, the phone rang.

Annoyed by the interruption, Riley grabbed the phone to dispense with the jerk who was calling so early on a Saturday morning so he could continue his assault on Alvin. He screamed "HELLO" through the receiver with clenched teeth. His head pounded and his stomach churned.

"Riley? This is Sean. I don't know how to say this, so I'll just come right out with it. You need to come home. Mr. Murphy is dead."

EIGHT

Riley Lynch, Donnie Brack and Carmine Mantano took the train from Penn Station in New York City to Back Bay Station in Boston to attend the wake and funeral of Mr. Mark Murphy. Mr. Mantano had left Mici and Lorenzo in charge of the restaurant for the three days he would be gone. Weeknights at Americo's were never as busy, and he felt it was about time the two took on more responsibility anyway -- he was becoming too old to keep up the hectic seven-day-a-week pace of running the place. To Riley, Mr. Murphy had been a part-time surrogate father -- always there on important days and holidays, offering his mother companionship, and keeping an eye out for him and his brothers and sisters when they started to mix it up with the wrong crowd on the street. And to Mr. Mantano, Murph was the son he never had. Both took the news of Murphy's death hard and the four hour train ride was filled with sad reminiscences and stories exchanged between the two. Donnie knew Mr. Murphy from his time in the old neighborhood, but didn't consider him family.

"I haven't seen Murph in person in over ten years." Mr. Mantano began. "And now I'm gonna see him lying in a coffin. He came to New York for a weekend and came to the restaurant for dinner. Such a nice boy. He ordered the scampi posilipo, you know with a little tomato sauce, and I told him it was a very classy choice, that living in Boston hadn't ruined him yet. I told him I'd be coming up to see him in Southie in a few months, but I never did it. He said he wanted to take me to the North End restaurants and show me what real Italian food tasted like. I was always so busy. Boys, you listen up to me now, make time for your friends and family. Don't wait until they're gone and it's too late."

"But he did call you?" Riley asked.

"Oh yes, he never missed a birthday or Christmas or important date or anything like that. When he called me about you he said you where smart as a whip. He said you would make us lots of money. He was right. You are smart and work hard just like Murph said you would. You remind me a little of him. I think I told you I was friends with his father. His dad was an assistant to a construction union boss, and he got the plum jobs working on the big skyscrapers every summer. Murph would come down to the city with him, but he got into trouble. Those were bad times, and Murph ended up working as a bagman for a small protection racket in the neighborhood. He was a skinny, little shit of a kid. The problem was, he'd go in to pick up the protection money and they would beat him up instead. Broke his nose once. He was a very bad mobster."

"Mr. Murphy was in the mob? He worked for the mafia?"

"You did what you had to do to survive. And you stuck together. His father got tired of seeing him get beat up all the time. He figured someone was going to shoot him. That's why he sent him to me -- to earn an honest living. The owner had just hired me to run his new Italian restaurant in the Irish West End; the restaurant was a gift from one gang to the other."

"Are you in the mob Mr. Mantano?"

"Oh, my, what a question! Do you work for the FBI or something? Are you wearing a wire?" Mr. Mantano laughed. "Like I said, you do what you have to do to survive. Did that make me a mobster? Put me in the mafia? Part of a gang? Well, kid, I never signed up for nothing. I never made no deal. No one ever gave me no membership card, I'll tell you that. Those were real wise guys back then and they were bad news but they are all gone now... wiped out. There is no mafia. It's just in the story books."

"But Lorenzo told me you were well connected."

"Oh, Lorenzo, that idiot. Don't listen to him. Connected... what the hell does that mean *connected*? I've lived in this city my whole life. How could I not know lots of people? Lorenzo plays it like he's a tough guy out on the streets. He's just a bored, spoiled rich kid from New Jersey. Lorenzo goes out and buys a pair of white shoes and a white belt and thinks that makes him a mobster, that shithead. He should have lived my life, through my eyes. I like having him in Americo's though. The people who come, the regular customers, they like the atmosphere. Our food is good, but there's a lot of good food in

New York. Some of them come because they think we're a mafia restaurant and it's fun to eat in a dangerous place. Others come because they think an Italian restaurant in the Irish West End is the safest place to be. Lorenzo fits right in. If people think we are connected, it's good for business, and say what you want about Lorenzo, but he looks like he is connected, too. He plays a good game, that's all. To him it's a game."

"For as long as I knew Mr. Murphy, he was always dead against the street gangs. I can't believe he was ever in one of them. He'd always be looking out for me and my brothers and sisters. He would chew us out if we were even talking to the wrong people. There was a lot of violence in Boston when I was little, people always seemed to be getting shot at. There was a lot of pressure on my older brothers to get involved with my dad not around. Did I tell you my brother Sean got arrested? He didn't do a thing. The police just grabbed him and all his friends. But he was found innocent of all the charges. They let him go."

"Listen... any time a group of people come together -- Italian, Irish or anybody else -- they should work together. Help each other out. Find each other jobs, help each other make money and do business together. Protect themselves and their community. Is that a gang? Or is it just smart? It's too bad some of them go too far, and it's sad that some people can't tell the difference."

The train pulled into the station about a half hour late this time, and Sean was waiting in the station to meet them. Riley and Sean embraced, and bittersweet introductions were exchanged all around. Donnie excused himself and flagged down a cab to head back to his parents' house, who would be concerned that he was already overdue. Sean brought Riley and Mr. Montano to a twenty four hour coffee shop at the top of the train terminal on Dartmouth Street, and Sean suggested the three of them stop there for a bit to discuss the arrangements. When they arrived, they were the only patrons in the dank establishment, and a tired and scruffy waitress poured them each a cup of lukewarm coffee.

"Is this necessary, Sean?" Riley asked. "Mr. Mantano is tired. We should get him to his hotel."

"I know, I will," Sean answered. "But there are a few things I need to fill you both in on before you get home and see Mom. I spoke to Mary, Mr. Murphy's daughter, early this morning. She and her family are flying in from Beijing and should be here late tomorrow morning. Mom is responsible for handling all the funeral arrangements until she gets here."

"Oh, come on!" Riley whined. "Why is it Mom who always gets stuck with this stuff? Can't somebody else handle it?""

"You know Mom. She insisted. She wouldn't have it any other way."

"I haven't seen Mary since I was about four years old. The reason I know what she looks like is from the pictures in Mr. Murphy's office at the store," Riley complained.

"Well, I know her a little better than that, and Mary was pretty upset when I spoke to her -- which is understandable. But she asked that Mr. Mantano here be filled-in, too, about what happened. She said you two were close. I don't know you sir, so I am sorry to drag you into this."

"Look," Mr. Mantano interrupted, "Murph was like a son to me. Mary was like a granddaughter. I want to help any way I can."

Sean continued, "Thank you, I appreciate the help. According to the police, Mr. Murphy died when he was struck by a car getting the mail out of his mailbox at his house in Waltham. It was a hit-and-run accident. The driver came up over the curb and hit him head on, then took off. At the moment, the police have no leads."

"Oh, how horrible," Mr. Mantano cupped one hand over his mouth, and performed a solemn Catholic sign of the cross with the other.

"One of the neighbors told Mary the aftermath of the accident was quite gory and horrific -- the car hit him very hard, it was an awful mess. They are sure he died instantly, thank God."

"Oh poor Mr. Murphy." Riley said as his eyes began to tear up. This is too unbelievable. It's a nightmare."

"It gets worse," Sean warned them. "The police are still investigating and want to prosecute the driver for leaving the scene of the accident once they find them, but the chief said it was just one of those things and it looked like nothing more than an unfortunate accident. But Mary isn't so sure."

"What are you saying? Mr. Mantano interrupted. "That somebody murdered Murph? Who would do this?"

"That's what Mary wants to know."

Riley sat up straight. "This sounds crazy. I know she must be devastated -- we are all upset -- it is quite a shock, but where is the logic in this theory?"

"Mary questioned why her father would be checking the mail at six in the morning. The mailman always comes through the neighborhood early in the afternoon. She asked the police if there was any mail found as part of their investigation at the scene, lying in the street or whatever, and they said no they didn't find a thing." Sean said.

"Then why do they think he was checking the mail?" Asked Riley.

"The driver hit Mr. Murphy and the mailbox at the end of his driveway together, and he was wearing his pajamas and slippers at the time of the accident. The assumption by the police was that he must have strolled out to check the mail."

"So that's her evidence for murder? Pretty flimsy. I think she's just upset and letting her imagination run wild, that's all."

"Mary also said her father had been getting a lot of threats. He owed a lot of money on the bookstore. The bank stopped loaning him money years ago, so he had to turn to some of his old friends for help."

Mr. Mantano still couldn't accept the premise. "Loan sharks have been around for centuries. You can make good money at it if you can keep yourself out of jail. But why kill him? You can't pay back a debt when you're dead."

Sean agreed, and continued Mary's story. "She has been paying down the loans for her father for years. The way his business had been faltering, he couldn't keep up with the payments. He was in so deep he had drained all Mary's savings and she was struggling to keep her own family afloat. She had reached her limit and insisted he close the store and rent it out -- and create at least some positive cash flow to pay off the debt. It broke his heart to close that shop, it was all he had."

"But I still don't see murder." Riley insisted.

"That's all I know. She wants to speak to you, Mr. Mantano, when she gets here tomorrow."

"Sean? How is Mom? News of Mr. Murphy's passing must have come close to killing her."

"She took the news better than I expected. She cried, of course, and has spent every spare moment at her altar praying for his soul."

75

"I can't believe she is coordinating the funeral."

"You don't know the half of it. The wake is tomorrow night and it will be held in our apartment."

"Oh my God, please Sean, please tell me you're joking!"

"Sorry... she got help from the funeral director and special permission to do it. They will be bringing the casket over at around four. Calling hours begin at six."

Riley spent much of the remainder of the night staring at the peeling ceiling of his childhood bedroom, fighting anxiety and insomnia. He was hot, then cold, then both at the same time and he felt as if the walls were closing in upon him. He would doze for a few precious moments only to be awakened by the tiniest little creek or the sound of a car whizzing by on East Broadway. When sleep did overtake him, for a few uneasy seconds, he dreamed of senseless violence. Perhaps it was all the mafia talk on the train, or the image of Mr. Murphy's innards being splattered across so many suburban lawns, or maybe both. In the dream, he was present at Mr. Murphy's wake there in his family's apartment. Everyone he knew was present -- his mother, brothers, sisters, neighbors, friends and family. Magnolia was there too, and so were Mici and Alvin, and even Lorenzo and Armand. They partied and laughed in a great circle around Mr. Murphy's casket. Riley grew more angry at them with every passing minute as they acted more and more rude and disrespectful. The sharp blasts of gunshots were ringing out all over the neighborhood, and with each blast Riley would wince and become flush with fear. His friends and family, however, would instead cheer and laugh louder after each of the bursts. Riley's anxiety was rising, and he would plead and beg each of them to follow him to safety before they were killed. But they would mock or ignore him and laugh even louder. Riley answered a knock at the door, and a man dressed in a gray pinstriped suit and a white banded fedora, a ghost delivered straight from Al Capone's mob, stepped in with a black Tommy gun and opened fire, mowing down the revelers in a hail of bullets. Riley dove for cover behind the sofa and watched as one by one his most dear friends and family would take bullet after bullet, opening wound after wound, and fall with blood, organs and gray matter splattering the walls and buffet table. He opened his mouth to howl in terror but could not scream, as if his vocal chords had been detached. He watched his friends fall one by one into an evil, mass of quivering flesh and broken bone. Then as fast as he came, the gangster just disappeared, and Riley found himself standing in a river of blood and human juices that stained his shoes and ran in a steady stream through the door and down the stairs behind him. All fell silent and his eyes scanned the room. The corpse of Mr. Murphy had sat up in his casket and was staring at Riley. His eyes were black and cavernous and his skin gray and pale. Riley writhed in horror, but his legs and feet were paralyzed, as if cemented in place. Mr. Murphy smiled at Riley, then giggled, then reached out to him and broke into uproarious laughter.

Riley awoke in a cold sweat, rolled over in bed, arched his back and screamed into his pillow, over and over. Once he caught his breath and recovered his senses, he wrapped himself in a blanket and went downstairs to the street. It was still dark and peaceful, and a soft mist had started to fall from the heavens. Riley curled up out of the weather in a corner of the front stoop of the vacant bookshop and stared straight ahead, self appointed sentinel to his family for the remainder of the night.

Mary Murphy, her husband and her two little girls had arrived at Logan International Airport right on time the next morning from their long and grueling flight from Beijing via Toronto, and headed to the Lynch apartment so as to not lose another moment. Sarah greeted Mary as she emerged from her cab, and the two embraced on the sidewalk. Both women burst into tears at the mere sight of each other.

"Oh, Mary it has been so long, too long. I am so sorry."

"Thank you for being here Mrs. Lynch. This means so much to me and my family." Mary waived the cab containing her husband and exhausted little girls on to their hotel to refresh, and the women went inside to talk. Mr. Mantano arrived at the Lynch apartment a few minutes later. Mary and Sarah sat inside with Riley, while Siobhan was prep cooking in the kitchen behind them, preparing for both the wake and after-funeral gathering under Sarah's careful direction. The sweet, peppery smell of a large corned beef at full rolling boil filled and warmed the stale air of the apartment.

"Oh Mr. Mantano, you haven't changed a bit," Mary smiled and hugged her father's great old friend.

"Oh Mary, you are still a terrible liar! But look at you. I can't believe how you grew up. You are so beautiful. A nice family and a nice husband. Your father was so proud of you. He loved you so much." Mr. Mantano answered.

Mary was a short round woman, several years older than the Lynch children, who had the unfortunate luck to inherit her father's rugged face and barrel body type -- and looked like a younger version of him with long blonde hair. She did, however, possess a good sense of fashion and dressed with extravagance, with meticulous attention paid to her make-up and jewelry. Her decision to learn to speak Chinese as a high school student, on a playful dare from her father, led to a very lucrative international career. And though her family had looked drawn and beaten, the long trip from China was not showing any effect on her appearance.

"I am not afraid to tell you that my head is spinning right now," Mary confided in the group. "The last few days have all been a horrible dream."

"Don't you worry, my dear, everything is in perfect order," Sarah explained, squeezing Mary's hand. "I have taken care of everything. You just tell us what you need us to do."

Riley offered his services, too. "That's right, Mary, I'll be here all week. Just let us know what you need. I owe it to your dad."

Mary smiled in appreciation, still teary-eyed. "There is something I need Mr. Mantano's help with, which is why I asked to see you. I need to find some of my father's papers."

"Oh, Mary, I'm sorry, but how would I know where to look?" Mr. Mantano said.

"Well, maybe Riley could help me find them. The papers detail loans and certain accounts my father maintained over the years. My father was a great and wonderful bookseller, but a very bad businessman. He would write important information on scraps of paper -- names, phone numbers, amounts -- and hide them to keep them safe. When I was little, I would come across the papers in the bookshop, folded up and stuffed in the oddest of places, under floorboards or even in the ceiling. I am looking for a red ledger book that includes the names of his creditors and debtors. When I last asked my father about the old ledger, he couldn't remember where it went. He said he left it behind somewhere when he closed down. Mr. Mantano, I am hoping you will recognize the names inside -- if we can find it." Mary explained.

"Oh, mio dio!" Mr. Mantano exclaimed. "I think I now understand. I pray to Jesus I cannot help you."

"I know, but I think it could tell us who murdered him."

Not eager to start an argument, and trying to be sensitive to Mary's frayed nerves and fragile emotions, Riley leaned forward and inquired with great care, "Do you think *murder* might be too harsh? I mean, the police said they were sure it was just a horrible accident."

"Riley, I hope you are right. But trust me on this... I know better. I feel it."

Riley, Mary and Mr. Mantano walked downstairs from the Lynch apartment to the front stoop of the old bookshop. Mary rattled a big key in the lock of the heavy door, and the door swung open with a slow, reluctant creak, as if even the shop itself was conspiring to refuse to submit to her paranoia. The floor was strewn with thousands of tiny glass shards from the broken window Donnie and Liam had repaired a few days earlier, as well as leaves, dirt and debris blown in from the busy street. The seal around the doorway had rotted away, which had allowed the rain to seep in creating shallow puddles and mud around the front of the old cash register stand. Trash, old magazines and empty boxes littered the floor of the showroom, and Riley was amazed at how small and old his beloved shop had become, having been raped of its intrigue and charm. Mildew was evident on all the bookcases and everything wooden, and the smell of mold was unmistakable and burned their nostrils. Mary stood in place, sighed and frowned.

"Growing up, I spent more time in here than I did in my own bedroom at home," she said. "This is so painful to see. Let's do what we need to do and get out of here."

The three of them started searching, opening drawers and cupboards around the cash register, revealing not much more than trash and the nest of an annoyed field mouse. Riley could see something on the floor well beneath the cash register stand, but couldn't quite reach it. He and Mary both pushed at the stand hoping to slide it over a few inches, but the base of the big piece of furniture gave way, and it tipped over causing a momentous crash, startling the three and causing them to recoil. Underneath, they found the most amazing collection of items representing forty years of business that had been lost, fallen into the thin crevasse behind the cash stand. There were dozens of ball point pens, two old credit cards, a crisp twenty dollar bill, bookmarks, a 1980 Popular Mechanics Magazine, petrified mints, and what looked like hundreds of dollars in nickels, dimes and pennies -- all fallen from the dainty hands of little old ladies who would search their purses every day for just the right change -- but no ledger book.

Mr. Mantano had discovered some of the dozens of little papers Mary had talked about, stuffed into the slats between the paneling along the wall. He read them aloud as he unraveled them, careful not to tear them.

milk, tuna, cat food, batteries

half a league, half a league, half a league onward

Red Badge of Courage, Life on the Mississippi, something by Voltaire

(555) 778-2915, Rosemary $500

Ferdinand, Bold Arrangement, Broad Brush, Rampage, Badger Land

Miss Lee's Asian Spa, Tremont Street

Notre Dame plus four and a half, over Georgia Tech

sugar, gin, lime juice, soda water, fresh lime

The Wapshot Chronicle, John Cheever, Harper Perennial

"I am sorry, Mary, none of this looks very helpful," Mr. Mantano said, holding the notes whose meanings had been lost years before. Mary had moved on to the business office adjacent to the cash register area and was pulling up loose floor boards, finding all sorts of forgotten curiosities, but nothing useful.

"Is this a staircase? This looks like an old staircase." Riley announced peeling back a loose piece of paneling behind Mr. Murphy's dusty, old abandoned desk.

"Oh, I'm sure it is," Mary said." This old building has been remodeled who knows how many times in the last hundred and fifty years. If you look, you'll find boarded up windows, doors and even a chimney that goes nowhere behind these old walls. It's all a real mess."

Riley pulled back on the wall board and he found it wasn't nailed to anything. He slid his thin body into the drafty enclosed space and flipped the light switch expecting nothing to happen, except a dim light at the top of the stairs did in fact come on. Riley ascended the tight swirling staircase, creaky step by creaky step, careful not to trip, and reached the top to find a recliner and small end table holding a half-filled Styrofoam coffee cup -- and nothing else. Riley pulled at boards and pushed on the walls, but there was no give. Just before he gave up and headed back down to the others, he heard something familiar causing him to pause.

"Mom, this cabbage is rotten. You gave me another rotten cabbage."

"Hold on, Siobhan, hold on. Please be patient. I'll be right there."

Riley sat, and glanced around the tight space, and came to realize that he was behind the wall of his mother's bedroom. From his seat in the old recliner, he could see through the molding at the corner of her closet into the bedroom itself with a clear view of his mother's bed. He watched as his mother whisked by him on her way to assist his cranky sister, and Riley felt a sudden chill go up his spine, and a queasiness in his belly. Riley noticed more of those small slips of paper stuffed in the cracks of the wall. He pulled one out and struggled to read it in the dim light.

red bra, white underpants, hot tea, Readers Digest

"Hey kid, anything up there?" Mr. Mantano shouted from below.

"No... nothing. I'm on my way down." Riley responded, mindful to not reveal his find, and pulled more notes from the wall. He realized there were dozens to choose from.

blue nightgown, slippers, heating pad, cinnamon toast

pink slip, leftover pizza, extra pillows, knee socks, Excedrin

The most dreadful, evil, immoral thoughts spiraled through his mind. Had Mr. Murphy used this space to peep on his mother in bed? It was a horrifying and perverted concept, and Riley shook his head in anger and disbelief. He had to be mistaken. But could there be any other explanation? He felt a torrent of fury rise within him, as he clenched his teeth and looked for something to destroy.

After a time, Riley made his way back down the staircase in a numbing cloud of perplexity and anger.

"Are you OK? You look like you saw a ghost," Mary asked.

"Yes, I'm fine," he answered inhaling a deep breath. "Mary, did you find anything down here yet?"

"No, not yet. But I'm not giving up that easy. I know it is here somewhere."

The trio continued to search and tore apart the store for most of the afternoon but failed to achieve the results Mary had hoped for. Riley kept his word and did his duty, but remained both furious and confused by his bizarre discovery in the stairwell. He didn't know what to do about it, and couldn't even decide who he should tell, or could tell -- if anyone. Riley looked up and noticed a black Cadillac hearse had parked itself in front of the building.

Mr. Murphy's corpse had chosen that moment to arrive. If he were not already dead, Riley might have killed him.

Preparations for the evening's wake had been underway throughout the day. Sarah and Siobhan had been cooking for hours and had created all manner of delicacy. Several families and friends were bringing dishes as well, and though Riley felt guilty about it, he looked forward to the many culinary delights that would be on display. Mr. Murphy's coffin was placed in the living room against the wall, and most of the family's furniture was pushed aside to make room for the large number of mourners who were expected to visit. Mr. Murphy's casket was opened, and to everyone's immediate relief, Hennessey's Funeral Parlor had done a masterful job preparing the top half of his mangled body for public view. There was no sign of the horrific trauma he had suffered. Mr. Murphy wore a dashing black tuxedo coat, white shirt, gray vest and tie. He had never looked better. In his hands, he grasped a rosary. The window next to the coffin was left open, a traditional gesture to allow the spirit of the deceased a way to escape to the heavens (it was considered rude for any visitor to block the path to the window.) Several of Mr. Murphy's friends had sent beautiful flower arrangements, and they were displayed around the coffin. In the kitchen, Sarah set-up a makeshift bar complete with beer, wine, whiskey, rum, schnapps, vodka, brandy and all manner of other liqueurs and spirits. Sarah did not drink, did not approve of drunkenness, and had maintained an alcohol-free home for her children through the years. But this was a special occasion. The boys' bedroom had been cleaned and cleared to allow a place for the little children to run around and play games. (To Liam and Riley's disgust, Deacon Sabol from the soup kitchen volunteered to chaperone the little ones.) And the girls' bedroom was designated to serve as the coatroom and storage.

All the Lynch siblings were given steadfast duties. Sean and Liam were assigned to be doormen outside, to help guests find parking spaces on the busy street, and to help elder visitors make their way up the Lynch's tread worn second-floor apartment steps. Erin served as the obedient barkeep, while Meghan and Siobhan cooked, warmed plates in the kitchen and hustled dirty dishes and trash. Sarah and Erin greeted guests at the front door, took coats, and served as hostesses. And it was Riley's job to circulate among the guests and keep an eye on anyone drinking too much or acting out of the ordinary -- including Deacon Sabol. It was a complete family affair. Mary and her family sat in a pre-assigned row of chairs to the left of her father's casket, assigned to do nothing more than represent the unexpected loss of the Murphy clan.

One by one at first, then several at a time, well dressed mourners filed into the Lynch apartment for Mr. Murphy's calling hours. The atmosphere in the room began very respectful and solemn. Each visitor would offer their condolences to Mary and her family, then cross themselves and drop to their knees in a moment of quiet prayer before the casket, in honor of Mr. Murphy's soul. There was much sobbing. The Murphy family was small, as Mr. Murphy was an only child, as well as Mary, and poor Mrs. Murphy had died when Mary was still an infant. So most of those coming to pay their respects were neighbors, friends and long time business associates, and included several dedicated customers who had shopped the bookstore for decades.

Mr. Mantano spent the early part of the evening alone, holding up a wall at the back of the Lynch's apartment. He looked quite uncomfortable and out of place, and Riley went out of his way to make sure he knew he was welcome.

"Come on, Mr. Mantano. Let's go get you something good to eat."

"What? You have something *good* to eat? This may come as a shock to you Mr. Lynch, but I didn't grow up eating corned beef. That stuff is terrible. Terrible! Who would eat meat that you have to boil with cabbage to make it taste good! *Cabbage!*" Mr. Mantano joked. "And that soda bread with the raisins -- why is it always stale? Where is the *zeppole*? Where are the *cannolis*?"

Riley laughed, and Mr. Mantano smiled.

"Riley, your mother did a wonderful thing here, hosting this party. I like her. She is a good woman, a strong woman. I'll bet she is part Italian."

"I wouldn't let her hear you say that."

"Hey Riley, look over there. See that tall man in the white shirt standing behind your mother? I know him. That's Matty Quinn, an old friend of Murph's. I don't remember why, but he spent a long time in the slammer, I think it was ten, fifteen years or more. And over there talking to him, that old guy is Tenny Doyle. I remember him as an old wise guy from Hell's Kitchen in New York back in the Sixties."

"You're saying this place is full of mobsters?"

"No, I'm not saying any such thing. Though since they are here, maybe Murph was in a lot deeper than I thought. I can't help but wonder what they would be doing here."

"To pay their respects to an old friend?"

"Maybe... maybe. Or maybe as cover. If whatever is left of that old gang did knock off Murph as Mary insists, they would want to have a presence here at the wake so the police would be less likely to suspect them, and they would be seen by others in the neighborhood as the heavies... as a warning to everyone not to cross them."

"Or..." Riley paused. "Or maybe they just want us to *think* they had something to do with Mr. Murphy's death, making us think they are in the mob and are all powerful. The police of course couldn't arrest them because there wouldn't be any evidence. There might be some advantage for them in that."

Mr. Mantano smiled. "Kid, you learn real, real fast."

"I have a good teacher."

As the evening wore on, fewer people arrived but everyone seemed to stay, creating a very noisy and bustling atmosphere in the undersized apartment. The liquor had been flowing with fortitude for a couple of hours, and the crowd was becoming louder, looser and more animated. Someone found a dusty Clancy Brothers CD, popped it into the player, and a small group alternated between singing rounds of *Whiskey in a Jar* and *Danny Boy*. Large party bowls of potato chips and pretzels had been moved to the top of the coffin, where no one could resist nibbling at them as they drank, and someone tucked an open bottle of Guinness under Mr. Murphy's right arm. The little children had escaped their playroom (and Deacon Sabol's oversight) and were chasing each other around, about, under and between everyone's legs, and even underneath the casket itself. More than once, the elegant red flower arrangements and their easels toppled over sending a gentle snowfall of flower petals on top of the giggling, offending child of the moment. Whenever the din of the crowd became too loud, the revelers responded by turning up the music. Several clapped to the rhythm, and a few began to dance.

"These people are nuts. They should all be locked up!" Mr. Mantano kidded Riley. "This is disgraceful. When we get back to New York, I'm taking you to an Italian funeral, even if I have to kill somebody myself. Very respectful, very proper, not like this."

"But they didn't come to mourn, they came to celebrate... celebrate Mr. Murphy and his life, as dictated by old Irish tradition." Riley tried to defend the revelers. "Tomorrow at the burial, at church, the ones who come will be more respectful. You'll see"

Loud, angry male voices emanating from the kitchen cut through the thick air and turned several heads. Some sort of squabble was underway, and Riley knew the voices -- the disturbance came from Erin and Meghan's slack-jawed new boyfriends who were having an argument. But before he could fulfill his obligation and get to the kitchen to intercede and quiet them down, all hell broke loose. A thunderous crash of dishes was followed by the site of Erin and Meghan, each in their Sunday best dresses and each with a right hand full of the other's hair, swinging at one another with their left fists. The two pirouetted in the center of the living room scattering guests to all corners. A few of the more inebriated visitors started chanting and egging them on *go... go... go..!* while Sarah and the more sophisticated attendees shrieked and gasped in embarrassment. A left hook from Erin caught Meghan in the ribs, sending her sprawling, knocking over chairs and the CD player on

85

the end table bringing the music to a screeching halt. Her response was a left hook that clipped Erin on the jaw, pushing her backwards and against the coffin, bringing the heavy lid crashing down on Aunt Eileen's hand in an impressive shower of small yellow potato chips and cheese doodles. Eileen howled in obvious pain, but the battling young ladies didn't miss a beat and kept swinging and shrieking, until a much larger Erin found her leverage and pushed Meghan against the open window, bringing the sill crashing down, and sending broken glass like a sudden summer shower of tiny daggers down upon the sidewalk. Sean and Liam reached the girls before Riley could, snared them each in their own bear hug, extracted their clenched fingers from each other's hair, and dragged them kicking, swearing, spitting and screaming through the apartment door and down the narrow staircase.

Without instruction, the guests began picking up debris. Someone righted the table and plugged the CD player back into the wall, and someone else bellowed a boisterous cheer. The wake resumed right where it had left off.

Guests stayed until well after one in the morning, leaving behind a God-awful flotsam and jetsam of party debris. Even Sarah the perfectionist threw up her hands and elected to get some much-needed sleep rather than stay up all night trying to restore the environment that she worked so hard to create. Mary had escorted her family back to the hotel hours earlier, as all needed to be at St. Finian's by noon for the Mass of Christian Burial, to be followed by interment in the cemetery in back of the churchyard. Tomorrow was another big day.

Riley stood alone in the wreckage of the apartment with his arms folded, facing Mr. Murphy's closed casket. Mr. Hennessey had drank a little too much and went home early, so Hennessey's Funeral Parlor elected to return to collect the casket early the next morning for transport to the church. Mr. Murphy would spend his final night above ground in the Lynch's living room.

Riley opened the lid of the casket, propped it up, and he stared at Mr. Murphy's pale, cold face for the final time. Riley had not had an opportunity to mourn for the old man as the responsibilities of the day had been overwhelming. But Riley was also confused and angry. Most of his day had been spent trying to decipher the riddle of who

Mr. Mark Murphy, mild-mannered bookshop owner, father and friend truly was. His voice quivering, Riley spoke to his friend.

"Hello Mr. Murphy, "Riley began, "I need to talk to you. I am sorry you died, we all miss you. It was very nice seeing Mary again after all these years, by the way. She is very nice and she loves you very much. Did you see Mr. Mantano? He came today, all the way from New York City, to see you. He told me he feels bad the two of you never went to the North End for dinner."

Riley paused and waited for acknowledgement from the lifeless body. There was none.

"I need to ask you two questions, Mr. Murphy, if that's OK. I need to know the answers. It's important."

Riley paused again.

"First, I need to know where that red ledger book is. Do you remember where you left it? Mary is very upset. She thinks you were murdered by somebody. I think she's nuts. It would make a big difference to me, and to her, if you could just tell us where it went off to. If somebody murdered you, we will get them, I promise. If not, Mary should know -- it will make her feel a lot better. You need to help her get on with her life."

Riley stared and waited a long time for a response, but the deceased Mr. Murphy did not answer. The room remained silent.

"And second," Riley began again, "what is up with all these notes you left in the staircase behind my Mom's bedroom? What's up with that? Why were you spying on her?"

Mr. Murphy remained stubborn and quiet. Riley felt his fists clench and he wanted to punch him. A minute of time ticked by, and Riley bent over Mr. Murphy's lifeless body, slid his hands apart, moved the rosary aside and unbuttoned his jacket. Riley reached into his own pocket and pulled out several of the scraps of paper he found in the staircase earlier that afternoon. He squeezed them into a tight ball then stuffed them into Mr. Murphy's exposed empty pocket. Then Riley re-buttoned the jacket and repositioned his hands and rosary with care upon his chest.

"There... if you refuse to tell me, then when you get to heaven, you can explain it to God."

The day of the funeral was warm and windy, and the family walked down the block for the mass and burial at St. Finian's holding their hair and clothing worried it would blow away. The church was as grand and somber as ever, and each mourner entered, genuflected their respect and then sat in silent prayer. The crowd from the evening before was nowhere to be seen, as the church pews were populated by a few dozen of Mr. Murphy's closest family and friends. Ryan had arrived that morning from the seminary (Sarah was now grateful to fate that he could not attend the riotous wake the evening before) and had been invited by Father O'Connell to assist and participate in the mass, and offer a brief eulogy on behalf of the family. Ryan was honored, and Sarah was very proud.

There were two callers present in the church audience who had not been at the Lynch apartment for the wake the evening before. The first was Mr. Malcolm Ward, Esq., the white-haired, diminutive attorney who had sprung Sean and his friends from their trumped-up charges, who sat alone in the back row. The other guest was a mystery to almost everyone -- a fat, sloppy mound of a man with short black hair and a mean grimace. A mystery to everyone except to a concerned Mr. Mantano.

Following the mass, the casket was carried outside into the graveyard. Communicants of St. Finian's had been buried here for generations, and the head stones were old and squeezed close together, with barely enough room to walk among them. Riley and his brothers served as pall bearers, and escorted Mr. Murphy through the maze of ancestors to his final resting place at the far corner of the sacred grounds beneath an old maple tree that bent in the strong breeze. It had been many years since Riley walked through the cemetery. The last time might have been when he, Donnie, and Anthony were playing war, dodging and hiding behind each erect stone, gaining protection from the hail of invisible gunfire. A sparrow chirped overhead, and the clear blue sky offered solace. At the conclusion of the brief graveside ceremony, everyone left except Mary, who offered her final goodbye to her father alone.

The march back home was done with profound sadness and in near silence, as everyone took a moment to ponder their own mortality. There was a lot to absorb. Ryan walked out ahead of the rest, and Riley, still bothered by many things, raced to catch up with him. When he caught him, Riley looked at him but said nothing. Ryan was puzzled.

"You look like you want to say something."

"I do, I want to ask you something."

"OK, what is it?"

"It's more like a confession."

"I haven't been ordained. I'm not allowed to hear confession. Go talk to Father O'Connell."

"Then maybe it's just an admission."

"Oh for goodness sake, spit it out kid. What's on your mind?"

"We were inside the bookshop yesterday, and I found something."

"OK... so what did you find that has you so upset?"

"A staircase. A hidden staircase."

"You mean the one behind the wall in Mr. Murphy's office?"

"Yes! You know about it?"

"That staircase was a second exit from the upstairs apartment. It was remodeled over before Mom and Dad moved in years ago."

"So... when I got to the top of the stairs, I could see into Mom's bedroom through a gap in the boards. Then, I found notes."

"What kind of notes?"

"Mr. Murphy wrote things down about what Mom was wearing, or eating, or reading. He saved the notes and stuffed them in the wallboards. I think he was peeping on her."

Ryan paused and took a deep breath. "Riley, I know."

Riley charged out in front of Ryan and stared him down, walking backwards, but kept his voice quiet so the others could not hear him.

"What do you mean you know? You knew and didn't do anything? Why didn't you do something?"

"Hey calm down. This may be a surprise to you, but Mom knew about it, too."

"Oh please... you want me to believe she let him do this to her? That's crazy. I can't believe that."

"Riley, there is a lot that you don't know about Mom, and a lot I don't know either. I don't always know why she does what she does, it's as much a mystery to me as anyone. But she was so grateful to Mr. Murphy who looked after us and watched out for us all those years, and who kept us out of trouble. She knew she couldn't do all that alone, she needed him. We all needed him. Please keep them dear in your heart, don't judge them. Let it be."

Riley looked back at his mother and saw her in a different light -- not so much as a mom but more of a mercenary for her family, part matriarch, part negotiator, part dictator, part lioness, part whore. He was not comfortable with what he saw, and was struck with a wave of old-fashioned Catholic guilt as if he alone was responsible for her life of misery, for making the mistake of being born -- his own original sin. Behind her, his rotten battling sisters Erin and Meghan walked together, hand in hand like schoolchildren, as if nothing had happened the night before, nameless boyfriends each one step behind them. Mr. Mantano walked along with them, cell phone pressed to his ear.

Before long, the family arrived back home. Sarah went off to her altar to pray, and the girls were dispatched to the kitchen to begin preparation for the post-funeral luncheon for Mary and her family, and a few invited guests, who would be arriving at any moment. Riley assigned himself the task of picking up the debris still strewn about from the previous evening's festivities.

"Riley, I just spoke to Mici. Problems last night, big problems at Americo's." Mr. Mantano confided, with a tone of concern in his voice. "She says Lorenzo had an argument with a customer and someone called the police. I'm going to catch the first train and go back to New York so I can be there tonight for the dinner rush. I am going to slap that shithead senseless."

"I understand. I am sorry you couldn't stay longer with us. I will be back to work as soon as I can," Riley promised.

"No, you don't worry about work. You take care of your family, you hear me? I don't want to see you until this is all blown over and everyone is OK."

"Thank you, Mr. Mantano."

"But there is one other thing I want to talk to you about. Don't tell anyone yet, I want to make a few phone calls to make sure."

"Make sure about what?"

"At the funeral just now. Did you see that big fat guy?"

"Yes. Did you know him? I didn't recognize him."

"His name is Giovanni Marcellino. The used to call him The Chef. That's all I want to say right now until I know more. But look, remember Matty Quinn and Tenny Doyle, those two-bit wannabe gangsters from the wake last night? The Chef is no pretender like them... he's the real deal. He used to be an important, dangerous man. I just don't know how dangerous or important he is any more. Don't say anything to Mary just yet, until I find out more."

90

"Meghan! Erin! Come help me!?" Siobhan wailed from the kitchen, squeezing a round loaf of bread under each arm. "I can't find the sweet potatoes -- and the coddle is boiling over!"

"Oh, shut up Siobhan," Erin interrupted, now sitting in her boyfriend's lap, petting his greasy hair. "Nobody cares and you're giving me a headache. Just go sit yourself somewhere and let Mom worry about it."

The inquisitive and quiet Riley, never known for drama or emotional outbursts had heard enough, and turned away from his conversation with Mr. Mantano and blasted into Erin.

"Listen to you! Why is Mom always the one to have to do everything around here? Mom knocks herself out day in and day out with no help from you. Why don't you get off your lazy ass and do something for a change."

"Oh, so listen to Riley, now! And who are you to tell me what to do?" Erin fired back. "You're never here, then you show up like a stuck-up rich kid from your big, fancy college and order me around? Why am I supposed to care what you think? Fuck you!"

"Don't swear at me! Mom almost killed herself yesterday to make sure that the wake went off without a hitch, she worked her fingers to the bone, and you and Erin show your appreciation to her by brawling like a couple of barroom drunks in front of all her friends, and Mr. Murphy's family last night. She was humiliated."

"You don't have to tell me, tell Meghan -- she started it. It's her fault. Go yell at her."

"My fault? My fault?" Meghan jumped up and charged forward, chest pumped out. "Screw you, you bitch! You're the one who said...."

"Damn it... the coddle is burning! Someone please help me!" Siobhan pleaded, stomping her right foot.

A knock at the door interrupted the family spat. Guests had started to arrive.

"Where's Mom?"

"She's still at the altar praying, I think."

"Somebody go get her."

Riley thought it odd she didn't come charging out hurling lightning bolts at them when they started arguing, but through the years, Sarah sometimes let her kids fight it out to get it out of their systems. So many people in such a small place provided seasoned fuel for short hot tempers, so controlled burns were often smart

91

parenting. Riley entered his mother's private sanctuary. The room was lit by the yellow flames of two small candles. He gazed up at the large crucifix whose gold trim shimmered in the candlelight, then he gazed down.

Sarah was lying on the floor, motionless.

NINE

Mici is not my real granddaughter."
Mr. Mantano confided in Riley, "At least not by blood. I never had children of my own, never got married. When I was young, I had no interest in being nailed down to one person -- didn't make sense to me. And kids? No, not me. No way. I wasn't responsible enough to take care of myself, never mind be responsible for the needs of another person."

"So if she isn't your granddaughter, who is she?" Riley asked. Mr. Mantano had invited Riley to have lunch at a new trendy Italian restaurant that just opened a few blocks away from Americo's. Mr. Mantano wanted to try the food and spy on the new competitor.

"Mici's mother died at the hospital in child birth, very sad, heartbreaking, and she was being raised by her father alone. Her father was a very nice man, my good friend, an older gentleman. He was as surprised as anyone to find out his girlfriend was pregnant, but he did the right thing by her. He married that sweet girl right away, got himself a real job, and started planning for Mici's future. When Mici's mother died, he took her to Queens and rented an apartment, but he could not afford it -- his job didn't pay enough to cover daycare and since he was the new guy, they would screw around with his hours. So I told him I would help him out. I got him a second job as a driver at night for a local wise guy named DelVecchio -- I cashed in a personal favor. DelVecchio would check-in on the family's gambling interests, keep the bookies under control, and make sure the money didn't disappear -- that sort of thing. Nothing too dangerous."

Mr. Mantano paused to cut another bite of veal parmesan. "This veal is too dry, it needs more vermouth... But I made a big, big mistake. I didn't know there was already a contract out on DelVecchio from some other deal that went bad that he was involved in years earlier. One night as DelVecchio got in his limo down in the Bowery, someone pulled up alongside and unloaded six shots into the car killing both DelVecchio and Mici's father. A single bullet pierced his heart and the coroner said he died instantly. I was devastated, it felt like it was all my fault. I blamed myself that I orphaned little Mici and sent him to his death."

"But that wasn't your fault. You couldn't have known."

"Yes... I hear you say the words and I understand them, but in my heart, I cannot accept what they mean. I had to do the responsible thing. The State of New York took Mici away and put her in a state home to wait for an adoption. I went and got her and brought her to live with me. She was less than a year old. I decided to raise her myself."

"It sounds like you're saying you kidnapped her."

"Well, kidnapped is a strong word, Riley. I had an old friend downtown take care of the paperwork."

"Does Mici know any of this story?"

"Oh yes, she knows. And more. I told her everything. What a tragedy. Mici's mother was the most beautiful woman I have ever met in my life. Mici looks just like her. She was all energy, full of life, always smiling. I remember dancing with her at the wedding as if it were yesterday, so happy and light on her feet, breezing around the dance floor. A highlight of my life. You felt special if she just looked at you."

"Just like Mici."

"Yes, just like Mici. And I will tell you, Riley, Mici saved my life. If I had not brought her to live with me, I would have died. My life was a mess and I was involved with all the wrong people. I wouldn't have survived. She made me clean up my life. She saved me."

"It sounds to me like you saved her, too."

"Ah, nonsense. I could never be a mother and father to her at the same time. She missed out on a lot, and as I got older I didn't have the energy that kids need in their parents. I wish I could have done more. I should have done more."

"Mr. Mantano, with all due respect, you did a wonderful job raising Mici. Just look at her! She is beautiful, she works hard, she's smart, and she loves you very much. She is devoted to you. You are her *Nonno.*"

"Thank you, Riley, thank you for that. I just don't know what the future holds for her. Is she going to be a busboy her whole life? I hope she meets someone nice like you who will take care of her and love her. She is attracted to the worst kind of boys. She doesn't think I know, but oh yes, I know. I see how she looks at them, then she sneaks out when she thinks I am not looking. It's very painful. I worry."

"You don't need to worry, I will help keep an eye on her for you," Riley said with some embarrassment, as the image of Mici standing naked in front of his bathroom flashed before his eyes. He did his best to ignore it.

"You are too good, Riley. Too good. I think I need an army of Rileys to keep an eye on her! But there is a reason I am telling you this story. It's the real reason why I asked you here for lunch today. I thought you should know something."

"Is something wrong?"

"The man who put out the hit on DelVecchio, who also killed Mici's father, was The Chef -- Giovanni Marcellino. He was that strange fat man at Murph's funeral."

"I remember... my God. Why would he know Mr. Murphy?"

"I don't know yet. But it worries me. I made a lot of calls and talked to a lot of people and nobody wanted to admit to me what Marcellino was up to these days, which means he's up to something no good. I had to be careful, too, since I didn't want anyone to think I was sniffing around Marcellino's business. They said he had been buying up real estate in several cities, including Boston, and had opened some new restaurants in Los Angeles, and nothing else. No one was ever convicted of the DelVecchio murders, and I wonder if the police were on the payroll back then, too. And it was a rumor on the streets that Marcellino ordered that hit, it was never proven. No one knows for sure. I but I do know that Marcellino is bad news."

Riley finished his calamari, afraid to tell Mr. Mantano that it was superior to Americo's signature dish. He was fascinated by Mici's life story, and his heart broke for her, the poor sweet girl, as no one deserved such calamity, especially someone as nice as she.

"But Riley, I must apologize. We have been sitting here all this time and I have not asked about your mother. How is she doing?"

Riley's good mood sank. Sarah was not doing well. Her collapse at home after Mr. Murphy's funeral was determined to be a symptom of brain swelling associated with a cancer that originated in the back of her head and continued down her spine. The tumors were malignant and inoperable, though Sarah would have refused any operation whatsoever if it had even been an option. The doctors said she had been carrying the affliction for years, and had they caught it way back then in its earliest stages, they may have been able to operate and given her a better chance. Under questioning from the doctors, Sarah admitted to exhaustion, severe headaches and fainting on several other occasions, but she had never told anyone. The spells had become much worse and more frequent as of late. Riley had watched her slow decline over the last few years. He was not surprised.

Six months earlier, the doctors had given Sarah no more than three months to live.

They warned the family that fainting spells would increase, and she would become weaker as time wore on. They also warned that pressure of that nature on her spine could cause her to lose her motor skills, costing Sarah her mobility and putting her in a wheelchair. She would need round the clock attention. The suffering she would have to endure and the prognosis could not have been worse.

Sarah, of course, accepted the grim news without blinking. She was a woman of deep faith, and believed God would call her home when he was ready -- and she was not afraid to let everyone know that. It took a substantial amount of cajoling on the part of all her children to make her accept even the need for medication. Sarah had no insurance as neither of her menial part time jobs offered it, and since she could no longer work anyway, all the money for her expensive medications, living expenses and care would come out of the shallow pockets of the Lynch children.

Sean agreed to coordinate everyone's contributions and keep the bills paid. When the children met to sort out the sad financial arrangements, they knew the burden would be a temporary one. Sarah did not have long to live.

Riley came back to New York to pick up as many extra hours as Mr. Mantano could provide. The new play at the Six Star Theatre had run its course and announced it would close soon, and everyone at Americo's worried about the effect on business. But Mr. Mantano obliged his promise and kept Riley busy.

96

"So far, so good," Riley answered. "My mom is getting by. I try to call her every day. She is in great spirits. She's still walking around the apartment, and goes out for short strolls in the neighborhood, but that's all she can handle. All the medication drags her down, but so far, it looks like it's helping a little."

"She's an amazing woman, Riley, amazing. She's a real fighter."

Riley hopped on the subway to get back to his dorm, and as the noisy train rattled along its familiar dark subterranean trail, he thought about how his brothers and sisters would survive without their mother hanging on their every movement. He believed he would survive and be OK and he could fend for himself just fine, and that Ryan would be alright too, with the church to be there to look out for him. (Riley also wagered his mother would survive just long enough to see Ryan's formal ordination ceremony during Lent in the spring.) Sean was the most responsible of his brothers and sisters scratching out a living with his girlfriend across town, Sean even proposed marriage to her just to pacify Sarah's never-ending nagging, but Sean's girlfriend wouldn't hear of it. Liam, however, was another story. Although the only remaining male in the household after Sean moved out, Liam had been outgunned and defeated by his dominant sisters and spent much of his time hiding in his bedroom. Liam couldn't hold a job and didn't want to, and his behavior had become tense, anxious and unpredictable. Erin was the oldest, and Sarah relied on her for quite a lot -- always, it seemed, to her disappointment. He figured Erin would just marry one of her greasy, sleaze ball boyfriends and re-direct her bile toward him. Meghan was recognized as the laziest of the family, and expected Sarah to wait on her hand and foot, and without her mother, he expected she would be rudderless. But it was Siobhan who worried Riley the most. With little Brian to look after, Siobhan had perhaps matured more than any of them, but had no means of support outside her apartment. Siobhan wasn't qualified to do anything and the father of her child (who Sean referred to as her Spanish sperm donor) had disappeared.

Riley had walked out of the subway station and turned the corner toward home when he was struck by an unnerving realization and stopped dead in his tracks. He was supposed to have met Magnolia at three at Cafe Marie Anne. She said there was something important she wanted to talk to him about. He swore he would be there. He was now over an hour late.

Riley sprinted toward Amsterdam Avenue at full gallop, rounded the corner, and ran headfirst into a Volvo parked with two tires on the sidewalk. He ignored the sudden pain in his knees, and wondered why Magnolia hadn't called him on his cell phone. He thought maybe he should call her, but abandoned the idea until he could contrive an acceptable excuse. He decided the best measure was to just get there fast. He wondered if she would still be there or not when he arrived, and considering her temper, he wondered which he would prefer.

Riley reached the cafe just as Magnolia stepped outside. She was dressed in full Catholic school girl regalia, wearing a tight white blouse, red and black plaid skirt well above the knee, white knee socks and black patent leather shoes. Her hair was set in pigtails, and she had exchanged her everyday purse for a jet black metal lunchbox. She saw him running toward her and hopped up to greet him outside as he arrived at the front door.

"Oh, hello asshole." Magnolia said, and she planted a big wet kiss on Riley's sweaty lips.

"I am so sorry, Magnolia." Riley bent over, put his hands on his knees and gasped for air like a goldfish plucked from its bowl. "I got hung up with Mr. Mantano at the restaurant. It was important."

"And I'm not important? Maybe what I want to talk about is important, too. So did Mr. Mantano steal your cell phone?"

"You're right, I know. I should have called. It's all my fault. You have every right to be upset. I got here as fast as I could."

Magnolia dropped her black lunchbox, spilling its colorful and eclectic contents on Riley's sneakers and across the cement sidewalk. A bottle of Prozac rolled to the curb. An annoyed Magnolia bent over to gather her belongings back up, and Riley, as well as a few wide-eyed patrons seated near the glass window of the cafe, noticed Magnolia wasn't wearing underwear beneath her short plaid skirt.

"Let's go back inside," Magnolia suggested. "I do still want to talk to you."

"Umm... no... no. I think we should go somewhere else right now," an embarrassed Riley insisted, hurrying her along as she gathered up her things.

The two walked hand in hand down Amsterdam Avenue and turned back toward campus. They stopped and sat on a bench beneath a large red maple tree not too far from Riley's dorm. The tree had been stripped of its leaves as was its annual autumnal rite, and several fat gray pigeons demanding handouts pranced around at their feet on the scattered red leaves.

"Riley... I have decided that I'm going to drop out of school."

"You're going to do what?" The news couldn't have hit Riley any harder had she struck him upside the head with her retro lunchbox.

"I'm dropping out. I want to go back home."

"What are you talking about? You hate being home. You said it was the worst place on Earth. You called it a Siberian gulag."

"So shoot me, I miss it. I miss being there. I miss the farm. Plus my grades are bad and getting worse. I think I should leave before they kick me out anyway."

"Don't worry about your grades. I can help with that, I'll tutor you. We'll get you through it. No big deal."

"Riley, I haven't even been to class in three weeks. I hate this place. I hate New York. Everybody sucks. I don't fit in here."

"And you fit in back at home? You'll hate it there. And your parents will kill you."

"Oh, I doubt that. They never wanted me to come to New York in the first place. They told me I wouldn't make it here. They wanted me to go to the community college in Glens Falls near home instead and learn a skill that would be useful to society."

"You need to think about this. Attending Columbia is a great opportunity -- not everyone gets to come here. Don't throw that away. Show your family they are wrong about you, that you can make it here. Show them how strong and smart you are."

"You sound like one of those self-help pamphlets my shrink used to give me. Maybe your family gets off on that crap, but not mine. Your family is proud of you -- those hundreds of brothers and sisters of yours always calling: *Oh, we miss you Riley! Oh, come home soon Riley! Oh, we are so proud of you Riley!* I still can't believe you told them my name was Maggie -- *yuck!* What you do matters to them. I could cure cancer and my parents would still find something in me to criticize. They would tell me to skip the Nobel Prize awards ceremony because they needed me to shovel the chicken shit compost over the new garlic bulbs."

"You matter to me."

Magnolia sighed and frowned but didn't respond. She stared down at the pigeons and when one pecked too close to her shoe, she punted it out of the way. The pigeon squawked in anger, and might have flipped her a New York middle finger salute, if it had ever bothered to evolve one.

"I am leaving tomorrow. I'm taking the bus. I have to go and pack, now. I'm sorry, Riley, I don't see how we can be together anymore. Goodbye." Pigeons waddled, scattered and flew in all directions in self defense as Magnolia stood, tucked her lunchbox under her arm, and marched away and out of Riley's life, wiggling her plaid-skirted bottom behind her.

Riley sat stunned, yet puzzled and sad. He had been flat out dumped. He sat alone for a long while formulating what he could say that would keep Magnolia in school and change her mind, and keep them together as a couple. He wondered if he should have done something different, or if he said or did something that caused this to all happen so fast. Maybe it was all because he was late getting to the cafe. Magnolia always overreacted in stressful situations, maybe she would come to her senses tomorrow, he thought. He decided to call her later, then he changed his mind. He would instead wait for her to phone him. She always called, even after they would argue, when she would explain how she was right after all and could prove it. But Riley felt her tone and manner were quite different this time. He knew she was dead serious. And he knew, for some reason that made sense only to Magnolia, she wanted out of school and for the relationship to be over.

Magnolia's call never came.

Riley's track record of relationships with girls throughout his life was bleak, at best. He had never experienced a true or meaningful relationship in high school, and whenever he started to like someone and it looked like things had the potential to blossom, he would find a way to screw it up, often by paying more attention to his latest literary find than his supple new teen squeeze. As he sat on the park bench with the pigeons, he thought back to his eighth grade dance at South Boston Middle School. In May that year, the pressure was on for each of the boys to find a real "date" for the end-of-the-year school dance. The dance was a long held school tradition, a rite of passage into high school and pre-adulthood, and included a live band, a sit down meal, and elaborate party decorations -- something akin to a mini prom. The students were expected to even dress up a bit, and the girls tittered on for weeks about what they would wear. It took a month for Riley to manufacture enough courage to decide to ask

Tammy Meeks -- his one true secret love -- to the dance as his date, as he had no defined interest in any other girl. He was infatuated with Tammy, and no one else. And at last, when she stood alone at her locker at the end of a warm spring day sorting out her books, Riley stood tall and approached, took a deep breath, and calling upon his innermost store of strength, like Samson praying to the heavens in his final moment of glory... he chickened out. Getting home later that night, he kicked himself for being such a loser and utter failure after working so hard and long to muster the courage. He decided on one final assault. At school the next morning, he elected to take a more literary and intellectual approach, an approach more suited to his feeble personality -- he would write her a simple note and stuff it in her locker, then run away. He stood in the hallway, pulled out a pencil and a crinkled piece of small gray math paper and began to compose, careful to be certain no one could see over his shoulder: *"Hi Tammy, how ya doin? I love you..."* That was as far as he got when Anthony approached from the back and startled him. Fearing his love note would be discovered, he stuffed it into his frayed notebook in embarrassment, and clutched it to his chest as he was whisked off to class by his pal. He never finished or delivered that note and later abandoned all plans to ask Tammy. He went to the illustrious dance alone that year. Tammy stayed home.

Magnolia's absence left a significant void inside him. He missed her companionship, friendship and quirkiness. And on some level, he did love her. For the next several months, Riley's life fell into a dull routine of school, study and work, followed by more school, more study and more work. His humdrum days were interrupted by predictable periodic calls to his mother, which always served to perk him up to hear she was doing well on the other end of the phone line. The conversation was almost always the same, and was something like:

"Hi Mom, everything OK?

"Hello Riley, yes, everything is fine, dear."

"Are you still taking your pills?"

"Yes, I never miss one. How is school?"

"School is fine. I'm studying hard."

"That's wonderful, dear. I am so proud of you."

"I'll send a check home this Friday. Love you, Mom."

"Love you too, Riley."

The medical bills were piling up back at home, as Sarah's medication was very expensive, and Riley found purpose in working at Americo's every waking hour he was able. He was all but running the entire operation now by himself, juggling finances, ordering supplies, paying bills, and even organizing the grumpy wait staff. And an old and tired Mr. Mantano didn't mind one bit. Business at Americo's was down since the play closed across the street, and it was Riley's wise financial decisions that kept the restaurant profitable and in business without it. Riley had also learned much about how to maximize tips, and had become a better hawk than even the more experienced Lorenzo, to Lorenzo's continual annoyance. Customers had even started to request Riley by name when they came in for dinner.

Mr. Edward Fabrizi and his elegant wife, Mrs. Imelda Fabrizi had been regular patrons of Americo's for several years, were creatures of routine, and tipped very well. Mr. Fabrizi was a large, square jawed man with deep eyes and a salt and pepper goatee. It was obvious he had money and wanted people to know that it was a lot. On each of the meaty fingers of his large, manicured hands he wore multiple diamond and gold rings. He would wave them around his head when ordering and talking so he could allow you an opportunity to admire them. His shoes were leather, square-toed and imported, and Riley surmised they were worth more than his annual salary as a waiter. Mr. Fabrizi's personality was very large and his voice boomed. When he spoke, it was because he was saying something important, and he expected everyone in the room to hear it and pay attention. Most people found him intimidating and obnoxious, if not outright terrifying -- but no one who valued their life would dare tell him so.

Lorenzo was always Mr. Fabrizi's waiter of choice -- no one else -- and he would ask for him by name the minute he walked through the door. Mr. Fabrizi refused to ever wait in line, and Mr. Mantano made sure he would come right to the front the moment they walked in the door.

Imelda Fabrizi was a demure picture of elegance. Her daintiness stood in comic contrast to her husband's intimidating mass, and when he escorted her to their table, her hand would disappear within his like a child's. She, too, was well-jeweled, wearing a shimmering string of white pearls around her thin neck, several rings, and huge diamond earrings that shimmered like the flames of two small candles. As if rehearsed, or playing to some unseen camera and audience, she would stand by and wait for her husband who would pull out her chair and she would sit, then he would push her chair back to the table, and peer around the room as if expecting applause in recognition of his chivalry. In her youth, Riley figured, she must have been stunning. But despite her heavy make-up and thousand dollar salon hairstyle, the emerging crow's feet around her eyes and a slight sag to her chin bore witness to her journey into middle age.

Then on yet another slow Saturday night the Fabrizis entered the restaurant with their usual imperial flair and approached Mr. Mantano who stood at the host's stand with his arms outstretched, welcoming their arrival.

"Oh Edward, let's have that nice Irish boy tonight." Imelda requested.

Surprised, Mr. Fabrizi looked at her and raised his eyebrows. Changes of routine were not acceptable. He blinked twice. His expression revealed that he did not approve of the idea, but paused and soon conceded to his wife's whim. "You heard the lady Carmine, have that Irish boy take us to our table."

Riley and Lorenzo both overheard the exchange and were shocked. Lorenzo fumed and stormed out through the back door into the alley where he was alleged to have broken a toe destroying several trash cans while disrupting the lives of a family of New York City's finest rats.

"Right this way, sir and madam," and Riley extended an elbow to Imelda who smiled and was flattered to accept it, and the couple was escorted with the usual fanfare to their usual table.

"Tell me Riley," what should I order?" Mr. Fabrizi began, having read his name from his gold nametag, "the sea bass or the veal?"

Riley paused. He learned later that Mr. Fabrizi never asked a question to which he did not already know the answer. Riley also knew he always ordered the sea bass which the kitchen would prepare with extra sun-dried tomatoes to his personal taste. He figured it to be a trick question to put Riley on the defensive. Riley elected to be bold.

"I would suggest the veal, sir."

"No kidding." A surprised Mr. Fabrizi responded, thinking he had tripped him up.

"While the sea bass is always a very smart choice, the veal is very moist and has a very delicate flavor. I selected it myself when I met with the butcher earlier this afternoon. You will not be disappointed, sir."

Mr. Fabrizi was impressed, and nodded. He liked to be privy to inside information. "Really, you met with the butcher? Then I will order the veal. My dear Imelda, what will you be having?"

"Oh, how exciting!" Imelda said with a mischievous smile. "Riley, what would you recommend for me?"

Riley knew Mrs. Fabrizi preferred pasta, and ordered the scampi on most visits. "If you enjoy shrimp, I would highly recommend our shrimp ravioli. It is very light and prepared in a wonderful and unique vodka rosa sauce you won't find anywhere in the city."

"Ooh, how decadent!" she purred, impressed by the exclusiveness. "I'll have that!"

Riley marched the orders to the kitchen and encountered a limping and still fuming Lorenzo, clothes and hair tussled, just returned from his tirade in the back alley. Lorenzo saw the order ticket, pounded his fist on the counter, and lost his temper all over again.

"No! No! No! Change this to the sea bass and the scampi right now before we piss them off! I'll go out and smooth it over before they walk out of here." Lorenzo demanded, combing his hair.

"Oh no you won't," Riley shot back. "You leave them alone. That's my table out there now."

"Fuck you! You're going to screw-up the best customer I have ever had in this dump. It took me years to cultivate those rich bastards, you little Irish asshole."

Riley wasn't sure if it was all the long hours and effort he had put into perfecting Americo's, or the stress of his mother's advancing illness, or the loneliness he carried from his break-up with Magnolia, or all of the above, but something strong and sinister deep in Riley's core emerged that evening and without uttering a word, Riley spun around and grabbed Lorenzo by his white-starched shirt with both fists and pinned him against a stainless steel refrigerator with an astonishing force. The kitchen staff fell silent and froze in place as a few steel spoons flew in random directions and rattled to the floor. Reacting on instinct, Mici slid into the shadows of a corner to cower.

104

Riley spoke loud and slow in a near homicidal tone with teeth clenched, and stared into Lorenzo's wide, surprised and terrified eyes. "You listen, and you listen to every word I say very carefully. First, you will not speak to the Fabrizis or change their order. Second, you will never scream or swear at me again. And third, if you do any of those things I will break your scrawny, greasy Italian neck and leave you dead in the alley as food for the rats." Riley paused, "Do we have an understanding?"

T E N

Good evening. I'm Marcia Small and this is the Channel 9 News Center with a Breaking News Alert. A Boston police raid on Dorchester Street in South Boston tonight has resulted in the arrest of several suspects, as well as a drug dealer police are describing as a major kingpin in the Boston drug trade. Let's go live to News Center 9 organized crime reporter Everett Craven for an update at the scene. Everett? What more can you tell us?

Thank you, Marcia. A Boston police spokesman is telling us tonight that fifteen people have been arrested in connection with a raid focused around a known drug kingpin named Alberto Lopez. I have been told that Mr. Lopez had been under investigation for several months for dealing crack cocaine, and it is believed that his influence in the drug trade around Boston is substantial. Fourteen others were arrested in this sweep including his girlfriend Siobhan Lynch who is alleged to have hidden two vials of crack cocaine in her child's shoes to avoid arrest. A spokesman tells us a charge of child endangerment is expected to be added to her drug charges. The raid was conducted in cooperation with the FBI and Massachusetts State Police, and they say further arrests and details will be coming in the next few days. A complete list of those arrested will be made available later this evening. I am organized crime reporter Everett Craven, live at the scene, for the Channel 9 News Center.

"Dude, your sister's a cute little thing." Alvin said, as Riley shut down his laptop's video player. Riley had watched the news clip at least a dozen times over the past week, and the sight of his sister's mug shot on TV unnerved him and broke his heart a little more each time he saw it.

"You are not getting anywhere near my sister," Riley insisted. "Unless you're planning to break into jail."

Siobhan was being held in the Nashua Street Jail in Boston, and little Brian Seamus Lynch-Lopez whose shoes his stupid mother had stuffed with crack in a moment of panic and desperation, was whisked off by the state and was staying with an anonymous foster parent until Siobhan could be exonerated -- which seemed a long shot at best. Sean and his girlfriend had offered to take Brian in and care for him, but as Sean and his girlfriend had never bothered to marry, and his girlfriend's record was less than terrific, Brian had to be absorbed into the state system. Sarah was in no condition to serve as primary caregiver for the child as her strength was slipping further away with every passing day, making it a challenge to even care for herself, and the money coming in from the responsible Lynch children wasn't making ends meet as it was. Siobhan had hired Malcolm Ward as her attorney further draining the family's parched financial accounts, and Sarah was now skipping medication and slipping on rent payments. Malcolm warned the family that although he would do everything in his power, the charges against Siobhan were severe and she was looking at a significant jail sentence.

The saga broke Sarah's heart.

Sarah's sagging spirit didn't need the added weight. She continued to defy doctor's expectations and had not yet lost her ability to walk around, though simple strolls around her own apartment would exhaust her. She would make multiple trips per day from her bedroom to her altar for sessions of intense prayer, and then return back to her bed to recover and nap each time. Meghan had caught her more than once skipping her medications, and the girls would try different methods of hiding pills in her favorite foods like one might do with a fussy puppy. But even that wasn't working as Sarah would only nibble at her meals eating less each day.

Riley found escape from the depression and drama of his family and anemic personal life in his academic endeavors, excelling even by his own lofty standards. He immersed himself in 800 page texts on international finance, tax law and economic policy during every idle moment. A paper he wrote for Professor Friedman comparing and contrasting European tax laws was submitted to *International Finance Magazine* and accepted for publication (though Friedman gave him a B+.) His pointed classroom questions and viewpoints would dominate his professor's scheduled mundane lecture, gaining him a colorful array of allies and enemies within the student body and faculty alike. His reputation was unproven but growing, and his future potential was seen as unlimited. Riley also excelled in his core courses as well -- such as English, History and Philosophy -- and the idea of becoming a sort of Renaissance man who is knowledgeable and proficient on multiple intellectual levels intrigued him. He also decided to register for Italian classes the following semester. He was getting to know a lot of Italians.

Mr. & Mrs. Fabrizi adopted Riley as their personal, exclusive waiter. Each Friday night, they would breeze in, ask for him by name, and order the veal and ravioli. But Riley was more than a mere replacement waiter for Lorenzo and his bruised ego. Riley sensed an unusual loneliness and sadness in them, something he couldn't quite pinpoint or explain, but he felt comfortable chatting with them and they enjoyed small anecdotes from his personal life. Visit after visit, he would entertain them with stories about his mother, his brothers and sisters back home, his friends at Columbia, and Alvin -- they loved his stories about stupid roommate Alvin. Each week, Mrs. Fabrizi would insist upon a nice story from Riley before ordering their dinner. *Oh, tell us about Christmas in Southie again! What has Alvin been up to this week? Have you heard from your brother, the priest?* They hung on his every word, and would laugh with approval at the conclusion of each installment, even if he had to make something up. He felt he had produced their own private Irish soap opera.

Seeing him become more friendly with the Fabrizis, Mr. Mantano pulled Riley aside one night to fill him in. Edward Fabrizi had a checkered past, and he felt Riley needed to know about it.

Edward Fabrizi was born in Sicily in the late 1950's, and came to the United States with his family as an infant, settling in a poor, rundown neighborhood of Yonkers. His parents named him Edward in advance of their immigration to give him a more American-sounding name and to help him fit in. His parents were penniless and spoke the native tongue, so as a child, he proved his value to his family by learning broken English on the streets and serving as the official family translator. Edward never went to school beyond the 7th grade, dropping out to work in his uncle's bakery on Riverdale Avenue. The hours were long and the work was hot and dirty, and when business was off or when the mafia was shaking his uncle down for protection money, Edward would work weeks without pay. The little money he did earn went to supplement the paltry wages his father would bring home from his job at the Otis Elevator Factory, which would serve to maintain their meager, subsistent lifestyle. It was obvious to Edward, as it was to many of the impressionable youth of that era, that the people in town with money, nice clothes and fancy cars were the wise guys. So when he stumbled across an opportunity to be a runner for a local gang's numbers racket, he jumped at it. Edward was a big boy -- much larger and more intimidating than his schoolyard friends -- so he was able to fit in with boys twice his age. Edward excelled and became a trusted soldier and confidant, moving up through the hierarchy and cultivating contacts that would serve him his entire life, but he would not accept his role as a mere servant to the syndicate. Edward also learned about the real value of money and how it bought influence, lessons he would master years later. He was impatient, and wanted to carve out his own piece of the action. In his early twenties, Edward befriended a Ukrainian political nationalist named Budnik, a leader in the small Yonkers Ukrainian community, who was working to save families from the abject poverty of their home country and bring them to the United States. In Budnik's cause, Edward saw financial opportunity. And from his days as a runner he had an insightful knowledge of and connections in every New York City strip club, peep show and massage parlor. He and Budnik concocted a "business proposal" for desperate Ukrainian families, allowing them to pay to send their teenage daughters ahead to the United States, to earn untold riches which they could either send back to their families or bankroll to bring the family to the United States later. In truth, the business proposal was nothing more than a scam to lure the girls into the burgeoning American sex industry, as white slaves, to perform like monkeys in the clubs if they were lucky, or be auctioned off to pimps as prostitutes if they were not. The girls were imprisoned not only by their domineering new masters, but also by their inability to speak the language, the humiliation they were bringing on their families, and the vastness of their new, mysterious nation. Budnik travelled back and forth between New York and Kiev or Odessa securing eager new recruits, while Edward would serve as the employment placement specialist in the city when the wide-eyed, terrified girls arrived. For years, the authorities had no active investigation into the practice, in fact, there weren't even any complaints. And the other mob bosses either didn't understand the racket or were put off by it. Edward and Budnik became rich in a hurry.

All the money Edward was amassing started to get some attention from several of the other crime families -- including an up and coming capo named Giovanni Marcellino -- and they all wanted their cut. When Edward refused to cooperate, the police detectives on the mob payroll were tipped off to the enormity of the enterprise. Budnik, the only person with deep enough knowledge of the business to harm Edward by providing evidence, was killed in Kiev during one of his recruitment trips -- a result of either the well documented political unrest, an incensed Ukrainian father, or a well placed hit -- no one would ever know for sure. Though Budnik's death brought a sudden end to the business, it didn't matter. Edward had already diversified and bought several strip clubs of his own, started a lucrative loan-sharking side business with his new Irish Westie friends, and made wise investments in a new and successful casino that was attracting thousands of visitors each day on the Las Vegas strip.

The organized crime crackdown in the 1980's decimated most of the known New York mob enterprises, putting many of the former bosses either out of business or in prison. Edward did not escape the sweep, and was sentenced to 30 years for racketeering, loan sharking and a laundry list of lesser charges. The FBI moved to seize his assets, cars and Long Island mansion, but was not able to touch most of the fortune he had amassed and hidden. Edward was able to manage his empire from behind bars, leaving his new and pregnant wife Imelda to handle the day-to-day tasks of what was left of the operation. Then in a surprise to everyone, Edward was released after serving just a few years of his sentence. Some said he had provided important evidence to the FBI in exchange for his freedom. Edward denied it. However, he was clear with everyone he met from that day forward that he was "through" with organized crime. He was a "legitimate businessman" and when the subject of organized crime was raised in his presence, he would always insist he was "out" for the sake of his children.

Riley was fascinated by the story, but wasn't surprised. He thought the Fabrizis looked the part and could be cast to play themselves in the Hollywood movie -- an invitation he was sure the Fabrizis' bloated egos would accept with enthusiasm. Riley promised Mr. Mantano he would be careful.

Riley took the following Saturday night off. Considering his large financial headaches, he couldn't afford it. But he had a complicated paper due in his economics class and needed quality time alone to get it done right. Alvin was heading to Atlantic City, so Riley took the opportunity to make the most of a quiet and productive weekend.

Books and notes were scattered around the floor of the room, and every piece of furniture or empty counter top served as a resting place for the next page of his thesis. Riley ran around the room like the metal ball on the playfield of a pinball machine, scribbling notes, lacking only the reward of a buzzer or bell, as he zigzagged from one direction to another organizing the project. The room was near silent, except for his incessant shuffling, and he read his notes aloud as he created his masterwork, sometimes sounding nonsensical as he spoke with a clenched ballpoint pen between his front teeth. The weather outside was calm, and most of his classmates were using the pleasant evening to enjoy the city. The occasional rustling of a passing coed in the hall distracted and annoyed him.

By 2 a.m., his masterpiece was nearing completion, and he even impressed himself with how much he had accomplished. Again, a noise in the hallway broke his concentration and he did his best to ignore it. A moment later, he heard something yet again, as if a returning drunken student was trying to sleep against his dorm room door, and a muffled groan followed. Enraged, Riley yanked the door open prepared to eviscerate the offender only to have a beaten and bloodied Mici fall across his bare feet. Riley stood in shock.

"Dear God, Mici!"

"Help me, Riley."

Riley lifted her from the floor and the two staggered to his sofa. Mici's mouth was full of blood, and it drooled down her chin in a ghoulish trickle and onto her yellow satin blouse. She had scratches on her arms and a large bruise on her right cheek. Mici's shoes were missing, and her thin stockings had worn off leaving her small, pale feet poking through and exposed. Her skirt was torn and there appeared to be a bite mark on her left shoulder. Mici bent over the edge of the sofa and vomited blood and bile across Riley's economics project. She fell back and wrapped her arms around her stomach. A frantic Riley grabbed the phone and started to dial.

"I'm calling 9-1-1. What the hell happened?"

"No, Riley don't... don't call anyone... please wait." Mici struggled to catch her breath and Riley, against his own better judgment, put down the telephone. He then ran to the bathroom to get her clean towels.

"I was attacked. They beat me up."

"Who beat you?"

"They said to tell *Nonno* to close the restaurant."

"What are you talking about?' You're not making sense. Who did this?"

Mici struggled to retain her composure. She closed her eyes and sucked on Riley's towel to help absorb the blood that was still trickling from her mouth.

"He said his name was Marcus. He had dinner at America's last night and asked me out on a date. I thought he was nice. He picked me up at the restaurant late tonight. When I got in the car... I think it was a Porsche, there were three of them. They took me to Morningside Park and did this to me." Mici burst into tears.

"Let me take you to the infirmary here on campus, and let them check you out. Please."

"No, I don't want anyone to know about this, please, Riley. They said to bring a message back to my grandfather. They said the restaurant needs to shut down or things will get messy."

"I think this is pretty messy already! Why do they want the restaurant to close? I don't understand."

"I don't know, I don't know. That's all they said."

"And why would they beat up a girl? What's wrong with them?"

"They didn't. They took me to the park and I didn't know what was going to happen. I didn't know who they were, at first I thought they were going to rape me." Mici burst into tears again, then took another deep breath and swallowed to regain her composure. "Now I think they just wanted to scare me to get at *Nonno*. I started swinging at them first to get away and the three of them grabbed me. I messed up Marcus' face pretty good. I almost pulled his eyelid off, I think. He screamed and got mad and hit me in the face. They pinned me on the ground and gave me their message, but I kept fighting them. Somehow I broke loose and started running away."

"You should have gone to a hospital."

"I knew you were nearby, and I knew you would help me. I didn't know where else to go."

"Mici, we have to tell your grandfather."

"I know, I know... but don't say anything yet. I don't want him to know they hurt me. He has a terrible temper sometimes. He will overreact and kill them. You know he will."

Riley collected all the towels and blankets he had in his room and spread them across the sofa. He undressed Mici like a child might undress a favorite Barbie doll, and she submitted to his care and laid motionless before him. Together, they inspected her body inch by inch stopping to inspect each bruise and scratch and anything that might look more serious. Riley suppressed powerful feelings of both rage and arousal as he analyzed her lissome form. Mici was lucky. Except for the gash in her mouth and painful bruise on her cheek, the rest of her wounds were superficial. And ever the gentleman, Riley would not consider taking advantage of her. Riley helped her stand and limp into the shower, and Mici's hands and legs trembled with each step. Riley left her alone, and she sat in the steaming hot water for what seemed like hours, allowing the water time to soothe and heal both her ragged nerves and torn flesh. Every so often she would be heard to weep or emit a whimper, and Riley would dash in to check on her to ensure she was still OK. When she did emerge wrapped in a white bath towel, her curly black locks straightened down her shoulders, she appeared to have re-centered herself, and had regained some control of her emotions. Riley grabbed a gray jogging suit from his closet, and procured a pair of Alvin's old sandals from his dresser so she would have something clean to wear the rest of the night. The two walked outside, Mici appearing to be adhered to Riley's arm. He hailed one of the many cabs screaming past, and Riley escorted a fragile Mici home.

The Sunday morning sun was starting to rise over the east horizon as Riley made his way back to his own room. The place smelled of a creepy mixture of vomit and Mici's favorite perfume, which hung in the air as if her whimsical ghost had just meandered by to tease him. Her tattered clothing remained strewn about the floor and across his project glazed in a horror of dried blood. Riley was exhausted from stress and lack of sleep, his nerves frayed, and his psyche injured by what had just unfolded. The mob wanted

Americo's to close for some reason and their willingness to pick on a sweet young girl was shameful, even for an advanced criminal syndicate. He fell back on his bed, mind swirling in all directions debating what he should do next. Contacting the police was not an option, and Mici wouldn't let him tell Mr. Mantano -- she was firm on that -- but he had to say something to somebody. Riley felt an obligation to both Mici and Mr. Mantano to help. He had failed in his duty to keep an eye on her as he had promised. Mici was able to tell him her date's name was Marcus and that he drove a Porsche. He was thin on facts, but it was a start. Mici also told him she had injured his eye and Riley hoped a gouge or scratch would give away his identity.

Riley awoke a few hours later not realizing he had even fallen asleep. It was late Sunday morning now, and Alvin was standing over his bed with a very concerned look on his unshaven face.

"Dude, you OK? This place is a total wreck." Alvin glanced around at the vomit, blood stained underwear and torn skirt. "I should take some economics. You guys know how to party."

"It was not a good night, my friend," Riley explained sitting up in bed, forehead throbbing in pain as if someone was in his skull with a pick axe working to escape. His brief dreams were disturbing and left him in even more of a foul mood, and though the mood remained, the specifics of the dreams faded.

"Mici was here. Some guys grabbed her and beat her up pretty good last night. She was very upset."

"Oh... no, that's awful. I like Mici. Is she OK? She is a very nice girl. What happened? What did the police say?" Alvin rambled and fired off question after question.

"I think she'll be OK. We didn't call the police." Riley admitted. "It's complicated."

"Riley, you really should call the police."

"Mici wouldn't let me. It was her choice. But I do want to find the people who did this to her. I have to. Alvin, will you help me?"

"Sure, dude... what did you have in mind?"

Americo's didn't open until late on Sunday, and Riley utilized his personal key to let them in the back alley door. Riley charged toward the messy stack of receipts left from Friday night, assuming that if this Marcus fellow paid by credit card, he could at least figure out his last name. Bingo -- Marcus paid with an American Express card, spent over $200, and his server was Lorenzo. There was no tip listed. Riley didn't remember him as his evening had been dominated by the Fabrizis' visit. Riley held the receipt straight overhead in victory.

"So what's it say?" Alvin asked.

"Marcus Etruscan."

"What kind of name is that?"

"I don't care," Riley said as he booted up the sauce splattered old office computer. A quick Internet search revealed that there was just one Marcus Etruscan in the New York area, or in fact anywhere in the United States for that matter, and he lived at 59 Washington Street in Hoboken, New Jersey.

"Sounds like a road trip!" Alvin exclaimed like a little boy whose dad was taking him for ice cream.

"Relax, it's only Hoboken."

"This is like playing Sherlock Holmes.... or Harry Potter!"

"Oh my God, Alvin... we need to rent a car so we can make a quick exit."

"I haven't returned the rental I took to Atlantic City if you want to use that."

"Perfect! But before we leave, I need to take care of something else." Riley pulled Marcus' receipt aside and typed with force at the computer, appearing to bruise each key as he proceeded. His eyes were glazed and focused, and Alvin could feel the waves of fury radiate from him with each angry key stroke.

"There, all set now." Riley said. "Let's go."

"What did you just do?"

"Marcus just made an extra $10,000 purchase on his credit card at Americo's. If we don't find him, maybe he will drop by later to dispute it."

Alvin and Riley retrieved the car and passed through the Lincoln Tunnel on their direct route to Hoboken. The traffic on this late Sunday afternoon was building as the city day trippers were retreating from their holiday and heading back to their bleak suburban realities. Riley was hell-bent on finding this Marcus character fast, but in his haste and impetuousness, he had developed no real plan, and had no idea what he would say or do if he really did find him. The idea that this could be a dangerous endeavor did occur to him, but he convinced himself that there was nothing to worry about since he had little chance of finding Marcus anyway.

The car pulled up near a row of apartment buildings along Washington Street and the two noticed a snazzy red Porsche parked along the curb in front of the targeted address across the street.

"We found it dude! That's got to be it. That was easy, now what?" An excited Alvin exclaimed, enjoying his Scooby-Doo adventure.

Riley paused and didn't answer. He figured he should go up to the door and ring the bell, or something. The realism of the situation had landed upon him with vigor and he was overcome by an instant flash of self doubt and fear. Was he contemplating interrupting a known mob assailant? And what was he going to do, scold him like a naughty child? His nerves and mind were conspiring to convince himself that turning back now would be the best course of action before he got hurt or in trouble.

"So what's the plan, dude? You do have a plan, don't you?" Alvin asked.

"Stay here."

Riley exited the car and stood on the sidewalk, peering over at the Porsche. It was a superb vehicle, and the sun now low in the sky, fired sunbeams that twinkled off its chrome bumpers and hubcaps making it appear studded with tiny well-polished diamonds. Riley crossed the street and crept up to the car, pausing to avoid oncoming traffic, pacing around it with a slow and deliberate gait, squinting and peering in its windows, searching for clues -- all ploys to buy himself enough time to formulate either an honorable retreat or a sensible plan of attack.

Behind him, a short, skinny man dressed in black burst through the building's main door and jogged down the front steps appearing to be in a hurry. The man fumbled with his rattling keys and trotted toward the Porsche. Riley stiffened, and walked away pretending to blend into the surroundings as a mild-mannered Hoboken pedestrian out for a Sunday afternoon stroll. The man's expression indicated he was preoccupied with something, and didn't notice him as he hopped into the car and revved the engine. It was Marcus. If there was any doubt, the thick patch of crooked white gauze taped over his left eyebrow gave him away.

Alvin and Riley watched the Porsche glide down Washington Street, and take a right onto the Observer Highway. Riley sprinted back across the street and jumped into their rental, and instructed Alvin to hurry and follow.

Alvin and Riley had fallen well behind the speeding sports car, and lost sight of it up ahead of them more than once. A bit of luck kept them from losing the vehicle altogether when a careless Mack truck driver backed his rig out of a gas station and into traffic without looking, causing several annoyed drivers to screech to a temporary stop. It saved just enough time for them to catch up and watch the Porsche turn left into an abandoned multi-stall car wash and slip out of sight. Alvin pulled their rental car into one of the empty trash-strewn stalls and cut the engine.

"What should we do now?" Alvin inquired.

"I don't know. I guess we should find out where he went." Riley answered.

The boys exited the car and started forward, then dropped down behind several abandoned boxes of rotting and stinking refuse when they realized that Marcus and a group of others were walking toward them, and had stopped a few feet away. Riley crouched and peered through a hole in the pile that gave him an obstructed view, while Alvin laid flat on his stomach and stared around the opposite corner. Riley's heart was pounding so hard he feared it would explode out of his chest, and he prayed no one would hear it when it did. There were five men altogether.

"Where the hell you been, Marcus? You were supposed to be here twenty friggin' minutes ago," the fat one said.

"Yea, well unlike you, I have a life." Marcus responded.

"I got Hanratty here like you said." The fat one continued. "What do you want to do with him?"

Hanratty was an older, refined looking gentleman, in great shape for his advanced age with silver hair and a strong chin. He scowled at Marcus.

"Excellent! Mr. Hanratty? A pleasure to meet you, sir. My name is Marcus Etruscan. First, I want you to know I am a big fan of your hotel. My ex-wife and I celebrated our honeymoon in that hotel twenty-five years ago. The food -- oh my -- the food was incredible, I think it was the best filet mignon I have ever had. And the service was the best in New York, too. I remember my wife told me that night..."

"Oh, cut the bullshit." Hanratty interrupted, staring down at the diminutive Marcus like he wanted to start a fight. The others all tensed, and their backs stiffened. "I don't give a shit about you or

117

your wife. You're shaking me down, you two-bit asshole thug, and I won't stand for it. You can kiss..."

A right hook from Marcus landed dead-center of Hanratty's stomach that let out the most inhuman *oomph* sound, like a broom knocking the dust out of a tenement carpet, and he fell to his knees onto the hot asphalt parking lot. Within a few seconds, he vomited, and gasped for air. The others circled around him. Alvin and Riley both held their breath now curled into fetal positions in their hiding place. Riley was making plans to run like a coward even if it meant abandoning Alvin. He was not proud of that thought.

"It hurts me that there is no civility in this town anymore." Marcus continued, pacing around him in a circle like a hyena surrounding its fated prey. "Here I invite you for a brief business meeting on this warm, sunny evening, and you call me a bad name, completely unprovoked. What has our society come to?" Marcus kicked Hanratty in the chin sending a fine mist of blood onto the shoes and trousers of the fat one, leaving Hanratty sprawled on his back moaning and coughing.

"We brought you here tonight, Mr. Hanratty, to deliver a message from our boss and good friend Mr. Marcellino -- and nothing else. Mr. Marcellino would like you to consider closing your midtown hotel and putting it up for sale. That's it! That's the whole message! See how simple and painless that was?" Marcus smiled and stretched his arms out wide.

"Fuck you, and fuck Marcellino." Hanratty responded, in obvious pain, spitting blood as he mumbled his words and struggled to speak.

The fat one reached into his jacket and pulled out an old pearl-handled pistol. He aimed it at Hanratty whose bloodied mouth opened and eyes widened. The fat one fired as Hanratty tried to roll away, and the blast startled them all as everyone recoiled from the noise. The bullet struck Hanratty in the chest a few inches above his heart and caused an instant geyser of thick red blood to shoot straight up out of him. Hanratty fell silent.

"You stupid fat shithead!" Marcus screamed, his voice in a panic. "You weren't supposed to shoot him! We were just supposed to scare him!"

"I know! I know, I was trying to scare him! But he moved! I was shooting at the ground and he moved! It's not my fault! Maybe he's not dead!" The fat one pleaded.

"Oh, he's dead! He's dead! Look at him, look at his eyes! Oh my God! Marcellino is going to kill us both! We need to get out of here."

Marcus and the fat man ran toward the Porsche. Until that moment, as everything had been happening so fast, Riley never bothered to consider the other two hoodlums whose backs had been to him and out of his view the entire time.

At that moment he realized it was Lorenzo and Armand.

Riley wanted to scream out at them in a rage, but sat shivering in terror and silence instead, praying they would all leave and not notice him lying in the trash. He heard something and realized Alvin had pulled a big cardboard box over his head and was bawling. His face was stuffed in an old oil-soaked rag, trying to muffle his cries and not be heard. Lorenzo and Armand must have realized at that moment they were standing alone over a fresh murder scene and started running away at full speed in the other direction. A thin stream of blood had snaked its way across the lot and had reached the hiding place. Alvin's patience had run dry and he jumped up from the trash and sprinted back toward the car. Riley hopped up and followed Alvin as fast as his feet could carry him. Riley looked out at the backs of Lorenzo and Armand, hair tussled by the wind, sprinting for their lives across the vast, flat parking lot, and noticed that Armand had turned his head and was looking back in Riley's direction.

Riley dove into the car head first and ducked low in the seat as Alvin shifted into reverse and sped away. He prayed to God they had not been seen.

<u>E L E V E N</u>

Alvin sat against the head board of his bed and hugged a pillow. Riley paced back and forth across the floor of the narrow room whose walls seemed to be moving in on him. Both boys had skipped class that Monday, too upset and disturbed and still coming to terms with the horror they had witnessed the prior afternoon. Alvin was more upset by the grisly scene than Riley. Nothing in his sheltered upbringing could have prepared Alvin for the revulsion of watching a man die a few feet from his innocent eyes. Americo's didn't open until late afternoon, but Riley called ahead and asked Mr. Mantano to meet him there early. He had to tell him what was happening. He was the only person who Riley knew who was experienced enough to have even a remote idea about what to do next. The two boys' eyes met often but they did not speak to each other. They didn't need to.

The television had been blaring all morning to offer up a diversion for their tortured souls, but instead the mindless blabber served to irritate their nerves even more. They waited for the news at noon to see if there would be any mention of the murder, and there was.

Good Afternoon and welcome to New York Action 5 News. We have a breaking news alert for you on this Monday at noon. The body of a midtown hotel owner was found dead of a single gunshot wound at a Hoboken car wash early this morning. Sixty year-old T. Wallace Hanratty, owner of the L'Hotel Inspire in midtown and several other high-profile properties in New York, Philadelphia and Boston, was discovered by passing children on their way to school this morning in what appears to be a gangland style slaying. The Hoboken Police are on the scene and investigating, and no motive or suspect has yet been named. The police will be holding a press conference later this

120

afternoon. Stay with Action 5 News for the press conference which we will broadcast live when it happens...

"Awww. Little kids found him. That's not right. We should have called the police," Alvin complained.

"No, no police until after I talk to Mr. Mantano. He will know what we should do."

Riley could have sworn the dorm room clocks were moving at half speed, and the afternoon refused to wear on. Anxiety filled his lungs and stomach as his body rejected relaxation. He watched Alvin hug his pillow until it began to drive him crazy and he couldn't stand it anymore. He grabbed a jacket and headed uptown.

Riley and Mr. Mantano arrived at the restaurant at about the same time. They went inside and Mr. Mantano poured them each a glass of wine, while Riley turned up the lights and pulled two bar stools over from the corner.

"OK, so I'm here. What was so important that you had to drag me away from my shows, you know, the soap operas. I have been watching the same shows for thirty-five years and now I'm going to be lost. You know when you miss one of those episodes, it takes weeks to catch up," Mr. Mantano said joking, annoyed and a little worried about what Riley was about to tell him.

"I don't know how to explain this other than just to come right out and say it. You and the restaurant are in danger."

"What are you talking about?" Mr. Mantano sat back on his chair and sighed. He had to know what was coming next.

"It's that guy Marcellino. He wants..."

"Riley, I know. I know what he wants. He wants me to close the restaurant and move out so he can buy the property without any strings attached. Anyway, this is none of your business. Why do you know these things?"

"One of his men came in the other night, and..."

"Oh no! Did he threaten you? He threatened you, didn't he? Are they trying to get to me through you? Oh, those dirty bastards! I will put an end to that right now!" Mr. Mantano said as he jumped up, tipping his wine glass.

"No, no wait there's more." Riley thought for a moment about filling him in about Mici, then reconsidered. "I followed him last night, this guy named Marcus, back to New Jersey where he lives. I needed to know what was going on. We saw something."

"What did you see? And what do you mean *we?*"

"I was with my roommate Alvin. We followed him to a car wash, they were shaking down this guy." Riley's eyes filled with tears, and the corners of his mouth turned down. "They killed him Mr. Mantano. They shot him!"

The color in Mr. Mantano's face drained to pale, and his thin lips gaped open.

"You saw them kill someone? This was that Hanratty murder that was on the news, wasn't it?" Dear God, Riley! What are you getting yourself into?"

"There's still more, sir," Riley continued, sobbing between each word. "Lorenzo and Armand were there, they didn't see me, but they are messed up in this too."

Mr. Mantano stood up and threw his wine glass at the far wall of the restaurant. Riley had only ever seen him this angry once before, and the image was terrifying.

"I thought you were smarter than this, Riley! I really did. What the hell is wrong with you?! Mr. Murphy, your family, your mother... they would all be furious. You're getting caught up in something you can't handle. Leave this alone. It's very dangerous. You're smart and have your whole life ahead of you. These violent animals do nothing but ruin lives. These aren't characters from some Hollywood movie you're dealing with here, they devour people. This so-called mafia, these mobsters, organized crime -- whatever you want to call it -- devastate lives and families. They're garbage -- all of them. It destroyed Murph's life and follows him now even after he's dead. It killed Mici's father and changed her life forever -- they stole her family from the poor girl. It has infected my life, and it shattered hundreds if not thousands of other lives all over the city, and all over the country. These criminals come in all races, too. Don't think this is just some Italian thing. You've seen for yourself what happened to the Irish community in Southie. The Blacks have their Bloods and Crips. Is that any different? Or the Born to Kill gang over near Chinatown, or even the Hispanics and those Latin Kings? It's all evil, Riley, all of it."

Mr. Mantano paused. "So Marcellino is behind the Hanratty murder? I shouldn't be surprised, but I am. Why would he resort to murder? It doesn't make sense to me. He has a big bankroll and he's trying to buy up property like he lives on a Monopoly board. He doesn't need to murder anybody."

"They shot him by accident. I don't think they meant to do it."

"Did anyone see you there?"

"No, sir... well, maybe. I think Armand may have seen me."

"Oh my God. So you can be ID'd, and I have three stupid fucking employees hanging around a murder scene. Oh my God, oh my God. You go home and study or something and get a hold of yourself. Don't come in to work tonight, it will be slow -- we can handle it without you. And I will deal with Lorenzo and Armand myself."

"Do you think they are involved in this?"

"They are as harmless as butterflies. It's all an act with those two clowns. They are nothing to worry about. Please, you must trust me."

When he was little, confession with Father O'Connell at St. Finian's always made him feel better. He would sit on the bench in the narrow wooden confessional box awash in anxiety waiting for the wooden window to slide open so he could begin his prepared statement. Father O'Connell's cool and caressing voice always put him at ease, and he imagined it sounded much like the voice of God himself, and when finished, Riley felt as if he had accomplished something important. But confessing what he saw in the carwash to Mr. Mantano made him feel worse. He felt guilty for being such a profound disappointment to him, and he felt guilty for not telling him about Mici and the assault. And he knew that when Mr. Mantano found out about that, there would be hell to pay all over again. He wondered and worried about how Mici explained away her cuts and bruises to him. He felt disloyal. He would have to create his own penance.

Riley debated what to do with his free evening as he wandered the streets kicking at trash, and elected to go to a movie since he had unearthed a stack of free passes that his sister had given him long ago from under some dirty laundry. Riley walked down to the big multi-screen theater on 42nd Street near Times Square to consider show times and what he might want to see. He tried to decide, but he struggled to motivate an interest in any of the selections. The large neon signs juxtaposed on the old gray stoic building offered a comforting Manhattan feel, and the smell of calorie-rich buttered popcorn filled the air even out on the sidewalk, enticing all who bustled past.

Riley's cell phone rang and vibrated in his pocket. He chose to ignore it. A few minutes later it rang again. His paranoia was winning the internal battle over his melancholy, so this time he answered.

"Hello, Riley? Hey kid, it's me Sean."

"Hi Sean, what's up?"

"Umm, well....."

"Sean, why are you calling?"

There was a long pause.

"I wanted to fill you in on something. First, Mom is still doing fine -- not much has changed. No need to worry about her."

"Well that's good to hear."

"Umm.., but we do have a little problem. Mom got an eviction notice in the mail today. They told her she has until the first of the month to bring her rent up to date, or they are going to take her through eviction proceedings. They want to kick her out."

"What the hell? Why hasn't she been paying the rent?"

"Money's tight, kid, that's all. Between the meds, Siobhan's legal fees, and all the other bills, there isn't enough to go around. We were hoping you might be able to help her out and wire us some cash right away."

"I sent everything I had last week. But I'm sure I can scrape up a few hundred more if you need it. How much does she owe?"

"We need to come up with about four thousand dollars."

"Jesus Christ, Sean!" Riley swore into his cell phone loudly enough for several passersby to hear him, making a wide cautious arc around where he leaned against the wall of the theater.

"I know Riley, it's not good. And that will only catch up her rent. The bill collectors are calling, too, looking for payment on some of Mom's medical treatments. Mom answers the phone and promises them the world, and sends them whatever they ask for. And then last week, I gave her two hundred dollars to buy groceries and she donated it to the Salvation Army."

"You have got to get that money away from her!"

"I know she can't manage it. She would rather go hungry than pass over a good charity. She refuses to see herself as the charity."

"And what about everybody else? I'm not the Royal Bank of Ireland down here!"

124

"I know that, I'm sorry. I haven't been able to help much. I feel bad about that. I buy her food when I can. But my own rent is way behind and I am working as many hours at the plant as they will let me. Ryan is at the seminary and has taken that vow of poverty thing way too serious -- he doesn't have a penny to his name. Meghan is still unemployed, and Erin brings in what she can as a waitress, but it's not that much."

"So you're telling me I'm supporting our whole fucking family?"

"I'm sorry Riley, you're right. It's not fair. Don't get mad, I'm just trying to figure this thing out. There wasn't anyone else to call."

Riley grew more angry. "What about Liam? What's his sorry ass excuse for freeloading off my money?"

"We don't know where Liam is. He packed his bags and took off several weeks ago. Erin seems to think he went to Los Angeles."

"Los Angeles? What the fuck? Why didn't someone tell me?"

"We didn't expect him to be gone that long. You know how he is, he can't commit to anything. We thought we would hear from him any day."

"Oh God, then, what about the church? Call Father O'Connell. Mom donated half her life to St. Finian's over the last thirty years. I don't see why they wouldn't jump to help her out now.

"Because Father O'Connell is an asshole."

"Umm, Sean, did you just call Father O'Connell an asshole?"

"Riley, I went to him first. He promised me all kinds of assistance from the food pantry and the ladies aide committee and they were putting together a couple of fundraisers and even a pancake breakfast. Then he called me back and said it was off -- all cancelled. Now he won't see me or return my calls. I don't know what the hell happened. I'm trying to get Ryan to talk to him, but Ryan has been hard to reach. I don't know what Mom told him at her last confession, but it must have been good."

"I'll put together as much money as I can and send it in the morning. But it's not going to be enough.

"Thank you, Riley. Thank you. Every little bit helps. Mom and I appreciate it, even if no one else does. And I am sorry, I never asked you how things were in New York. How are you?"

Riley took a breath. In an instant, disturbing images of Magnolia, Mici, Hanratty and Marcus all pin wheeled through his brain at once. Then he wondered if he even had a job anymore.

"Everything is great here, Sean. A fucking utopia."

"That's great kid, talk to you later..."

"Sean, wait... tell me, how is Siobhan?"

"Not good, kid. Not good." The tone of Sean's voice changed from depressed to dire. "I took Mom to see her last weekend. It's ripping both her and Siobhan apart. The two got together and cried for the hour we were allowed to be there in the prison family room. They both miss little Brian and the state won't tell us where he was placed -- it's a security thing so we don't kidnap him, I guess. Malcolm is hoping for a reduced sentence but doesn't see her getting out for a long time. This crisis has aged her years, Riley. It's horrible -- she looks like she's sixty. I try not to think about it. There isn't anything we can do. But I do know I will slit the throat of her rat bastard boyfriend if he ever gets out."

Riley took his sinking heart home and scratched together every penny he had, and even managed to guilt Alvin into cleaning out his secret keg fund and sent it all back to Southie. It wasn't much, and Riley resigned himself to a permanent diet of white bread toast, ramen noodles and whatever leftovers he could pilfer from America's kitchen when the cooks had their backs turned.

He went back to work Tuesday night, and toiled alongside the regular staff of Mici, Lorenzo, Armand and even Mr. Mantano as if nothing had ever happened. The atmosphere was strained and the crew spoke to one another only when it was necessary. Business had never been worse and good tips were fewer and farther between with each passing hour, increasing the unspoken tension that fouled the rich, garlic-laden air.

Riley's long stressful week was limping to a merciful end when the Fabrizis came in Saturday night for their ceremonious weekly dinner. Riley knew it was his one chance that week for a great tip and gathered up as much enthusiasm as he could muster, from deep within his suffering core, to shower upon his favorite affluent customers. His effort was noteworthy, but his heart, overflowing with worry and depression, just was not into it.

"Oh Riley, tell us, how is your mother?" Imelda Fabrizi asked as she did every other week, anticipating a new and amusing tale. Riley had wanted to prepare a quick anecdote in advance to entertain them, but this week it had been a chore. Without thinking, he answered the question with honesty.

126

"Not so good. My mom is having a hard time. The costs of her medication and treatments are too expensive, and now the rent is overdue. We're worried they might even evict her from her apartment."

Imelda's eyes widened and her facial expression stuck in an uncomfortable place somewhere between shock and anger. She did not come to Americo's to feel upset, she was here to be entertained. She fired a quick offending stare at Edward expecting him to say something supporting her slight, but Edward said nothing right away. He waited a bit, then looked up at Riley and with a disappointed and intimidating tone, and he said, "Bring us a bottle of the Pinot Noir."

Riley was humiliated and wanted to crawl under a table. He looked out through the window of the kitchen doors at them whispering back and forth knowing he had violated one of their sacred, unwritten laws, and also knowing they were whispering about him. Mr. Mantano had prepared the wine bucket with ice shavings and a corkscrew but Riley was afraid to bring it to them at the table. He considered apologizing but wasn't sure if that might annoy them even more. He couldn't stand in the kitchen and wait forever, so he dug deep for a fragment of courage and approached the table with the wine preparing to pay the price for his indiscretion.

"Riley," Edward spoke, with his hands raised like a priest conferring a blessing "...we are very sorry to hear about your mother. No one should have to endure such a thing. It's terrible. How is your family going to pay for her care?"

Riley froze and felt suspicious. He already knew that Edward, like a seasoned trial attorney, would not ask a question for which he did not know the answer.

"I spoke to my brother the other day. We are working something out. All my brothers and sisters are chipping in, and we are hoping for a little help from St. Finian's Church, too, that would make a big difference. It will all work out just fine, no need to worry, sir." Riley responded with as much false optimism as he could create.

"What do you study at Columbia, finance and accounting?" Riley had told him this many times.

"Yes, sir. And I enjoy it very much."

"And you tell me you almost run this place, and you help Carmine with his books and operations, is that right?"

127

"Yes sir, I do. I help the restaurant and Mr. Mantano any way I can." Riley poured them each a glass of wine.

Edward rubbed his goatee and closed his eyes. "I..," he paused for a moment to create an atmosphere of dramatic tension, "... have an idea. Why don't you come to my office on Monday where we can talk? I think I can offer you a position in my company where you would make a lot more money than you make here. Maybe this will help you and the situation with your mother."

Riley could have been knocked over with a breadstick. He had no idea how to respond. "Oh, sir, thank you sir. But, no, I couldn't leave Mr. Mantano. He needs me here. That wouldn't be fair to him."

"See, what did I tell you?" Edward glanced at a loving Imelda who offered an approving nod. "I told you he would say that. He is a smart and a loyal kid. Just the kind of person I need in my company, on my staff. I want you to come see me on Monday afternoon in my office, after school." Edward handed him a business card. "And don't worry about Carmine, I'll talk to him. He and I are old friends. He'll understand."

That evening, the Fabrizis left no tip.

After careful thought, Riley decided he would skip the meeting with Mr. Fabrizi on Monday. He couldn't do it, he couldn't leave Mr. Mantano like this. But the restaurant's struggles were so serious that even Riley's financial wizardry wasn't enough, and he was haunted by images of his weak, frail mother being tossed into the street, laying dead in a gutter abandoned by her seven adoring children. And if he didn't show up on Monday, Americo's best customers, Edward and Imelda, would never be seen again. He had to go see Mr. Fabrizi on Monday whether he wanted to or not.

When Riley arrived back at home, Alvin met him at the door of his room hugging a sofa cushion, since he had spent the previous week flattening his pillows into uselessness.

"Riley, we were on TV! We are so screwed!"

Alvin flipped on the television with the remote and cued up a news recording he had made earlier.

Good evening and welcome to New York Action 5 News. We have a breaking news update for you tonight as part of our top story: Mob Hit in Hoboken. Hoboken Police have released the following video tape and need your help. The tape from a security camera mounted a block

128

away shows what appears to be a blue Ford Taurus which can be seen entering and leaving the car wash around the time when police believe millionaire hotelier T. Wallace Hanratty was shot to death last week. The police are asking for your help in identifying the car and occupants who are persons of interest in the investigation. Viewers can contact police at...."

"They saw us Riley! They saw us!" Alvin cried.

Riley was upset, but tried to appear unconcerned to save Alvin from certain panic. "Oh for God's sake Alvin, calm down. The quality of that video is awful. It's impossible to make out the license plate or the drivers. And since it is a rental car, no one would ever think to connect you or me to it anyway."

"Maybe you're right and I should calm down. But I can't go to prison Riley, I just can't."

"No one is going to prison."

After classes on Monday, Riley went back to his room and pulled out his best white shirt and a fire-engine red power tie to wear to his meeting with Mr. Edward Fabrizi, president and CEO of Lafayette Street Enterprises, or LSE for short. LSE was a profitable conglomerate of over twenty smaller companies that dabbled in a myriad of industries, including publishing, wholesaling, toxic waste removal, gentleman's clubs, and so many others that even LSE's own CEO would become confused when trying to discuss them all. LSE was a big company, but not considered to be among the country's elite, or even among the elite in just New York City, to the continual consternation of Mr. Fabrizi.

After his release from prison, Mr. Fabrizi was able to pull together all his hidden but legal assets and established himself as a legitimate businessman (though he preferred the term "entrepreneur.") He made his new fortune and established his foothold in the business community by buying up the assets, companies and properties of his old cash-poor mob associates who were languishing in prison or who were struggling to pay their mounting legal fees. He did not consider his methods of preying upon the weak and less fortunate as a negative, in fact, it was quite the opposite. He saw his business activities as acts of charity and compassion -- or at least that is what Imelda believed and what he told people.

129

Riley walked along the sidewalk on bustling Lafayette Street past Federal Plaza and the FBI offices on his way to his interview. The sun was bright and the sky cloudless as he stood and stared up at the tall gray structure whose rooftop antenna shined, ablaze like a giant matchstick. He sucked up a lungful of the city's best air and taxi exhaust and marched through the revolving door and into the lobby.

Riley walked into the executive offices of LSE and was directed by Mr. Fabrizi's secretary to take a seat. The oversized, stuffed chair was upholstered with some sort of authentic animal print, maybe leopard. Mr. Fabrizi was on the phone with someone whom Riley assumed to be Imelda. Without any visible human assistance, the heavy, opulent door closed behind him as if commanded by thought alone.

"Just buy him a cheese. You know one of those giant cheese stick things." Mr. Fabrizi barked into the phone.

The office was as elegant a room as he had ever seen. Behind him sat an enormous, stocked aquarium featuring a wonderful array of exotic tropical fish. To his right stood a stocked wet bar that included over a hundred selections. And on the opposite wall from where they sat, was mounted the most intimidating collection of framed and autographed photos of famous villains -- an impressive who's who from the history of organized crime -- that included Dillinger, Lansky, Siegel, Hoffa, and Gambino all surrounding a much larger portrait of a beaming Al Capone. Riley wondered if these photographs were there to idolize Mr. Fabrizi's heroes, to intimidate his office guests, or as a front to be used to tow the line between his legitimate business enterprises and his former criminal history.

"No, I said cheese. *Cheese!* Jesus Christ, cheese, cheese, cheese!! One of those big cheese sticks, you know, that you can cut up in those nice thick slices." He paused again, this time, puffing his cheeks and letting his large eyes roll skyward.

"How the fuck do I know? Mozzarella? Maybe some Provolone? Something *nice*. I don't care. Just pick one." His left hand was waving the air now, as if he was trying to hurry the caller along.

"Jesus Christ, Imelda, it's only a fucking stick of cheese. I haven't even spoke to the son of a bitch in a year. I don't know why I am buying him a present anyway."

Another pause. He was growing more irritated.

"Fine, OK, fine, fine, OK. I'll get the fucking cheese myself, OK? I got one of those cheese catalogs in the mail... it's around here somewhere, I'll pick one out."

"I didn't say you were stupid. But Jesus Christ, I gotta wonder when you can't even pick out a simple stick of fuckin' cheese!"

"I love you too baby, you're beautiful. I'll be home soon."

He put down the phone and without even the luxury of a sigh or deep breath, in perfect rhythm, he looked into Riley's eyes and started the interview.

"So what makes you think you can work for me? You think you're good?

"Yes sir, as you know, I attend...

"Yea, I know, I know. I know all about your school and your resume. You think I would have you in here if I didn't know that? What I need to know is, can you work for me?"

"I'd love an opportunity to show...

"I'm a very demanding businessman, you know. I'm an entrepreneur. I'm not interested in yes men. I got those comin' outta my friggin' ears. I need someone who will tell it to me straight. No bullshit."

"Well, I promise that I....

"I'm a visionary, I'm telling ya'. I built this company with these two hands. No one sees the potential in this business like me. I'm on a rocket ship and I'm stuck in here doin' everything myself. I can't trust nobody to give me anything except bullshit."

Mr. Fabrizi hesitated and looked Riley over like one might inspect a new piece of furniture right before pulling out the credit card. "One more thing... don't get any crazy ideas in here. I run a clean operation, and everything is legal and honest. No funny business. Those days are long gone -- history. I will not allow you or anyone else to put my family, my business or my money at risk. Do you think you can handle that?"

"Yes sir, I think I can..."

"Good. Then go downstairs and tell that girl.... the new one in HR I hired yesterday ...what's her name.... Jill or Julie or something I think. Go tell Jill you're hired and I want you to start right away."

"Yes, thank you. I look forward to working here."

"Yea," he said forcing a smile, "and tell my secretary to get in here right away."

His concerned secretary charged into the office in a sweat, and as Riley walked away and the door closed behind him, he could hear the conversation continue.

"Katie, where the hell is that God damned cheese catalog that came the other day. I can't believe this. I got a million dollar deal going down the crapper and I gotta drop everything to order some friggin' cheese."

Riley strolled down to the human resource office considering that he had not been offered anything -- he was *told* he was hired and didn't appear to have any choice about it. He had no idea how many hours he would work, how much money he would make, or what his responsibilities would be. He also respected how much of a change this would be in his lifestyle, and how hard it would be to break the news to Mr. Mantano that he intended to quit -- though it was less intimidating than marching up to see Mr. Fabrizi to decline the offer. He also thought about Siobhan in jail and all the accumulating bills and eviction notices. And the image of his mother's crumpled body at the foot of her altar continued to haunt him.

"Hello, my name is Riley Lynch. I was asked to come down here and see Jill?" Riley said as he poked his head in the hiring manager's office. "Mr. Fabrizi sent me."

"My name is Jane, not Jill. And who are you again?" A middle-aged woman surrounded by foot-tall stacks of paper and wearing wire-rimmed glasses waved him into the office.

"I am Riley Lynch. Mr. Fabrizi just hired me."

"To do what?"

"Well, I'm sorry but I'm not sure," Riley responded a bit embarrassed.

The woman sighed in frustration and eased back in her chair, an indication to Riley that she had heard this story before. She dialed upstairs to find Mr. Fabrizi and to request clarification.

"Yes, sir. Yes, sir. Yes, sir." Was all she would reply. It was evident that Mr. Fabrizi had been anticipating her call, and Riley could hear a variety of loud four-letter words fired back at her through the receiver. The phone conversation was brief, and despite the abuse, she never flinched.

"Mr. Fabrizi would like you to start tomorrow afternoon. He would like you to report to his office at three o'clock -- sharp.

Following that, you will meet with José for your orientation. Now fill out this paperwork and get it back to me as fast as you can."

Riley walked into Americo's that evening for what would be his last shift at the famed restaurant. He stood in the ornate dining room and looked around for one last time, like a tourist might look over a Smithsonian museum, working hard to remember every nuance and detail for his internal scrapbook. He had collected many fond memories of the place in a short time, and might have been content to work there forever had circumstances been different. It had treated him well, and he felt at home. He remembered that first time he came in and how important the restaurant job made him feel; he remembered Magnolia, Alvin and Donnie making a mess of the place that night they dropped in on him unannounced; he remembered pinning a bewildered Lorenzo against the kitchen refrigerator in a rare moment of bravery and defiance; he considered Mici and her warm eyes and affectionate personality and eulogized his secret crush; and most of all he remembered all the long conversations he enjoyed with Mr. Mantano and how his stoic advice guided him and gave him solace through a scary and exciting time of his life. He would miss him.

He had asked Mr. Mantano to meet him early so he could break the news that he planned to quit and go to work for Mr. Fabrizi at LSE. The butterflies in Riley's stomach were in a full Capistrano flutter when Lorenzo walked in, coat over his arm and a hand-rolled cigarette dangling from the corner of his mouth. When he saw Riley he stared, froze in place, yanked the cigarette from his mouth, and pointed the butt at Riley's nose.

"You are a fucking coward," Lorenzo fired. "You are a piece of stinking shit."

"Screw you, Lorenzo. What did I do to you? What's your problem?"

"That little old man needs us right now, and you're bailing out on him. Look what he did for you -- he gave you a job when you had no experience, he put money in your pocket, he lets you drool over his granddaughter like a starving puppy, he even fed those ignorant street bums you call your friends. And now you repay him by walking your candy ass out the door when he might lose his whole business. You are nothing but a yellow Irish coward."

133

"Lorenzo, please.... it's not like that. I need more money. My mother..."

"Your mother... your mother... your mother. One more word about your mother and I'm going to throw up. Like the rest of us don't have problems, or sick mothers, or families, or bills. Grow the fuck up, will you? We all work for a reason. And now the minute you see that Mantano has a problem and might lose this place you abandon him, and go off running away with your tail between your legs."

Though cruel, everything Lorenzo said struck a nerve of truth in Riley, as if he were listening to his own conscience yell back at him, and it hurt. But Lorenzo wasn't some sainted guardian angel either, and Riley had not forgotten he and Armand were present at the scene of Hanratty's murder. He wasn't going to let him off the hook that easy.

"So you want me to believe you work here just to help Mr. Mantano? Is that it? Fine. Then you're nothing but God's gift, raised from the scorched earth by a lightning bolt from the heavens, to save old Italian restaurants. Oh, please. Maybe I think you're a big part of what's bringing this place down."

Riley had chosen to cross the line. If Lorenzo knew Riley and Alvin were at the murder scene, he would understand the direct insult. If not, he expected Lorenzo might slug him. Lorenzo paused. Riley had his attention.

"You think I'm bringing this place down, do you? You're sneaking around and plotting behind Mantano's back, slithering through the garbage like a maggot, with that other nitwit Hardy Boy friend of yours, and I'm the bad guy. So tell me, whose payroll are *you* on, Riley, Mantano's or Marcellino's? You seem to be in an awful hurry to quit and get out of here, aren't you?"

It was now clear that Lorenzo knew he was at the carwash. And Riley was offended he would accuse of him of such a despicable and disloyal act.

"Well I wasn't the one buddying-up to that murdering slime ball Marcus now, was I? It looked to me like you and Armand were in pretty tight with those thugs."

Lorenzo lowered his voice. "For your information, moron, Armand and I were ordered to be there -- against our will. Marcus came in for dinner, threatening the restaurant and told us we had to go to

Hoboken and see something. We were told to meet him there when Fat Jack showed up with that hotel owner. We didn't know what he had in mind or what he was going to say. I'm guessing he wanted us to watch him beat the guy up, then we would quit -- like you -- or pressure Mantano into shutting down."

"So you had no idea he was going to kill Hanratty?"

"Will you keep your voice down! That's all we need is for your big stupid mouth to put us in fucking jail. Of course I had no idea. I didn't even know who Hanratty was before we got there. Marcus is an idiot. If he wanted to get to Mantano, all he needed to do was slap Mici around a little bit and this place shuts down overnight."

Riley took some comfort in that fact that at least Lorenzo didn't know everything. But Riley didn't believe for one second Lorenzo's story of altruism, or of being a victim. He knew Lorenzo didn't do anything unless something was in it for him.

"Lorenzo, who told you I was leaving?"

"Fabrizi called Mantano this morning at home. Then Mantano called me and accused me of being an asshole and chasing you away. You need to know you broke that old man's heart."

Mr. Mantano and Mici appeared in the doorway at that moment.

"Ahh, Riley my boy, come here," and he gave Riley a hug and kissed his cheek as if he were a long lost friend. "I hear things... I hear that you are moving on away from us, on to bigger things, better things. This is true?" he asked.

"Yes, sir, I'm sorry sir. Mr. Fabrizi offered me a position today at his company. He wants me to start tomorrow."

"Congratulations, my son. Eddie will teach you everything you need to know about business. He is very smart. Very clever. You will be very successful under him."

"I swear I am only leaving for the money, my mother's not doing so well. Maybe I can come back here someday when things get better."

Mr. Mantano chuckled, "You know you are always welcome here, you are part of our family now. But don't think you can come back and things will be the same. Times change, and people grow -- like an old pair of comfortable trousers that don't fit anymore. I want you to promise me that you will never forget us here after you are rich and famous, and that you stop by sometimes for dinner."

"I promise, sir, I will miss all of you.

Tears welling in her eyes, Mici placed her head on Riley's shoulder and gave him a big hug seeping with emotion, and Riley wondered how her small frame could be so strong as to squeeze all the air from his lungs. "I will miss you *piccolo orso*," she said sobbing. Riley never remembered her lips so red or the smell of her hair so sweet and stimulating. He would miss her, too.

"Oh Mici, we should stay in touch. We should stay friends."

"Oh, of course, Riley," she responded, but Riley could read through her forced smile and knew that she didn't believe they would ever meet again.

TWELVE

Katie Cubbage was Mr. Fabrizi's trusted private secretary and had been for ten years or better. She was a professional, fine-looking, dark-haired woman in her mid-thirties and in fabulous shape. Katie's skirts were always tight and expensive and her hair wrapped in a perfect bun atop her head making it appear to come to a point. No one was sure how she could stand Mr. Fabrizi's constant foul mood or his perpetual obscene insults, but she would persevere, crisis after crisis, year after year, providing the continuity and stability to the company that her boss was unable to offer.

Katie ushered Riley into the LSE boardroom and instructed him to take a seat. The room was wide and stylish, with a stunning gold chandelier which sparkled above the bulky oak table that was surrounded by twelve high-backed leather chairs so large they made their occupants feel insignificant. A rare assortment of antiques was placed throughout the room, each displayed upon its own ornate pedestal, and a large oil painting of a stern Mr. Edward Fabrizi, CEO, was mounted at the far end of the room in that precise position so he could gaze upon himself while he conducted his meetings. Riley believed that the room was so perfect and well-equipped, that the President of the United States could carry out world affairs from here if necessary.

Riley sat and looked around the room at the occupants of all the other chairs. All were older men of various ages, and were all dressed well with little variation -- black suits, black shirts, red ties -- and each emitted their own unique foul attitude even as they sat in silence. Riley folded his hands and sat in silence along with them, attempting to blend in. This was not the chatty Ladies' Aide Committee at St. Finian's.

Two chairs remained vacant. The chair at the head of the long table belonged to Mr. Fabrizi, of course, while the chair next to it, a smaller version of the others, belonged to Katie. Katie was allowed to enter the room when Mr. Fabrizi was ready, and not one second earlier or face his wrath. Riley was nervous and self-conscious, his hands were sweating, and he felt as if he should say something to break the searing silence. Riley sat up straight and cleared his throat to get their attention, and the board members all looked in his direction.

'Ahem... Hi. My name is Riley Lynch. I thought I would introduce myself to you while we waited since I am new. Mr. Fabrizi hired me yesterday and asked me to be here with you this afternoon."

The room remained silent. Two of the men smiled back to him and looked away, two others looked at each other and shook their heads. Another rolled his eyes. The rest elected to ignore him. However one of them, a Hispanic man, thinner and a bit shorter than the rest, smiled and extended his hand in friendship.

"Pleased to meet you Riley, my name is José-Alejandro Martinez Villanueva-Zapata. But you should just call me José. I am Mr. Fabrizi's, and LSE's, operations director. I believe I am scheduled to give you the official company tour after our meeting today."

"It is a pleasure to meet you Mr... umm.., José. Is Mr. Fabrizi running late?" Riley asked, and someone guffawed.

"You will see in time," José responded, "Mr. Fabrizi likes us to be present and ready to conduct business fifteen to twenty minutes before he arrives. You will become used to the delays."

Mr. Fabrizi marched into the room as if hurried or being chased, the dutiful Katie three feet behind him. He slapped the papers he was carrying down at the head of the table, and fiddled with his cell phone. Katie sat in her chair, crossed her legs, opened a yellow legal pad and prepared herself to take notes.

"I want every cell phone turned off, now!" Mr. Fabrizi barked taking control of the stiff and tense room, and all complied. "I don't want any interruptions."

Mr. Fabrizi looked up and saw Riley sitting at the end of the table, his white shirt and black tie in stunning contrast to the rest of the better dressed board members. Mr. Fabrizi shot him a wide toothy grin.

"Hello Mr. Lynch, nice to see you made it. Has everybody met Riley Lynch? Good. Let's get down to business."

In fact, no one had yet met Mr. Lynch except maybe for José, but none of them saw Riley as important enough to correct him.

Mr. Fabrizi looked down the table at Riley again, and added. "A white shirt and black tie, huh? I like it! It looks like Wall Street." Everyone swallowed and fidgeted and gave Riley an annoyed critical stare. The only sound in the still quiet room was the shuffling of Mr. Fabrizi's papers. He then raised a fist high overhead and brought it crashing down on the hardwood table with a bang, coffee cups jiggled, and everyone's eyes widened as they sat up straight.

"What the fuck is going on in distribution! Mr. Fabrizi's voice was so loud and piercing Riley thought the chandelier might shatter. "We sat in this room for three fucking hours last week to come up with a new distribution plan and nobody did a God damned thing about it."

Mr. Fabrizi looked to the heavens for guidance, "Why do I have to do everything myself? Buckner, you're supposed to be the fucking distribution manager, what the hell is going on?"

"Well, sir," Buckner began, "I have one warehouse manager on medical leave and another on vacation, I thought I would wait until they..."

"Wait? I can't afford to wait. Who told you to wait?" Mr. Fabrizi shot back. "Why not just re-assign someone else?"

"Because you told us we couldn't spend one extra dollar of payroll. We're barely keeping up with shipping, and you said you'd fire the whole loading dock staff if they fell behind again," Buckner begged, hoping for leniency.

"And did my phone ring? Did you call and ask me for more payroll? Or for permission to delay some shipments? Your title is distribution manager. You're supposed to *fucking manage!*" Mr. Fabrizi shot back again. "And what the fuck is going on with the truck fleet? I got a call from my close friend in Philadelphia this morning and he tells me our trucks didn't show up to pump the wastewater out of his plant. Then I find out they got lost. Hooper, you want to fill me in on why we don't know where Philadelphia is?"

"I'm sorry sir," Hooper began. "Only the lead driver had the directions and the convoy separated on the New Jersey Turnpike in a construction zone -- traffic was heavy. The lead driver tried to double-back to find the others and then he got stuck in more traffic. They didn't get there until ..."

"Anybody in your department ever heard of a cell phone?" Mr. Fabrizi joked.

"But sir," a concerned Hooper shot back, "you had the company phones confiscated to save money last quarter."

"Oh. So it's my fault the truck drivers don't know how to drive trucks. What the fuck! Does anybody have any good news before I slit my own fucking wrists and bleed to death?"

"Yes sir, I do." Flagg, LSE's chief financial officer interrupted. The investment you made in that Gibraltar fund overseas has matured as of this morning. You should see a net gain of fifty thousand dollars, tax free."

"There! That's what I pay you all for. To make me money!" Mr. Fabrizi leaned back in his chair and interlocked his fingers behind his head.

"And the funds will be split and reinvested between The First Bank of Barbados and the Union Bank of Switzerland first thing in the morning." Flagg added proudly, and Mr. Fabrizi unleashed a rare, controlled grin and nodded his approval.

Something didn't sound right to Riley, and he thumbed through the dense file cabinet in his brain to find the term paper he wrote on this very subject. In fact, it was the very part Mici had vomited upon, and he knew it well since it was written twice. Once he had it, he drew upon it for confidence and interrupted the conversation. "Excuse me, sir? You don't mean to invest in the Union Bank of Switzerland funds, do you? There is a new tax treaty that goes into effect between the United States and Switzerland on the first of next year, and not only will your accounts be subject to government review, but you will be taxed at a fairly severe rate if you are a United States citizen. And though Barbados isn't a bad location for an investment fund, the Caribbean Islands are losing their luster because of their double-tax policies which can be worrisome for the average investor. I would suggest Cyprus... or better yet Panama who can't seem to come to a tax treaty agreement with the United States at all, and are very welcoming to foreign investors -- they don't ask any questions. Now if you're looking long term, the Netherlands has written some creative law this year when it comes to transferring assets to other members in your immediate family. You could..."

Riley stopped cold when he realized he was rambling, like he often did in Professor Friedman's class -- and it didn't make him any friends there, either. The room was quiet again, including Mr. Fabrizi who cocked his head to one side and stared at him, sort of squint-eyed as if he lost his glasses, then Mr. Fabrizi shot a nasty stare at Flagg and addressed him, all the while pointing at Riley.

"Do you know about this, Flagg? What he's saying?"

"Well, of course I do, sir. Umm....I think," Flagg responded. "But I will double-check all that when I get back to my desk, I promise. Things can change very fast sometimes." Flagg's face had changed from a glowing pride to an alarming shade of dark pink in his embarrassment. Riley hoped he had not gone too far, and felt bad that he had harpooned Flagg and didn't even know him. He didn't mean to humiliate the poor man.

"Here's what I want you to do Flagg, go check into it like you said. Then I want you to bring the documents over to Lynch's desk and have him check them over. That money doesn't get transferred until Lynch signs off. Got it?" Mr. Fabrizi ordered.

"But sir," Flagg responded with a defensive tone. "I appreciate Lynch's opinion on this, but I am the CFO of this company."

"And it's my fucking money!" Mr. Fabrizi shot back, pounding the table with his fist yet again. "You'll do what I fucking tell you to do. You've been a fuck-up as CFO since the day you got here. This was the first thing I thought you were ahead of me on. Then I pull this kid in off the street and he shows me more in one meeting than you have in a year. What the fuck am I paying you to do, anyway?"

Mr. Fabrizi looked back at Riley, "You OK with this, Lynch?"

"Yes sir" Riley answered, heart racing. "Except there is one little thing."

"What is it?"

"I don't think I have a desk yet."

The torturous meeting wore on for two excruciating hours, but in the minds of its participants, it felt much longer than that, and followed a predictable pattern. Mr. Fabrizi would scream and humiliate each of his directors one at a time, and they would make excuses which always seemed to point back to a bad decision Mr. Fabrizi made at a previous meeting. When the meeting did adjourn, the group would fall over each other to get down the elevator to the sidewalk where they could heal their battered egos and frayed nerves by inhaling a fast cigarette. Riley was never one to approve of smoking, but he understood why they needed it, and wondered if he should start. Over time, Riley would learn that these meetings were less about getting chewed-out and more about letting Mr. Fabrizi blow off steam about whatever ailed his soul, and it allowed their CEO to re-charge his batteries and locate a feeling of accomplishment within his dysfunctional organization. Whatever the directors thought about Mr. Fabrizi, no one questioned his commitment or his loyalty to his company.

José met up with Riley after the meeting to give him a personal tour of the Lafayette Street Enterprises home office, top to bottom, as promised. Riley had already visited the top floor during his interview which included not only the ornate CEO's suite, but also a private lounge, movie theater, Jacuzzi and sleeping area where Mr. Fabrizi could nap or spend the night if he felt the need. The floor directly beneath the penthouse was divided into several small private offices reserved for each of Mr. Fabrizi's directors, so as to never be too far away from the chief executive. The three floors below that belonged to a strange and wacky array of administrative assistants, pencil pushers, accountants and telemarketers who offered functional support to the directors. The first floor was the main entrance with a small reception area, and hidden behind it, was a fully-equipped modern gymnasium complete with treadmills, weight machines, a small track and even a sauna. Mr. Fabrizi had invested close to half a million dollars in creating the gym as a gift for his best employees, but he had yet to allow any of them to use it. Though, it was often shown to clients and out-of-town visitors as an example of how progressive and legitimate Mr. Fabrizi and Lafayette Street Enterprises had become.

"So tell me José, are all of Mr. Fabrizi's meetings that crazy, or did I start on a bad day?" Riley asked.

"Oh my." José responded. "They can become much worse and much longer than that. Don't let the drama get to you or your arteries will explode from the stress. I know it's hard, but let it roll off your back."

"I don't understand why you all don't quit on him."

"They can't quit. Don't you know? Every one of them, or I should say every one of us, works here because we have to. Flagg, for example, spent a year in federal prison on tax evasion charges. Who else would hire him as a CFO? Hooper ran his own telecommunications company in Denver until he caught his wife fooling around with his vice-president and beat the poor bastard to near death with a fireplace log. And I should warn you about Katie, too."

"What's wrong with Katie?"

"She might be the most talented executive assistant in the city, and you will need to rely on her for a lot to survive here. But if you see a bottle of alcohol on her desk, or smell it on her breath, get away."

"Why?"

"Just get away. She is a binge alcoholic and becomes unpredictable. Just trust me on that one."

"I don't mean to get personal, but can I ask why you work here? You seem to be a level-headed guy."

"My mother was the Fabrizis' family housekeeper. Several years ago, when he was in prison, my mom helped Imelda run the household and she became like a nanny to the Fabrizis' two children. Then after my mother died, Mr. Fabrizi made sure my brothers and sisters were looked after and cared for, and he found us all jobs. He is like an uncle to me. My family owes him everything. My title of operations director doesn't mean anything official, I guess I'm more like an executive gopher. Whenever Mr. Fabrizi has a special errand, or needs something done by someone he trusts, he calls me. That's my story. So now it's only fair that I ask you, why did you accept the job here?"

Riley had been pondering the same question all afternoon. He had no criminal record or severe personality flaw that he was aware of. Though he now wondered if his decision to leave Americo's had been a mistake.

"I was offered the job after I told him about my mother. She is terminally ill and struggling to make rent payments. I'm trying to go to school at Columbia and support my family back in South Boston."

Ah ha," José said and smiled, "I get it now. You have no choice but to work here because of your mother's condition, and you are educated. Mr. Fabrizi has an obsession with education. You need to understand that the man never made it out of grade school and regrets that. He's not stupid -- not by a long shot. But he wants everyone to think he is brilliant. He surrounds himself with successful and educated people so they will compliment his ideas and achievements. Another bit of advice -- don't ever make him feel stupid, even if it's deserved."

José and Riley stopped in front of a small empty cubicle. "This will be your desk. You will be assisting Flagg for the next few weeks pulling together supporting documents for the quarterly tax filing. His office is over there in the corner."

A short chubby Hispanic man was in Flagg's office sorting through papers, he looked over at José and Riley, blew a kiss, and offered an effeminate wave and smile. Riley was taken back.

"That's just José, he's Flagg's personal secretary," José responded.

"You're both named José?"

"Yes, my name is José-Alejandro Martinez Villanueva-Zapata. His name is José Ballesteros Padilla-Luna. I am José A, and he is José B. To keep from being confused, call me *Hose-A* and him *Hose-B*, get it?"

"You're kidding."

"Mr. Fabrizi came up with the joke years ago and still thinks it's funny when he says it. It was insulting and demeaning at first, but we got used to it. I know he means it with affection."

"So who do we have here?" Hose-B had come over looking for an introduction and stood smiling with his hands behind his back, batting his eyelashes.

"This is Riley Lynch. Mr. Fabrizi just hired him as an associate to Mr. Flagg to help with the quarterly filings."

"Riley is such a nice name," Hose-B responded, extending his hand and limp wrist in an act of friendship. Riley grabbed his hand and gave it a brief, awkward shake.

"I'm looking forward to working with you," Riley responded in a forced professional tone. Hose-B nodded, smiled and skipped back to Flagg's office like a cheerful six year-old girl.

"You don't need to worry," José said, noticing Riley was uncomfortable with Hose-B's over-the-top flamboyance. "He's into blondes."

The journey from Lafayette Street near China Town back to campus took much longer than the trip from Americo's in the West End did, and it wasn't as direct either. The subway ride gave Riley some time to absorb and analyze his new found existence. LSE was no Americo's and Mr. Fabrizi was no Mr. Mantano, this was for sure. There would be no slacking-off or showing up late or taking a last-minute day off because of a forgotten term paper. And as rotten as Lorenzo and Armand could be, he was on a whole other level with Flagg, Hooper, Buckner and the others -- including both the Hoses. He saw no reason to trust any of them. And though his ego and intellect were riding on an all-time high, his emotional self was spiraling into an abyss of solitude. He didn't have Mr. Mantano's wisdom and even temper or Mici's charming disposition to comfort him any longer. He also wondered how Magnolia had made out back home, upstate. As hard as he tried, he could not picture her in bib overalls farming garlic. (And he could picture her in many things.) He longed for her off-beat companionship.

As his train scurried through the dark tunnels, he thought about the sub-zero Saturday afternoon he and Magnolia spent at the Metropolitan Museum of Art. Unbearable cold had blown in from the northwest the evening before, and though the sun was bright and the sky cobalt blue, the frigid air brought searing pain to any exposed skin it found. Magnolia's fashion statement of the day included a green army jacket, blue French cavalry pants, brown mukluks and a Russian fur hat with ear flaps-- outfitted to survive any international incident. The two made the brainless decision to walk to The Met from the dorms at Columbia which under normal conditions would have been a delightful and healthy stroll, but the walk on this day had turned into a death march along slippery, glazed sidewalks as their flesh turned red and froze numb in the wind. The two squeezed together, each trying to crawl into the other's skin for warmth, until they reached the icy marble stairs that led up to the main entrance. The couple spent hours winding through the wondrous galleries that day, considering each of the works on display in turn, and Magnolia immersed herself. Riley couldn't recall another time when her focus was so intense and unyielding. To Riley, after staring at a dozen or so paintings, they started to look a lot alike. He accepted their value and significance but was too much of a pragmatist to get so worked up about them. Riley would have figured Magnolia to be a fan of modern art, but as it turned out, it was on the second floor among the French Impressionists where she enjoyed her time the most. Riley found a soft gazing couch to relax upon and finish thawing while Magnolia spent an exorbitant amount of time staring at Edouard Manet's *Dead Christ with Angels*, pacing back in forth in front of it like a lawyer facing down a difficult witness.

"Riley, look at this. There's something wrong with this painting."

"It looks fine to me."

"No, it's not. There is an awful problem here."

"Oh, wait. I see it now. The Met has been exhibiting a forgery all these years, and Magnolia Fair, brilliant art history undergraduate from Columbia University, has broken the case. Should I call a cop?"

"You are such an asshole."

Riley sighed. "So, Magnolia, what is wrong with the painting. Maybe you should have said something to Manet before he painted it?"

"Look at it! It's crooked."

"No, I doubt it's crooked. This is The Met after all, not City Hall."

"You're a stand-up comic all of a sudden, huh? Shut up and come over here and help me." Riley realized Magnolia intended to remove the painting from the wall and reposition it.

"Jesus Christ, Magnolia, you can't do that!' Riley said in a stern, scolding tone. And though it really didn't matter to him, when he looked at the painting again he noticed that Magnolia was correct. It was crooked.

It didn't take more than a few seconds for the two of them to be surrounded by a half dozen security guards. Riley wasn't sure if they had tripped some silent alarm when Magnolia pulled on the painting or if they had been observed on one of the many security cameras. Magnolia in her Russian fur hat and mukluks no doubt drew their attention the moment she walked into the building anyway. But no matter now, the gig was up.

"What's going on here? The lead guard questioned, the only guard armed of the bunch. Magnolia's answer was calm and direct.

"Your painting was crooked. But I fixed it."

"You two need to come with us down to the museum security office."

Riley had visions of arrests, prison time and expulsion from school. But Magnolia was a pro, with years of hands-on experience, at getting in trouble and wiggling out of it.

"Fascists!" She screamed. "You're all fascists! You are desecrating the greatest works of humankind! May God punish you and your families! You have institutionalized the great masterworks! You are treating humanity's greatest achievements with all the respect you give a caged monkey at the zoo! Shame! Shame on you capitalist pigs!

Shame on the almighty dollar! Shame on The Met and its commercialization! Shame on you all!"

"Oh for the love of St. Peter!" The guard snapped, seeing clear through her act, staring her down. "Be goddamned quiet! There must be a thousand people in here today, including two hundred school children from an art school in Cincinnati. Not one of them came all this way in this freezing weather and paid their admission to listen to your lunatic ravings. I will make a deal with you. If you shut your trap now and leave *quietly*, I would be willing to forget the whole thing and we can all get on with our day."

In under a New York minute, Magnolia and Riley found themselves back out on the marble steps of the museum in the cold, under orders to never return to the museum again. Riley this time was so hot he welcomed the rush of freezing air across his exposed face.

"Magnolia, you scared the shit out of me. What the hell was that all about?"

"Nothing. I just had to think on my feet. Those guards only make about ten bucks an hour, right? So if we go with them quietly to the security office, we become their trophy, something to show off to their bosses about how big and tough they are. If we act crazy -- as long as they realize we aren't international terrorists or art thieves -- they'll just push us out the door to get rid of us. They don't want the headache or the paperwork. You see, Riley, I understand what motivates people. That's why I always get what I want. It's all about comfort. Most people are weak and when faced with a decision, they take the path of least resistance -- the path that's most comfortable. If I can make them feel uncomfortable, I can predict what they do and how they will act."

"You are demented. You do know that?"

"Would you have me any other way?"

"Not a chance. Though sometimes..."

"But that's why I like you Riley. The night we met, the most comfortable thing for you to do would have been to kick me out of your room or just walk away. But you didn't. But you overcame that inner voice of yours that told you to run, and you were good to me instead. It showed me you have character."

"I hope I was a little more than good," Riley quipped.

147

"I'm hungry. How about some hot cocoa and stuffed mushrooms? And maybe sushi?"

"Sounds like a plan. But let's take a cab."

Thoughts of Magnolia and their wacky escapades tended to cheer him up. But perhaps the most shocking moment of Riley's crazy day came when he opened the door to his dorm room to find Alvin sitting in a chair and reading a book. There were no girls hiding in the bathroom, or underwear draped over any furnishings. In fact, Riley didn't even see an empty beer bottle or potato chip bag anywhere in sight. Fueling the unusual scene was the television news which blabbed low in the background. Something had to be wrong.

"You feeling OK, Alvin?"

"I feel great, dude." Alvin answered.

Since Hanratty's murder at the carwash, Alvin had not been himself. The incident was disturbing and horrific to all who witnessed it, including Riley, but it seemed to etch into Alvin's core a little deeper. Alvin now lived always on edge, irritable and short tempered. He contracted a chronic case of paranoia and would flinch at loud sounds, or the cries of police sirens at any time of day or night. He had also become an eagle-eyed news junkie, scouring the daily papers and scanning the television channels for any word or rumor surrounding the murder, Hanratty or the mob in general. The television news channels, without knowing, became an accomplice to his crusade and fed his hungry inner demons with tasty daily offerings. Mob news got ratings, and they went to extremes to report an organized crime story whenever they could, whether the story was true or not.

"So what are you reading?"

"Hamlet." He answered. "Big English paper due this week. Hey dude, you got mail over there by the refrigerator."

"You always make me nervous when you study," a bemused Riley responded. "It's like a front and you're up to something no good."

Riley shuffled through the crumpled ad flyers, credit card offers and mail-order catalogs and pulled out a letter addressed to him from his brother Ryan at the seminary. He grabbed a butter knife from beneath a week old pile of dirty dishes and used it as an impromptu letter opener, splitting the unassuming envelope in two causing it to unleash its contents to flutter to the floor. The letter from Ryan was short, and it was unusual for Ryan to write in the first place rather than call. Riley dove into the letter. Alvin's attention, however, was riveted to the TV.

Tomorrow, in a report you will see only on New York Action 5 News -- "Inside the New York Mob: A Special Report." We will take you inside the city's gritty, criminal underworld and introduce you to the characters who not only run the modern New York mob...

"Hey. That's Marcellino on the news!" Alvin jumped up out of his chair. Riley looked up as a fuzzy, black and white image of a frowning Giovanni Marcellino stared back at him.

"Yea, that's him alright. He'll get his someday." The next image caught Riley by surprise -- it was Edward Fabrizi, and though Riley couldn't be sure from the grainy background, he appeared to be standing in front of Americo's.

""But I don't know that guy at all," Alvin said. "I'll record the report tomorrow night."

Riley said nothing to Alvin, but felt his stomach flop over, and wondered how much trouble Mr. Fabrizi could be in, praying Mr. Mantano was not involved. And it concerned him that his new career could be over before it started. He doubted there was much call in the business world for an unemployed former financial consultant to a mobster. He turned away from the television and his elbow struck a brown lunch bag on the corner of the counter sending it to the floor with a loud metallic crash, and small gold bullets rolled in every direction.

"What the hell are these?" Riley shouted, surprised.

"They're bullets for my new gun." Alvin stuck his hand in his pocket and produced a small black pistol.

"Have you lost your mind? Where did you get that?"

"I bought it from my buddy Teddy at the fraternity party the other night. Like it?" Alvin smiled and spun the gun around his index finger like an old-west outlaw, then puckered his lips and blew across the top, dispersing the make-believe smoke.

"You have got to get rid of that thing, man! You'll get us both expelled -- or arrested -- if they find out we have an unregistered gun in our room."

"Chill. Don't worry, Riley. No one will ever find out." And Alvin put the gun back into his pocket, showing off his now empty hands. "You didn't see a thing."

"I'm not kidding, Alvin. I don't want a gun in this place. It will bring no good."

Alvin's docile mood turned cool and angry. "You saw what happened to Hanratty just like I did. What if they saw us? They will be looking for us. All that Marcus guy had to do was watch the news and he would know there was a car in that carwash stall that wasn't his. It's a dangerous world, dude. New York is a dangerous place. I'm not taking any chances. They're not taking me without a fight. And I think you should get one, too."

Throughout Riley's childhood, both Mr. Murphy and his mother railed against guns and violence as the path to all evil. Gun violence was not uncommon in his neighborhood, and each time there was a shooting or incident, Sarah would use it as further evidence to support her lifelong commitment to pacifism. He could hear his mother's words echo in his head, and he spit them out at Alvin.

"Guns have no other purpose than to kill other people. God has declared, *though shall not kill.* So why have a gun? To threaten? To persuade? To steal? Or to kill?" What greater good is there in any of that?"

Riley turned away from Alvin, thinking about where he could hide Alvin's bullets. Persuading him to ditch the gun would take some time. But Riley still felt the responsibility and drive to continue to protect Alvin from his most viable and immediate threat -- Alvin.

In the heat of the moment, Riley had crumpled Ryan's letter with so much force that his fingernails were now poking through it. He laid it out on the counter and smoothed it over, attempting to read it once again without interruption.

"So... is that letter anything important?" Alvin asked, trying to bring normalcy back to the room's atmosphere.

"It's from my brother Ryan. He says his ordination as a priest is scheduled for April first, in Providence, then he is off to Nicaragua. Wow, he really is going through with it. For some reason, I never thought he would."

Riley clung to the hope his mother would live until April to see it. And now he hoped he would, too.

THIRTEEN

Riley was worn out. For almost a year, he had been juggling not only a marked increase in his school work load, but also an increase in the layers of responsibility piled on him by Mr. Fabrizi.

His performance at LSE was exemplary. Mr. Fabrizi looked to him for an informed opinion on almost everything now -- from tax issues and financial matters to hiring, distribution policy and even warehouse operations. Hose-B had been re-assigned from Flagg's assistant to now be Riley's, as even on a half-time basis, Riley's responsibilities had mushroomed and were more important to the corporation in Mr. Fabrizi's opinion than Flagg's as CFO. Riley had now watched everyone in the building get chewed-out and humiliated in fits of rage at least once, except him. He was grateful that Mr. Fabrizi continued to show him the highest level of respect. And he worked hard to give him no reason to act otherwise.

Riley was riding the train from New York to Boston to visit Siobhan in jail. He wrote her often, but never had an opportunity to see her in person since her incarceration so many months ago. He was anxious about visiting the Nashua Street facility since he had never been anywhere near such a place before. He considered prisons to be scary places. He spent a good amount of time reading and re-reading the jail's visitation policies so as to not bring any undue attention to her or himself while there, and planned to stay only as long as necessary. After visiting Siobhan, he was then heading straight down to Providence for Ryan's ordination ceremony to be held in the great Cathedral of Saints Peter and Paul the following day. There, he would join most of his family including his mother whom he had last seen at Christmas when Riley first realized she was losing her battle and slipping away. He also wondered who from his family wouldn't show up.

To keep himself busy on the three-and-a-half hour trip, he brought along about fifteen hours worth of work. A major economics project was due to Professor Friedman upon his return, and he had yet to begin a single bit of research or touch pen to paper. Mr. Fabrizi also gave him a stack of folders for him to review on LSE's modest strip club empire. Mr. Fabrizi owned or had a financial interest in more than fifty "gentlemen's clubs" located up and down the east coast, and some of them were losing money without explanation. Mr. Fabrizi fired his national club director from the board in New York, and suspected his local managers were skimming profits -- strip clubs never went into the red. Riley was to analyze the files and look for any patterns or curiosities that might explain the downturn in business and suspicious losses of cash. It was also an exercise to get Riley up to speed and informed on the operations of one of LSE's most lucrative divisions. Riley opened the thick manila files and spread their contents -- spreadsheets, letters, memos and photographs -- over his lap.

But somewhere near New Rochelle, just minutes away from Penn Station, Riley leaned his head back and dozed off. Sleep had been staved off for several weeks, and now it had invaded and conquered him without permission. His dreams were short and disconnected, and made little rational sense as dreams often do. He dreamed he had lost his pack of cigarettes, and was frantic to find them, but in reality he didn't smoke. Then he dreamed he was angry at Alvin for something which wasn't clear as the two of them bagged groceries at the local supermarket. He dreamed he was back at Columbia looking for a classroom that didn't exist, only to open a random door and be back in Mr. Murphy's bookshop during the busy Christmas season with joyous carols dancing in the air. And then he dreamed he walked upstairs and saw a bleeding Mr. Hanratty on the floor of his mother's apartment, writhing in pain, with a glorious Marcus standing over him. Riley's heartbeat increased and his arms flinched, slapping a young woman sitting across the narrow aisle. His spastic movement shocked Riley awake.

"I'm sorry, did I just hit you?" Riley asked, groggy and slurring his words.

"I'm fine. It's OK," the woman giggled, with a wide toothy but friendly grin.

Riley looked down and the contents of his manila strip club folders were spread all over the train floor, including an 8 x 10 nude color photo of "Miss Aurora Ample, 46EE" which laid in the aisle between the two of them. In fact, pictures of nude women had found their way up a few rows of seats. Riley jumped up and scrambled to collect the contraband together and stuff them back in the folders from whence they escaped. Warm waves of embarrassment swept over him.

"I really am so, so sorry." He continued to apologize, and when his foot felt cold, he realized he was also missing a shoe. The young woman, still smiling, pointed it out for him hiding beneath an adjacent seat.

"Thanks, I guess I was more tired than I knew," Riley said, tucking in his shirt and re-focusing his eyes toward her. "My name is Riley."

"Yes, I know."

Riley looked at her again and knew he recognized her but couldn't place her. He first considered that she was the girl Alvin was sleeping with the night he met Magnolia, as she was about the right height and age. She was an attractive girl, not too tall but thin with long legs, and bouncy short dark hair without a strand out of place. She wore a very smart blue business suit and round wire-rimmed Harry Potter glasses.

"I'm sorry again," I recognize you and can't place your name. I am still trying to wake-up I guess. I am such an idiot," Riley apologized once more, still groggy, trying to ease the pain of his growing humiliation. He wondered if she might be one of the regular patrons at the Cafe Marie Anne, as he thought he may have seen here there. Then he thought he remembered her from his calculus class at Columbia. He just wasn't sure. She continued to beam an energetic smile at him.

"I'm flattered you remember me at all. It's me, Tammy. Tammy Meeks? Do you remember?"

In Riley's universe, for the briefest of moments, time stopped cold and his five senses refused all input as his big brain churned and attempted to process the words she had just spoken. A wave of joy and surprise replaced his acute embarrassment for a moment, only to be swept back into embarrassment again when he realized he had a large wet drool stain on his left shoulder. Without thinking, he tried to wipe the drool away, then reached his wet hand out to shake hers, reconsidered and pulled it back, and cupped it over his cheek.

"Oh wow, Tammy! How are you? I haven't seen you in so long. Look at you!" Wispy recollections of school days gone by and secret old crushes flickered in his mind's eye. Riley searched to find words that made sense to string together in a sentence. His eyes scanned her from bottom to top. She turned out nothing like he had imagined she might. But she looked wonderful all the same, and he could see the small, pretty, shy girl he remembered etched into her larger grown-up face. His stomach fluttered, and he took in a deep breath, and Tammy's smile somehow grew even wider.

"I knew it. I knew it was you the second I got on the train in Stamford," Tammy said.

"I see the train has stopped, so where exactly are we right now?"

"We're just past Kingston station in southern Rhode Island."

"So then you have been watching me drool for over an hour?"

"Umm, yea. That's about right. And I have been working on a crossword puzzle."

"Wow, it is so great to see you again."

"I'm so relieved you remember me. I almost got up and switched seats a while ago. I was afraid to say something and make a fool of myself." Tammy said, clutching her chest as if feeling for her own heart beat.

"Looks like I took care of that for you."

"You looked so content and happy asleep. I guessed you must be having the most sweet, magnificent dreams."

Riley remembered bits and pieces of the dreams he just endured, but they were neither sweet or magnificent, and with mercy, they were fading. He tried hard to think quick and ask her something poignant and thoughtful, but drew a blank.

"So Tammy, tell me about yourself? What have you been up to since Middle School?"

"Well, I'm afraid my life isn't all that exciting. I'm in a pre-law program at Northeastern at night right now, and work for my father's law firm during the day. He works with all the big, New York Fifth Avenue publishers on copyright issues, so I feel like I ride this train all the time -- I guess I'm cheaper than hiring a courier service. I like to stop at the Town Center in Stamford when I have a little free time and do a bit of shopping. Do you remember my brother? Benny just got his law degree this winter, so he works in my dad's law firm now, too. What can I say, it's the family business. Even my mom is doing the paralegal stuff. So what about you? You look like you have an interesting job."

Riley glanced down at his folders, as did Tammy. Miss Ample was peeking out at them both from beneath his forearm. The humiliation Riley had booted out was doing its best to crawl back in.

"Oh this is nothing," he said, trying to explain it away. "I work for a company on Lafayette Street in Manhattan part-time and my boss sent me with some work to review. He owns a chain of strip clubs -- among a bunch of other things. I go to school at Columbia during the day. I'm studying international finance."

"Columbia? Good for you! That's a great school. How exciting it must be to live in New York. I doubt I will ever escape from Boston."

"New York would be the greatest place on Earth if it wasn't for all the Yankee fans." He looked up to see if Tammy had smiled, but realized she had yet to stop.

"Tell me about your family, Riley. You had such a big, wonderful family. I always wished I had sisters to play with growing up. I have always been so jealous of big families."

"Oh, sisters!' Riley looked at the ceiling of the train. "If you had asked, I would have given you the whole bunch of them. Meghan and Erin still live at home in Southie with my mom. Siobhan, though..." Riley stopped, realizing how awkward he would feel if he told her she was in jail.

"Oh Riley, I'm sorry, I forgot," Tammy cupped her hands over her mouth as if she had wanted to push the words back in. "I did hear about what happened to Siobhan on the news. That was horrible! I couldn't believe it, I remember her as such a sweet little girl."

"I'm on my way to visit her this afternoon." Riley tried to dismiss the Siobhan issue as fast as he could. "But there is better news in my family. Do you remember Ryan? He is becoming a priest. His ordination is in Providence tomorrow."

"A priest? Oh, you're joking. That's amazing. I didn't see him as the type but truth be told, I didn't know him that well. He hung around with Benny once in a while when I was little, so I only remember him as this annoying kid from down the street. That's too

155

funny. Isn't it fascinating where kids turn out when they grow up? It sounds like you're doing well for yourself, Riley. I missed you and all our old classmates when we moved -- I ended up going to Gloucester High School, I was a *Fisherman* -- how's that for a mascot? My father had reached his limit with all the stupid problems in South Boston -- the crime, the busing controversy, and the rotten teachers."

Tammy's smile had gone, and her tone turned more serious. But she continued and Riley hung on her every word.

"I was such a lonely, weird and sad little kid, I couldn't make any friends, and I got bullied and beat-up all the time. My life was miserable and I hated myself. The people who ran the middle school back then like Principal Leonard and Mrs. Beckmeir didn't care one bit, either. There were some dark times for me in those days. Looking back at it, I'm sure my parents wondered how I was going to make it -- or if I was going to make it at all. And to be honest, there were times in high school when I wasn't sure if I would make it either. When I graduated from high school, my father wanted me to do something, anything other than law. In fact, he pushed me toward art and music so I could have a better appreciation for the beauty and majesty in the world. But I felt like law was my calling -- I wanted to help people. Maybe it's a product of what I endured all those years. I don't know, I never enjoyed self-psychoanalysis. Down deep though, it's who I am. You can run from anything, and you can change, but you can't escape who you are."

Riley was grateful for her candor. He could sense the honesty in her voice, and he regretted not embracing her as his friend all those years ago.

"I have to be honest with you, Tammy. You said a few minutes ago you would have been embarrassed had I not remembered you. I am surprised you remembered me, or my name. I didn't realize you knew I was alive back then."

"Oh, Riley, you were the most considerate, charming little boy. And smart, too. I always kept my eye on the smart ones." Tammy blushed a bit. So did Riley. "How could I forget you? I used to hope back then we would become friends, you were always so nice to me, and that's about when my father moved us out of Southie and up to the North Shore. It was heartbreaking for so many reasons."

"I have often wondered where you went and how you turned out."

"You did?" Tammy blushed a little more. "I'm flattered. And I always wondered where you ended up, too. But I knew it would be good. Isn't that funny."

The train creaked, then lurched and restarted its journey to the north. Tammy and Riley spent the rest of the trip chatting about school, old friends, the neighborhood and long boring train rides. Riley was immersed in the conversation, and had escaped the pressures of his school and family for the moment and felt sad that he didn't have more true friends in his life to talk to. School, his family drama and his job had executed a hit on his personal life as of late, and since Magnolia had left and he had witnessed that murder, he had tried to live as unemotional and detached a personal existence as possible. Tammy's willingness to share and her openness about herself was refreshing and authentic and filled a void in him he had forgotten existed.

The train was a few miles from Boston's Back Bay Station, and Riley knew Tammy would be getting off there. He enjoyed their long conversation and was distressed it was about to end. He was compelled to share more about himself, and yearned to know more about her. He couldn't remember the last conversation he had where someone didn't want something from him. Their time had but a few precious moments remaining.

"My mother isn't doing so well," Riley blurted out, surprised he had even broached the subject. "At Christmas time, we didn't think she would make it to April to see Ryan's ordination. It's a miracle she will even be there tomorrow."

Tammy made a sharp turn toward him as if he had struck her again. Her eyes were big, dark and filled with care and compassion. Riley regretted mentioning it as soon as he said it, as it wasn't fair to hit her with such a heavy topic and demand her empathy. He thought he was being selfish. His mother's condition weighed on his heart more than he would admit.

"Oh no, I'm sorry to hear that. Is there anything I can do?"

"Thanks, but I don't think there is anything anyone can do. Her condition is serious and she won't make it much longer. I do worry that tomorrow will be the last time I see her."

Riley felt his throat tighten and his eyes well up, emotions he had buried were emerging. Tammy's presence had brought it out of him. Now he was feeling like a fool, humiliated once again. The train slowed as it pulled into the station.

"I need to get off here, Riley. It was wonderful to see you again after all this time." Tammy shot him a warm smile, gathering up her bags and belongings.

"I really enjoyed our talk. Good luck in law school."

"Good bye, Riley"

In a matter of a few seconds, she was gone, absorbed into the bustling crowd of the station. Riley felt very alone. He kicked himself for not asking for her phone number, then figured a smart and pretty girl like her had a boyfriend anyway -- though he thought it was curious she didn't mention a relationship. If she was working at her father's law firm, he figured she would be easy enough to find later. But why would she want to hear from him again, anyway? Their meeting was pure coincidence, and he hadn't exactly come off as dashing Prince Charming, though the drool stain on his shoulder had dried and his porn was out of sight.

Reality had started to creep back into his day. Though well worth the investment, his time with Tammy meant his economics project and his paperwork from Mr. Fabrizi were in deep trouble. He was thankful he had chosen to reserve a hotel room for the night at the Marriott in Providence and not try and hook up with his family before the ceremony at the cathedral. Although he wouldn't get much sleep, some quiet time in the hotel, and maybe a swim in the pool, would help him catch-up some work and balance his nerves and beaten emotional state.

He arrived at Science Park Station earlier than expected, and strolled along the long, thin park that abutted the Charles River waiting for the visiting hours to begin at the jail across the street. The local kids called the park "The Eggs" in honor of several bizarre oval shaped stones that were placed about in a pleasing artistic pattern. Although the effort of the artist is lost on most visitors who stroll by, the work is a favorite of the local skate rats who have invented a number of unique skateboard jumping tricks over the top of the artwork, to the continual frustration of local police. Riley sat on a park bench surrounded by blue azaleas and stone eggs. The sky was gray and the air warm, and the Charles River remained calm and dark as it always had been. With skateboarders darting around him,

Riley alternated his thoughts between what he planned to say to Siobhan, and relishing each piece of his conversation with Tammy.

At 3:30, he walked across the street and entered the Suffolk County, Nashua Street Sherriff's Office. He checked his personal items into a locker, tolerated a quick search from the guard on duty, then was led to a small white cubicle and sat on an uncomfortable plastic stool for an unreasonable amount of time. Just when he thought she wouldn't appear, and it was time to find someone to complain to, Siobhan was escorted into the other side of the cubicle. The two were separated by a thin glass window with a small round speaker so they could hear each other. Siobhan sat, saw Riley, and burst into tears.

"Oh, Siobhan, don't cry."

"Thank you for coming Riley," Siobhan choked on each word, struggling to speak. "I've missed you so much."

Sean was right, Siobhan looked as though she had aged twenty years. Her small, youthful, chirpy demeanor was long gone, replaced by a gray and dour scowl. Her hair was short now and ratty and looked like it needed a good shampoo, and her eyes had sunk in as if she needed a good sleep. Riley promised himself he would stay positive no matter what she said, and leave her feeling positive with some hope. It would not be easy.

"How are you doing?" Riley asked. "You look good."

"I'm fine, considering." Siobhan sniffled and cleared her throat after each word. "It's hard in here, and so depressing."

"Have you heard from Malcolm lately? I know your sentencing was delayed again."

"Malcolm has been a wonderful lawyer. He works so hard for me. He has managed to get my sentencing delayed three times now, and believes if he can throw enough motions and paperwork at them, he has more control over them, and can get them to react the way we want them to."

Riley briefly remembered Magnolia's similar explanation for her behavior after being evicted from The Met. He wondered if she should have abandoned garlic farming and become a lawyer.

"Just do whatever Malcolm tells you to do. I know he's a good lawyer."

"Malcolm thinks he can get me less than two years since I have no priors. The harder part will be getting custody of Brian back after I get out." Siobhan burst into tears again, and cried louder than before. "I miss my little boy so much, it's killing me."

"Hey now, you stay focused. The best thing you can do for Brian and yourself is stay positive. You won't be in here forever, you'll get to see Brian and your life will come back together eventually -- you just need to be patient. You can do this. You are a Lynch. You're tougher than all of them put together."

"Thank you. I needed to hear that. You're right. It's just that it is so unfair. Alberto and I were screwed. It was all a big set-up, but we can't prove it. Malcolm has been trying to find witnesses that back up our story but no one is willing to talk. Alberto liked to hang out down at Gulliver's Bar, and every few days, this old guy would come in and try to sell him drugs to set him up as a dealer. The guy claimed he had big-time connections. Each time he came by, he offered something different -- pot, crystal meth, coke, crack -- trying to find Alberto's tipping point I think, and he always told him no. I guess the guy got impatient trying to wear him down, because he showed up at our apartment unannounced one night with a suitcase full of crack vials. He dumps them out over the kitchen table telling Alberto that they were worth a half million dollars, and hands Alberto a printed list of people willing to pay big bucks for them. Alberto got really pissed off and ordered him out, and the guy excuses himself to use our bathroom. Next thing I know, the police are busting through our front door in full riot gear, guns pointing at us, dogs -- oh, it was the most terrifying moment of my life -- I thought we would all be killed. They even brought a photographer who is snapping pictures of everything. The police make us lie on the floor, and little Brian is screaming in the next room -- and I'm screaming at the officer who won't let me move because his boot is on the back of my neck. I could hardly breathe. Then the police start searching the place and come up with more vials -- in the bathroom, in a flower pot, even in Brian's shoes. We figure the guy realized Alberto wasn't going to play, planted the stuff all over the apartment, then went out the bathroom window and down the fire escape. The police had to have been tipped off before this guy ever showed up. It's like they were waiting outside for the word go. The police arrested us and everyone on that list."

"What was the name of the guy? The guy who brought the crack?"

"He said it was Tenny Doyle. Who knows what it really is."

The name was a little unusual and rang a bell. Riley clanked it around for a few moments in his head and remembered a man at Mr. Murphy's wake named Tenny Doyle. Mr. Mantano had pointed him out that night. He didn't tell Siobhan, but made a mental note to call Malcolm Ward later.

"The district attorney and police made a big deal about our arrest on the news, like they had been following us undercover for weeks. That's total bullshit. The only part I don't understand is why us? Why pick on us? We don't own anything, we don't have any money. Alberto and I aren't part of any gang. We just wanted to start a family and we struggle to get by like everyone else. I don't understand. I think I could handle this better if someone just told me why?" Siobhan's eyes turned to fire, and her anger was intimidating.

"I don't know, Siobhan. It doesn't make sense to me either."

"And I miss Alberto, too. Malcolm says even though I might get out, we need to prepare for the reality that he could be in for ten years or more. I know Mom didn't like him very much, but he is a sweet man." Siobhan appeared to cry again, but her eyes stayed dry. Riley wondered if she had run out of tears.

"Here's what I will do. When I get back, I'll call Malcolm and volunteer whatever help I can to help crack the case. I'll find the time. And I know a few people now. Remember Mr. Mantano I introduced you to at Mr. Murphy's wake? He knows a lot of people. I bet he will have a few ideas."

"Thank you, Riley. And give everyone a hug for me tomorrow at the ordination. I want to be there so bad."

"Hey, now, don't feel bad about that. Everyone understands. You'll be with us in spirit."

Riley left Siobhan behind and wandered the streets of downtown Boston alone for some time that night thinking, wondering how much of her story he could believe. His mother didn't like Alberto, and he didn't either, and he found it hard to swallow that the same Alberto who got his teenage sister pregnant was some poor, innocent bystander in this crime drama. Boston's city streets were clogged with traffic in what looked like a gridlock impossible to unweave. He noticed how narrow the streets felt, and how much older they were, as he walked up Tremont Street toward Boston Common. Riley had walked these streets many times as a teen and never stopped to appreciate the history and splendor of his own hometown. Boston

Common was no Central Park, but likewise, Central Park was no Boston Common. Each possessed their own unique charm and ambiance. Central Park was larger and offered more attractions, but Boston Common felt more like home, and the random passersby felt to him more like family. Riley watched the random Bostonians ramble by him and wondered if any of them had the problems that weighed on his mind. Up ahead, Riley saw a sign for Suffolk Law School, and an arrow pointing farther ahead toward Fenway Park and Northeastern University. Tammy, he assumed, must be home long before now, telling her mom and dad about her chance encounter with one of the nice boys from the old neighborhood. Riley checked his watch and panicked -- he only had a few minutes to get the last train south to Providence for the evening.

Riley arrive at the Marriott late, and rose early. He took a cab from his hotel on Orms Street over to the cathedral a couple of miles away, and wasn't surprised to find he was the first to arrive. He thought it unfair that they charged him at all for use of the room since he used it for such a short time. He considered it would have been a better use of his funds to wander the streets all night. But at least he was able to shower and shave.

Behind the cathedral there was a large open brick courtyard, and Riley sat on a bench and seized the opportunity to review his economics notes. The weather remained warm and the morning sunshine felt pleasant on his cheeks. The sturdy New England maples and oaks that stood above him had yet to produce their first leaves of the season, but little red buds were growing from the ends of their gray spindly branches, a sign that spring and summer were well on their way. Red tulips and yellow daffodils dotted the courtyard, the morning sun extracting vibrant colors from their fragile petals. As the morning wore on, human activity increased. Men in dark suits shuffled back and forth across the courtyard, and an occasional nun or priest would materialize as well. Riley was impressed by the abundance of gray squirrels, unthreatened by the activity or nearby traffic, who darted and tumbled with one another everywhere, carefree, as if the courtyard belonged to only them.

Guests for the ordination ceremony had started to arrive. There were ten priests being ordained by the diocese at this ceremony, and Riley expected it would draw a big crowd, though he was yet to recognize anyone coming for Ryan. A little blonde girl ran by him in a bright yellow dress and white sweater trying to catch a chattering squirrel. A whiff of cheap cologne wafted by him following to two old men with red boutonnieres. A fat man with a large camera bag strolled past next, looking uncomfortable in a suit and black shoes a few sizes too small that he probably had not worn in a while.

"Riley?" A familiar voice inquired from behind.

"Sean!" Riley jumped up and the two brothers embraced. Though Riley had been loathing his latest family reunion, it always felt good to see them.

"Wow, I thought I was early. I can't believe you beat me here."

"I came in last night and stayed in town. Where's Mom?"

"The girls are bringing her down. We took separate cars. They were right behind me. They should be along in a minute."

"How is she doing?"

"Not good. We're going to lose her, kid. It's only a matter of when."

"Thank God she lived to see Ryan's ordination."

"It's all she's talked about for months."

"Anyone heard from Liam?"

"No. Still nothing."

"Hey Sean, do you remember the Meeks family back in Southie?"

"I think so. Didn't they live on the corner where that used car lot is now?"

"Yes. You won't believe it. I just rode the train up here with Tammy. Tammy Meeks. I haven't seen her since middle school. She's studying law at Northeastern." Riley's enthusiasm was getting control of him. He was dying to talk to someone about his chance meeting. Sean was not interested.

"Sorry kid, I don't remember her that well. She had a brother who was Ryan's age, and she was a fair bit younger, so I don't think our paths crossed much."

The boys turned as Erin and Meghan were rounding the corner, pushing Sarah along in a wheelchair that bumped over the uneven red brick pathway. Riley was struck by how ghastly his mother looked. He had seen her at Christmas a few months before, but it was clear her condition had worsened still. Her frail physical self consisted of nothing more than skin and bones, and her head hung relaxed, as if lifeless, to one side. His sisters had dressed her in her Sunday best olive suit, and it hung on her like it was still on the wire

163

hanger. Riley strode over to her and gave her a big hug. She returned a big wet kiss on his left cheek.

"Oh Riley, look at you, so handsome in your suit."

"It's nice to see you again, Mom. Are you excited for this? I know you and Ryan have been waiting a long time for this day to come."

"I couldn't be any prouder."

The group walked around to the front of the brownstone building, as Riley volunteered for the duty of pushing the wheelchair along to the relief of his sisters who didn't have to be asked twice to step aside. As they entered the Victorian gothic-style cathedral, they each gazed up at the twin brick towers at the front entrance that when observed from directly below, seemed to reach the heavens at a single point, no doubt where God sat. Until that moment, Riley had been too distracted to notice, but his sisters were dressed like a couple of common Dublin streetwalkers in tight skirts, high heels and black fishnet stockings. He was surprised his mother let them out of the apartment dressed this way though he knew there wasn't much she could have done about it. He wanted to slap them on her behalf and send them back to their rooms.

The entrance to the sanctuary of the cathedral was grand. The marble floor stretched far ahead past dozens of oak wood pews to a grand marble altar. The church was large and could seat nearly two thousand when full. The mammoth and elegant stained glass windows that lined each side of the room humbled and captivated all who entered with their arrays of brilliant color. Riley started to push his mother's clunky chair up the center aisle, and she stuck her foot out to stop him.

"No, I will not be rolled into a cathedral like some entitled Italian princess. I intend to walk."

Sean looked at Riley, and Riley looked at Sean. They knew objecting to their mother's wishes on this day was suicide. The boys stood on either side of her, and summoning strength no one knew she had, she rose with grace and poise from her chair.

Watching her wobble, Riley was convinced that each step she took forward would be her last. But somehow after each painful advance, she was able to find the energy and spirit for one more step. Their pace up the aisle was slow, and the other guests had begun to notice their time consuming pilgrimage with anticipation. Sarah had become an opening act to the ordination, and her dainty frame appeared ready to collapse at any moment as the congregation hung on her every move, rooting her on in silence. She fought and persevered through her weakness, step by step, until she reached a pew she felt appropriate for her family. And then to everyone's surprise, she dropped to one knee in a perfect genuflect to the altar, crossed herself, stood then fell exhausted into her pew. The guests burst into a warm spontaneous applause.

"How disgraceful they would all act that way in God's great palace." Sarah mumbled and grouched. Riley and Sean each let out a great, coordinated sigh of relief.

Riley had taken his seat between Sean and Erin where he had sat since he was five so the other two could keep him from fidgeting. The deep, soulful cathedral organ hummed with piousness as a line of ten young men, all graduates of the seminary, marched in a single line toward the center altar. At least two dozen priests and deacons, including Father O'Connell from St. Finian's, sat together off to one side. Riley caught Father O'Connell's eye, and the good father offered a brief smile and wink Riley's way. Still seething that the parish refused help to his mother in her time of need, Riley smiled politely back, nodded and shot a quick middle finger back at him. A shocked Father O'Connell's eyes widened and his gaze spun back to the ceremony at hand.

The diocesan bishop offered everyone welcome, and began the ordination mass. Sarah's attention was riveted and she absorbed each moment as if recording it for replay later. Just a few moments into the ceremony, Riley was already bored out of his mind. He had not been to mass since he had left for Columbia, and hadn't missed it. His mind shuffled back and forth through his economics project, Mr. Fabrizi, Tammy and Siobhan.

"Hey, Sean, I went to see Siobhan last night."

"You did? How was she?

"Shhhhhh!" Their mother hushed them as if they were still naughty toddlers. Riley lowered his voice to a near whisper.

"Not good. She looked like hell. I didn't expect that."

"She's having a hard time in there."

"She told me she and Alberto were set up."

"I don't believe it. That Alberto is a shit."

"She said the guy's name who set her up was Tenny Doyle. Does that name ring a bell to you?"

"Tenny is this old guy who hangs out at Gulliver's. He always has some get rich quick scheme up his sleeve. He's been hanging around Southie for years. The guy is a bag of hot air. I don't believe for a second he could be capable of everything Siobhan is accusing him of doing."

"Did you know that guy Tenny also came to Mr. Murphy's wake in our apartment?"

"Yeah, I saw him. So what? Lots of people knew Mr. Murphy, and lots of people came to the wake."

"Yes, but Mr. Mantano recognized him that night and said that he had underworld connections, that he had been part of a gang years ago."

"Mantano knew him? Wow, that is strange. I don't know what to make of it. Maybe old Tenny has more gusto in him than I thought."

"I'm going to talk to Malcolm. Don't say anything to Siobhan... yet."

The ceremony had advanced to the Litany of the Saints, and as the congregation sang and prayed, all ten priests-to-be lay prostrate on the cold, marble cathedral floor in their flowing white robes to symbolize their humility to God and devotion to the church. The bishop then conveyed all manner of blessing upon them, and anointed them with holy water and oils. The scene, even for a jaded Riley, was profound and moving, and as the candidates stood, each professed their love and conviction to their calling. When Ryan's name was announced and he stepped forward, Sarah gasped and her eyes swam with delight.

Ryan was now a priest.

Following the pageantry of the official ordination, the ceremony veered off into the familiar pattern of a traditional Catholic mass. The first assigned responsibility and honor of every new priest is to provide Holy Communion to his assembled guests. Sean and Riley assisted their mother to rise from her pew and join the line. She staggered toward the front with great anticipation waiting her turn as a child might wait for a special present on Christmas morning, and Riley was struck with a significant dilemma – should he take Communion also? He had not attended a mass in years, and to be cleansed to receive the body of Christ, he was supposed to attend confession first. If he skipped communion, his mother would know he had not been attending services. If he accepted, he would be leading her to believe he was going to church when we was not, and would risk eternal damnation. His genetically programmed Catholic guilt weighed the problem. He chose to risk damnation and let God get even with him later.

The moment Sarah accepted the host wafer from her son the priest at the cathedral, as witnessed by the Bishop and her family, marked the proudest moment of her life. Riley, Sean, Erin and Meghan thought of the moment as a celebration of Sarah's achievement more than a celebration of Ryan's.

Following the mass, the new priests and their families met in the function room of the cathedral basement for an informal reception. Crepe paper streamers affixed with pushpins circled the large rectangular room, and urns of coffee percolated on tables piled high with finger sandwiches, small bags of potato chips, apples and chocolate chip cookies. The Lynch family and the guests of all the other priests mulled around and nibbled politely on the humble offerings. Sarah was now behaving again and was seated back in her wheelchair, to the family's relief. The Bishop mingled and worked the crowd like a politician. The room was crowded and hot, and the ceiling hung low -- not the place for a claustrophobic.

Out of nowhere, Ryan appeared before them like an apparition. Cheers and hugs greeted him.

"We are so proud of you, Ryan." Sarah told him as Erin and Meaghan affixed themselves, one to each of his arms.

"I have some good news," Ryan began. "I got permission to work at St. Finian's for the next few weeks. I'll be back at home for a while."

"Oh, it will be wonderful to have you home," Sarah cooed. "I will need to pick up a few things at the market on the way home. I'm not impressed with how that seminary has been feeding you. You are too skinny."

"Oh Mom, no. It's not necessary. The parish will take care of my needs."

"So then what happens after a few weeks?" The always inquisitive Riley asked.

"Then I will be off to Nicaragua."

"Nicaragua sounds so far away," Erin complained. "Why don't you be a priest closer to home? They need priests everywhere nowadays."

"It's my calling. It's the path that God chose for me. I saw a presentation by a farmer who lives on the outskirts of Managua. The Catholic population there is poor and live on rural farms with very few priests to manage the day to day needs. I was moved by their condition and unwavering faith, despite the hardships, and knew that's where I needed to be. I don't know why. Someday, I'm sure I will come home."

"We will miss you, Ryan." Meghan sobbed into his flowing white cotton sleeve. "We will all miss you."

The Lynch family emerged back in the courtyard without their new priest Ryan in tow, having escaped their clutches to return to the seminary with the rest of his classmates. Riley was eager to catch the train back to New York, and Sean was late for work. Meghan interfered with all their plans when she announced she had plans to hit the mall and do some shopping.

"I have been waiting all week to get to Providence Place." She exclaimed.

"Oh no you don't. You have to get Mom back home. I have to get to work at the plant. I am already late." Sean complained.

"Mom can come with us," Erin suggested, hoping to join in on Meghan's mall spree.

Sarah remained slumped in her wheelchair ignoring most of the conversation about her, and fell in and out of brief, unrestful naps. It was clear to all of them Sarah did not have the energy to do anything except return home to her bed and rest. The emotional day had sucked everything out of her. Riley sensed a standoff was looming among his siblings, and interceded in hopes of striking a compromise before a fight broke out.

"What if..." he began, "...I drive Sean to work and then take Mom home. Then, the girls can have the other car and go shopping."

"That's pretty far out of your way, kid. And do you even remember how to drive?" Sean asked, annoyed that Erin and Meghan were being so selfish.

"It's been a while, but I still have my license. After all, who says you need to know what you're doing to drive a car in Boston? And I really don't mind." Riley was lying, irritated his projects and paperwork would be delayed yet again, and furious that his sisters could even consider dragging his ailing mother through a shopping mall. He looked at Erin and Meghan and continued with a sarcastic tone, "Besides, why would I mind sacrificing my education and career so the girls can shop?"

Meghan kissed him and the two ran off, oblivious to his needs or his sarcasm.

The ride from Providence up to Boston started out a quiet one, and the typical heavy New England traffic wasn't so bad for a change, to Riley's relief. Sean spread himself supine across the back seat of the sedan and was sound asleep in minutes. Sarah nodded in and out of consciousness up front, so Riley had some time to think and fight off profound drowsiness of his own.

Riley's mind wandered to his brother, and Siobhan's twin, Liam. He wondered where he had run off to and what had become of him. Liam had always been the devoted and reliable kid but had become distant and aloof after Mr. Murphy's passing, isolating himself from the rest of the family. He had to know his absence was causing concern and paining their mother, and it angered Riley that he wouldn't call and let his mother know he was OK -- that is, if he was OK.

"Where are we?" Sarah asked, having emerged from her nap a bit disoriented.

"We should be home in about half an hour. How are you doing, do you need anything?"

"I'm just wonderful," and Sarah smiled and flashed a look of contentment. "But I am very tired. I expect I will sleep well tonight. Will you be staying at home with me tonight, Riley?"

"No Mom, I have to get back to New York. Between work and school, I am buried."

"Oh, that's too bad. The apartment has become a very lonely place as of late. It would have been nice to have you around for a while. While all you kids were growing up, there was always so much noise and activity -- people were always coming and going. Now only Erin and Meghan are left in the nest, and they aren't home very much anyway. And I pray every night that Liam will come home safe someday soon."

"Have you heard from Liam?"

"No, not in a long while. But I have asked God to keep him safe and look after him. Of all my children, Liam is most like your father, Seamus. He was the quiet one. He would never admit when something was bothering him and reveled in being mysterious. And he was so thick-headed, too. Once a notion started banging around in that thick noggin of his, it would stay in there until he went to do something about it."

Riley dared broach a subject he had avoided for years with his mother. "Part of me hoped Dad would show up today. With you sick I mean, and Ryan going into the priesthood, I thought maybe..."

"Your father left our lives a long time ago and won't be back. You surprise me Riley. All these years and I don't remember you ever asking or caring about your father one little bit. Sean, Erin and Ryan are older and his absence hurt them much more."

"I couldn't miss somebody I never knew, I guess." Riley answered, not sure if he should feel insulted. "But I feel like the family could sure use him right now. He would find Liam in no time, and be able to take care of you while you're sick. And with Erin and Meghan..."

"Oh your sisters! Don't get me started on those two."

"And I can't help but think he could have done something to keep Siobhan from getting pregnant and going to jail." Riley felt a resentment building within him that he didn't know existed. He felt his blood pressure rise. It surprised him.

"Don't you dare go blaming your father for the poor judgment of everyone else. That's too easy, and it's lazy. You are all adults now and responsible for your own actions. And so is he."

Riley pulled the car into the plant parking lot and roused Sean who was still snoring in the back seat. Sean sat up straight as if he had been awake all along, grabbed his bag and opened the car door in one fluid motion.

"Thanks, kid. Leave the car in the street and I'll come back and get it later." Sean staggered off, zigzagging across the pot hole filled asphalt lot like a zombie. It appeared to Riley he was no amateur at staggering to work.

Riley spun the car around and headed for the apartment. Every visit home to Southie featured more changes to the neighborhood he had left behind. Someone might have cut down an old tree, while someone else might have planted a new one. Someone might have demolished a building, and someone else might have remodeled a duplex. Someone might have opened a new gift shop, and someone else might have closed and hung a "for rent" sign. Others might have painted a fence, trimmed back a row of shrubs, or installed a satellite dish. Everything was changing, and to Riley it entered the surreal, as if he was travelling into a parallel dimension, somehow warm and familiar yet somehow foreign.

The car turned the corner and glided down East Broadway as if it knew the way to the apartment. Riley could see a couple of moving trucks ahead and a flurry of human activity in the street. He felt frustrated since now he had to park the car farther up the street and worried that Sean would never find it later. He stopped to let one of the workmen cross in front of him, and realized the front door of their building was propped open with a big stick. All the activity centered around his mother's apartment. Workmen were carrying boxes and furnishings out of the doorway and loading them into the moving trucks. Both he and his mother shrieked in shock.

Riley flung the car up in front of one of the trucks half on the sidewalk, bringing it to an uncomfortable stop, and jumped out screaming and waving his arms like a madman. The workers coming through the door at that moment froze, worried they were about to be attacked.

"Stop! No!" Riley cried over and over, and the concerned workmen did their best to arch around him as he flailed his arms. As he charged to enter the building, an older gentleman in a gray suit stopped him and told him to calm down.

"What the hell is going on?! This is my mother's apartment."

"I am a representative of the Suffolk County Sherriff's Office. We are executing an eviction on this premises as issued by the county court."

"You can't just do this! There is supposed to be a hearing! Who is doing this!"

"There was a court hearing, sir, and no one showed up. A default judgment was issued against the residents of this apartment. Several registered letters have been served on this premises without response. The court is merely carrying out the law on behalf of the building's owner."

"This is insane! My mother is old and sick and has no place to go."

"I'm sorry, sir, but there is nothing I can do. I am here to enforce this court order. I suggest you contact your attorney as soon as possible, or the local family services office."

As Riley ranted and raved at the sheriff, pacing back and forth with hands laced on top of his head, watching his family's belongings come down the apartment stairs item by item in the arms of strangers, Sarah sat in the car screaming at the top of her fragile lungs, pounding on the glass window with her white studded handbag, demanding to be freed. Riley had no intention of freeing her since the car was the safest place for her at that moment, and he didn't see how she could be of any help. The veins on his forehead popped and throbbed as he tried to think fast and do the right thing. The moment that the sheriff turned his head, Riley charged by him and headed into the building and up the staircase.

"Stop, you can't go in there!" The sheriff hollered.

When Riley reached the top of the stairs, he saw a crew of disinterested workmen shuffling from room to room loading things into boxes. The Lynch homestead would never have been described as sparse in the first place, and stacks of magazines, random papers and personal items were spread everywhere, made worse by the callous workers. Riley pulled out his cell phone and called anyone he could think of who could get him the number for the attorney Malcolm Ward. Even if he couldn't help, he could direct him to someone who could. After repeated tries, he managed to get through to Ward's answering service.

"We are sorry sir, Mr. Ward is on vacation in Jamaica."

"I need to speak to him! My mother is being evicted!" Riley grew more frantic.

The sheriff had made it to the top of the stairs and grabbed a passing workman and pointed at Riley. "If that guy gives you any trouble, let me know and I'll have him arrested."

"I'm not interfering with anything. I'm calling my fucking lawyer!" What little patience Riley possessed had expired. The answering service told him that either Mr. Ward or another attorney would contact him in a few minutes. Riley hung up. The seconds that ticked by felt like hours. He wandered into the kitchen debating what to do next, perspiring and angry, and on the counter in plain sight, he noticed a stack of blue letters and envelopes addressed to Seamus Lynch from the county sheriff's office. He shuffled through them like they were a deck of cards and saw not only had the sheriff outside been correct, his mother had been notified, but most of the letters had been signed for by his sisters and never opened. The letters held

172

postmark dates that went back over two months. He tore open one of the letters at random with vengeance, sending bits of blue paper into the air, and realized that his mother had not been paying the rent at all -- she was several months behind. Riley had been starving himself to send every available penny home to Southie all this time, and no one paid the rent? A puzzled Riley could only speculate as to where the money could have gone. He wondered what the hell Erin and Meghan were doing to allow this to happen right under their noses. He had never felt more exasperated and helpless. Riley's cell phone rang.

"Hello, Riley? This is Malcolm Ward."

"Oh thank God, it's you. My mother is being evicted! What can I do to stop this?"

"My office told me what was happening. I just made a call to my buddy in the sheriff's office over there. I asked for a verbal stay of execution on the eviction. They owed me a favor, but the best I could do was get them to stop now and wait until Monday to finish. It will buy you a couple of days to find out what is going on and talk to your landlord and the sheriff." Riley could hear Malcolm slurping on something on the other end of the line, and could hear giggling female voices. "I need to go now. Keep my office up to date on your progress. I'll do what I can. Good luck, Riley."

As Riley hung up his cell phone, the sheriff's cell phone rang behind him. The sheriff said nothing to the voice on the other end, but listened and nodded.

"OK boys, stop right where you are. We got orders to hold on this expulsion until next week." The frustrated sheriff announced, throwing up his hands like a football referee, and everyone dropped whatever they were carrying and stood in place.

From behind them, one of the workmen screamed.

Riley would piece together all the agonizing details later. He discovered his mother had pounded on the window in the car with such force that even in her weakened state, she somehow managed to break the glass and cut her hand. The activity caught the attention of a dim old man who was out shopping and looking for Mr. Murphy's long-closed bookshop, who came to her aid and let Sarah out of the locked car. She somehow managed to stagger and drag herself from the car across the sidewalk to the front door, losing her shoes and leaving a trail of blood droplets along the way. Several of the workers must have stepped over her decrepit, struggling body as she dragged herself up the steps of the confining stairwell one tortuous step at a time, and one of the men even swore at her as her presence lying on those steps caused him to stumble and almost fall over her with his overloaded box. Another man even stepped on the hem of her favorite olive dress with his large heavy work boots, tearing it, but he kept moving offering her scorn, but no help. Sarah crawled from the top of the stairs into the apartment on all fours, blood now smeared across her cheeks and filthy dress as Riley stood in the kitchen yelling into his cell phone, distracted and unaware of her suffering pilgrimage behind him. Sarah used her last ounce of energy to crawl into the closet where her precious altar now stood in shambles, interrupting a surprised workman in the midst of dismantling it. The man took one look at the silent determination and fire in Sarah's eyes and retreated back into another room. Sarah used the altar to pull herself up and adore and address her large bronze crucifix one last time.

Sarah's dead body was discovered lying across her Bible on her altar, her rosary beads wet with blood were draped across her shoeless feet.

FOURTEEN

Sarah's passing had been anticipated by everyone for months, but it still hit Riley quite hard, as if he had been struck in the forehead with a hammer. Sarah had served the family as both matriarch and patriarch, a true rudder, and without her, Riley expected his siblings to drift with even less direction than they were drifting already. His mother had not died peacefully as she deserved, but died fighting like the final, loyal soldier on the field of a battle gone wrong, bullets depleted, fighting hand-to-hand to her final breath. Riley missed his mother from the very moment she died in the apartment that day, and her passing further opened a cavern of isolation that felt bottomless.

Riley's Aunt Eileen handled all the details for the wake and funeral. Sarah had entrusted her with carrying out the arrangements since she wisely knew her children were incapable of handling it. And Riley was content to stand in the background in silence and not interfere. From the moment Riley informed his brothers and sisters of their mother's passing, squabbling and infighting broke out among them punctuated by emotional outbursts and bouts of hysterical crying. Riley turned his anger and sorrow inward. He had also been responsible for notifying Siobhan in jail since no one else wanted to do it. He did it by telephone, unable to bear another visit to the facility to watch Siobhan disintegrate before him, so near yet out of his reach. Riley was employing his own retreat. He couldn't handle any more.

The sheriff's office delayed execution of the eviction order for two weeks, either a sympathetic gesture considering the sad circumstances, or a selfish act to distance themselves from the embarrassing drama. Either way, it provided a brief respite to allow Erin and Meghan to find a new place to live -- initial phone calls pleading for mercy to the landlord, who was preparing to sell the

175

building, were useless. Both girls were stewing in their own juices, terrorized by the concepts of independence and maturity, but Riley knew it was time they grew up anyway -- whatever the conscquences.

Sarah's wake and funeral saw many of the same old visitors who had attended the services held for Mr. Murphy, but this time the wake occurred at Hennessey's Funeral Parlor instead of the Lynch apartment. Notably missing this time, however, were any of the pseudo-mobsters who came to see Mr. Murphy -- Tenny Doyle, Matty Quinn or Marcellino -- and Riley didn't miss them. He wondered and worried about Liam, wherever he was, and wasn't sure he even knew their mother had passed. He started to wonder if he was still alive. He vowed to himself to find Liam as he promised his mother he would.

Riley had no sooner arrived at the wake than his cell phone rang.

"Hello, Riley? This is Katie from Mr. Fabrizi's office."

Riley had neglected to tell anyone outside of Boston about his loss, and didn't care to. He figured he would be in hot water with both his job and his school but chose to worry about it all later when he was better suited to deal with it.

"Hi Katie," Riley answered, expecting to next hear he had been fired for disappearing on them.

"Mr. Fabrizi asked me to call to relay his condolences on the passing of your mother. He said to not worry about work and to take as much time as you need to get your affairs in order. He asked that you contact him immediately if you need any assistance."

"Thank you, Katie. Please let Mr. Fabrizi know I appreciate that."

Riley was struck by how charitable Mr. Fabrizi's offer had been. He was not the type of boss to extend charity, in fact, most of his employees thought of him as more of a Mr. Scrooge badgering them about when they would be returning to work. Riley felt appreciative, but the positive feeling was suppressed by his profound, overwhelming grief. It also occurred to Riley that someone must have told Mr. Fabrizi all about this. But who? No one outside of Boston, except his family, was aware of his mother's passing -- he hadn't even told Alvin yet. By the time the funeral began the next morning, not only had Mr. Fabrizi sent a beautiful flower arrangement, but so had the staff of Americo's Restaurant. Riley thought this all very, very odd.

Ryan accepted the honor and duty of conducting their mother's funeral mass at St. Finian's. Father O'Connell was conspicuous in his absence. It was only his second official ceremony -- the first being at his ordination where he gave communion to his mother. And now he was burying her. Ryan had a difficult time making it through the ceremony and choked up more than once, but as the trooper he was, he got through it, and would have made his mother proud. Riley passed over the opportunity for communion this time without any regret or concern.

Just before the casket was sealed for the final time, Sarah's children gathered around her weeping, paying their final respects. Meghan was near hysterical, Erin stood stoic but her moist eyes had sunk and she looked shell shocked, and Sean smelled of Irish whiskey and acted a bit drunk. Riley had worn the gold crucifix Ryan had given him as a present when he went off to Columbia. His mother's pale emaciated hands clutched her rosary beads tight, and Riley placed the crucifix across her chest, with Ryan's approval. It had received an official blessing from the pope after all -- and meant much more to Sarah than it ever would to Riley. He figured whomever Sarah was about to meet in heaven might be impressed.

The night following the funeral, Riley slept in his old bed in his family's apartment for the final time. The place was a shambles, as the half-filled boxes the workmen had filled dotted each room, and over thirty years of family personal items and artifacts were spread around the floor scattered and broken. The kitchen where Riley ate his corn flakes every morning growing up looked ransacked, the refrigerator magnets had been brushed off the door and the kitchen table had suffered a broken leg in the mayhem. Pieces from his mother's altar were strewn aside, as several white candles had been squished by the heels of the black boots of EMT's who responded to their frantic call for medical help. Meghan and Erin slept in the next room, but Riley could not find sleep, and he stared up at the ceiling tracing patterns with his eyes as he did when he was small. He listened to the familiar chorus of the building's pipes that creaked and popped each time the boiler fired up, and he listened to the traffic patterns outside as cars sped by every few minutes. He got out of bed and browsed through his old comic books that were now spread on the floor, many torn. Each had been a friend to him in his childhood, and now they lay assassinated and abandoned beneath his feet.

Riley wandered around the apartment for an hour in the dark, examining it inch by inch in the moonlight, allowing memories to stream in, unsure if he should clean and straighten things up, or maybe just light a match and end his self imposed torture. His meandering brought him to his mother's bedroom. The workmen had only begun to pack-up her things before being halted, and her medication and tea cups were still arranged in a perfect line across her dresser, and the photograph collection of her children on the wall had survived the onslaught unscathed so far. He glanced at her closet, and at the crack in the wall where he discovered Mr. Murphy's secret stairwell, and relived his anger and disgust all over again. He turned and walked into his mother's tiny bathroom, turned on the light, and saw a fine stream of water shooting from the back of the toilet -- it looked like one of the movers must have cracked something in their enthusiasm to evict the sick old lady, and the tiny flood was advancing and dampening the bedroom carpet, and most likely dripping into the vacant store below. Riley reached down behind the toilet and with a little effort, he was able to shut off the water. The water pipe entered a hole in the wall at an odd angle, and Riley noticed a small slip of paper jutting out from that hole. He unraveled it and read it.

third board from the wall, red ledger, loan documents

It was one of Mr. Murphy's insane little notes -- in his mother's bathroom wall of all places. Riley's heart pounded and his mind raced. The floorboards in the apartment were wide, and his eyes darted across the floor to the third one from the wall. He crawled over to it and pulled, and the board came up in his hands with ease. All sorts of curious items and papers were stored beneath the board, including what appeared to be the infamous red ledger book that he, Mary and Mr. Mantano had once spent so many hours searching for in the bookshop. He noticed several envelopes -- the very same envelopes he had mailed himself from New York to help pay the bills. The envelopes were filled with cash, thousands of dollars all together, and Riley surmised that his mother had been cashing the checks and stowing the cash here for some reason. He was flabbergasted -- she had the money to pay the rent all along and chose not to. Also in the hole was a metal box that when opened, revealed his mother's marriage certificate, a photo of his father Seamus, a diamond broach, a few random pieces of jewelry, locks of hair, and old immigration documents from her family's history. Riley pulled out the red ledger book next and opened it from the back end. Riley's jaw hit the floor. The last entry was dated just two weeks earlier.

Not only did his mother know about Mr. Murphy's financial problems, she knew the whereabouts of the infamous red ledger book. She had kept it a secret from all of them, including Mr. Murphy's daughter Mary. She had watched them search the bookstore top to bottom the day of Mr. Murphy's wake and said nothing. The entries in the book indicated she was not only an accomplice, but indeed a perpetrator. The handwriting in the ledger was hers and the entries went back several years. At first glance, Riley's training in finance and accounting offered no help, as the entries were unprofessional, messy and confusing. But it was clear she was paying off large loans to someone. Riley shuffled through more documents and letters until he found the payee -- City Point Properties, Inc., the very same company that was about to purchase the building, causing the eviction of his mother and sisters.

He continued to rifle through the paperwork looking for names, phone numbers, addresses, or any clue that could point him in some direction. It was clear that payments were being sent to a local post office box, and there was little more information than that. Riley opened a tri-fold brochure that had been inserted into the ledger book many years earlier. It was a yellowed real estate sales pamphlet for "City Point Properties" and pictured artists' renditions of modern condominiums, swimming pools and tree-lined boulevards. It boasted affluent living, great schools and the great history of Boston in your backyard. The City Point developments had been expanding for years, invading and replacing buildings and raising rents in the old Southie neighborhood. In fact, it was residents of the City Point neighborhood who accused Sean and his friends resulting in his false arrest for burglary. The brochure instructed the customers to contact Sales Manager Tennyson Doyle. Could Tennyson Doyle be Tenny Doyle, who had attended Mr. Murphy's wake and who Siobhan claimed had set-up her and her boyfriend? Could he also have set-up Sean and his friends? Riley didn't believe in coincidences. His discovery that evening meant two things. First, Mary's instincts may have been spot on and her father may have indeed been involved in much more than

179

anyone realized, and second, Riley needed to talk to Malcolm. There was so much more he needed to know.

It was now six in the morning, and Riley sat in his underwear on the chilly and wet bathroom floor surrounded by his dead mother's secrets. He begged the documents to tell him more, but accepted sifting through and understanding all the papers would take some time. He started to collect them together and understood he had better hide his find before Erin or Meghan started asking questions. He elected to keep the money for himself, as he deduced most of it was his to begin with, and estimated it to be over fifteen thousand dollars. It occurred to him that there could be other hidden treasure troves around the apartment and began hunting. He crawled around on all fours looking for more little notes and secret compartments, pulling on floor boards and molding. He was successful finding more notes -- all irrelevant or trivial messages about food or the barometric pressure, and he wondered how much time Mr. Murphy spent with his mother when he was not around. Erin was now awake and wading through the debris in the kitchen trying to make a pot of coffee. Nothing was where it was supposed to be, and she wept frustrated, with pressures from the funeral and loss of her mother still fresh on her mind. Riley turned on the television, surprised it still worked at all. He caught the tail end of a morning news report on overnight drug raids in nearby Dorchester and a murder investigation in Mattapan (that the locals called Murderpan), that police were investigating and focused on a crime ring centered in South Boston. Riley was interrupted by the ringing of his cell phone. He had ignored all his messages for days, but answered to find out who was calling him so early.

"Riley? Dude, are you OK?"

"I'm fine Alvin. Everything is fine. Why are you calling me at six in the morning?"

"Because you don't answer you phone if I call you at any other time, and I have something important to tell you. I must have left you a dozen messages since last week. I heard your mom died. Is that true?"

"Yes, it's been a difficult week. We are all coping, and the funeral was yesterday. So who told you about my mother?"

"Professor Friedman called yesterday looking for you. He told me. I explained you had not been here in a week."

"How the hell did he find out?"

"I don't know. He only said that I should tell you that you are missing a lot of class work, but he understands and not to worry, that he will work with you when you get back."

Riley felt bad that he was giving Alvin a hard time. It was not intentional. Alvin was calling because he was concerned and Riley knew the list of people who cared about him was getting shorter.

"Alvin, I'm sorry I didn't call. Things have been crazy."

"That's OK, dude. I understand. But did you hear the news? Did you hear what happened?"

"I've been a little distracted. What are you talking about?"

"Remember that guy, Marcus Etruscan? The guy from the carwash?"

Hearing the name caused Riley to sit up straight as if someone had poked him from behind with a needle. Riley lowered his voice in case either of his sisters were eavesdropping. "Of course I remember, Alvin. What about him?"

"They found his body floating in the East River the other day. He's dead, Riley.... dead, dead, dead!"

It was big news. But Riley was too depressed to care, and tried to create some enthusiasm for Alvin's benefit. "Wow! Holy shit! Do they know who did it?"

"They have no idea. I can't tell you what a relief it is to have that guy out of the way, even if he didn't pull the trigger. He was one bad dude."

Riley told Alvin he would be back in school in a few days, and asked him to thank Professor Friedman for his kind offer. But that was all the good will Riley was able to muster. Riley was worn down, his spirit was still in a shambles and he was in no mood to chat it up with Alvin or anyone else. But he did need to call Malcolm Ward, and once again enjoyed the pleasure of leaving a message with his cranky answering service while he vacationed on some Caribbean island. He slumped back on the family sofa, covered his face with both hands, and massaged his forehead trying to find inspiration to even put on a pair of pants. Erin appeared in front of him and offered him a cup of coffee.

"Here, you look like you need this." She said as she handed him the cup, her eyes also damp and bloodshot. "But I couldn't find any cream or sugar. I think the movers took all the food first."

"Thanks." Riley accepted the offering without looking at her. He had been avoiding a confrontation with Erin all week. She was the oldest child in the family, and in Riley's opinion, should take the blame for all that had happened. Erin was never a looker, but had gained a lot more weight and had cut her hair short, giving her the appearance of a troll. Though only in her late twenties, she could pass for fifty, and showed the scars of leading a hard life. To Riley, her crass appearance was indefensible -- she had grown up under the same roof with the same values that he had. But it wasn't her appearance that bothered him most, it was her negligence that allowed their mother to be evicted that stuck in his craw.

"I need you to explain to me," Riley began still massaging his forehead, "how you didn't know they were coming to seize this apartment?"

"Mom always took care of those things. I saw the letters. I'm not stupid. But she said she was taking care of it."

Riley spun his head around and stared her down. "The woman was sick. She could barely walk. What the hell makes you think she could take care of anything? You should have been watching out for her!"

Tears glided down Erin's cheeks. "I waited on her hand and foot, I brought her pills five times a day, I cooked her meals, did her laundry and ran all her errands. And where were you while I did all this, huh? Living the high life in New York City on some permanent vacation?"

"No, I was working my ass off, sending all my money home to pay for your food and your bills." Riley realized he sounded like Mr. Fabrizi. "And you couldn't be bothered to open a goddamn letter."

Erin threw her coffee cup at Riley and it glanced off his shoulder, sending lukewarm black coffee over the sofa and floor. Riley caught the distinct smell of whiskey emanating from the mess. "Fuck you, Riley. Get out of my house and go back to all your little rich kid friends. In a few days, Meghan and I will be homeless. Will you care?"

"No, I won't. Not one bit. You will get what you deserve."

Riley stormed into his room and started packing. Anger oozed from every pore of his body, and he exhaled fire with every breath. He grabbed the paperwork, money, ledger and family mementos he had discovered in the bathroom. He rifled through his childhood toys and collections and selected a few pictures and comic books that held personal meaning and stuffed them in his bag. He scooped up his dirty clothes and suit that hung over his chair. He slid on the last clean pair of pants and shirt he had remaining and started for the door. His cell phone rang again. This time it was Malcolm.

"Hello, Riley. First, please accept my condolences to you and your family on the passing of your mother. She was a fantastic woman."

"Thank you, sir." Malcolm's timing, and Riley's mood, could not have been worse.

"And second, what is the emergency? I am out of town still on vacation, and only have a few minutes."

Riley tried to pull his emotions together and give Malcolm a quick summary of what he knew.

"Sir, I went to the jail to visit Siobhan the other day. She told me she and her boyfriend were framed by Tenny Doyle."

"Riley, I can't discuss specifics of her case, you know that. It's the attorney client privilege thing."

"I know, I know. But the Tenny Doyle she's talking about came to Mr. Murphy's wake. I know a guy in New York, Mr. Mantano, who tells me Tenny is involved in organized crime."

"Do you have any evidence of Tenny Doyle framing your sister?"

"I found some documents in my mother's bedroom. Mr. Murphy owed money to City Point Properties, and Tenny Doyle used to be their salesman. City Point is the same company that's about to buy this building, and I think they must have murdered Mr. Murphy."

"Riley, I appreciate what you're trying to do for your sister. You are a very loyal brother. But none of what you are telling me makes any sense. So here's what we should do. I will be back in Boston next week. Collect together all your paperwork and conspiracy theories and make an appointment with my secretary. I'll be glad to work through all this with you at that time. How does that sound?"

Riley felt condescension in Malcolm's tone, and he didn't appreciate it. He hung up his phone without acknowledging Malcolm's offer or saying goodbye, and stormed out of his family's apartment for the final time, slamming the rattling door behind him.

Thick black clouds hung on the western horizon of Boston, and the air was rich with moisture, threatening a cool spring rain at any moment. It was about eight blocks to Malcolm's law office, and Riley marched to it like a soldier ordered to complete an urgent mission.

When he arrived, the office door was still locked -- too early for Malcolm's secretary or paralegal to be there yet. In a pique of frustration and raging anger, Riley kicked the door hoping to smash it in, but he failed and only succeeded in denting it. Now his big toe ached, and he screamed and swore at the top of his lungs to the sky, which had begun to scatter raindrops on his face and around him, producing little dark spots on the sidewalk. He pulled out the red ledger book and papers from his bag and dropped them on the law office's front stoop. The papers instantly absorbed the small droplets of moisture from the sky, the corners of the papers curling from the light breeze. Riley didn't care. He was done with it. He was done with the conspiracy theories, the mobsters and the drama. He was done with his sisters, his missing brother and his paranoid roommate. He still had an envelope full of cash in his pocket -- his money -- that he could put to good use. He needed time to himself, for himself and with himself. He was leaving Boston and going somewhere, anywhere. He didn't know where he wanted to go, but he was confident that he would know it was the right place when he got there.

FIFTEEN

A direct drive from Boston to Ticonderoga, New York takes a
little over four hours straight up assuming there is no traffic
to contend with as there is no direct highway route, but Riley
didn't care how long it took as he was in no hurry to get there. No one
was waiting for him or knew he was coming, and he didn't bring a
map. His anticipated destination of Ticonderoga was no accident. Not
only was it the home of the historic Fort Ticonderoga, famed
stronghold of the French and Indian War as well as the American
Revolution, but was also home to the Scarborough Fair Garlic
Company, owned and operated by the proud parents of old flame
Magnolia Fair.

As soon as he found himself in the rural expanses of western
Massachusetts and out of the depressing and greasy confines of the
urban seaboard cities, Riley veered off a highway exit ramp and
dedicated himself to following the back roads. His path would carry
him through quaint villages and past rolling farms, over babbling
brooks and by dark blue lakes. His family had not ventured much
beyond the city when he was little, so much of the land of even his
home state was foreign to him and he discovered it to be worthy of
exploration. He had never enjoyed listening to music very much, to
his friends' frequent chagrin and needling, as he believed music
served to distract him from thinking. On this day, the cheap radio of
his rental car was at full volume, distorting the music, and he sang
along to every song whether he knew them or not with enthusiasm,
making up lyrics as it suited him. No one was there to offer a critique
or give him a grade -- except for an occasional passing motorist who
would flash him a perplexed disapproving look.

Spring in New England and upstate New York is forever in
transition, and the warm weather he had enjoyed just a week earlier
was gone, replaced by the biting north winds and fast-moving snow

flurries of a winter that would not surrender. The round gray western hills of Massachusetts were as unfamiliar as a Martian landscape, and Riley felt some appreciation for what the first explorers must have experienced every time they ventured over the next peak in anticipation of what was on the other side, which looked to Riley unremarkably like what they were seeing on the side they were already on. The roads were narrow and signs warned truckers of steep grades, deer and even rock slides -- it sounded so dangerous. And for a while, he fantasized he was a race car driver hugging each bend and guardrail, searching for the perfect driving line that would propel him to the lead and glory. Ahead on a telephone pole he saw a sign for the Crispy Biscuit Diner and made the spontaneous and uncharacteristic decision to stop for lunch.

The Crispy Biscuit Diner was an old, grungy aluminum rectangle of a place that from the outside didn't look wide enough for a row of tables, never mind large enough to cook and serve people meals. Riley entered and noticed the glass vestibule hadn't been swept in an age, filthy with fingerprints and streaks, month old newspapers were stacked in the corner surrounded by an inch tall drift of sand and road salt. Fliers advertising a dance at the VFW, cord wood for sale, and a lost cat name Scrapper were taped inside the windows. Remnants of tape attached to triangles of paper from fliers long gone speckled the glass. Postcards for sale at the cash register showed what the restaurant looked like thirty years earlier, all shiny and new, surrounded by large new, metal automobiles full of happy families with nice haircuts. On this day, aside from two beat-up pickup trucks and Riley's rental car, the place looked deserted.

Inside, two elderly fat men wearing red flannel jackets and baseball caps sat at the counter eating sandwiches and drinking coffee, but not saying much. Riley sat in the first booth by the door and gazed out the window. The trees on the hill across the street were leafless and appeared lifeless, and a snow squall was pushing through the area, whipping the spindly branches in violent, random directions. A large bird's nest clung to a branch at the top of one tall tree, listing back and forth, and Riley wondered what sort of superior craftsmanship the bird had spun to make it stick and not blow away in the gale. Then as soon as it started, the squall was over. The ground was too warm to support snow, and the large puffy flakes melted away in seconds. An occasional hole in the dark clouds even permitted a swatch of blue sky to peek through and taunt him.

Riley ordered a mushroom burger, fries and chocolate milk. The perfect all-American lunch for an all-American boy. The food was greasy, but juicy and full of flavor, and the burger left a little warm puddle on his plate as he ate. If Americo's served this, he surmised, Mr. Mantano would never worry about business.

Riley looked into the kitchen at the scruffy short order cook who looked up at him from his griddle. From where he sat, it looked like Lorenzo.

But it couldn't be.

He then looked up at the waitress who had just returned to his table, pitcher in hand, to refill his water glass, and he swore it was Siobhan. The two men at the counter turned his direction as they prepared to leave, and he recognized them as Marcellino and Mr. Fabrizi.

Riley stopped chewing, his mouth bursting with fries, and felt the color drain from his face. He felt a shivering chill all over. He knew right away he was hallucinating, and blinked over and over trying to re-focus himself. He attempted to suck a deep breath through his mouthful of food without choking on it. He made an embarrassing grunt noise.

"You OK, honey?" The waitress asked, bending down placing a kind hand on his shoulder.

"Yes, I'm fine," Riley answered, swallowing again and again to catch his breath.

"I thought I'd have to do that Heimlich maneuver on ya there for a minute. Only had to do it once before. It didn't go so well."

"Thanks, really, I'm fine. I think I'm just a little tired."

"You should order a slice of apple pie. Just came out of the oven. That'll fix-up whatever's got ya beat down."

The waitress was right, and the pie was warm and excellent. Riley paid for his food and left the waitress a twenty dollar tip, which worked out to more than the entire bill itself. After his experiences as a waiter at Americo's, he vowed to leave his servers excellent tips for the rest of his life.

Riley hopped back in the car and headed west toward New York State. The disturbing images of the ghosts he saw in the diner were still clear in his mind, and it unnerved him. He felt like he was being followed and he needed to drive farther to escape them. He spent the next several hours weaving through small town after small town, more similar in design than they were different. At each village he would first pass a gas station, followed by some sort of sports bar or pub and a bank. Then as he traveled farther along, Victorian houses would appear, at first far apart and then more numerous and closer together. This would bring him to a downtown area, featuring angled parking and two full blocks of two-story red brick buildings. The buildings' construction was similar to those found in Southie, except with second-hand shops and antique stores on their street levels in neat, organized rows. After traveling no more than a mile, the village would disappear behind him except for another gas station, sandwich shop and an expanse of road that led ahead into the forest. Another village was always no more than a few miles ahead.

When he got there, he learned that almost no one in Ticonderoga had heard of the Scarborough Fair Garlic Company, and Riley needed to stop four times to ask if anyone knew where it was, receiving only one useful response. A befuddled old woman told him she knew of a farm near the municipal airport along Lake Champlain that sold garlic and other things, but she didn't know its name. It was the only lead he had, so he had nothing to lose.

The old woman was right. A long, bumpy gravel road and small wooden sign led Riley to the general store of the farm. Most of the land had been stripped bare of trees generations before, replaced by long, expansive flat fields that stretched to the lake in the east and orchards in the west. Spring crops at various stages of growth surrounded him for acres in long green rows and quilt-like patterns. The store itself looked like more of a garage than a place of business, dark red and peeling, and in need of a good painter. Year-old hay bales were stacked out in front and dozens of empty bushel baskets were strewn in the field behind them. Riley turned off the engine to his car. A small neon sign indicated the store was open for business, and Riley sat and wondered if this had been a good idea after all. His heart was picking up speed and his stomach felt queasy, unsure if he was nervous or was feeling the inevitable effects of his mushroom burger. He questioned why he was putting himself through this drama, and why he was compelled to find Magnolia. He re-started the engine and grasped the gear shift, and thought about heading back to an efficiency motel he had passed in the village a few miles back.

He then realized a woman was peering at him through the window from inside the store, no doubt wondering if he was planning to come in or just stalk her from the parking lot like a serial killer. Trapped, Riley turned off the engine again and went inside.

Riley was amazed to see the interior of the store didn't meet his low expectations as portrayed by the dowdy exterior. The shop was neat and fully stocked with all kinds of interesting items. There were stacks of fresh-baked pies, a few bushels of apples, bins of walnuts, hazelnuts and chestnuts, jars of giant pickles, a wide variety of spices, and an odd collection of dried gourds crafted and painted to resemble police officers, firemen and teachers. The store smelled of an inviting blend of warm cinnamon and potpourri, and complimentary hot cider was available on a rickety card table at the back of the room. And the whole store was decorated by hundreds of bunches and braids of garlic that hung from every available ceiling joist.

"Was there something I could help you find?" The woman asked, brandishing a warm ear to ear smile.

"No, thank you... just looking." Riley responded sheepishly, trying to be small and invisible. The woman was tall and rail thin with long straight white blonde hair. Her blue jeans and blouse fit loose, and a wide-brimmed floppy sun hat shaded most of her face. Her skin was tanned and wrinkled far beyond her age, no doubt he thought, a result of years of abuse working in biting wind and sunshine. Although they didn't resemble each other much physically, Riley knew she was Magnolia's mother just from the glimmer in her eyes and how she tilted her head to the left when she spoke. There was no doubt.

Riley poured himself a cup of warm cider. The flavor was biting and hot, and he allowed the mulling spices to waft upwards through his nose which made his eyes water. The soothing brew calmed him for the moment and like magic awakened fleeting thoughts of the comforts of home, which energized him with a spike of sudden confidence.

"Is Magnolia here?" Riley asked her, before he knew his mouth was moving. The woman's head spun around and she pulled off her hat.

"Oh my! Are you here to see Magnolia? Are you a friend of hers?" The woman responded with more enthusiasm than Riley expected.

"Yes ma'am, we met at school. At Columbia."

"How nice you came out here to see her. Is she expecting you?"

"No, it is a surprise." Riley was sure it would be a surprise alright, but he didn't know if it would be a good surprise or a bad surprise.

"Come with me."

Mrs. Fair took him by the hand and dragged him out the door and through the field closest to the parking lot. She glided across the field like she was on ice skates, while behind her Riley tripped and stumbled on every lump, hole and rut along the way. The ground was damp and muddy from the recent rain and melted snow and it didn't take long before Riley's loafers and feet were covered with mud up over his ankles. They waltzed together across the brown raw earth until they reached a man and a woman loading a trailer with firewood. The man was in his late fifties and had a large frizzy graying beard and wire rimmed glasses. He wore a baseball cap on top of his head with a gray pony tail that hung half way down his back. The woman with him in blue jeans covered in sawdust was Magnolia. The two looked up to see them arrive.

"Oh my God." Magnolia declared under her breath, just loud enough for everyone to hear. She wiped dirt and sawdust off her face with her sleeve and approached Riley's outstretch arms. The two embraced in a friendly but restrained hug.

"What are you doing here?" Magnolia inquired smiling, though her suspicious nature was evident on her face.

"I was in the neighborhood," Riley answered.

"You never were a very good liar."

"I took a couple of weeks off from school and work to do some traveling and just found myself here in Ticonderoga."

"I heard about your mom. That was so sad. I'm sorry." Magnolia squeezed his hands. Riley rolled his eyes and couldn't fathom how everyone was hearing news about his family. He was starting to wonder if some reality TV crew was following him without his knowledge. "Riley, this is my dad Rowan, and it looks like you already met my mom. Riley is a friend of mine from Columbia."

"My name is Gwen. It is wonderful to meet one of Magnolia's college friends." Her parents stood together holding hands, each projecting a sappy smile at them.

It's nice to meet you both Mr. and Mrs. Fair." Riley answered.

190

"You're so polite, but please call us Rowan and Gwen." Riley nodded and smiled.

"I thought we'd be done hauling wood for the season, but this winter doesn't want to give up. We're looking at a late spring." Rowan said smiling, straining to make a little small talk. "Did you say your name was Riley? In Gaelic, that would translate to *valiant*, would it not?"

"Yes sir, I have been told that it does. There was snow in the air on my drive up here today. I'm looking forward to the warm weather."

"Let's walk back to the house and warm up," Gwen suggested, "It's about dinner time anyway. Riley, can you stay and join us for dinner?"

"Of course he will," Magnolia answered for him. Riley didn't object and was relieved at Magnolia's initial acceptance of his uninvited presence.

The four walked toward the rambling Fair family farmhouse located behind the store. Rowan and Gwen walked ahead giggling, and kept looking back at Riley and Magnolia. It occurred to Riley that neither of her parents recognized his name -- it was clear Magnolia had never mentioned his name to them, and he wasn't sure if he was insulted or not. And despite Magnolia's horrid descriptions of her parents and their loathsomeness, Riley thought on first impression they seemed quite nice. He liked them.

"OK, so why are you really here?" Magnolia asked, the surprise of the moment wearing thin and her true personality re-emerging.

"I'm not sure. I just felt I needed to see you."

"I'm not buying it. You're here to try and put our relationship back together."

"No, I swear, I'm not. My life has been a mess the last few weeks... even longer than that, maybe months. After my mom's funeral, my family was in a shambles and I didn't want to go back to school. I don't know if I want to go back to school ever again."

"What about your job at that stupid restaurant."

"I quit that months ago. I work for LSE enterprises as a financial consultant now."

Magnolia's eyebrows perked up. "Really? No more *Goodfellas*? No more *Meeecheee*?" Magnolia's sarcastic mock Italian tone surprised him.

"I haven't seen or heard from Mici in several months, I swear." Riley realized Magnolia still carried a whole lot of jealousy and resentment.

"So what about this new job? Don't they want you back?"

"My new boss, Mr. Fabrizi, is very understanding. He gave me some time off to sort out my life."

"So you have come to a garlic farm in Ticonderoga to sort out your life? And it happens to be the one owned by my family?"

"The way our relationship ended, the way we broke up -- it wasn't right. I haven't been able to feel at ease about it all. I thought there were some things that needed to be said -- that I wanted to say. I felt we needed closure. Just before my mother died, I ran into an old childhood friend named Tammy Meeks on the train to Boston. She is a wonderful girl, and a lot of people did wrong by her, she had a tough childhood. She got me to thinking about my life and the people you leave behind, all the people who are important to you and bring it meaning."

Before Riley could finish, he found they had completed their trek across the muddy fields and arrived at the Fair farmhouse. They kicked off their muddy shoes, left them in a pile at the door and entered. Inside, Riley marveled at the decor -- it was akin to a museum, something torn from the pages of his mother's *Good Housekeeping* magazine. Every furnishing in the home was made of wood, and as far as he could tell, it was all handmade, too -- tables, chairs, picture frames, countertops -- and even a pine chandelier that clung to the dining room ceiling. The home was heated by a roaring woodstove and the dry, intense heat was welcoming to his chilled toes and fingers. Magnolia excused herself and went upstairs to her room to clean up and change. After running over to lock up the store, Gwen returned with a couple of pies and a pickle jar and quickly put herself to work chopping things in the kitchen in preparation for dinner. Rowan and Riley sat in the living room on two exquisite hand-made rocking chairs and watched Gwen whistle to herself and dart around. Rowan pulled out a wooden pipe and stuffed it with tobacco. Rowan's first question was a doozie.

"So tell me, Riley, how did you two meet?"

Riley thought about finding Magnolia naked and drunk in his bed. Then he erased the image.

"We were introduced by my roommate Alvin. I think he and Magnolia took a class together."

"What are you studying at Columbia?"

"International Finance and Accounting."

"Fascinating! When do you graduate?"

"Next May."

"Where do you expect to work?"

"Well, I am working part-time for Lafayette Street Enterprises in Lower Manhattan right now as a consultant. I would like to stay in the city after I graduate."

"Where is your family from?"

"South Boston. I have six brothers and sisters."

"That's great. I came from a big family, too."

Riley was being grilled much like a parent might interview a future son-in-law. Riley looked into the kitchen and noticed Gwen had stopped whistling and was peering around the corner, hanging on his every word, as if there was going to be a quiz. Riley squirmed in his wooden seat.

"Magnolia doesn't get many visitors way out here on the farm," Rowan explained. "She keeps to herself most days, and leads a quiet, conservative life. She does so much for us here with the business, I don't know what we would do without her. I can't tell you how much it means to my wife and I that you made the drive to see her."

"She was a good friend to me. I was sorry to see her leave Columbia."

"Oh, we were disappointed, too, as you might guess. But she hated that place. It was our fault for sending her there. She is so smart, near genius, and when she was accepted we were elated thinking it would change her life and offer her an escape from this world. We pushed her to go... she didn't want to. But we learned an important lesson: you just can't take the country out of the girl. This farm had become more of who she is than we realized."

Riley wondered for a moment if they were talking about the same Magnolia.

Magnolia skipped down the wooden stairs and returned to the dining room clean and refreshed, wearing a pretty pink flowered dress and sandals -- not an outfit Riley was used to seeing on her -- and took her seat at the table. Riley overheard Gwen whisper to Rowan, "*Oh, look she's wearing make-up!*"

It turned out that Gwen was an excellent cook, and all the dishes and ingredients on the table were made from scratch -- from the butter she churned herself to the asparagus grown and picked from behind the barn. She served a delicious sweet potato casserole and warm buttermilk biscuits. There was no meat dish as Gwen was a vegetarian, however Rowan offered to sneak him a venison steak from his secret stash in the freezer later.

"So where are you staying tonight?" Gwen asked.

"I plan to grab a room at that motel back in the village."

"Oh no, that place is disgusting! Filthy! Why don't you stay here with us tonight?" Gwen offered.

"You've all been too kind already. I can't impose on you like that."

"Nonsense. We have a guest room we never use. You are welcome to it. It will be fun to have someone new and interesting in the house. Our routine around here can get pretty dull." Magnolia nodded her wide-eyed approval to Riley, otherwise he would not have accepted.

"I'll give you a complete tour of the farm in the morning," Rowan explained with enthusiasm. "I'm proud of our little operation here although not many people get to see it. It's more than just a garlic farm. We have a full apple orchard, grapes, five kinds of nuts and all kinds of vegetables. The goats and chickens give us all the milk and eggs we need. We pride ourselves on being self-sufficient. I would say we venture to the market no more than about once per month just to pick up a few necessities."

"But of all things to farm, why garlic?"

"Because, my boy, it's the greatest crop in the world. It enhances the flavor of any food or dish and makes it delicious. It can be used as a medicine, and it can even keep vampires away. We grow a special New York long neck variety here that thrives in this crazy weather. The bulbs and cloves are smaller, but the flavor is much more intense. Real chefs prefer it over that flavorless, imported Chinese variety you get in the supermarket. It's taken me years to discover the right combination of mulch and manure that helps nature produce the perfect garlic bulb."

"His big secret is chicken shit." Magnolia taunted.

"Chicken manure, my dear. Manure. Compost. Fertilizer. And must I remind you we have been in first place five years running at the Saugerties Garlic Festival?"

194

"There's such a thing as a garlic festival?" a bemused Riley inquired.

"Oh yes there is. And Maggie was even crowned Garlic Queen when she was twelve. Hey, Maggie, pass the cherry pie down this way, would you?" Rowan asked.

"Maggie? Garlic Queen?" An amused Riley snickered.

Magnolia raised her spoon toward Riley like a weapon. "If you laugh or say one more word I promise I will gouge out your left eye."

Riley enjoyed all the innocent family bantering and it took him back to his more innocent childhood days when his mother and siblings sat around their Southie table inhaling their dinner. No matter what activities the children were involved in, Sarah made them pledge to be home to eat dinner together every night. No one left unbruised, unbattered, or unscathed.

After dinner, Riley followed Magnolia up to her bedroom to collect some extra pillows and blankets for him to use in the guest room. At last he found the Magnolia he remembered. The museum atmosphere of the house ended at her bedroom door. Inside were piles of dirty laundry, grimy dinner plates and empty soda cans. Above her bed, as Riley anticipated, was her cherished and infamous gravestone rubbing, and at the foot of her bed was one of the decorative fireman gourds from the farm shop, except Magnolia's had a meat clever embedded in its forehead. Riley winced at the sight. What was different from her dorm room at Columbia, however, were several oil paintings she had been working on each set upon its own easel, all unfinished, that were either landscapes of the farm or self-portraits.

"Do you prefer Strawberry Shortcake, Barbie or Tinkerbelle sheets?" Magnolia asked.

"I'll take Barbie."

"You are *soooo* predictable."

"These paintings are amazing. I knew you were studying art history but I had no idea you could do this kind of work. Do you have any that are finished?"

"No, I don't. I love starting paintings and new projects. I don't have the desire to finish them. Too boring."

"Even a self-portrait?"

"How can I finish an honest self-portrait with any integrity if I am not finished myself?"

195

"Ah, such a paradox. Perhaps you have uncovered the key to immortality. Until, the final brush stroke touches that canvas, you will live forever."

"So I can kill myself by finishing this painting?"

"Exactly. Or at least, figuratively speaking."

"But I've been dead on the inside for years."

"Oh, come on now. Your parents seem like such nice people. They aren't close to the tyrants you told me they were. You seem to have settled into a peaceful existence here."

"You are falling for their evil spell. They start by enticing you with sweet potatoes and pickles then before you know it, you'll be up to your knees in fermenting chicken shit whistling Peter, Paul and Mary tunes."

"Your parents seem glad I came. Are you?"

Magnolia paused and gazed out the window. A single tiny light could be seen a couple of miles away at the airport, otherwise the world was black. "I am very happy to see you, Riley. I really am. But my parents still see my as sixteen years old waiting for my first date. But see that little light? That's the real me. I am comfortable being alone. In the city with all those people around, I missed my emptiness and loneliness -- it fit me like a wool sweater. You know, always itchy and uncomfortable but damn glad you have it when the wind blows. My mom and dad don't get that I am a happier person being miserable. And that's the big difference between you and me. You need people around to validate you -- brothers, sisters, a mom, a girlfriend -- and I don't. It's why I knew our relationship was doomed -- you are predictable. Fire and ice. Oil and water. They won't mix together. See that rubbing over my bed? That's Magnolia, too, who died a hundred years ago. She keeps me company. She's the only person I need to validate me."

"That gravestone rubbing of yours creeped Alvin out. He didn't know what to make of it when he saw it."

"Alvin is such a... wait a minute." Magnolia's tone changed and the pupils of her eyes shrunk. She put her hands on her hips, spun around and tilted her head to the left. "Are you saying Alvin told you about my bedroom?"

Riley feared he had misstepped. He should not have mentioned Alvin's name. He believed Magnolia cheated on him with Alvin, but he had done all he could to suppress the anger and jealousy long ago for the sake of keeping the peace with everyone."Well, yes. Umm, he did. But he only mentioned it once."

"You think I cheated on you, don't you?" Magnolia was indignant. "Then I have a question for you. Why didn't you ever ask me *why* I was in your bed that night we met?"

Riley was stuck. He didn't want to know the answer then, and didn't want to know it now. It was a relationship he didn't go looking for but instead found him, and he had come to terms with that.

"Alvin was my date that night. Surprised? He came to pick me up in my room and we were going to a movie -- and by the way, it was the only time he had *ever* been in my room. As we were leaving, a friend of mine came by who was real hot and Alvin liked her better. So the three of us go to the movie and he invites her, and not me, back to your dorm room. Suddenly I'm the third wheel on my own date. I refused to concede my date to her or anyone else, so I follow them back and while they are making out in his bed, I got to watch TV, drink every drop of alcohol I could find, and even take a shower after I threw up. The booze made me sleepy and I started to doze off in your bed. Alvin tells me you are a tight ass and will be pissed off if you find me, so I should leave, that asshole, but I was too shitfaced. Then you come in and for the first time all night, or since I had been at Columbia for that matter, someone was nice to me. You have no idea how much I needed you to hold me right then at that moment. If I had a self portrait to finish, I would have applied the last brush stroke that night."

Magnolia sniffled as if she was fighting back tears. Riley felt horrible. All this time he had believed she had been unfaithful. He hated himself, and Alvin more. He reached out to hug her, and she fell into his chest. He gave her a tender kiss on top of her head. She was a true paradox -- he now understood her so much better, and yet had never been more confused.

Riley spent the rest of the week living like a migrant worker at the garlic farm. He rose each morning at five, ate a hearty breakfast as prepared by Gwen, then assisted with the assigned task of the day -- chopping wood, mucking stalls, or flinging chicken manure compost. The city slicker in him struggled at first to adapt, and his shoulders ached badly by nightfall, but overall he enjoyed every moment of the escape. Each night after supper, Rowan brought out his twelve string guitar and they sang folk songs until the woodstove burned down to pulsing orange embers. Riley even showed Gwen how to bake authentic Irish soda bread as his mother had done so many times before. Gwen liked it so much she made an extra batch to sell in the store, and her regulars loved them and bought them right up.

"So Riley, you want me to ask Mom and Dad to adopt you?" Magnolia teased.

"Sure that would be great. You think they will give me your room? You have the better view."

And each night as he lay in bed before sleep overtook his tired flesh and bones, he would think of his mother and weep himself to sleep. He missed her, the loss still fresh and powerful, and it weighed heavy upon his chest.

Riley cherished his time with the Fairs, but his reality was slowly creeping back in. The family owned a television but rarely turned it on. The one time he succumbed to temptation, Riley was greeted with a news story about a police raid on an illegal gambling hall in Greenwich Village. He switched it right off. He was also running out of clothes and had not arrived prepared for a week of manual labor. The three pairs of designer slacks he packed for the trip were not standing up well.

At the end of the week, Riley took out his cell phone and turned it back on -- something he had been avoiding. The friendly automated voice informed him he had seventy-five messages. He pulled out a notepad and sat at the Fair's large wooden dining room table, beneath the wooden chandelier, and started to transcribe.

"Hi Riley, it's Meghan. What the hell happened between you and Erin? She's a wreck. Call me. Bye."

"Hi Riley, this is Katie. Mr. Fabrizi wants to know where you put the quarterly financials. Hose-B can't find them and the auditors will be coming tomorrow. Let us know right away. Thanks.

"Hello, Mr. Lynch. This is Hose-B. I need those quarterlies or Mr. Fabrizi is going to kill me. Call me back and let me know where they are, please. Thanks, sweetie."

"Hey dude, it's Alvin. Everything OK? Where the hell are you? Lots of people are looking for you. Hit me on my cell. Talk to you later."

The messages droned on and on and on, and Riley became more despondent with each passing communication.

"Riley, the movers have cleaned out the apartment. There's nothing left. I don't know where we're going to go now. Are you happy?

"Hello. This is Jack Wallace from Fenway Car Rentals. The Ford Taurus you rented was not returned and is now overdue. Please call us at 555-9012 to avoid criminal or civil action."

"Riley, it's Malcolm Ward. Please call me back at my office."

"Hello Riley, Malcolm Ward again. Call me right away. Thanks."

"Hey kid, it's Sean. Did you talk to Malcolm? I went to visit Siobhan at the jail today and she was asking. She's obsessing on this and it's driving her crazy. Call me tonight."

"This is the New York Public Library notifying you that the book you reserved is now available. You may pick up your items Monday through Friday..."

"Dude, Alvin here. Call me, man. You got problems. The police were just here looking for you. They think you stole a car."

"Good afternoon Mr. Lynch. This is Professor Friedman wondering if you had planned to return to school anytime soon. Please call my office before returning to class."

"Hi Riley, it's Malcolm again. I need to speak to you right away. I don't want to leave messages on the phone. It's unsecure, I need to see you in person. In short, those papers you left me indicate your suspicions may have some validity. Please call me, anytime, day or night."

Riley didn't realize Rowan and Gwen were in the next room and could hear every message. Rowan put his hand on Riley's shoulder and it startled him.

199

"Son, you lead a complicated and confusing life."

"I think it's about time I go home. I will leave in the morning. It's been wonderful here, but I have responsibilities. I can't continue to hide. There are things I need to do. I guess you could say I own a few unfinished paintings."

S I X T E E N

Riley drove at a high rate of speed from the garlic farm directly to Malcolm Ward's office in Boston, without stopping, in a Ford Taurus now reported stolen. His goodbyes with the eccentric Fair family of Ticonderoga were bittersweet. He adored Magnolia's parents, like a favorite aunt and uncle, and admired their resolve and commitment to their isolated lifestyle. He had fun on the farm and fantasized that he might try farming after graduation and give up his dreams of become a financial tycoon. Saying goodbye to Magnolia was hardest of all. His heart broke for the parts of her that were miserable and trapped, yet he was convinced the farm gave her a sense of place and comfort whether she wanted to admit it or not. He had passed the son-in-law audition with everyone except her, though she cried when he left which told him she did care. He was beginning to understand that her desire for a relationship was a prisoner within her own psyche. If her eyes were windows to her soul, he could see the prison bars in hers, and accepted her soul might never escape. He promised he would return to see them all soon.

And if his trip to God's country had any effect at all, Riley felt more confident and focused about what he needed and wanted to do with his life. He felt renewed and redeemed, as if having discovered and devoured his own Eucharist.

"So let me get this straight," Malcolm began, drumming his large maple desk with his fingertips. "Am I addressing the same Riley Lynch who called me twice during my Jamaican vacation only to turn off his cell phone when he didn't want to be bothered?"

"Yes sir, that was me. I am sorry Mr. Ward, or should I call you Malcolm?"

"You can call me anything you want if you are paying the bill."

"What did you want to see me about? Will you be able to help Siobhan?"

"First, do me a favor and don't leave legal documents and potential evidence on my front stoop in the rain ever again. Please, please be respectful and bring it inside. Do you know what it cost me to hire six paralegals with blow driers to hang those papers around my office?" Malcolm paused to rub his eyes, and an uncomfortable silence followed." Anyway... those documents did contain lots of fascinating bits of information."

"But will any of it help Siobhan?"

"There may be enough circumstantial evidence here to at least reduce her sentence, and if we are a little lucky, to time served. I am going to guess the prosecution will not want me to gum up the process with all this. Much of the evidence you provided connects to other cases, and they won't want me putting their other active cases at risk."

"What other cases?"

"It's complicated. If you watch the news, you'll know there has been a sudden increase in organized criminal activity in the city and it all seems to be pointing to South Boston neighborhoods."

"I have noticed. But I try not to watch television. My roommate follows all that stuff and lets me know whenever something big happens."

"Well I suggest you start paying closer attention. First I need you to understand that your evidence affects several of my clients -- not just Siobhan -- so I have to be careful what I talk about. The linchpin in this matter is Tenny Doyle -- you were right in your suspicions. He is bad news. Tenny Doyle is an old-school Boston mobster. He belonged to the old Winter Hill Gang and did time in the late seventies for fixing horse races in New Jersey, New York and Boston. His real job was being the owner and sales manager for a real estate company, City Point Properties, which as you know, is buying up and developing old brownstones into new condominiums all over Southie. Well, back in the seventies, City Point Properties only owned one actual property -- down on the waterfront. It had a beautiful view of the harbor and brought some well needed urban renewal to the old neighborhood. But Doyle wasn't making ends meet with it and for whatever reason, he found financial success and glory inside the gang. But the gang was so disorganized and undisciplined in those days, it cost Tenny his livelihood and his freedom for a while. Over the last ten years or so, several other companies have followed in his footsteps and have been converting old properties into more valuable, high-end living units. You've seen it -- pieces of the old neighborhood fade away, finding themselves replaced by shiny new upscale apartments. Tenny Doyle was, in many ways, a real estate visionary."

"I've seen it. I've lived it. All those snotty suburbanites invading the neighborhood. It's quite sad in many ways. But you're saying that old mobster is buying up all this property? I don't believe it. He'd be a millionaire by now."

"Not exactly. Tenny never expanded beyond that one single property. A few years ago, buried in debt and facing bankruptcy, he sold the company to Giovanni Marcellino."

"Marcellino!" Riley exclaimed.

"So you have heard of him?"

"Yes, I saw him on a television news report in New York. He came to Mr. Murphy's funeral, too -- a big fat slob of a guy. He sat in the back row of the church. In fact, Tenny Doyle came to the wake the night before, with a few other wise guys."

Malcolm stopped his story and scrunched up his eyes as if trying to interpret what Riley had just said. It made Riley sound well connected, and he figured Malcolm was calculating how much more he should tell him, and if he could trust him. Riley decided not to mention his friendship with Mr. Mantano, or the Hanratty murder at the carwash in New Jersey... at least for now.

"You do understand that what we speak about in this office, stays in this office?"

"Of course. I understand."

"Marcellino has been buying up real estate all up and down the Eastern Seaboard. He is using City Point Properties as his corporate operation in Boston. I am told he fancies himself the next Donald Trump. The difference is if he can't get the deal done, he threatens or intimidates his targets until they come around to his way of thinking and concede."

"Is that why he killed Mr. Murphy?"

"I don't know if you are aware of this or not, but Murphy owned half of the building you and your family lived in. Marcellino targeted that place for City Point Properties to acquire early on. Murphy's partner succumbed to Marcellino's intimidation right away, but Murphy refused to cooperate, even when threatened. Murphy couldn't stand the idea that he would sell-out his beloved bookshop and put your family in the street, even while his own business was failing. So Marcellino got to him another way. He loaned him two hundred thousand dollars to keep the bookstore business afloat and pay his wholesalers and other bills. Marcellino knew it would only be a matter of time before Murphy choked on the debt and the high interest rates. But Murphy refused to cave-in. He hung on. And Marcellino was growing impatient."

"So he killed him to get him out of the way."

"Well, at least that's my assumption. I think Marcellino learned Murphy was getting infusions of cash from China."

"That was Mary, Mr. Murphy's daughter."

"I don't know if Marcellino realized it was his daughter. Though he did perceive it as a threat -- he didn't understand where the money was coming from all of a sudden and became concerned that the big debt would get paid off. All I can tell you right now is that on the morning Murphy was killed, Marcellino has an airtight alibi, while Tenny Doyle is unaccounted for."

"Sounds to me like the police should be closing in."

Malcolm sighed again. He rose from his chair and paced around the room. "Unfortunately, Riley, the police have no interest in any of this. Marcellino is too smart for that. They are all too busy chasing this big crime wave that has come into vogue the past few years, sweeping the city. And the police are making arrests and big headlines, too."

"But isn't Marcellino responsible for the crime wave?"

"Yes, but not the way you might think. Marcellino is a master of playing the police, the prosecutors and public opinion. He knows what worked and what didn't back in the sixties and seventies and has no intention of repeating old mistakes. All the new tenants in the City Point neighborhood are protective of their expensive, new investments, and whether it's fueled by racism or raw paranoia, they find it too easy to believe there are criminals lurking in the shadows. Marcellino set-up burglaries and fencing operations against his own tenants to frame poor innocent residents in other parts of the neighborhood."

"You mean like Sean and his friends at Gulliver's Bar?" A wave of anger had been building inside him since the conversation began. Not only had this animal Marcellino been connected to Siobhan's arrest,

Mr. Murphy's murder, and his family's eviction, but he may also be behind Sean's arrest, too.

"I believe Sean was in the wrong place at the wrong time. Marcellino's crew engineered break-ins in the City Point neighborhood and fenced their bounty at the pawn shop next door to Gulliver's intentionally to entrap the Irish kids drinking there. What's more believable to the police -- that a bunch of Irish hoodlums from the poor neighborhood stole stuff, or that a real estate tycoon from Southern California did it?"

"But why pick on us?"

"Creating this mythology of organized criminal activity helps Marcellino on many levels. First, it keeps the police busy chasing nickel and dime problems and out of his hair, piling up arrests and convictions north to south. Second, the media loves it and are happy to divert attention to full scale coverage of a crime wave. The public always loves a good mafia story. Third, it drives poor people like your family out of the neighborhood creating vacancies. And finally, property values are now plunging in the crime-infested areas where he wants to make his purchases. It's all very simple when you think about it."

"So Marcellino has created a false mob for the reporters and police to chase while he operates a real one."

"More or less, yes.., you've got it."

"So is there enough here in Mr. Murphy's papers to bring to the Attorney General and bring Marcellino down?"

"Well, that's a problem. In one word, no. By uncovering this conspiracy, I implicate a lot of people. With your sister's drug bust, for example, I don't believe the police think it's legitimate. The evidence isn't there. There is no way Alberto is a kingpin -- that's just silly. What it tells me is that the police are enjoying these easy arrests, they look great on TV and all these uneducated poor people, and minorities are easy and believable targets. It's like shooting fish in a barrel. Why screw up a good thing? The only question I have is whether the police and AG's office are on Marcellino's payroll, or if they are just hapless, crediting themselves for all this remarkable good fortune? The public view of their police work has never been better. I just don't know how deep the conspiracy runs."

"So does that mean that you can't use all this to help Siobhan?"

"Well, that's where my craft as a brilliant defense attorney comes into play. If they think I am a threat to their good fortune, they will negotiate with me. They think I am this deep, connected mob lawyer -- what a joke that is. I can play this game as good as anyone else. I spent four hundred dollars on sunglasses last year -- I hate sunglasses. On one difficult case, I wore then to court and made a spectacle of myself by making the judge order me to remove them. It plays great in the papers. And if they think I am connected, they think I know more than I really do. They won't want to annoy me any more than necessary. It will work out."

Riley stared out Malcolm's window at a flock of crows perched on a building across the alley. With his luck, he imagined, every one of those birds would be dropping white blobs of crap on his rental car parked down in the street. It struck Riley that he had another urgent legal problem to solve.

"Malcolm, about you being a brilliant attorney? Umm, I need some legal assistance. It's sort of urgent."

Malcolm closed his eyes, placed his forehead against his bookshelf, and took another heavy deep breath.

"And what will this piece of free legal advice cost me? Can you at least estimate the number of paralegals I will need this time?" Malcolm answered with sarcasm.

Riley reached into his pocket and drew out a roll of twenty dollar bills, about a thousand dollars altogether, part of the loot he uncovered under his mother's bathroom floor, and tossed it across Malcolm's desk.

"Will that cover it?" He asked. Malcolm's eyes were fixed on the stack of bills.

"You know, you'd make a helluva mobster, kid. So what is your problem?"

"I think I'm wanted for stealing a car."

"That would be a felony. You didn't cross state lines with it, did you?"

"Well, yes I sort of did. I took it to New York." Malcolm doubled over like he was in pain. Riley tossed him a crumpled piece of paper written at the Fair's wooden kitchen table.

"I was supposed to return a rental car a week ago. That's all the information. They left me messages that said I was going to get arrested if I didn't return it right away. They even left messages with my roommate. What should I do?"

"Oh God... let me see it." Malcolm unraveled the note, sighed again, picked up his phone and dialed. "Let's start with the rental car company and see where that takes me."

As Malcolm worked the phone, getting transferred around from person to person in a bureaucratic cyclone, Riley walked the perimeter of the office and studied the spines of Malcolm's immense legal book collection, much the way he used to browse the stacks in Murphy's bookshop. There were volumes on municipal law, real estate, family law, torts, civil litigation, and a complete set of novels by Mario Puzo. Riley supposed it all fit together. The anger he felt for his family's misfortunes at the hands of Marcellino was acute, and he was relieved that Malcolm not only knew but understood and was making things better. A true Southie patriot. But Riley also knew his mother had been part of the conspiracy, evidenced by the fact these documents were found in her bathroom, but she had never uttered a word to the family about it. And Riley also knew Marcellino's evil ran deeper. The rotting corpses of T. Wallace Hanratty and Marcus Etruscan would attest to that.

"OK, Riley, you are all set." Malcolm hung up the phone. "You are not going to jail."

"What happened?"

"The rental car company said your car was paid for through the end of the month. They apologized for any inconvenience and said to enjoy the vehicle."

"What? Who paid the bill!?"

"They didn't say, and they might not even know."

"That's crazy. Maybe my friend Alvin paid it? Or Magnolia? I have no idea."

"Well, all I can say is that was the easiest thousand dollars I have ever made."

SEVENTEEN

Months passed, and Riley fell back into his old, lonely routine of school and work, followed by more school and more work. After barely passing his spring classes, he spent a long, hot summer in New York working around the clock for the chaotic Lafayette Street Enterprises and the cantankerous Mr. Fabrizi. He even took a few summer courses at Columbia to jump ahead a little bit so he wouldn't fall short of his graduation date. He vowed to give his class work a higher priority as he surmised he had burned all his bridges and spent his goodwill that spring. Not only had he disappeared for almost two weeks from Columbia without explanation, but the research paper he turned in included an eight by ten glossy of a topless Miss. Aurora Ample, which was accidentally mixed in when he dropped his papers on the train. He took a crack at laughing it off but the department chair, he learned that day, possessed no sense of humor.

His mother's death continued to haunt him and he often found himself lost in long daydreams about her, longing for her strength and selfless reassurance to get him through difficult moments. And anytime a newspaper or television reporter mentioned a crime, mobsters, the mafia, or South Boston, he would fly into a rage. Alvin learned to keep his obsession to himself after Riley snapped a favorite skateboard in half one evening after a mere mention of the name Marcellino. Riley understood now why Mr. Murphy and Mr. Mantano both warned him so often of the dangers. Organized crime had victimized and decimated his family. And Riley was equipped with the flaw to never forget anything.

By late Fall, with holidays fast approaching and isolated within his festering anger, Riley tried to swallow the reality that he would be spending Christmas in New York City. He had not heard a whisper from any of his brothers or sisters since he left Boston in April, as he believed they somehow blamed him for the fiasco and tragedy at the apartment. He felt alone and took some strength from Magnolia's seclusion and her ability to cope. Perhaps it could suit him, too. On Thanksgiving, he strolled over to the big Macy's Parade, as he believed all good New Yorkers should, that he had watched so many times on television growing up. He was amazed at the thousands of people who lined the chilly sidewalks, all families with children huddled together in bunches in the numbing November cold, warmed by big eyes watching the wondrous floats and balloons float by. Instead of cheering him up, the parade depressed him and served to remind him of how alone he was.

About a week before Christmas, Mr. Fabrizi ordered Riley to attend an important meeting on a Friday night, unusual even by Mr. Fabrizi's inconsiderate standards. Rumors had been circulating for some time that the government was investigating LSE for something, but no one was sure what was happening. Riley arrived in the board room on time, prepared for the anticipated twenty-minute wait before Mr. Fabrizi's heralded arrival. This time however, Riley opened the heavy board room door to find Mr. Fabrizi already there, pacing in circles around the room in his Gucci print shirt and black designer loafers, sunglasses perched on top of his head. And he was upset about something. Two other well-styled men sat at the board room table. Riley would learn the first was Eli Solomon, a publishing tycoon from Las Vegas who made his fortune in the seventies printing slick hardcore porn magazines out of the backroom of his mainstream warehouses. The other was Johnny Katz, a dealer of exotic automobiles who built his fortune selling large, expensive American-made automobiles to Middle Eastern oil barons, though he denied rumors that had him brokering arms deals as well. Riley knew of them and had heard Mr. Fabrizi speak of them, but he had never met them in person before. The two men were not employees or lackeys to Mr. Fabrizi. They were his friends -- his contemporaries and his equals -- who had flown in to New York to advise him on this special problem. Riley sat at the far end of the room feeling invisible, wondering why he was there, as the conversation between the three rich and influential men continued.

"I'm telling you, I'm selling. The whole fucking business, Eli. Everything." Mr. Fabrizi barked. "I have fucking had it."

"Think, Eddie, think." Eli tried to reason. "You've been in tougher spots than this before. Why are you flying off the handle now and throwing it all away?"

"Do you think I like seeing my face on television, telling everybody I'm a criminal?" Mr. Fabrizi paced quicker. "I have been legit for years. I paid my debt to society. I pay my fucking taxes. I employ hundreds of people. But they won't forget, they won't let me escape. I'm trapped."

"What's done is done. You can't just erase your past. It's part of who you are. You were able to build this empire because surviving those problems made you tough. It made you strong." Eli said, playing on his ego, trying to calm him down.

"I have had to make decisions in my life that you can't even dream of!" Mr. Fabrizi threw his hands in the air, growing more angry.

"Hey... don't forget who you're talking to here," Eli reminded him, as he pulled an expensive Cuban cigar from his pocket and rolled it between his fingers. "Johnny K and I have been through this. We've made the same sacrifices you have. You don't get to where we are without a little adversity."

"Adversity? You call this adversity? What happens to my kids when I'm back in prison, huh?"

"You're too emotional, Eddie. You're not thinking clearly. This is just another business problem. Deal with it like you deal with every other business problem." Eli said.

Riley laughed to himself. Mr. Fabrizi was dealing with it like he deals with every other problem.

Johnny K had been leaning back in his chair as if bored and napping and had yet to say anything. He cleared his throat and leaned forward, and placed his bony, wrinkled elbows on the table.

"Listen to him, Eddie. Eli's making sense. Let's break this down like a business problem. The Queen of Diamonds Cabaret opens Wednesday night, correct?" Johnny K asked. Riley was aware of Mr. Fabrizi's new investment, the Queen of Diamonds Cabaret, a high-end strip joint just off the strip in Las Vegas, and knew he had dumped millions into it. And he also knew it had suffered nothing but delays and setbacks.

Johnny K continued. "I see no reason to interfere with it. Let it open on time, as scheduled. You have good lawyers, let them worry about the charges from the FBI or IRS if they ever materialize."

"It was in the paper and on TV that I am paying a tribute to that union official who doubles as a gangster. You know the IRS won't let that go. They watch everything I do. Every move I make. The Feds are convinced I am dirty and the strip club industry is run by organized crime. They're going to bring me down!" Mr. Fabrizi leaned over and crushed the table with his fist.

"Eddie, there aren't even any charges yet... just rumors from an overzealous asshole reporter. You're overreacting," Eli pleaded."Just how much did you pay this guy anyway?"

"Sixty thousand dollars. It kept me out of trouble with the unions and the local capo. If I don't pay him, there is no way this place opens and I lose millions. They even stooped so low as to threaten the girls. So tell me, how am I expected to run a clean honest business when everyone else is crooked?"

"So tell me Eddie," Eli interrupted, pointing at Riley. "You wanted this kid invited into our meeting tonight. Now that you've admitted committing a felony, you want to tell me again why?"

"Lynch here is the most loyal and important employee I have. He keeps a close eye on my books. And he's smart -- very smart. He advises me. If there is anyone who can prove that my business is clean, it's Lynch. He also knows business and tax law better than all those expensive fucking lawyers downstairs. I wanted him to hear this. He needs to know."

Mr. Fabrizi's trust in him was admirable, and gave Riley a sense of strength and value that he needed to hear to raise his spirits. Despite his silence through the meeting, Riley hadn't been a mere spectator. The problem was that Mr. Fabrizi had indeed paid a tribute -- extortion money -- to local mobsters, and it was off the books. His mind had been thumbing through tax law and case studies, trying to find some alternatives for his embattled boss to wiggle out of this.

"Sir, I do have an idea. But I am not sure if it is legal or if it will work. I need a day or two to do some research. I need to get over to the law library."

"See? I told you he would help." Mr. Fabrizi said. Eli and Johnny K exchanged skeptical glances as if they were patronizing them both. "Let's meet back here first thing Monday morning. And it's getting late, let's go get some dinner. I know this restaurant called Americo's..."

Riley apologized and backed himself out of dinner with the power brokers, a terrible idea for a variety reasons, and flew back to his room to start his research. He spent all night surfing the Internet from website to website searching in vain for the right tax code entry, or the right case law study to validate his theory. But he was not a lawyer and much of the detail and confusing citations escaped him. In desperation, he sent email to a few lawyers and CPA's he knew -- including Malcolm Ward -- but received no responses. He thumbed through case after case, citation after citation, opinion after opinion, until he swore he could feel his retinas start to bleed from the intensity. The United States tax law was the most boring, circular and mystifying subject yet conceived by the human mind. Alvin snored with voracity behind him as he struggled to stay focused, and Riley succumbed to exhaustion falling asleep stretched across his keyboard.

The next morning, functioning on only a few hours sleep, he hustled downtown to the county law office library still wearing the same clothes from the evening before. It was only open a few hours on Saturday morning, so he needed to work fast and effectively. He jogged up and down the aisles of law books grabbing what he needed at a furious pace. The librarians and staff were watching him with intent, and he half expected to be asked to leave. Riley scribbled notes, recorded citations, made copies, researched and reviewed until the library closed and he found himself back on the street with an armful of worthless paper, still without his answer.

By Monday morning, he had abandoned all hope. He had worked all weekend and was no closer to a solution for Mr. Fabrizi's problems than he was on Friday. He was furious at himself for allowing Mr. Fabrizi's kind words to inflate his ego and convince him he was competent to do this. He thought about how ugly and humiliating his meeting with Eli, Johnny K and Mr. Fabrizi was about to be. He could hear Eli and Johnny K uttering "I told you so" in his mind. Riley's skin was white and drawn as he passed by Katie's desk on his way to the board room for his execution. He was not only about to embarrass himself, but he would do so in front of Mr. Fabrizi's powerful and influential associates.

"Oh, good morning, Riley. I have a package for you." Katie passed a thick manila envelope to him as he walked by.

"Thanks. Who is this from?" Riley inquired.

"No idea. A courier delivered it about twenty minutes ago," Katie said disinterested in his crisis, shuffling her own project around her desk.

Riley entered the board room and was relieved to find out he was the first to arrive. All was quiet, but wouldn't be for long, and it gave him a few minutes to compose his nerves and focus. He tore open the envelope and let the papers fall across the table in front of him. Distracted, it took him a moment to realize what he was looking at.

And he was stunned.

In his hands he held the very documents he had searched for all weekend. Here in front of him were the specific tax law citations he needed, along with opinions, and examples of case law, all organized, circled and highlighted with careful precision. There was no indication of who had sent the package, however. He flipped through the papers and his eyes scanned the pages twice as fast as he could read. He fumbled in his pocket for a pen, flung open his notebook, and began scribbling with shaky fingers in short notes and half sentences. Mr. Fabrizi, Eli and Johnny K burst through the door at that moment, just returned from breakfast. Mr. Fabrizi's guests were staying at the famed Waldorf Astoria on Park Avenue, and were unhappy with the service. All three were offended and complaining at the same time, and the three rich men reminded Riley of his pathetic sisters at dinner each night in Southie.

"So Mr. Lynch," Johnny K began. "We very much enjoyed that restaurant of yours Friday night. Very nice place."

"It was OK." Eli added, "I think Johnny here has a crush on that barmaid."

"Mici?" Riley asked

"Don't know her name, but she was a sweetheart, no doubt." Johnny said.

"Not bad for an east coast girl." Eli kidded.

"I know how to take care of my friends," Mr. Fabrizi pointed out, fishing to take credit for their good time. He tossed his leather briefcase on the table with a thud, and placed his sunglasses back on top of his head like a tiara. He inserted what appeared to be half of a bagel in his mouth in one bite, chewed twice, and swallowed.

213

"So this morning, Riley, I made my decision. I am selling my interest in the Queen of Diamonds in Vegas. I want out. I'll take my lumps with the lawyers and IRS later, but I need to distance myself from this problem. I have to get it off my desk and out of my hair... all I got is problems! So here is what you need to do today. Get José to draw up a contract..."

"I don't think you should sell," a confident Riley interrupted him, clutching the mysterious envelope. Mr. Fabrizi was annoyed with the comment, stared him down and raised his voice.

"Look, I made my decision. It's my money I'll be losing."

"But it's not necessary. I have an idea."

"Let the kid talk," Eli advised. "I want to hear what this whiz kid of yours came up with. This should be entertaining."

"First of all," Riley began, "there is no reason for you to sell, unless you want to lose money. I know exactly how much you've poured into this project, down to the penny. There is no chance you will recoup it all back."

"OK, so I don't sell it. I just lose it when the IRS takes it away from me."

"No, I don't think so. The first step will be to find this person you paid the tribute to. And get him on the payroll."

"His name is Romano, and he's already on the payroll! I gave him sixty thousand fucking dollars!"

"No, no. I mean hire him. Make him an employee, just like me or Katie or José. Call him a project manager for the new club. Give him health care and vacation time for him and his family."

"You gotta be shittin' me. Why do I want to do that?"

"Because then the laws change. What he does for you changes. He needs to be a legal part of this enterprise, and you become his superior. Then the second step is to declare in writing, on paper -- on the books -- every penny you gave him as that tribute to the mob."

"Are you trying to get me a life sentence?"

"No, no sir. Put it on the books before the quarter ends and it becomes just another business expense. I have in my hand a dozen Internal Revenue Service case histories and court documents that prove beyond a shadow of a doubt that all strip clubs and adult entertainment venues in the United States are controlled by organized crime."

"But they aren't all owned and operated by organized crime. I'm clean!"

"I know, but their evidence -- the government evidence true or not -- says otherwise. Therefore, follow the law and the precedent. The law says without question that you can claim and deduct any ordinary and necessary business expense under IRS code 16a. Therefore, if it is fact that all strip clubs are operated under the influence of organized crime, and strip clubs are legal businesses, bribes and tributes now become ordinary business expenses -- by the Fed's own admission -- and can be claimed, recorded and used as a tax deduction in the next tax year. It's just a normal part of doing business in this industry. The Feds can't deny it, they came up with it. And it's all legal -- they can't touch you."

"So for me to be clean and legal, I have to lie and claim I'm not. Unbelievable. You are fucking crazy, Riley. Fucking crazy."

"It's an option. It's the way the law reads. And if the Feds don't buy it, there is enough legal gray area to keep this tied-up for a long time, letting the profits from the club catch up with the expenses."

Eli and Johnny K had pulled Riley's documents away from him and were studying them, flipping through the same pages Riley had a few minutes earlier. Their sarcastic tones were now gone, replaced by stoic concentration, and they whispered between themselves.

"Hey Eddie, I'm going to overnight this stuff to my lawyer in Beverly Hills. I want to see what he thinks about all this." Johnny K offered, rubbing his chin.

"Are you telling me you're buying into all this crap? What the fuck! You gotta be kidding me!" Mr. Fabrizi was incensed, hands in the air again.

"I don't know if he's right. But I'm saying there is enough here to consider. It won't hurt to get a qualified legal opinion. Hey kid, you want to come work for me in Beverly Hills? Eddie's right, you do nice work." Johnny K laughed.

"Thanks anyway, but I have plenty to keep me out of trouble here in New York."

In less than a day, Mr. Fabrizi had not only warmed up to Riley's crazy plan but was now telling his staff how he thought it up and assigned Riley to do the legwork. José and Hose-B were now chained to their desks, both assigned to working on the new project around the clock, preparing documents, and revising budgets and projections to account for the sixty thousand dollars in extortion money. But there were still two significant problems with the plan. First, the opening of the club was one day away and many of the dancers had been scared off by the news reports and unfounded rumors of possible violence -- and obtaining quick cash from the big club was critical to the success of the plan. The second problem was that the union official and capo Mr. Fabrizi paid, a gentleman by the name of Romano, had to be convinced to sign on as an LSE employee. Mr. Fabrizi put together a package with salary and benefits that included good company health care for him and his family, a Florida vacation club, and a lucrative cash signing bonus. For all this money, Romano had to do nothing but accept Mr. Fabrizi's illegal payments and pass them on to his local mob boss. In short, it was an offer Romano couldn't refuse.

"Listen to me Riley," Mr. Fabrizi demanded. "Not many people know about all this yet, and I want to keep it that way." Riley thought it ironic since Mr. Fabrizi had been bragging to everyone he encountered. He pointed his ring covered meaty fingers at him. "I want you to go to Las Vegas first thing tomorrow. I need someone I can trust to deliver the offer to Romano. Don't come back until he signs it."

"Me? Las Vegas? Are you sure?" Riley was astonished.

"Of course I'm sure! I know what I'm doing. You said you had nothing to do this Christmas. You told me that you were staying in New York." Mr. Fabrizi smiled and pointed to his own temple. "See, you don't think I remember these things! Get Romano to sign and you'll be back before Christmas Eve. In fact, when you get back, I want you and your girl to join me and my family on Christmas Eve at my home in Queens. We throw a big party every year for my friends and family -- *La Vigilia* -- it's the Feast of the Seven Fishes. You will come as my guest."

"Thank you sir, this is all so sudden. I'm not sure what to think. I guess I need to go home and pack." Riley felt a burn in the pit of his stomach. His preference would have been to spend the holiday cultivating his depression, rolled into a ball in the corner of his room covered by a blanket.

"Katie will take care of the tickets and arrangements. And she will set up an appointment for you with Romano. You and the girls will stay at my casino, The Desert Intrigue, on West Tropicana Avenue, just off the strip."

"Girls? What girls?"

EIGHTEEN

The arrival of the mysterious envelope that contained the tax documents was the final straw. Riley was now able to add paranoia to his increasing list of personal deficiencies. He had been curious as to how Professor Friedman heard about his mother's passing, and shocked to find out his rental car bill was paid without his knowledge. His emotional state at that time was so brittle that it was easier to chalk such things up to coincidence, error or random happenstance -- and he had not invested any time in figuring it out. But now Riley sat holding a thick manila envelope full of paper, analyzing the handwriting, looking for clues to its origins. He even sniffed the contents revealing a clean, vanilla scent he found familiar, but couldn't place. All this talk of mobsters had him believing he was being followed.

Mr. Fabrizi did not own a Las Vegas casino, but he was an important investor in The Desert Intrigue which had opened just off the strip during the great Vegas building boom of the nineties. As usual, Mr. Fabrizi's timing, money and blind lady luck had somehow collided to add to his fortune. Not only did revenues from The Intrigue help keep his bank accounts full and help mask the losses from mismanagement of other LSE enterprises, but it quenched Mr. Fabrizi's thirst for the lights, glitz and pageantry of Las Vegas, seduced like the generations of criminals, charlatans, mobsters, gamblers and shrewd businessmen before him. Within his circle of friends, success in Vegas represented not only success in business -- it meant everything.

Riley was not excited to be off on this new assignment and adventure. He had never been to Las Vegas, to the desert, or outside the Northeast in fact, and had never traveled on an airplane. And then to complicate matters more, he had been assigned to bring three top "performers" from LSE's lucrative strip club operations along with him on the trip. The grand opening of the Queen of Diamonds Gentleman's Club was threatened by a lack of female talent -- strippers, exotic dancers, adult entertainers, or whatever you want to call them -- and Mr. Fabrizi had ordered his top three hard-bodied money-makers to drop everything and get out there as soon as possible. Mr. Fabrizi viewed these girls as business assets, and by reputation, they were unreliable and known to wander off from time to time. Riley was assigned to see that the unpredictable talent made it on time and as scheduled. After hastily collecting his clothes and stuffing them in a suitcase, Riley hopped into the company's limousine darting back and forth across the five boroughs snatching up the three exotic dancers like an entomologist would collect butterflies.

The first girl he picked up went by the stage name of Shyla Bright, and by Riley's standards, she wasn't very. Shyla was in her early twenties, but her cherubic face and small size screamed jailbait, and she played the part for all it was worth. Her petite and perky ninety pound frame, long blonde hair and summer complexion, along with her stage props of school girl uniforms, hair bows, oversized lollipops and rag dolls played to raves on the dirty old man circuit. When Riley let her into the limo, he learned she had no idea where she was going, and was following the instructions of her manager-boyfriend who was pissed off he couldn't come along. Throughout the trip, she would alternate between texting, swearing into her cell phone and combing her doll's hair.

At the second club, Riley met Sienna Ferrari, a long-legged and vivacious model on the fast track to adult industry stardom. Sienna had become the most sought-after men's centerfold model in the country, and it was easy to understand why. Sienna was physically faultless in every way -- from the tips of her meticulously manicured toes to the top of her raven-haired head -- and Riley could find no flaw. She walked and carried herself like a Hollywood starlet might, and he surmised it must take her hours to apply her make-up just so. Sienna viewed her career as an exotic dancer as a temporary one -- high-paying mainstream films and music contracts were just around the corner, or so she believed.

Riley's final stop was a dingy strip club called the Raw Bar situated next to a large cemetery in Queens. The neighborhood smelled like dead fish and trash was strewn across the cracked asphalt parking lot. At the sole, peeling red door, an enormous and bald Black man in an oversized leather trench coat stopped him and demanded a ten dollar cover charge. The man's name was Mikeé Evans, the very same Mikeé Evans who Riley would befriend and work alongside later in prison, but neither would remember their brief chance meeting on this cold, stressful December afternoon. Riley was focused on collecting his bounty at this club and making it to JFK Airport before they all missed their flight. Once he explained his intentions, an older woman carrying an overstuffed bag lumbered out and flopped herself into the limo.

Aurora Ample could have passed for one of Riley's mother's friends, or even his aunt. She was a grizzled performer, a veteran of years worth of dancing, stag films, magazines and private performances, and wore baggy gray sweats that covered her middle-aged hips and celebrated, oversized breasts. Riley would not have believed she was who she claimed to be if not for the obvious resemblance from the glossy photos he had been carrying around in his folder, photos it was clear to him were taken many years earlier. Aurora was a polite and focused business person, and in her bag, she carried extra glossy photos, souvenir underwear to sell to fans, stage props and a laptop computer. The computer was for her webcam shows that she could set-up and plug-in anywhere she found herself. With Aurora, it was all business, all the time.

The three girls knew each other. And with each stop, hugs and giddiness ensued. They all looked forward to going to Las Vegas -- Shyla for the fun, Sienna for the exposure, and Aurora for the money -- and Riley thought it odd that they didn't seem to care that they were leaving family and friends behind for the holiday. They lived and worked in another dimension.

The limo hopped onto the Van Wyck Expressway, drove about a mile, and came to a dead stop in traffic. The airport wasn't far, but the traffic was dense and Riley felt anxiety tighten in his bowels for fear they would miss their flight. Riley sat stoic and motionless in the car as the girls who sat across from him became reacquainted, chatted and talked shop. Riley had dressed for the trip -- black shoes, black suit, black shirt and sunglasses that he wore to hide his eyes. If he was escorting strippers to Las Vegas to intimidate a mob capo, he surmised it was wise to look the part.

The girls immersed themselves in mindless chatter about eyeliner, blush, and some new expensive organic shampoo. Riley stared out the window at the slow moving cars around him already looking forward to the end of the assignment. Many men Riley's age might be excited to be in the company of three sexually uninhibited women, and the girls impressive physical attributes were not lost on him, yet Riley wouldn't allow himself even a guilty pleasure, and remained content to be bathed in melancholy and watch the seconds tick by on his digital watch. He noticed the cars around the limo had started to move forward, but the limo wasn't budging. He looked forward toward the limo driver and saw the man's wide eyes in the mirror looking back at him. When Riley looked to the rear of the vehicle to see what had captured the driver's attention, he understood the delay. All three girls had pulled out their breasts.

But this was no moment of sleazy male fantasy, the girls were talking shop. Each had undergone some sort of recent breast augmentation surgery and they were comparing notes and results much the way three widget salesmen might discuss the finer points of the latest new widget specifications.

"My doctor in Chatsworth prefers to hide the incision here," Aurora showed them. "He believes the scar heals more naturally. The girls peered close and nodded.

"My implants are textured," Shyla said, inviting the girls to feel them. "My doctor said this would be a safer option."

"Mine just healed up," Sienna added, now I wish I had gone to one size larger."

"But they look so real," and Shyla reached over and squeezed them both. "They're cute. They did a nice job."

"You're better off keeping them smaller," Aurora advised. "Mine are 46 EE and even my best customers want them bigger. You'll never get them big enough to satisfy everybody. Keep them small and firm and in proportion to your body. You'll appreciate it later."

Riley stared in disbelief. It was a crude and unerotic moment. He had never given any thought to the life of a sex performer, and had subscribed to the popular notion that they were all drug users, alcoholics and drunks with low self-esteem. He wasn't convinced their vocations were healthy, but the attention they paid to their business was surprising, more so than many of the employees at his own office on Lafayette Street.

221

"How about you girls doing a cameo for my website?" Aurora asked and both girls nodded their approval. A wild flurry of activity followed. Aurora stripped off her sweats and pulled a revealing outfit from her bag. Sienna and Shyla rifled their handbags for eyeliner, brushes and make up, and bits of false eyelashes, tissues, hair and press-on nails showered around the cabin. There were now so many varied bits of debris on the floor, Riley wondered idly if he could save them and construct his own girl later. Aurora powered-up her laptop and snapped a webcam to the top. The three girls huddled together and smiled.

"Hi boys, it's Aurora here! Welcome back! I'm heading to Vegas with my sexy friends Shyla and Sienna... say hello ladies." The girls smiled, licked their lips, waved and blew kisses at the camera. "Why don't you boys all check back later and I'll update you on all the fun I'm having in Las Vegas and at the grand opening of the new Queen of Diamonds Gentlemen's Club. Remember, only members get to see all the hot, explicit action. See you later!"

Aurora shut down her computer and packed it away. The girls relaxed and went back to chatting

"On your website... do you have a lot of members?" Riley inquired, trying to insert himself into the conversation.

"Oh, hundreds." Aurora responded. "I keep them happy. I always try to give them something fresh, something new to keep them interested." Riley peered down into her big bag and saw several small webcams.

"Oh, those... I'll set them up all over my room when we get to the hotel. Guys will pay ninety-nine cents an hour to watch me walk around in my undies and eat pizza all night. In fact, I can make two hundred dollars an hour just sleeping."

"That's creepy," Riley responded in horror.

"You're new to all this aren't you." Aurora deduced, blowing his cool cover. "It is creepy. This whole industry is creepy, but you get used to it. Guys will email me about how many times I roll over every night, how many times I sneeze, or how many times I scratch my ass. I'm too old for porn now, and almost too old to dance. So if I can continue to milk these sweet perverts, I can retire on this."

"My boyfriend is making my website," Shyla chipped in. "He says it's going to be awesome when it's done. For now, I work with his brother who runs a lingerie modeling agency out of Brooklyn."

"I tried private modeling," Sienna interrupted." It was OK if they just jerked off while I danced around, but I didn't want to turn tricks. I want a mainstream career someday and didn't want that following me."

"Once you start in this business you stay in this business. You're better off grabbing the money now while you've got that tight ass, because after age twenty-four, honey, it's all downhill." Aurora advised.

"That's why I want to go into porn now. I want to work for one of those big studios outside L.A. I hear they pay you thousands," Shyla said.

"You'd better get that contract fast and pimp yourself to that studio. There's no money in it otherwise. Do whatever they tell you to do. You don't see many rich porn stars. And make sure you never stop loving the money more than the sex."

Riley had received an education. He was gazing down Alice's rabbit hole. He had no idea any of this world existed.

The limo finally reached the JFK terminal, and the place was jam packed as holiday week travelers were queued up everywhere. He and the girls elbowed and shoved their way through the crowd and found themselves standing in an endless line of grouchy, noisy voyagers. But from within the deafening cacophony of random chatter, he distinctly heard a familiar voice.

"Riley, Dude!"

It was Alvin.

"What's up, man! What are you doing here?"

"I'm going to Las Vegas on business for LSE. I should be back by Christmas Eve." Riley told him.

"Well, I'm heading back to L.A. to see the family for Christmas. My flight is delayed." Alvin looked at Riley's companions, his eyes widened, and then he glanced back at Riley.

"Are these your sisters?" Alvin inquired.

Sienna and Aurora looked at each other stupefied, observing Riley's dismayed reaction and sensing Alvin's acute stupidity, as the three girls could not have looked any more unalike. The girls had crafted careers out of identifying and manipulating unsuspecting marks like Alvin. Sienna pulled Riley toward him and erotically licked the side of his cheek. A passenger standing in line behind them swallowed his chewing gum.

223

"So is that your sister or not?" Alvin asked a second time.

The Desert Intrigue Casino was as opulent and as grand as any in Las Vegas. Its wide marble steps lead up to a shimmering wall of glass where white-gloved doorman greet overconfident gamblers and masses of wide-eyed tourists as they enter. Down below, the steps lead to a spacious, multi-leveled veranda populated with small white tables that overlook a breathtaking array of water fountains and hand-crafted topiary. An interesting and never ending societal cross section of pedestrians pass by in the street, each carrying an alcoholic beverage of choice, and each handed escort service business cards by Hispanic men in Santa hats. The weather was cool and dry, but far warmer than New York City could ever be in December. Classical instrumental Christmas carols played everywhere they went, from unseen speakers as if floating about the desert air, and as night had fallen on the city, its gluttony of neon dwarfed anything Riley had experienced back in Boston or Times Square. Riley didn't know which direction to look, and felt all five of his senses were in danger of overload.

Each of the girls had arranged separate plans for the evening while they traveled. Sienna was invited by a Hollywood producer to accompany him to a high stakes poker room at the Bellagio, an offer she couldn't pass up, as she was on the lookout for her big break. Shyla was going to The Venetian to check out the Tao -- an exclusive, high-energy, high-profile nightclub that plays regular host to A-list music and movie celebrities. Had Riley not been intimidated by everything around him, including his own shadow at this point, he might have accepted her kind invitation to join her. Riley sensed Shyla felt sorry for him.

Aurora had worked her fingers raw during the flight arranging special meetings via cell phone and email. Several members from Aurora's website and fan club were in the Las Vegas area, and the sudden news of her visit prompted a flurry of personal inquiries as to her private availability. Aurora had booked two-hour blocks of these meetings with her members like McCarran Airport had planes in a holding pattern, and she planned to be working every available free moment of her week, maximizing her earning potential.

Riley left instructions for each girl to meet him at the bar in The Desert Intrigue lobby at ten a.m. sharp, where they would walk together over to the King of Diamonds to meet the club manager and receive their performance schedule and instructions. The club opened at noon and a huge crowd was expected with all the pomp, circumstance and spectacle Las Vegas could muster. Once the girls made it to the front door of the club, the first half of his assignment would be complete, and then he could concentrate fully on his meeting with Romano. A VIP booth had been reserved for them to discuss, negotiate and sign Mr. Fabrizi's generous employment offer. Riley found his way through the maze of halls to his room, fell across his bed and passed out.

But at 10:15 the next morning, Riley stood alone in the lobby. All three of the girls were nowhere to be found, his stomach was doing flips again, and it was starting to hurt. He spied a gift shop across the lobby where he could buy some antacid, but didn't want to abandon his post for fear of missing one of the girls. He paced in circles around the casino lobby's immense Christmas tree that was decorated with silver angels and gold VIP frequent player cards, and dialed his cell phone. Only Aurora answered that she was on her way down.

Aurora arrived in the lobby with a middle-aged couple. The three exchanged affectionate hugs and kisses, and the couple walked away hand in hand.

"That was my fan club vice-president," Aurora said. They are very nice people.

Riley was confused, "Your vice-president brought his wife with him to rendezvous with you last night?"

"Oh no," Aurora explained, "My vice-president brought her husband."

Sienna turned up in the lobby next, confirming Riley's intuition about how long it would take her to get ready. She was miffed that Riley considered her late as she was conducting important business that he didn't understand. The three waited for Shyla for some time, all dialing cell phones and leaving messages trying to track her down, until she walked through the main doors from the outside carrying full shopping bags.

"Oh my God! You'll never guess! I found out last night my picture is in this month's *Penthouse* Magazine." Shyla was as proud as a child whose name was in the newspaper on the elementary school honor roll. "I need to buy a copy right away."

"Is there a store nearby?" Aurora chimed in. "I'm out of tampons."

The girls spied the gift shop across the lobby and started toward it like a herd of cows after a bale of fresh hay. Riley stopped them in their tracks.

"No! You all stay right here, and don't move. I will go get what you need."

The girls were a bit taken back by Riley's harsh tone. He was feeling the pressure of his upcoming meeting and it showed. They thought it wise to stay put.

"I need a chocolate bar!" Sienna shouted after him as he approached the shop.

In a frantic rush, Riley grabbed a *Penthouse* Magazine, a box of extra large, extra absorbent tampons, a chocolate bar and the antacids. He threw them with haste and disgust on the counter.

"I'm in a hurry," he told the clerk.

"Yes, sir," he responded, looking over the peculiar selection of items. "I understand... and I am sorry."

Security at the Queen of Diamonds was high. Not only had a police detail been hired and put in place, but Mr. Fabrizi had seen fit to employ a dozen plain-clothed private security guards to keep an eye on the business. The adult entertainment atmosphere in the city was competitive, and the other club owners were less than pleased that a new high-end establishment was opening in their backyard. It was the reason Mr. Fabrizi paid the tributes in the first place -- to guarantee protection so he experienced no interference from any of them.

The grand opening was a huge success. Patrons circled the entrance in all directions while sexy, young, scantily-clothed women danced outside near the front doors. Mr. Fabrizi's strategy of offering the cab drivers fifty bucks a head to bring patrons to the new club worked like a charm. Riley was waved through the crowd with his three ladies on his arm, black suit and sunglasses in place, and spectators whispered about who he was to have three women like that and receive such treatment. He took his seat alone in the elevated and stanchioned VIP area, with a clear view of the club's three new immaculate stages. Red neon lights bordered everything and the brass and chrome trim on the bar and fixtures shined spit-polish clean.

The club's doors opened to live music and cannon fire, and throngs of drunk, horny men rushed the stages and bar. Riley's three special friends were scheduled to appear on each of the stages first that day, as the club's regular girls were working the crowd hustling for lap dances and making new friends.

Riley sat alone for some time, milking his fifteen dollar beer as the girls started the show. Watching them gyrate and grind to the guttural beats, oozing in lust, each in their own unique style, he became impressed by their professionalism and baffled as to why he had not even tried to hit on one of them -- they looked incredible -- nothing like the girls he picked up the day before.

"Mr. Lynch?" A security guard interrupted his daydreaming. "I have someone here to see you. This is Mr. Romano."

The two men exchanged pleasantries. Romano was a small, wiry, rat-faced man who appeared wrinkled as if retrieved from a gutter that morning. In contrast, Riley had dressed the part of the gangster and was sharp and pressed. Riley was nervous and out of his element, but he could tell Romano was scared to near death, perspiring and breathing heavy, pupils darting around the room. This was not the fearsome mob capo Mr. Fabrizi had prepared him to meet.

"Did you bring the money?" Romano asked, appearing to be in a hurry to leave.

"Before we discuss that, I want you to sit down and talk to me, and enjoy the nice show." Riley did his best to impersonate Mr. Fabrizi. Of all the people he knew, who would best handle the situation, Mr. Fabrizi would have been a natural.

"Why, what's wrong?" A skeptical Romano wrung his hands.

"Nothing is wrong. I have been empowered to make you an offer to join our company. On this paper, it describes your pay, benefits and responsibilities. All you need to do is sign it and we will be all set."

"Are you nuts? I'm not signing anything. What kind of set-up is this?"

"We want to hire you, Mr. Romano, as a security consultant for this club. It is a very generous offer."

"Security consultant? What the hell does that mean?"

227

"It means that you will continue to relay messages and payments on behalf of Mr. Fabrizi to keep this club safe and in legal, proper business operation."

A puzzled Romano scanned over the documents, then his eyes darted around the room again as if looking for an exit or for someone to sneak up behind him and slash his throat. Riley sensed the deal wasn't going well but he wasn't intimidated by Romano in the least. Romano was an emotional car wreck.

"It says here you want to pay me a thousand dollars every week, just to extort money from you?"

"You will be providing an important service to our corporation. And not only will you be paid on the second and fourth Fridays of each month, we will provide full health coverage to your wife and your children. We are excited to have you on board." Riley held out a pen, hoping he would take it.

"I don't know.... I don't know about this." Romano kept repeating. Behind them, Aurora was wrapping up her show with one of her famed and popular stunts. She was lying on her back on stage with legs spread wide, and she had inserted a shot glass into her pussy. She was inviting patrons to wrinkle up dollar bills and shoot. The first successful basket won her underwear and a free website membership. The crowd noise increased with each close shot. She was a master of flexing her most sensitive muscles just enough to cause unsuccessful rim shots until she deemed the pile of scrunched-up dollars lying about the stage sufficient.

Romano looked both intrigued and disturbed by Aurora's spectacle, and wasn't focusing on their conversation. Riley seized the opportunity when Shyla walked by, and he called for her to come over. The girls were aware Riley had an important meeting and had been asked to make themselves available as needed. On cue, Shyla walked into the VIP booth, dropped her robe, and sat nude on Romano's lap.

"I wanted to introduce you to one of your new co-workers. This is Shyla." Romano's eyes bugged and he sat motionless. "Though, I should remind you that we do have a progressive sexual harassment policy that I will need you to read and sign."

Romano's eyes were inches from Shyla's surgically enhanced twenty-something right breast. He looked up just as Sienna walked by and winked at him.

"Is there anything in this offer that you don't like?" Riley asked.

"I still don't know about this. I need to ask Mr. Marcellino."

"Did you say Marcellino?"

Riley felt the oxygen in the room disappear as if sucked out the door, and his skin went cold. Fury returned to his veins, and even the hair on the back of his neck tingled and stood at attention. He could not escape Marcellino and he was in disbelief that the money he was carrying would be going to the man who had destroyed his family. He was now terrified and felt way over his head, much as he did at the carwash when Hanratty was shot dead. Shyla was smiling and chirpy, but when she saw the color disappear from Riley's face, she sensed something was wrong and tensed.

"Will you be giving this payment to Mr. Marcellino yourself... in person?" Riley asked, sounding out each word and vowel.

"Yes. Yes I suppose I will." Romano said, fidgeting and wondering what would happen next.

Riley sat for a moment and examined his options as he did whenever solving a challenging calculus problem. But it wasn't helping -- he was out of his element. He reached into his pocket for an antacid and froze, looking Romano square in the eye. The two exchanged glances of terror. Without thinking, Riley jumped up startling Shyla who fell naked to the floor, and without removing the extra large package of antacids from his pocket, pressed the roll into Romano's shuddering shoulder as if he held a gun as he had seen done in the movies. Romano gasped and stiffened.

"I've had enough of this crap. Here's what you're going to do. Fill out this paper now and sign it. It's that simple. Or do I need to find Mr. Marcellino myself and explain how you disrespected me and threw this pretty young girl to the floor?"

"Please don't hurt me, I'll sign it." Romano said panicked, as his breathing increased, and a small droplet of sweat fell on to the page. Shyla curled up into the corner, clothed only by her own blanket of fear, baffled as to what was happening. Romano scribbled and Riley made sure he didn't miss a blank.

"Thank you, Mr. Romano. It will be a pleasure having you join us as a co-worker." Riley wiped his own moist brow. Then Riley remembered one thing Mr. Fabrizi insisted he mention before he leave, as he gathered up the documents and covered over his faux pistol.

"Mr. Fabrizi asked me to mention that your Disney family vacation club enrollment form will be in the mail next Tuesday."

NINETEEN

A lthough his assignment in Las Vegas couldn't be described as anything but triumphant, Riley returned to New York beaten and broken. His stomach hurt, he popped antacid tablets like candy, and the searing pain had ruined his appetite and was giving him headaches. He had grown to hate his life, become paranoid, and felt trapped by Giovanni Marcellino's evil influence that hung over him no matter what direction he turned. He even felt bad for that dirt bag Romano who he threatened -- the poor guy had a wife and kids and worked for both Fabrizi and Marcellino now. He wished he could quit his job at LSE and go back to Ticonderoga with Magnolia and grow garlic. He wished his life had progressed more like Tammy Meeks' had, and he was back home in Boston planning a safe, dull, inconsequential life. He thought of Tammy often and how much he enjoyed talking with her on the train that day and how his childhood felt wasted and friends discarded. He thought of his mother and how she would know exactly what he should do, and would encourage him and stand behind him. He missed his family and was hurt they didn't call. He received obligatory store-bought Christmas cards from most of them, but not a single invitation to come home or join them for the holiday. He felt he had been forsaken by many, maybe even himself.

It was two days until Christmas, and Riley sat alone in his dorm room in silence. He almost forgot he had been invited to the Fabrizis' grand soiree on Christmas Eve. The thought of attending depressed him, and he wrestled with the idea of spending the evening tucked under his blankets in his bed. But there would be no insult greater than skipping out on his boss's annual extravaganza, and if he didn't go he might as well quit his job now. Siobhan's legal fees were piling up, and as the only financially responsible sibling she had left, he anticipated seeing Malcolm Ward's invoices arrive in the mail at any time. Quitting his job meant abandoning his sister in prison. And he just couldn't do that.

His invitation to the party included him and a guest, and he was expected to bring his "girl" as Mr. Fabrizi put it. Most of his classmates were home for the holidays, as he was one of a handful of students allowed to stay in the dorms over break, and he didn't even have Alvin around to rent a member of his fan club. Riley was also in a bind as he knew he would be judged on who he brought along. It was late, but on a whim, he pulled out his telephone and dialed a number he had saved long ago, but had never used before.

"Hello, Mici? This is Riley Lynch."

"Riley? Oh my God, hello, Riley! How are you?"

"I have a question for you, Mici. I was invited to a big Christmas Eve party and wanted to ask you to come with me... as my date."

"On Christmas Eve? Oh, Riley, that's very sweet... but I always spend Christmas Eve with *Nonno* and his sisters after we close the restaurant."

"I understand. The party is at Mr. Fabrizi's estate in Queens, and I thought you might enjoy a night out."

"*La Vigilia* at Mr. Fabrizi's? Oh my God, Riley! Yes! Of course I will go!" He had never heard Mici so excited, and he was well aware that she understood the social magnitude of the invitation. He could hear her explain to Mr. Mantano in the background what he had said, and heard him voice his enthusiastic approval.

"Oh my God! That's tomorrow night! I must find something to wear!" And Mici hung up the phone before he had a chance to arrange a pick-up time, or say goodbye for that matter.

For a brief moment, Riley felt content and almost smiled to himself. He had made someone happy, and couldn't remember the last time that had happened, and it was someone he liked, to boot. He now looked forward to the party -- a little. After all, he justified, it was something to do and something to make the holiday feel more like a holiday. If he was lucky, it would be fun. Instead of sleeping, he bolted into his kitchenette and rifled through the room's meager cooking staples. There wasn't much, but he found a couple of boxes of raisins and half a bottle of rum left from one of Alvin's late night private parties. He rummaged a bit more and found the rest of the ingredients he needed to whip up his mother's famous Southie rum pudding. He had watched her make it dozens of times, often helping, and he could recite the recipe from memory. It was his favorite. He would bring it with him tomorrow night.

Riley felt the night would be special and he rented a limousine to transport them to the party. Had Mici declined his invitation, he would have stayed in bed. The thought of her presence beside him awakened gentle feelings he had suppressed about her when he left the restaurant. He found her motivating. He arrived at Mr. Mantano's apartment in his best suit, and Mr. Mantano greeted him at the door with exuberance and a great hug.

"Merry Christmas, Riley!" He said. "I have not seen you in so long. You look thin. You need to come by my restaurant and eat more, eh?"

"Merry Christmas to you, too, sir."

Behind them, Mici stood waiting. She was a spectacular sight to be seen. She wore a Christmas-red dress with green and white trim that fit snug and warm around the curves of her breasts and hips. She was adorned with small green sprigs of holly in her hair. The light flickered off her necklace and her eyes as if synchronized, and her smile was as wide and dimples as deep as he had ever seen. Those surgically enhanced Las Vegas showgirls were nothing compared to this. Riley felt his heart skip a beat, and wanted to inhale her. He took her hands in his and she kissed him softly on the cheek.

"Now you kids have a nice time tonight, and you watch yourself, Mr. Lynch. I hear stories about you Irish boys." Mr. Mantano smiled.

"Don't worry, sir, I will return Mici to you in mint condition. And not too late, I swear."

"Oh... and here is an envelope from me for Edward and Imelda. It's a donation to Imelda's foundation for Christmas. Please wish them both a happy Christmas for me."

Mr. Mantano's estate was along an exclusive residential beach in an upscale Queens neighborhood. Despite the scores of beautiful homes in the developed area, his was the most grand, secluded and preserved behind high stone walls and a tall, gothic, black iron gate that discouraged visitors. Once inside the compound, the limo clamored along a lengthy cobblestone path, delivering its riders to the front door much the way a sleigh may have done a hundred years earlier. The house was colossal and built in the classic Mediterranean style, with a tan stucco exterior and large single-paned, arched brown windows. What used to be a barn with horse stalls had been restored into guest rooms, rambling from the rear of the main house and out of sight. Exotic shrubs dotted the landscape -- the only green lawn left in the city -- and were all hung with red and yellow lights for the holiday. A doorman approached the car and opened it so Riley and Mici could step out. It was Hose-B.

"Merry Christmas, Mr. Lynch." Hose-B gazed up and down the elegant Mici, "Ooooh, my, she is beautiful. You will have a wonderful time tonight."

Inside the great door of the house, many guests had already arrived and were mingling and enjoying cocktails. Riley noticed a coatroom had been set-up, near the door, staffed by none other than Buckner from distribution. Outside, the cars were being parked by Hooper from shipping. Riley checked in their coats and couldn't help but notice how Buckner stared at Mici, eyes full of both lust and disdain, and Riley wondered how many of Mr. Fabrizi's employees hated him.

"This place is even more wonderful than I imagined it would be," Mici said, pulling Riley toward her in an appreciative embrace, her smile now permanent, glancing at the tall silk pleated curtains and glass chandelier. Hand painted flowered tile stretched across the floor of the foyer to a large staircase at the end of the room. A four piece jazz ensemble played holiday music at its foot. A waitress offered them Champagne from a silver serving tray, and he and Mici sipped as their eyes latched together. His emotions were back on that rollercoaster. Last night he had been too depressed to move. And now he had never felt so rich and alive.

Without warning, the band stopped playing and the room fell quiet. All eyes looked to the top of the stairs where Mr. and Mrs. Fabrizi stood with their two daughters. The jazz ensemble began a song that Riley recognized as being from Verdi's Rigoletto which wasn't a Christmas song at all, and while no music aficionado, it sounded strange to him on saxophone. The family descended one step at a time to polite applause from the guests. It was an official royal entrance, pompous and pretentious even by Mr. Fabrizi's standards, and Riley wondered why he hadn't hired someone to throw rose petals at them.

The Fabrizi girls were dressed in matching white dresses, something more akin to a Confirmation than a Christmas party, and were the ugliest girls Riley had ever seen. They looked nearly the same age, twelve or thirteen he guessed, and they shared their dad's gruff, masculine facial features – as if someone had surgically removed their father's face and taped it on the bodies of these two girls – right down to his thick and bushy black eyebrows. The family reached the bottom of the stairs and greeted their guests with smiles, each with more theatrical flair than the next, with hugs, tears, and kisses on both the left and right cheeks. As Riley and Mici waited their dutiful turn, someone placed their hand on Riley's shoulder from behind. It was Eli Solomon, Mr. Fabrizi's good friend from Las Vegas.

"Merry Christmas, Mr. Lynch." Eli said with a welcoming and festive spirit.

"Oh! Hello Mr. Solomon. Merry Christmas to you, as well."

"So how was your hunting trip to Las Vegas? Were you successful in snaring your bear?"

"Yes sir, all went exactly to plan."

"Eddie has the highest degree of confidence in you. You impressed me, and I am not easy to impress. And who is this young lady? I think I recognize you... from that Italian restaurant?"

"Yes, sir this is Mici." Mici smiled and bowed her head. Her eyes sparkled. "Mici, this is Mr. Solomon a good friend of Mr. Fabrizi."

Eli kissed her hand. "You will call me Eli, my dear, I insist. Mr. Lynch, you have outstanding taste in restaurants and women. Trust me on this... those are the only two skills you will ever need to succeed in big business."

Mr. and Mrs. Fabrizi were making their way around the room, and made their way toward Riley.

"Heyyy," Mr. Fabrizi said with a smile, placing each of his meaty hands on Riley's shoulders and shaking him with vigor. "Glad you could come. You do remember Riley, don't you Imelda?"

"Oh, of course I do, and Ms. Mantano from Americo's. Thank you both so much for coming this evening." Mrs. Fabrizi's words were proper and polite, and seemed forced.

"Mrs. Fabrizi. This is from my grandfather." Mici handed her an envelope. "It's for your wildlife fund."

"Oh my! Carmine is the most generous man I know after Edward. Please thank him and give him a big kiss for me, dear."

"And here, I brought this." Riley handed her a plastic bowl with a big red bow. "It's a Christmas rum pudding, very popular in my Irish neighborhood at Christmastime."

Imelda held the bowl in her hands like she might hold a bowl full of feces. She scrunched up her nose and looked down on it with a quizzical expression.

"It's Irish?"

"Yes ma'am, and it's delicious."

Mrs. Fabrizi tossed him a short polite smile and handed it off to a passing waiter to deliver to the dining room table, wiping her hands on her legs.

"That was very thoughtful, Riley," Mrs. Fabrizi said. "Very thoughtful." He could tell she was not impressed.

"Hey Eli," Mr. Fabrizi interrupted, poking his good friend with his elbow. "Did Seamus here tell you about his trip to Las Vegas? He did a great job."

Riley froze and replayed the last sentence over in his head, and then replayed it again. Mr. Fabrizi had just called him Seamus. How weird, he thought. Mici giggled, and Eli laughed out loud.

"Don't worry kid, Imelda tells me he doesn't remember her name sometimes, either." Eli joked, and Imelda fired off an evil glare indicating that there may be a morsel of truth in his ribbing.

"If you don't mind, sir, I have to ask, why did you call me Seamus just now?" Riley asked, feeling unsteady. He felt paranoia, like bile, rising in his belly.

"Slip of the tongue is all. I knew a guy... a long time ago. His name was Seamus... Seamus Lynch. You reminded me a little of him just now. I've been drinking eggnog since four this afternoon, so you'll have to forgive me; I'm a little off, but we're still buddies, right?" Mr. Fabrizi smiled and gave him a hug across his shoulders.

Coincidence had not been Riley's ally for a long time, and he saw no reason to believe it was his friend now. Riley's mind was flipping twice as fast as his acidic stomach, and both were starting to throb again. Should he consider that Mr. Fabrizi could have known his father? Or was he being paranoid? There were lots of men named Seamus in the world, and several with a surname of Lynch, his estranged, dead-beat father being just one of them. Riley was still afflicted with a full dose of paranoia over his rental car bill and that mysterious envelope. This didn't help his condition.

Without prompting from the host, the band broke into a quirky jazz rendition of "Dominick the Italian Christmas Donkey" (later Riley heard the band leader was tipped fifty bucks by Eli) to the indignation of the Fabrizis. It took little urging for the alcohol-loosened crowd to break into the low-brow but festive *chingedy-ching, hee haw, hee haw* refrain. The more reserved guests had begun filing into the massive dining room to escape the ruckus and sample the evening's true feature -- the august buffet.

The dining room was long and wide, and a staff of attractive, dark-haired young waiters dashed around laying out the evening's courses. At one end of the room stood the Fabrizis' Christmas tree, so huge it rivaled anything found at Rockefeller Plaza, and it towered over twenty feet high bursting with vibrant color. At the other end of the room was a hand-carved wooden nativity -- called the Presepio -- with dozens of figures so well crafted one might expect them to hop up and start talking, perched along a wide shelf above a fireplace burning a Yule log. A wall of glass looked out over the back yard which stretched down to the private beach. All colors of twinkling lights decorated the long horizon of Manhattan Island. It was as if New York itself was decorated exclusively for this party.

"Before we eat, I want to bring my daughters Cara and Mia in here for a moment." Mr. Fabrizi had once again garnered everyone's silence and attention. His booming voice was not easy to chat over. "The girls will be singing *Tu Scendi Dalle Stelle* for you all this evening."

The sisters took their place in front of the fiery Yule log and broke into song. Their father swelled with pride as they had learned the classic Christmas tune in authentic Italian, or so Riley presumed it was what they were singing. It was clear from the first line that neither girl had been born with the gift of harmony or melody. Their voices were as harsh as their inherited profiles, and it took work to not cringe, cover one's ears or look away. Mici stood next to Riley and took his arm, placing her head on his shoulder. The crowd endured the performance with honor, and broke into uproarious applause upon its merciful completion.

"And now, before we enjoy this great feast, Cara here, the youngest of our family will honor us all by lighting the Christmas candle." Cara held her sterling silver candle lighter up to a white candle planted behind the manger in the Presepio and lit it. The crowd burst into applause once again. Riley pondered his own Christmas Eves back in Irish Southie, and how often he, as the youngest in his family, bore the honor of lighting the Lynch family candle in the front window each year. He felt sad that his East Broadway apartment would be dark on this evening for the first Christmas Eve in a hundred years. There was so much that the Lynch families and Fabrizi families shared, yet they were so different.

Without further invitation, the affluent yet ravenous crowd attacked the buffet table with less grace than vagabonds in a soup kitchen. *La Vigilia* -- The Feast of the Seven Fishes -- may have intended to include seven separate fish dishes, but Riley saw at least a dozen including calamari, cod, shrimp and all matter of smelts and whole fish. To accompany the seafood, the Fabrizis' cooks had prepared at least a dozen wondrous side dishes of pasta, meatballs, roasts, soups, glazed onions and herb roasted potatoes. In the middle of the orgy of food, sat the conspicuous plastic bowl Riley had brought from his dorm room overflowing with rum pudding. Guests were sampling it along with all the other delectable offerings, ignorant of its inferior origins.

Riley charged off in one direction, and Mici in another. Riley overflowed his plate with as many of the culinary delights as he could stack up, as he had not enjoyed a decent meal in weeks. Between the pain in his stomach, the stress, final exams and his dramatic Las Vegas adventure, food had not been a high priority in his life. Mr. Mantano had been accurate in the assessment of his weight loss. And if she knew, his mother would be furious.

As he cleaned his plate of a third helping of calamari and meatballs (and considering a fourth), he felt a warm head lay on his shoulder, and a hand massage the left cheek of his behind. Riley's back stiffened, his heart raced and he gasped. He turned expecting to see a radiant and affectionate Mici, but instead found Katie, Mr. Fabrizi's rigid and dutiful secretary. Katie was much older than Riley, and before this moment, had paid him no attention outside of obligatory shop talk. José had warned him to be wary of her, especially in the presence of an open bar.

"Hi Riley... what about you and me heading upstairs, huh? You look a little tense." Katie smiled and winked, her breath revealing her penchant for salted cod and martinis. Riley winced and recoiled in horror, nearly backing into Mrs. Fabrizi and a friend who were enjoying a heaping portion of rum pudding.

"Oh, Imelda, what is this dish? It is exquisite!"

"It's an old favorite. It's Irish!" Mrs. Fabrizi answered with pride.

"You have such an incredible intercontinental flair! I am so jealous! How do you do it?"

"Hey Riley," Eli interrupted. He didn't know Eli was standing nearby. "I was thinking. Why don't you come out to Las Vegas with me for a couple of weeks this summer? I know what you're thinking.., so I'll talk to Eddie, he won't mind. He owes me a favor. I was thinking about opening another dealership downtown..."

Mr. Fabrizi happened by next. "Riley, I have something for you here. And Eli, you stay put, I want you to hear this, too." He reached into his vest pocket and retrieved a wrinkled and folded piece of paper. "I hold in my hands a check for ten thousand dollars. And Riley, it has your name on it"

Riley's mouth gaped open. But before he could say anything, Mr. Fabrizi continued. "I'll be making a ten thousand dollar donation to Imelda's wildlife fund in your name which, so you know, is the largest donation she has received all year. Congratulations, kid! You're worth it. Merry Christmas."

Strange things were happening way too fast. He felt a rush of anxiety and another sensory overload and wasn't sure what to think or worry about next. He strolled over toward the kitchen to find some cold water or a rush of December air from an open window. When he opened the kitchen door, he was greeted by the sight of Mici in a passionate embrace with one of the waiters. Their bodies were entwined and grinding against the kitchen stove, eyes closed and lips fastened, her hands caressing his back, and his hands caressing her legs and thigh. They were oblivious to his presence, and Riley froze in place, staring in disbelief for several long, painful, excruciating seconds as what was left of the good in his world cart wheeled away from him. The other waiters darted in and out of the kitchen and dining room with dirty dishes and party debris as if the scene were invisible to them. Had Caravaggio been alive, he would have relished painting this tragic scene.

Riley felt a regrettable gurgle in his belly and knew what was about to happen next. He charged through the dining room at breakneck speed, coattails flapping in his wake, through the grand foyer and out the front door. Both Buckner and Hooper were enjoying a cigarette and leftover panforte when Riley screamed by them into the front yard and leaned over the shrubs. It was here Riley vomited his half digested calamari and meatballs into a manicured Japanese boxwood. He had not tried the rum pudding.

For the next hour or so, Riley hid in the dining room behind a great porcelain urn, unwilling to stay but unable to leave, hoping for either his stomach pain to subside or hoping he would succumb to it. Mici didn't show herself again until the bitter end of the evening.

"There you are," Mici said beaming, with rosy cheeks. "I have been looking for you everywhere. I think we should go. Remember, you promised *Nonno* we would not be late tonight."

Without uttering a sound, Riley gathered up their coats and called for the return of the limousine which had been waiting outside. He didn't know what to say to her. On one hand, she had betrayed him. She was his date and she spent it making out with some strange, greasy waiter. On the other hand, there was no formal agreement that they were in fact dating. He used her to get to this party and look important, and she used him for the same reason. Maybe they were even. Maybe he should forget about it. Maybe he should tell Mici he loved her.

"Oh, Riley, this was the most wonderful evening of my life," Mici said, clutching his arm in the back seat of limousine. "It was everything I hoped it would be. Are you OK?"

Riley still had not spoken. "It's my stomach. It'll be fine in a few minutes." His complexion was gray and he could feel his eyes sinking into his skull.

"And I have to tell you who I met," Mici beamed, even more excited than before. "His name is Jerome. He was one of the waiters from the kitchen. I swear he has the sweetest face I have ever seen." Mici sighed and looked up to the heavens. "And he goes to New York University at night."

New York University? Riley thought. *She's impressed by NYU? What about Columbia! Ivy League!*

"And he is studying art history. Isn't that interesting?"

Art History! What's he going to do, move upstate and grow garlic for a living!?

"And Riley, oh! How he could kiss! Oh!"

240

He felt Mici pound the spike deeper into his temple, and his heart was now limp, cold, and approaching death.

"Mici, why are you telling me all this?"

Mici laughed and held his hand. She placed her head back upon his cooling shoulder, breathed deep, and cuddled up close. "Because you are my best friend, silly. I missed you so much after you left Americo's and went to work for Mr. Fabrizi. Now I want you to know everything. Do you think I can tell *Nonno* about my evening? That I was kissing a sweet boy in the kitchen? He would kill me! I don't get to go out much anymore. I don't have many girlfriends because I work so many hours, and ever since that guy hurt me back at Morningside Park, I have been too afraid to date. You took care of me back then. You were the only one who cared about the real me. And I don't know how, but somehow, you knew how badly I wanted to go to this party tonight. You are so sweet. I know you do care about me, don't you?"

"I do, Mici. I do care."

"You are my best friend, Riley."

Riley's watch told him it was midnight. It was Christmas. The limousine was passing over the Robert F. Kennedy Bridge toward Manhattan. Riley prayed it would plunge over the edge into the icy river and kill them both.

TWENTY

"Tell me about that guy you knew named Seamus Lynch?" Riley asked Mr. Fabrizi for the third time that week. Mr. Fabrizi leaned on his elbows, hiding his face with his thick, hairy hands.

"Jesus, kid, you're driving me fucking crazy with this. I told you, I barely knew the guy. I'm sorry I mentioned it, it was just a stupid slip of the tongue, and you're taking it all serious. What did I say to make you think this guy was your father? You want some of this?" Mr. Fabrizi offered him a bite of a half-eaten steak sandwich that oozed melted cheese and grease. When Riley declined, the sandwich disappeared into Mr. Fabrizi's mouth in one bite, and he licked the end of each of his fingers.

"It could all be just a coincidence," Riley admitted. "I don't know. I never knew the man, in fact, I only ever saw one picture of him. My mom raised me alone, with the help of all my brothers and sisters and Mr. Murphy, our neighbor. By the time I was born, he was gone for good. I never knew him, and what happened to him has been a mystery to my whole family."

"Fine, then. Back in the early days -- and you know I hate talkin' about those fucking early days -- right after I bought that old club, the Raw Bar over in Queens. There were a few guys in the West End who helped me with some, uh, you know, creative financing. One of the guys was this guy Seamus, he was a runner for the Westies. All I remember was that he liked coming into my club a lot. He was hot for one of the Ukrainian girls I had dancing there. He couldn't keep his eyes or his hands off her. That's why he reminded me of you I think, it was the way you looked at that Mici girl. It was the same way he looked at that girl -- the exact same expression on his face. You know, it's no fun going to a candy store if you can't suck on some licorice once in a while. I caught him sleeping in the backroom of the club one night and chewed him out. He didn't want to go home. I have no idea where he lived, or with who, but I remember him complaining all the time that his old lady was a royal pain in the ass. She wanted him to be with her and the kids all the time and be a family. He was convinced she was two-timing him while he was away making real money and supporting the family, and it pissed him off. He probably would have put a hit on her if it hadn't been for his kids. He was a fun guy though, always the life of the party. He told a great joke. And man could he drink. That boy could suck down a bottle of whiskey like it was water. Now I ain't saying that he was a drunk because he was Irish or anything, but... he was Irish, after all."

"So what happened to him?"

"I don't know. He went home one weekend and I never saw him again. Maybe he went home to his family."

"Did he go home to Boston?"

"He could have gone home to fucking Timbuktu for all I know." Mr. Fabrizi's thin patience was about gone." That Ukrainian girl disappeared right after that, too. I thought for a while maybe they ran off together somewhere. But that doesn't mean anything. Those Eastern European girls ran off all the time. They cost me a lot of money."

"Is there anything else you remember?"

"What the fuck! You're like talking to a grand jury, and now you're pissing me off. Why don't you go torture Mantano. He knew more of those Irish guys than I ever did."

Riley had come to terms with the absence of his father long ago, even when his brothers and sisters had not. It was hard to miss something he never had. Seamus' disappearance became the stuff of family lore, and as children, his siblings concocted all sorts of tall tales to explain his whereabouts -- he was a secret agent, or on a military expedition, or an explorer travelling the African continent -- ready to call upon his family to join him at any moment. Their mother was uncomfortable when they glorified him, and she discouraged it. But to young, bruised and lonesome hearts, the stories eased their ache and made them smile. At no time did they fantasize he ran off with a Ukrainian stripper. Riley might never know if this acquaintance of Mr. Fabrizi's was his father or not as there was no way to prove anything. But if there was any damning evidence from Mr. Fabrizi's description, it would be all the poor choices

Seamus made -- a genetic deficiency he passed on to all his children. It surprised Riley how much he cared about his father and his disappearance. He didn't think he cared about anything anymore.

Instead of walking back to his dorm room to watch Alvin make-out with his girlfriend of the week, he chose to keep going and strolled over to the Cafe Marie Anne. It had been months since he had visited last, and outside of a freshman crop of skinny girls lining up for lattes, he couldn't remember what he liked about the place. And even they didn't interest him anymore. He ordered a cup of green tea, turned off his cell phone, then sat at the corner table behind a plastic fern and stared out the window. He hated green tea, but Riley figured if he was to spend the evening despondent, he would compound his misery every way imaginable. And there was such a rich, eclectic menu of misery in his life to ponder.

After enjoying a few hours of torture and self-pity, he grew weary and started the trek back home. The late December wind was harsh and biting, and felt more painful to him in the dark than it had been earlier. Off on a bench, a homeless man lay bundled and still. It was a sad and depressing sight and he wondered in this bitter cold if the poor man could survive the night. There had been a time in Riley's life when he would have stopped, or at least alerted the authorities, but there was a crack in his soul and his compassion and care had leaked out. He was aware he didn't care, and it worried him.

"Where the hell have you been, Riley?' Alvin was beside himself with frustration, and the accusatory tone reminded Riley of his mother chastising him for returning late after hanging out with his childhood friends. Alvin paced across the room, hands in his hair, as if trying to pull clumps of it out. "There was a big fire!"

"What fire?"

"I tried to call you, I did. You didn't answer your phone."

"What are you talking about, Alvin?" Alvin switched on the TV. Riley stood absorbed in stunned horror.

An elderly man is missing tonight following a five alarm blaze in the city's West End. Fire ripped through Americo's, a popular Italian restaurant, earlier this evening during the busy dinner hour, but all patrons are believed to have escaped safely. Police tell us that the restaurant's owner, Carmine Mantano, 71, is missing at this hour and is feared not to have escaped the fire. Fire officials tell us the blaze is believed to have started in a receptacle by the front door. The restaurant is a total loss, as well as an adjacent gift shop and several upstairs apartments. Americo's Restaurant had recently been listed for sale, and the fire has been classified as suspicious by the city fire marshal. The block is considered a crime scene at this hour. The Red Cross is also at the scene assisting displaced families.

You are now looking at pictures live from the scene...

Riley fell to the floor and lay on his stomach. He clenched the carpet with both fists and ejected horrific muffled scream after horrific muffled scream into the worn and stained fabric. Alvin sat next to him and wept, heartbroken for his friend, placing a compassionate hand on Riley's back. The television showed video of the neighborhood that included the flashing lights of emergency vehicles, gawking theater goers and the restaurant's blackened and smoldering exterior, hardly recognizable as the posh eatery it had been. Riley could hear, but couldn't bear to look, and with each sentence the reporter uttered, Riley would pound the floor and wail louder. Poor Mr. Mantano, he thought. Riley couldn't bear to lose anyone else. And then a deeper wave of horror swept over him -- he thought of Mici.

Riley shot up and brushed the tears and snot off his face with his forearm. He worked hard to locate his breath, and fumbled through his pockets for his cell phone. His hands were sweaty and they shook as he dialed and knelt on the floor with the phone clutched against his cheek, rocking back and forth. Alvin held him, both young men whimpering, praying Mici would answer on the other end. The line rang and rang, but Riley could only reach her recorded message. He tried again. And again. And after the fourth attempt, he fired the cell phone across the room and into the kitchen, skipping it across the table like a flat stone on a serene pond.

Riley jumped up, shoving Alvin aside. He snatched the phone off the floor and charged toward the door.

"Where are you going?" Alvin asked. "I will come with you."

"No, stay here," Riley responded, barely intelligible. " I need to be alone."

Riley took a cab from Amsterdam Avenue to Mr. Mantano and Mici's apartment, and chastised the clueless and indifferent driver for driving too slow. He ran to the door and rang the bell, but no one answered. He paced around in circles and rang the bell again, expecting a different result, and then he pounded on the door in frustration with his fists and swore at the top of his lungs. A police officer watched his suspicious actions from a car parked across the street and approached him from behind.

"Is something wrong? The officer asked.

"Are they OK? I just want to know they're OK," rambled Riley.

"Who are you talking about?"

"The Mantano's. From the fire! There was a big fire."

"I know, but I don't have any information about the fire. Who are you?"

"Does it matter?"

"I think you should show me some identification."

"I think you should fuck off."

"What's your problem, kid? Look, I'll give you one more chance before we have an issue here. I want your ID... now." Riley noticed the officer's hand had moved to the handle of his service revolver. At that moment, Riley would have welcomed a fight with anyone, armed or not, but he wanted Mici more. He clenched his teeth, acquiesced and turned over his license. The officer kept him spread-eagle against his patrol car for a while as he checked out Riley and his story, and the officer let him go with nothing more than a threatening, obscenity-laced warning.

By the time Riley arrived at the charred remains of the restaurant, it was late. All the pedestrians were gone and the street was closed off to traffic with long wooden police barriers. The bulky stench of fresh, wet carbon hung in the air. Debris was visible ahead in the street including a stool from Americo's bar, and much of the water used to douse the blaze now laid like a frozen blanket on the sidewalks, and hung like holiday decorations from the wires and trees of neighboring establishments. A public works truck was spreading sand on the pavement and sidewalks where the ice was thickest, and the front of the restaurant was visible, blackened and painted thick with fresh soot. He was surprised to find there was no investigation underway, and no coroner present, and only a solitary police car guarded the awful scene. Had they found the body already? Could Mr. Mantano have escaped and still be alive? Riley stared at the scene in a combination of reflection and loneliness. He could not bear to turn away. He had promised himself he would look after Mici

246

and he had failed. He had failed to look after his mother, too. In fact, he believed he had failed every family member and friend he cared about since middle school.

Riley spent the next several days in bed. He barely ate, didn't shower and spoke only when necessary. During his waking hours, the television was his only companion, and he scoured news reports hoping for more information on the fire investigation and the whereabouts of Mr. Mantano. After a few days, the reports became fewer as the media had moved on to other crimes, a murder and banal political bantering. Alvin had learned to give Riley a wide berth and stopped talking to him. Riley would rarely answer anyway, and Alvin spent as little time as possible in the dorm room. Classes had resumed for the second semester of his senior year at Columbia, Riley was a no-show at all of them, and a concerned Professor Friedman left a daily message that he never returned. Professor Friedman had always been one of Riley's biggest allies, but even that bridge was smoldering. At LSE, he told Hose-B he had the flu and needed a few days of sick time. Mr. Fabrizi knew better, understood Riley was mourning and extended whatever time off he felt he needed. Mr. Fabrizi was also as disturbed by the alleged arson at America's Restaurant as anyone, and whether the suspicions of the fire marshal were confirmed or not, he knew who had to be responsible for the fire.

Hours passed, and days passed. Messages he continued to leave for Mici remained unreturned. Even an unexpected phone call from Malcolm to report that his sister Siobhan had been granted parole and would be released in the next few days gave him no relief from his hopelessness. Malcolm was excited and he rambled on and on about someone who helped him execute some complicated legal maneuver, but Riley didn't care and wasn't listening. The room had become a pig sty and reeked of rotting food and body odor. Alvin was threatening to throw Riley out in the snow, have the room fumigated, and then change the locks. In his darker moments, Riley would remember Alvin's gun and the bullets stored in the kitchen, though he knew he was too much a coward to use them on himself or anyone else.

His phone rang again. Each time he heard the tone, he prayed it was Mici returning his call, and each time it wasn't his heart sank deeper. This time, it was just Hose-B.

"Riley, you need to come down to the office, right away."

"I'm sick. I am going back to sleep."

"No, Mr. Fabrizi wants you here right away. He told me to send a car to come get you. This is something big."

"Tell him I can't."

"You can tell him yourself when you get here. The car will be there in ten minutes."

Riley threw down his phone in anger and stumbled out of bed. He pulled on a pair of sweats and his slippers, and walked to the bathroom. He didn't recognize the dreary, emaciated, unshaven creature who looked back at him in the mirror. He attempted to run a comb through his hair and it got stuck in the mangle of dark knots on the back of his head. He threw a tantrum and brushed all the toiletries off the bathroom counter and onto the floor. A shampoo bottle lost its lid and leaked its contents across the tile. Alvin would be pissed. There was a knock at his door -- the driver had already arrived.

The car carried him to LSE headquarters. Riley walked down the long hallways that led to Mr. Fabrizi's big office looking like a street bum, and each employee stopped what they were doing to gawk at his disheveled sight. Riley mused that if they hated him then, they must love him now. Katie escorted him into Mr. Fabrizi's office and he took a seat on an animal-print chair. A moment later, Mr. Fabrizi and José appeared. José's presence concerned him -- he only showed up when Mr. Fabrizi wanted to fire or hire somebody, or there was a serious corporate issue to deal with. He accepted that Hose-B's assumption that something big was happening was dead-on correct.

The door closed, sealing them in and there was a moment of uncomfortable silence. Riley felt the stress and tension levels in the room rise. Mr. Fabrizi took a deep breath, stood, and began to speak. To Riley, the scene looked stiff and rehearsed.

"Riley, I'm going to ask you a question, and I'm only going to ask it once so I want you to think a moment before you answer. I don't think you have ever lied to me, so I will accept and believe whatever you say to me right now as truth. Is that clear?"

"Yes sir, I understand." Riley didn't recall ever lying to Mr. Fabrizi. He had no intention of starting now.

"Did you pull a gun on Romano in Las Vegas?"

"No sir."

"Are you sure you want that to be your answer?" Riley could tell Mr. Fabrizi was holding back.

"It was a package of antacids, sir." José and Mr. Fabrizi scrunched up their noses and looked at one another, confused by his response.

"Did you say antacids?"

"Yes, sir."

Mr. Fabrizi's heavy body fell back down into his leather chair with a thud and he stroked his face again. He looked out the window, then at Riley, then at José. Then he looked up at the ceiling as if pleading to a higher power.

"My company... is going bankrupt, and I am going to go to prison, over a package of antacids. Un-fucking believable." Mr. Fabrizi slammed his desk again, startling both José and Riley.

"What the fuck did you think you were doing?!" Mr. Fabrizi screamed at the top of his lungs. Riley had heard him scream at employees before, but never at him. And his psyche was in no mood for it, so he screamed right back.

"I was getting your stupid, fucking contract signed. That's what the fuck I was doing!"

In his younger days, Mr. Fabrizi might have made a fist and clocked him. No one screamed at the CEO of Lafayette Street Enterprises and walked out of the room to tell about it. But though Mr. Fabrizi was uneducated, he was no fool, and he saw the fire in Riley's eyes and his seething, uncontrollable anger. He had sensed the situation was escalating and he might lose control. Losing control was less acceptable than being screamed at.

"José, why don't you leave the two of us alone for a minute." Mr. Fabrizi asked calmly, and José complied. Once José was out the door, he looked Riley in the eye.

"Look at you, you look like hell. What's this all about?"

Riley had never had a father sit down with him and chew him out for breaking a window with his baseball, or denting the fender on the family car. He surmised it must feel much like this.

"It's the fire. Mr. Mantano and Mici. And it's a lot of other things." Riley confessed.

"Well I will tell you, you look like hell and smell like shit. Where is your self-respect? You are a smart kid, you know better than this."

"Yes sir, I know."

"Then why the act? And you know what? I'm not buying it. I know it's an act. You can't bullshit me. I know what that restaurant and the Mantano's meant to you, they were like your family. I don't mind telling you it broke my heart, and Imelda's too, when we heard the news about Americo's. I was stunned, I couldn't believe it either. So now, you tell me.... are you feeling sorry for them, or are you feeling sorry for yourself? This is all bullshit if you ask me." Mr. Fabrizi paused and Riley didn't respond. He could see Riley was hurting. "Have you heard anything from Mici or Carmine at all?"

"No sir, not a word."

"Sad. And very suspicious."

"But I know who did it." Riley exclaimed, surprised at even his own candor. "It was Marcellino."

Mr. Fabrizi looked concerned, and Riley wasn't sure if it was because Mr. Fabrizi believed him or Mr. Fabrizi thought he was insane.

"Riley, why do you say such a thing? You're talking crazy. Do you know something?"

"Mr. Mantano had been under pressure to close the restaurant, Marcellino's organization wanted to buy the building. Some of Marcellino's men came and threatened his staff one day. They even took Mici out and roughed her up. Mr. Mantano told me he was handling it and not to get involved. And you want to know something else? Marcellino was behind the Hanratty murder in Hoboken. Remember that one?"

Mr. Fabrizi looked very concerned. "Marcellino's little empire has grown from coast to coast too fast, he's out of control. When the feds shut down most of the mob operations years ago, it left a void and he just stepped right in. I don't care how much investment law enforcement puts into wiping out these criminals, there will always be the next dirt bag ready to take their place. There's just too much fame and money in it. But you gotta tell me, why do you know all this?"

"I just do."

"There you go again, you're pissing me off. You think I was born yesterday? Riley, you are like a son to me. Ever since I met you I thought, that's the kind of son I wish I had -- smart, polite, hard-working. I was blessed with two daughters, but I will never have a real son, Imelda and I are getting too old. In my family, having son --

a true male heir -- means everything. My girls will never have the same influence as a son would. So Cara and Mia will inherit this business from me someday. I do all this for them, no one else. And I hope when they are old enough, there will be good people here like you to show them the way, advise them, and look after their interests."

"Yes sir."

"And now I sit here and look at you, and you come to me a pathetic piece of shit. Am I supposed to put my family and girls' future in your hands? Look at you! You can't even comb your own goddamn hair."

"I'm sorry sir."

"Do you have any idea what I have been through in my life? I have had partners killed, I have been to prison, I have had a gun put to my throat and had my life threatened more than once. I have had to make decisions that you couldn't possibly even imagine. But I stayed strong, and it made me stronger."

"I am not as strong as you are. I never will be. This is too much for me to handle."

"I had hoped that you being so smart, you would understand more, and that big fucking brain of yours would keep you away from these problems. I never made it out of grade school and I have regretted that my whole life. Imagine how successful I could be if I was educated, if I had learned more. You have no excuse."

"You didn't call me in here today to yell at me about this. You called me here to find out what happened with Romano?"

"Marcellino is bullshit right now. He says I walked into his territory and pulled a gun on one of his associates, threatening to kill him. I can't believe you put me in this position, Riley, of all people that I trusted. He wants an explanation or I can expect him to retaliate. He could shut down the club in Vegas which would cost me millions, or worse. I don't need this shit. I worked years to stay clear of assholes like him and stay clean. Now I have to figure out how to fix this... how to make this right."

"Let me do it. I can fix this."

"No. You're all done with me and LSE. But I'm not going to fire you. You are going to be re-assigned to help Imelda with her foundation. She likes to help the wildlife, you know, like lions and bunnies and all those other animals, and you could do a lot to clean up her books and find more donations."

"What? No! I want to stay here!"

"No. You have proven to me you can't handle it. But I am not going to ruin you by just firing you."

"You need me here." Riley was right, he was needed in the office, and was the only person who not only knew the overall financial picture of the corporation, but also appreciated the former relationship Mr. Fabrizi had with the old underworld.

"I've made up my mind. I am heading out this afternoon to meet Marcellino in Boston. He's flying in from Vegas tomorrow to close some real estate deals, and I'm going to see what he is willing to accept from me as an apology."

"You can't do that. You know you can't be seen in public with a known criminal mob boss. Your whole company could be called into question. Everything you have worked for would be in jeopardy."

"What choice have you left me now?"

"You need to send me. Let me meet with Marcellino and talk to him. I will explain what happened, tell him it was all my fault, that I was acting on my own, and you had nothing to do with it. I will fall on my sword and beg for his forgiveness. I'll offer him anything he wants to make it better. This way, you'll get what you need and stay out of the spotlight. What chance do I have of rebuilding my self-esteem if you don't give me the chance to make this all right?"

Mr. Fabrizi considered what he was saying, mulling it over in his mind, and Riley sensed he was uncomfortable with making this decision. Riley knew Mr. Fabrizi hated leaving the comforts of New York City for any reason. He turned away from Riley and looked out his window at the sunny Manhattan skyline and sharp blue sky, and twirled a silver pen between his fingers.

"Alright, go to Boston. Pick Marcellino up at Logan Airport tomorrow and take him out to dinner. Don't screw around and don't go anywhere else. When you get back, though, you're still going to work for Imelda for a while. At least until I know I can trust you again."

Riley was given the company car and he went back to his room to clean himself up and pack an overnight bag. Mr. Fabrizi's words stung him, and he rolled them over in his mind again and again, piercing him each time. But even in this final bit of trust he had been extended, he found no solace. The center of the evil in his world was Marcellino, and fate now had him escorting Marcellino to dinner. He walked into the kitchen and retrieved Alvin's gun and bullets, considering solving this problem once and for all, for everyone's benefit. They would be alone in the car and he would have a gun. No more misery. Riley took a handful of cartridges and rolled them around in his hand like jellybeans -- he found them to have a surprising, calming effect. After enjoying his few moments of dark fantasy, Riley dropped the bullets back into their box and put the handgun away back into its safe hiding place. He would not be killing Marcellino.

That was crazy thinking.

TWENTY-ONE

R iley arrived in Boston as the frenzied evening rush of traffic was dissipating, and he looked around at the sights like a first-time tourist. The Boston city landscape was so different than New York's, it felt closer and more intimate, and he felt several conflicting emotions about being home. He checked into the luxurious Boston Harbor Hotel right away as he would need an upscale and comfortable place to suck-up to Marcellino the next day. But before heading up to his room, he walked through the hotel's great golden arch to gaze across Boston Harbor. He didn't want to be isolated while his mind was still so active. The wind was still and the sky was clear, and he walked along Rowe's Wharf as the planes flew in and out of Logan Airport across the still, cold water of the harbor. As a child he would think about the hundreds of passengers and hundreds of planes that would fly in and out of the busy airport each day, and he would try to assign an adventure story to each of them. The Lynch family never had enough money to travel or fly anywhere and as a child he was often jealous of them all. He watched a flight take off for an unknown, distant destination. He was jealous of them all over again, except now for a different reason.

Riley sat in the airport and waited for flight 755 from Las Vegas to arrive. Passengers darted back and forth in front of him as he sat in the uncomfortable plastic seat that was bruising his tail bone and making his legs ache. His stomach was acting up again, and he thought of finding himself a cup of tea, however the line at the coffee shop behind him was thirty people deep and he didn't have the patience to stand and wait. He felt fidgety, and he swore he saw the same person zigzag back and forth in front of him more than a dozen times and it annoyed him. In fact, everyone in the airport annoyed him.

Riley's cell phone rang, and his caller ID told him it was from an unknown source. He fumbled and answered fast. He still clung to hope that he would hear from Mici and learn that she and her grandfather were somewhere safe and sound.

"Hello, Riley? It's Lorenzo. Remember me?"

Riley shot up from his torturous chair and cupped the phone over his mouth. He had not spoken to Lorenzo since he left Americo's.

"Lorenzo? What do you want?" Riley asked, annoyed by the interruption. He was not in the mood to speak to anyone.

"I need to talk to you. Can we meet somewhere?"

"Lorenzo, I'm in Boston. I won't be back for a couple of days. Do you know where Mici is? Did they find Mr. Mantano?"

"I don't know anything. No one is talking about it like it's some kind of big secret. I don't think the old man made it out of that fire. But Riley, I need to talk to you about something else."

"Then where is Mici? Have you seen her? Is she OK?"

"The last I saw her she was hysterical. That little girl is strong, I'll tell ya. It took three New York City firefighters to hold that spitfire back from going back in that burning building after the old man. She fought a couple of them off and almost made it inside more than once. I think she broke the nose of one of them. The last I saw her, she was upside down and they were stuffing her into the back of a police car. Man, that girl can scream." Lorenzo's comments were cool and unemotional.

"Where did they take her?'

"No idea. I went home. It was a bad night. But Riley, I need to talk to you about something else."

"What the hell happened, Lorenzo? How did the fire start?" Riley refused to let the conversation wander away from the fire. He could hear Lorenzo become frustrated and sigh.

"We were shorthanded that night. Armand didn't show up for some stupid ass reason. Everyone was at each other's throats all night. The fire started near the front door, so it was slow getting out. The place filled up with smoke fast. A few people made it out the back door and got trapped back there because the alley was blocked and there was no way around the building. Mantano kept going back in looking for more people, then the last time he went in, he didn't come back out. It was total chaos."

Riley felt his throat swell and the tears welled up inside him again, but he couldn't lose his composure with Marcellino expected to step off his flight at any moment.

"Was it an accident?" Riley asked.

"What are you asking me? Are you asking me did Mantano set it for insurance money or something? No, no I don't believe he would do that while we were inside. Now are you asking me did someone else like Marcellino or his thugs set it? Who the fuck knows. I didn't see anything, and wouldn't tell you or the police if I did."

Riley could tell that Lorenzo hadn't changed. He was still an ass.

"Riley, look. I need to talk to you about something else. I need a job."

"You need a job? How can I get you a job?"

"I know you work for that Fabrizi wiseguy. Help me get my foot in the door over there. Fabrizi and his wife used to like me, too. My girlfriend had a little baby boy on Christmas Eve. I really need the cash right now -- I'm dying. The economy in the city sucks and there aren't any jobs anywhere. I've been knocking on doors since the day after the fire. For old times' sake, I thought you could help me out."

"Maybe it would be easier to find a job if you would stop being an asshole."

"Oh come on, kid. Do you have any idea how hard this is? I'm begging you, man. I'm on my knees here. Help me out. I'll make it up to you."

Riley searched his memory for one favor Lorenzo ever did for him, or one act of random kindness he ever saw Lorenzo deliver to anyone. "How are you going to make this up to me?"

"I know this girl. She works out of a club in Queens called the Raw Bar, she used to be a big porn star. I can get you a private session with her for free, I know her personally. Her name is Aurora, and she's incredible. She's got these huge ...."

Riley threw his phone at a trash can and it shattered. A few travelers looked at him with concern and a few others moved away. He shot them all threatening stares. At least he would not be bothered by any more inane phone calls.

Giovanni Marcellino was the first off his plane from Las Vegas and through the gate with the first class passengers. Riley had not seen him since Mr. Murphy's funeral sitting alone at the back of the church, but recognized him right away. He was an immense man, tipping the scales at almost four hundred pounds Riley guessed, and his suit was wrinkled and twisted around him like the stripes on a candy cane. The legs of his pants were too short, exposing his scaly-yellowed skin, short orthopedic socks and worn oversized brown loafers. Despite his wealth and influence, he looked like a slob.

"Mr. Marcellino?"

"Are you my driver?"

"Yes sir. My name is Riley."

"Where is Fabrizi?"

"He's not here. He sent me in his place."

"What? Who are you then? Are you Eddie Fabrizi's son?"

Riley paused for a moment thinking it amusing that he could be mistaken for his son, especially since he and Mr. Fabrizi looked nothing alike.

"Yes sir, I am Riley Fabrizi. Mr. Fabrizi's oldest son." Riley lied without thinking of the consequences.

"Nice to meet you. But I have to admit, I'm a little annoyed your father didn't come meet me in person like he told me he would."

"I know. He apologizes for the confusion. A big business deal came up at the last minute and he couldn't break away from it, so he sent me in his place."

"Eddie always did put money first. Whatever. It doesn't matter to me. I am closing on two properties tomorrow in South Boston, so I planned to be here anyway." Marcellino pulled a rolled up magazine out from under his arm and threw it on the floor near the trash can. He noticed Riley was a little put off by the rudeness of the act.

"Oh, come on now. They pay the monkeys good money to pick up trash in this place. I'm just keeping somebody employed." Marcellino laughed an evil laugh, and Riley smiled, going along with him as if he agreed.

"Mr. Marcellino, I made you and I dinner reservations at the restaurant in the Boston Harbor Hotel for seven o'clock tonight."

"That sounds good. I can't wait to hear your father's explanation for the stunt he pulled on me in Vegas last month. I always enjoy a good story."

"Yes sir. I understand. It was all a big misunderstanding..."

"No, stop. Don't tell me now, wait until later. With Eddie, there's always drama. I want to enjoy it with a cold glass of beer. For now, I need to go visit the properties I will be closing on. I have a couple of million dollars on the line in this city. I want to go down and take a look at them before I sit with the lawyers tomorrow."

"I can drive you sir. As it happens, I know the area pretty well."

Riley's car left the bumper-to-bumper traffic of the interstate and cruised down the ramp into Dorchester as if the car had been set on autopilot and knew the way all along. Marcellino sat in the passenger seat with his greasy reading glasses perched on the tip of his nose thumbing through paperwork and maps trying to determine exactly where his two new properties were located. He had been quiet since they left the airport, the silence broken only by the heavy man's wheezing as he exhaled.

"Do you know where Telegraph Street would be? I can't find it on the friggin' map."

"Yes. It's behind the South Boston High School near Columbus Park. I'll take you right over there."

"How come a New York City *Guido* kid like you knows all these old Boston city back streets?"

"I know a few people here, that's all. I have spent a lot of time in this part of the city."

"A little red-headed girlfriend, I'll bet. Why else would you hang around this dump."

"There are people here I used to care about." Riley took offense at Marcellino's insult, but dared not show it.

"You sound like your old man. He was too sentimental to make it in the old days. He'd fall in love, want to get married and settle down with some slut he'd known for one night. Women always get in the way of good business."

"I believe that as long as I can pick good restaurants and good women, I can succeed anywhere."

"I love it! Now that's the Eddie Fabrizi I remember. You sound just like him. Your father was something in the old days. He was one of the best. It broke my heart when he turned state's evidence, the bastard. But you know what? And don't tell him I said this – but I don't blame him. I almost envy him. He has a nice son like you, and a nice family. Oh... how's your mother? Imelda was such a pain in the ass. I have no idea what he saw in her."

Riley was amazed at how he could so casually insult Imelda to his face when he believed she was his mother. He was finding many reasons to hate Marcellino with each passing moment.

"She's great. Just great. When I get back, I'll be helping her raise money for her wildlife foundation."

"Oh that Imelda. A heart of gold but a personality like black coal."

"And I have two sisters, Cara and Mia. They both act just like her."

"Oh no! Ha, ha, ha! I feel bad for you and your father now! And what the hell was he thinking naming you Riley, like some piece of drunken Irish trash?"

Riley had to think quick on his feet. "It's short for Rialto. Riley is just a nickname some school kids gave me at school and it stuck."

"Rialto Fabrizi. Nice old-school ring to it. Does your father talk much about the old days?"

"Yes, all the time. He tells me everything." Riley felt he was gaining Marcello's trust. If he had any prayer of getting him to forget about the Romano incident, he had to continue to play the game and press on.

"Those were exciting times back then, not like today. We lived on the edge of the law every minute of every day. It was violent, too. You got your point across with your gun, and you had better know how to use it. It was the language of the streets."

"It seems to me those times are coming back. There has been a lot of violence in Boston and New York lately."

"There's violence everywhere, but nothing like the old days. You see today, all you have to do is point a finger and the law comes running. They're just out to grab headlines. And you got this whole melting pot of petty thugs, they're like insects, little bugs scurrying around, too stupid to get out of their own way. So now if you need to vacate a building, you don't shoot anybody, you just tell the police they're selling drugs and they clean them out for you. Piece of cake."

"I know what you mean. Set up all the Blacks and Hispanics. Get them thrown in jail." Riley said, playing along.

"Oh yes, and don't forget these Irish here in Boston. They came here as immigrants like the Italians, but they never moved beyond these ugly old neighborhoods. I'm doing a public service cleaning them out for everybody else. It's my contribution to urban renewal."

Riley stopped the car on Telegraph Street as Marcellino requested, a few blocks from the apartment where Siobhan and Alberto were arrested, and Marcellino exited the car to survey the property. It didn't appear he know what he was looking at, like someone kicking the tires of a used car to determine its drivability. He paced along the sidewalk back and forth in front of the building, pulling up his pants at the waist every third step when they started to slip down. Riley found him repulsive in every way imaginable, and his anger simmered beneath his unemotional exterior. The simple physical activity of pacing appeared to tire Marcellino, and he flopped back into the car, breathing heavy and wheezing.

"It's a nice piece of property. It will make a fine addition to the City Point Properties portfolio. I'm buying it from this guy who owns another property in New York -- his other property is an apartment building with a restaurant downstairs. He didn't want to sell that property to me either out of respect for his long time restaurant tenant -- a senile old mob capo. Not a good business decision on his part. He needed a little coaxing and persuasion to understand I was serious. There was a big, mysterious fire in that restaurant a couple of weeks ago, now the building is crap. He calls me all upset in tears, calling me all sorts of things. But it worked, and it convinced him to change his mind about this one -- this was the building I really wanted all along." Marcellino's expression was one of satisfaction, like the cat that swallowed the canary.

"A fire? In New York? It was that restaurant by the Six Star Theatre in the West End, wasn't it?"

"Yea.., how did you know that?"

"I watch a lot of TV."

"You kids today should read more books."

Riley was horrified and furious that Mr. Marcellino's death would be no more than a footnote to a real estate sale. His stomach hurt as much as it ever had.

So did you set it?" Riley asked, clenching his fists and staring straight ahead.

"If you were anybody other than Eddie's kid I would smack you in the mouth for asking me a question like that. What do you think?"

"I heard somebody died in there."

"Well, that's the price of doing business. Now, let's go over to East Broadway. Do you know where that is or do you need my map?"

Riley knew exactly where it was. It was his neighborhood. They were going to look at his old apartment building. His knuckles were white on the steering wheel and his jaw hurt from clenching his teeth.

Seeing his old neighborhood again made Riley feel even more anxious and uneasy. He wanted to be anywhere but here, and he resisted the urge to park the car and just run. Riley drove around the block and passed St. Finian's Church first. It looked exactly the same as it had when he was little, exact perhaps a bit smaller somehow. Then down the block a little farther he passed Gulliver's Pub where Sean had been arrested with his friends, and he noticed the old pawn shop next door had gone out of business. And then they passed the used car lot where Montgomery Meeks used to have his modest law practice and where his sweet little daughter Tammy used to hide from the bullies. Riley picked up the aroma of garlic and was reminded of Theodora's Greek Restaurant and craved the rich flavor of their world-class, magical pizza. Riley pulled the car up to Mr. Murphy's vacant bookshop and parked close against the curb. The building had been cleaned and painted, and looked as nice as he ever remembered it. Marcellino hopped out of the car and looked in the windows, fogging the cold glass with his hot breath as he peered into the darkened shop. Satisfied after only a few moments of looking around, he hopped back into the vehicle.

"There used to be a bookshop here," Marcellino explained. "A guy named Murphy owned it. I've been in this neighborhood once before. A lot of crazy people live around here." Marcellino chuckled.

"Oh, I can believe that." Riley stared straight ahead, fearful he wouldn't be able to contain his frustration or his tongue. He feared he would lash out at any moment.

"Hey Riley, you're gonna love this story. This guy Murphy, I'll tell ya, he was a piece of work. Over twenty years ago, he rents out the apartment over the bookstore to this young Irish couple. He finds out after that they got connections to the Westies gang in New York, and he catches a lot of grief from the Winter Hill Gang here in Boston, of which he is a member.

"They were Westies?" Riley knew he was speaking of his parents Seamus and Sarah, but his mother had always denied the gangs had any influence in the family.

"Yea, they were trying to get a foothold in New England. Really pissed off the locals. Hey, I'm hungry. Let's go find that restaurant you were talking about."

261

Riley pulled away from the curb and headed away from his neighborhood. He took his time. Part of him wanted to stay. Part of him had never wanted to leave.

"So Murphy gets the hots for this girl. He can't stop thinking about her. You know the kind. Every night he's downstairs in the shop and hears the guy kicking the shit out of her upstairs. They still end up with a shitload of kids, you know these people breed like friggin' rats. The girl can't take the abuse anymore and one day asks for his help."

"Why are you telling me all this?" Riley was getting upset, and his hands were shaking. He wanted Marcellino to stop but didn't want to blow his cover, either.

"Listen... this is a great story. Your father will get a kick out of this, too. So Murphy gets a video camera and hides behind their bedroom closet. He videotapes the guy beating the crap out of the girl every night. I don't know if they tried to blackmail the guy or if they were taking the tape to the police, but the guy finds the video tapes hidden in the wall of the apartment and threatens to kill them both."

"Why do you know these things?" Riley could feel his heart trying to burst from his chest.

"Because that's when Murphy calls me. He wants to put a hit on this guy for beating up his own wife, because his own gang is too chicken shit to upset the Westies. Now here's the funny part -- I already got a call from the guy wanting me to put a hit on Murphy!"

"You find that funny?"

"If I could have figured out how to get paid from them both after they were dead, I might have done it. I was still young and already a made man, so I didn't need to get caught up in that shit -- and then have two Irish gangs pissed off at me at the same time? Screw that. I told them both they were on their own."

"You were a made man? Was that because of the DelVecchio hit in New York?" Riley could see Marcellino liked to brag.

Holy shit, your father does tell you everything. No one was ever arrested for the DelVecchio incident."

"But everyone knows you did it."

"Shit, you are a pain in the ass just like your old man. Just let me finish this story. The guy ends up dead, and I don't hear from Murphy for twenty years..."

"The guy is dead?" Riley's head spun around.

"... then all of a sudden Murphy wants a big loan from me for his store that's failing. I guess I was feeling nostalgic, because I authorize it through City Point Properties. I know his little girl in China has big bucks, so I am pretty confident I'll see my money again. Plus I got my eyes on this sweet location and can have it almost free if he defaults. It was just a matter of time, of waiting him out."

"At some point, his daughter runs dry on cash and he can't pay the loan. So he calls me up and tries to blackmail me, that bastard. He says if I forgive the loan, he won't tell the police I killed that guy twenty years ago. I told him, I didn't kill anybody and you can go tell the police whatever the fuck you want to."

"So who killed him?"

"So we chat for a while and he says he knows I did the hit. He knows this because the girl who he has been shacking up with now for twenty years, the guy's wife, told him she hired me. He even helped her bury the poor bastard's body under the floor boards in the stockroom of the bookstore. And then the guy starts screaming and crying into the phone when he figures it out. She completed the hit herself to get rid of her husband and lied to him about it."

"So then you killed Murphy?"

"Oh hell, no. Why would I do that? I wanted to stay as far away from this mess as I could. Besides, I didn't need to. Murphy confronts her about it and one of her little brats hears the argument. He takes it upon himself to protect his mother and he drives a car right over the guy in front of his own house. Nasty mess. I heard the kid was distraught and ended up hanging himself later on. And they call me a criminal! Isn't this story hysterical? I love this stuff!"

Riley's attention was on anything but driving when a speeding car shot from a side street cutting him off. Riley shrieked and tires screeched, his car lurched to the left and came up on two wheels, then Riley over reacted and spun the steering wheel to the right. Marcellino flopped about like a rag doll, his arms and papers flying out of control in all directions. And then without warning, Marcellino's door flipped open and his big round carcass rolled out the open door like an evil humpty dumpty. Riley instinctively reached out to grab him and keep him from falling, but was only able to grab his left shoe as his body disappeared out the door. Marcellino bounced off the pavement, rolled once, and his bulbous, sweaty head slid under the right rear tire of Riley's automobile..

Riley stopped the car a few feet ahead. He had struck his face on something during the chaos of the accident and his nose was bleeding. Adrenaline had filled his veins and he shook all over and couldn't catch his breath. He closed his eyes for a moment and thought he might throw up or pass out. He looked behind his car through the side mirror but could only see Marcelino's stocking feet. He heard a woman scream, scream, then scream again louder. He noticed a crowd of bystanders with horrified expressions gathering around his vehicle. Frenzied people were darting around dialing cell phones. Many of the people were averting their eyes and looking away, and one man was on all fours vomiting.

Riley exited the car and staggered to where Marcellino lay in the street. The top of his head and forehead had been flattened, one of his eyes was missing, and the other was bugged out from the pressure. An advancing puddle of brain and blood stretched around him like a ghoulish halo. Marcellino's right leg flinched in a spasm, as did his right hand, and Riley looked toward his face. His lone eye shifted and looked up at him. Riley recalled reading in school that cockroaches could live for hours without a head. He surmised Marcellino, now dead, had proven his heritage.

Riley leaned over the trunk of his car and laughed.

TWENTY-TWO

Riley waited alone in an antiseptic white room for his attorney Malcolm Ward. His wrists and ankles were shackled, and the room was empty except for a table and two black chairs. A bored prison guard waited outside. Alone with only his thoughts, he reviewed in his mind what he wanted to discuss with his attorney. He knew that even though he had been charged with first degree murder and had been denied bail, he was no murderer. Marcellino's demise had been an accident -- plain and simple. It was just a matter of time before everyone would understand the truth.

Malcolm walked into the room, flopped his briefcase on the table, and sat. Riley could tell from his flat expression that he wasn't happy.

"The judge has set a trial date of August first. It will give us plenty of time to prepare a defense, unless of course, I can convince you to change your plea."

"I pled innocent because I am innocent." Riley insisted. "I will not change my plea."

"Riley, the evidence against you is impressive. I am advising you -- as both your lawyer and your friend -- that it will be a difficult case to win. Attorney General Calderwood has chosen to make an example of this case to cement his re-election bid. Right now, you are looking at life with no parole. If we deal, I could get you twenty years, twenty-five tops. When you get out, you'll still be in your forties with plenty of life ahead of you to live."

" I'm not interested in a deal. I didn't kill Marcellino. It was an accident."

"Just think about it, Riley."

"I know you're just trying to help me, and I don't even know how I'm going to pay you..."

"I told you not to worry about the fees, they are taken care of."

"...but I would rather rot in here than admit to something I did not do."

"Very well. I will begin preparing your full defense. Don't forget that criminal trials like these are about evidence and testimony, not truth. It may not be pretty."

"Nothing about my life has ever been pretty."

The guard walked Riley back to his holding area which was a cinderblock room that housed about thirty other prisoners at various stages in their own tenuous journey through the Massachusetts legal system. He was unshackled and sat on his cot. The room's single television was tuned to a news channel which blathered on about a political dispute. The jail's rules forbade television news, but when certain guards were on duty, he learned for the right price they could be persuaded to look the other way.

Marcellino's untimely death didn't just excite news channels in Boston. The story was picked up and exploited on a national scale. Marcellino owned property -- and exerted influence in a dozen cities including Los Angeles, Las Vegas, Chicago, Baltimore, New York and Boston. The Marcellino family hired a public relations firm to seed stories about his success in business and donations he made to youth groups. They even released a photo which became iconic of Marcellino buying a box of Thin Mints from a Girl Scout in front of a Salvation Army store.

In contrast, Riley was portrayed as either an insane and unstable mob wannabe who overstepped his bounds, or as a shrewd young capo in a rising Irish organized crime syndicate. He grew tired of seeing his embarrassing Columbia freshman record photo on the TV screen every other day. But most of the early media attention didn't focus on Riley at all, but on Mr. Fabrizi instead. The general public assumption was that Mr. Fabrizi ordered the hit and sent Riley to carry it out. News reporters now trailed Eddie Fabrizi wherever he went. Riley watched on television as reporters staked out his Queens compound, and was amused when one set of reporters somehow made it inside to knock on the front door. He recognized the Japanese boxwood the reporter straddled.

"I threw up all over that shrub last Christmas." Riley told a fellow prisoner bunking next to him. The irony was lost on the poor fellow who just nodded and smiled since he didn't speak English.

Mr. Fabrizi was followed back and forth to work every day, Imelda was trailed wherever she went, and even their two daughters were filmed exiting their weekly ballet classes. Riley didn't need to hear him swear to know he was upset -- he could feel the anger penetrate through the screen and into his soul. He could only imagine what Mr. Fabrizi would say to him now. It broke Riley's heart that he had become such a profound disappointment to a man who had done nothing but support and help him.

The hardest part of being accused and incarcerated in this manner, Riley learned, was being unable to explain himself to anyone. There were so many conversations he wanted to have. He wondered how many people on the outside -- his friends and family -- pitied him without knowing all the details, believing only what was said on the news. It was a humbling and humiliating experience. He thought about Alvin and the attention that must have been brought down on him in their messy dorm room at school. Riley could just picture him going insane, pacing the floors and bouncing off walls. He thought about Magnolia and her wonderful family up in Ticonderoga, and what they must have thought watching him being led to jail in handcuffs after his arrest. He hoped since they didn't watch much television, perhaps they could have missed the whole sordid affair. And then there was Mici -- wherever she was -- her heart still raw and hurting from the death of her grandfather -- now having to watch who she believed to be her best friend be accused and tried for first-degree murder. And there were his brothers and sisters, too, and though they had already disowned him after their mother had died, he guessed they would think him guilty of this as well and write him off. He wanted to already be dead in their minds.

He had not yet told a soul, including his own lawyer, about the incredible story Marcellino shared right before the accident. Each night before he fell off into brief, uncomfortable sleep on his narrow, rigid cot, he would replay Marcellino's tale in his mind, word for word, looking for clues and wondering how much of the outrageous story he could trust. He had so many questions for him that would now go unanswered forever. Was his pious mother Sarah a murderess? Did Seamus beat her? Did Liam kill Mr. Murphy and commit suicide? On good days, Riley dismissed the whole story as braggadocio from an eccentric blowhard and career criminal. On bad days, he would sob into his small blue prison-issued pillow for hours mourning his poor brother's life and his artificial childhood.

Riley looked up and realized the TV station was broadcasting a special expose on Mr. Fabrizi's life. They kept showing a mug shot of the man in his early twenties, maybe even younger than Riley, and Riley started to realize how far Mr. Fabrizi had come in his own life. To rise from his origins as a local hood with several arrests, to eventually gain control of such a large company, was impressive. Riley was both inspired and offended by the truth in the tale.

The trial began on a steamy August morning. Malcolm didn't bring the black suit Riley requested as he felt it made him look too Mafioso, so instead Riley was given a white shirt and wide, gaudy flowered tie. He was no fashion maven, but he knew he looked like a circus clown and was annoyed. Malcolm didn't care -- he wanted to portray Riley as an unsuspecting, innocent victim caught in a whirlwind of unconnected circumstances. Riley had little choice other than to comply, but expressed his disapproval whenever he could.

The case had become so high profile that Attorney General Calderwood contracted Veronica Birdwell, the most preeminent attorney he could find to handle the prosecution. Birdwell had successfully prosecuted corrupt political leaders, mobsters, and even child molesters. The case had also struck a nerve in the Boston political community, and several city councilmen were none too happy that such a high profile death occurred in their backyard, and Birdwell had the political savvy to juggle them as well. She was a rising legal star and next in line for Calderwood's political seat, and though he needed her to execute the case, he elected to sit at her table during the trial. He wasn't going to let her too far out of his sight. Both Calderwood and Birdwell saw Riley's conviction as a slam dunk, and they each wanted their own personal slice of the glory and attention -- in full color and in high definition.

Riley got his first look at the jury when he was walked into the courtroom. He had heard from Malcolm throughout the week that Birdwell found reason to object to every potential juror with an Irish or Italian surname, and as a counter maneuver, Malcolm raised objections about the rest. Riley knew the judge had already chastised the embattled attorneys more than once. Riley looked across the room and tried to make eye contact with each of the men and women sitting in the juror's box. In their hands was his fate. They all looked middle aged, and he wondered if any of them were secretly Southie. He saw no intellectual Ivy League students or young men. He wondered how they could be considered his peers.

"Before this trial begins," Malcolm whispered to his client, "you still have an opportunity to strike a deal and avoid this mess. Our chances have not improved."

"No deals. And what's with your suit?" Malcolm had elected to wear a suit entirely in white -- pants, shirt, jacket, tie and shoes.

"Because in the movies, the good guys always wear white."

As Birdwell stood before Judge Hoffman to begin the state's opening statement, everyone turned toward the disruption behind her. A team of lawyers that Riley recognized from Mr. Fabrizi's office were interrupting the trial, shouting for motions, and raising general havoc. They wanted the trial halted on behalf of their client, who they believed was about to be slandered. The surly Judge Hoffman was not impressed with the theatrics and ordered them to his bench. Neither the prosecution or defense was amused either. A heated argument ensued. The judge stopped the trial and ushered the jurors out, then ranted at the attorneys for their loathsome, unprofessional conduct. Reporters at the back of the room loved it, and pranced out to the lobby to deliver their first live report from the exciting and now chaotic murder trial.

The trial was off to an auspicious start.

Once order was restored and the jurors returned to their seats, Birdwell stood again. She was a long, thin woman with bobbed blonde hair that stayed in place as if ordered. She wore a conservative blue dress and pearl necklace. She peered at the jury over the top of her intimidating bifocals.

"Thank you, your honor, and thank you ladies and gentlemen of the jury for your commitment to public service and devotion to justice. What the evidence will prove to you beyond a shadow of any doubt in this proceeding is plain and simple. That the defendant, Mr. Riley Angus Lynch, did willfully and maliciously murder businessman and entrepreneur Giovanni Marcellino, who also is known by the nickname, The Chef. You will hear evidence that will prove Mr. Lynch planned the vicious act well in advance, carefully executed his heinous plan, and then executed Mr. Marcellino in full view of innocent men, women and children going about their business one typical afternoon in South Boston. You will hear evidence that immediately following Mr. Marcellino's death, the defendant not only lacked any shred of remorse, but instead celebrated his cold-blooded act, laughing and carrying on over the grisly scene of the deceased victim. You will hear evidence that will show how Mr. Lynch was attracted to and lived in a world of organized crime, idolizing felons and corruption, pursuing his selfish and violent..."

Riley listened amazed, and realized his mouth had fallen open. It was as if he was listening to some old radio play and he was beginning to wonder how it would end. It could not be possible for the jury to believe this hogwash about him being a mobster -- a lifestyle he had avoided and detested his entire life. It couldn't be proven, however without proof, and there surely would be none. Birdwell droned on for over an hour, outlining every detail and fact, and how the State of Massachusetts considered Riley an assassin and a danger to the general public. For the first time he felt confident Malcolm could easily persuade the jury to understand the real truth. His case would be a slam dunk acquittal. Birdwell's statement was delivered with style and drama, the jury hanging on every word, and someone in the gallery actually applauded when she concluded. It was a wonderful theatrical performance, worthy of an Oscar, Riley thought. Malcolm had been scribbling notes in his binder throughout the oration, and when Judge Hoffman offered his permission, Malcolm Ward stood, adjusted his white vest, cleared his raspy throat, and offered his own opening remarks.

"To my right, your honor and ladies and gentlemen of the jury, sits a broken and confused young man. At one time, just months ago, he was poised to graduate at the top of his class from Columbia University in New York, and now he has been caught up in a terrible tragedy, by no fault of his own. An out of control vehicle cuts him off at a busy intersection, and the passenger in his car is thrown out the door and killed. It truly was a tragic and grisly scene, and my thoughts and prayers, as well as the thoughts and prayers of the defendant, go out to the Marcellino family and to those unlucky enough to have been standing on that particular street corner at that particular hour on that particular day. Mr. Marcellino was a victim of circumstance and profound bad luck, as was each pedestrian who witnessed the accident. Also a victim of that moment is the defendant, Mr. Riley Lynch, Ivy League honor student, who is guilty of only running a business errand for his employer, and nothing more. Mr. Lynch is not only a victim of the accident; he is also a victim of circumstance and coincidence. The defendant had no control over the lifestyle that Mr. Marcellino chose to lead, or as the evidence will show, his connections to a nationwide organized criminal empire. The evidence will prove that Mr. Lynch is nothing more than a good boy who studied hard, worked hard and loved his mother..."

Since Mr. Fabrizi's attorneys had eaten up so much time with their annoying motions, the first day of the trial ended with just the opening statements. The prosecution would begin its case for murder in the morning.

Riley changed back into his uncomfortable prison jumpsuit and settled back onto his cot in the noisy and stuffy room. Two prisoners were arguing about a pillow behind him, attempting to out curse and intimidate each other, and the cartoons on the television became difficult to hear. His brief day outside the depressing confines of the jail had re-energized him, and he was optimistic about his chances for the first time. Someone changed the television channel away from the cartoons and over to the local news, and he recognized the woman being interviewed, but couldn't quite place her. When he saw her name flash on the screen, he jumped from his cot screaming at his cellmates to shut up, imploring the guard on duty to increase the volume.

The woman was none other than Ms. Wanda Beckmeir, Riley's eighth grade English teacher from South Boston Middle School.

"Yes... Riley was a good student. He was a little unusual, very quiet... kept to himself. You know the type -- a wallflower, a loner. But as suspicious as he always acted, I didn't think he'd be capable of a murder. But I have to admit, I always wondered what went on behind those beady little eyes of his. I guess now we know."

Riley felt the anger surge up from his gut, and he felt his hands tighten into fists. He was powerless to affect anything from his current location, and he watched the remainder of the newscast in a peak of frustration and horror. The scene switched to the front of his High School, and then on the screen appeared his old friend Anthony. He hadn't seen Anthony since his high school graduation when he fell flat on his face after delivering his graduation speech.

271

"Riley was a great guy. There is no way he could have murdered that mobster."

"Was he your friend?" The reporter asked.

"I wouldn't actually say he was my friend... I didn't know him that well..."

"You rat bastard!" Riley hollered at the screen. The other prisoners were gathering around, now wondering who this anonymous whacko was hollering at the TV. Father O'Connell from St. Finian's appeared next.

"Riley grew up with a difficult family life. His father disappeared before he was born and his mother raised him and his brothers and sisters alone. It is unfortunate, and a sad state of the poor in our neighborhood, that when faced with adversity, these families feel hopeless and are attracted to the criminal lifestyle, turning away from God."

"Asshole! You're an asshole!" Riley screamed, spittle flying from his lips. "My brother is a goddamn priest! And you fucking know it!"

A survey of his friends shows Riley Lynch was a quiet individual, but the warning signs were there, as a community mourns a vicious crime alleged to have been performed by a son of its own. This is Everett Craven, reporting for News Center 9.

One of the nameless prisoners approached Riley and looked him straight in the eye. "Hey man, you're that Lynch kid that knocked off The Chef, ain't you?"

Riley froze in place.

"Yes... I mean no. I didn't do a fucking thing." Riley's heart was racing, and his eyes darted around the room. Malcolm had threatened to slit his throat if he uttered one word about his case while he was incarcerated.

"Hey, everybody, this is the guy that whacked The Chef!"

The crowd of prisoners gathered around him like zombies seeking out a fresh brain. The prison guards had taken notice and Riley could see them moving into strategic positions, getting ready to react if something were to happen. The prisoner closest to Riley, a scruffy Hispanic man, extended his arms and gave Riley an affectionate hug.

"You are the man! You are the man!" He yelled. A few of the prisoners started to clap, and a couple of others hooted. One at a time, the men approached Riley and shook his hand, or slapped his back, and one Portuguese prisoner kissed him on both cheeks, a salute, the man surmised, that was customary for such a high ranking mafia celebrity. Riley didn't know how to act or what to stay. He accepted the kudos with grace, and took the advice Mr. Mantano gave him long ago. If they thought he was connected, he could use it to his advantage. For the rest of the evening, a number of prisoners offered him their stories of how Marcellino and his associates framed them or their family, hooked them on drugs, and stole their homes and livelihoods. It was a bizarre bonding from some of society's most ruthless and corrosive individuals, and Riley was the unwitting emcee, and star of the show.

Day two of Riley's murder trial began as expected, and the prosecution placed several eyewitnesses to the accident scene on the stand. They each took their turn describing the heinous sight, and each, in their own words, turned the jurors' stomachs with tales of blood, squished body parts and splattered gray matter. The descriptions were all different (and one man even denied the existence of the renegade car that cut Riley off) but all the witnesses agreed on one indisputable fact -- Riley's reaction to the accident was to laugh, which they all agreed was bizarre and unnerving.

Following the eyewitnesses, Calderwood and Birdwell produced Mr. Marcellino's widow. Riley wondered what kind of women would be attracted to such an obese, foul man as Marcellino, and he got his answer when she lumbered into the courtroom, looking just as foul and at least fifty pounds heavier than her rotund husband. The prosecution used her presence to foster compassion and help illustrate the victim's value to society – intended to offset the anticipated testimony of his mob world connections. Mrs. Marcellino spoke of his kind heart and generous soul. The widow wept and droned on and on about all the little children her husband adored, the Little League team he sponsored, the Girl Scout cookies he bought every year, and the retirement home he would visit every holiday to deliver presents. By the time she was done, Marcellino was ready for beatification.

José, Mr. Fabrizi's reliable assistant, appeared next. Malcolm considered him an odd choice for a witness, and evidence that there

273

was backroom dealing going on with Mr. Fabrizi and his legal team. After all, why wouldn't the prosecution just call old grumpy Edward himself? José represented a compromise, as someone near the top of LSE could testify yet keep Mr. Fabrizi out of the spotlight. Birdwell's questioning was brief and to the point.

"Was Mr. Lynch instructed by anyone at LSE to kill Mr. Marcellino?"

"No, ma'am."

"Was Mr. Lynch instructed by his boss, Mr. Edward Fabrizi, to murder Mr. Marcellino."

"No, he was not."

"Was Mr. Lynch ordered to meet with Mr. Marcellino."

"At first, no. Mr. Fabrizi planned to go. Then Riley insisted on coordinating the meeting himself."

"Then it was Mr. Lynch's idea to meet Mr. Marcellino in Boston?"

"Yes ma'am. The meeting was at his initiative. He said he had to fix things."

Malcolm had but one question for José.

"Did Riley here tell you he planned to kill anyone?"

"No sir. He did not."

When the next witness was announced, Riley didn't recognize the name. He didn't even recognize her when she walked into the room and sat at the witness stand. Birdwell readied her notes and addressed the nervous-looking girl.

"Please state your name and occupation for the court."

"My name is Sally Westbrook. I am a flight attendant for Northeast Airlines."

"Do you recognize the defendant?"

"Yes. I saw him meet Mr. Marcellino at the airport the day he was murdered."

"Would you explain to the court why you are here today?"

"Well... I was watching TV and saw the coverage of the murder and the arrest of that gentleman over there. I recognized him right away. I had been sitting next to him at Logan Airport. I remembered him because he was acting very strange. He was pacing around a lot and fidgeting in his seat. Then he was swearing very loudly into his cell phone which he threw across the concourse and smashed. I thought about getting a security guard when a fat man approached him who had just disembarked from a flight. The two exchanged greetings and he introduced himself to him. It turns out the fat man was that Mr. Marcellino who died in that accident."

"What did you hear them say."

"It was just pleasant introductions. But when I saw the TV report, the report showed his picture and said they had arrested a man named Riley Lynch. I thought that was very strange, since I heard him introduce himself as Riley Fabrizi."

"You heard the defendant call himself Riley Fabrizi?"

"Yes. It got my attention because my husband's middle name is Fabrizi. It's a very unusual name. I told my husband about the incident as soon as I got home. Then I saw the report on television of that terrible accident the next day."

Riley wanted to stand up and shout. He was amazed at how these disconnected moments were coming together to prove his guilt. He felt Malcolm's reassuring hand on his shoulder.

"It's going to get worse before it gets better. Stay calm."

Riley looked toward the door.

"Your honor, we call Siobhan Lynch-Lopez to the stand as our next witness."

Siobhan was escorted into the room weeping. Her arms were wrapped around her torso as if in great pain. She gazed at Riley with bloodshot eyes, and he could feel the embarrassment and regret emanate from her in waves from his seat across the room.

"Your honor, we are declaring Ms. Lopez a hostile witness."

"So noted, please proceed." Judge Hoffman said.

"Ms. Lopez, what is your relationship to the defendant?"

Siobhan mumbled something under her breath that no one could hear. She buried her face in her hands.

"Ms. Lopez? Could you repeat that please?"

"I'm his sister!" Siobhan shouted.

"Ms. Lopez, have you ever been arrested?"

"Yes," Siobhan mumbled again.

"Ms. Lopez, please speak up so the court can hear your response."

"Yes!"

"Thank you. The documents I am holding indicate you were arrested for possession of drugs and child endangerment. Is that correct?"

"Yes."

"Good. And were you guilty of these crimes? Were you guilty of endangering your son by stuffing drugs into his shoes?"

"No! I didn't do it. I was innocent. It was all a mistake."

"Ms. Lopez, why do you think it was a mistake?"

"Because I was framed. We were framed. A man named Tenny Doyle planted the drugs on us and called the police. He ruined our lives."

"Ms. Lopez, that's a serious accusation. Was Tenny Doyle convicted of this crime?"

"No, he wasn't. He wasn't even arrested."

"So the police, our courts, and our criminal justice system did not agree with your opinion?"

"I suppose not."

"And why, Ms. Lopez, would Tenny Doyle do such a horrible thing to you?"

"He wanted us out of the building so his company could buy it."

"Do you know who Tenny Doyle's employer is?"

"Yes."

"He works for City Point Properties in South Boston. Is that your understanding?"

"Yes."

"And do you know who owns City Point Properties?"

"Yes, I do."

"Please, Ms. Lopez, do tell the court,"

"Marcellino."

"When your brother, the defendant, found out you had been arrested, was he upset?"

"Yes, he was furious. My whole family was upset."

"Your whole family? Was your brother Sean upset?"

"Yes, he was."

"Let me ask you about Sean for one moment. Has he ever been arrested?"

"Yes."

"I hold in my hand Boston Police records indicating Sean was arrested for burglary and fencing stolen goods. Is that correct?"

"Yes, I suppose it is."

"Do you know what property he was accused of burglarizing."

"Yes."

"Was it the new condominiums on South Street in South Boston?"

"Yes."

"Do you believe your brother Sean was guilty or innocent?"

"He didn't do it. They set-up him and his friends."

"Someone framed him, too? Who set them up? Who would do this?"

"I don't know."

"Do you know who owns the building he was accused of burglarizing?"

"I'm not sure."

"Was it City Point Properties, Mr. Marcellino's company?"

"Yes."

"Ms. Lopez, do you love your brother, Riley?"

"What a stupid question. Of course I love him. I love him with all my heart!"

"In your opinion, do you believe your brother Riley is capable of committing such a heinous crime of murder?"

"Absolutely not! Impossible. Riley couldn't hurt a fly."

"So you think he is innocent?"

"Of course he is innocent."

"Was he set-up just like you and your brother?"

"I don't know! Riley, I'm sorry. I love you!"

"Ms. Lopez, does anyone in your family take responsibility for anything they do, or just blame Giovanni Marcellino?"

"Objection your honor! This badgering has gone on long enough." Malcolm interrupted.

"Sustained," Judge Hoffman ruled. "Ms. Birdwell, do you have any additional questions?"

"No, your honor."

"Mr. Ward. You may now question the witness."

After Birdwell's questioning, Siobhan was no better than a blubbering mass of raw nerves. She couldn't breathe or speak, and her tear-filled eyes could barely see. Her time in prison had aged her beyond her years, her perky, bright exterior had long been worn away. Malcolm knew Siobhan well since he represented her too, and knew her testimony had been damaging to Riley's case. He did his best to ease her nerves, and asked her all sorts of softball questions about how sweet Riley was growing up, how hard he studied at school, and how popular he was among his schoolmates. Siobhan even told stories about going to catechism classes at St. Finian's, and how proud she was when he was valedictorian and read his speech. Riley was heartbroken that his sweet, young sister was so used and broken. She didn't deserve it. It wasn't fair.

Throughout the proceedings, Riley had watched the faces of the jurors and saw them absorbing the drama. It worried him. But up until that moment, he had all but ignored the full gallery of guests, journalists and onlookers who thought the trial would make worthy entertainment. He glanced around the room at the faces in the gallery, wondering what sadistic pleasure they got from witnessing his lynching, when he noticed a pretty and familiar face in the back row.

It was Tammy Meeks.

Riley hadn't seen Tammy since the train ride up from New York so many months earlier. He had thought of her often, wondering how she was getting along. She represented the last good memory from his childhood, and now, her last memory of him would be as a convicted murderer. It was humiliating. She sat with her head down, not a strand of her silky, dark hair out of place, scribbling something into a black binder. She was dressed smart and professional, with a frilly white blouse and sleek gray suit. To her right, an attractive young man was paying close attention to every word she wrote. He remembered she was studying law and wanted to work in her father's small firm, and assumed her presence must be to work on some sort of school project. He stared as much at Tammy's dashing companion as he did at her. Riley was jealous and knew it, and wondered how his life's path could have led him so far astray. He should be sitting next to her in the gallery, working on a law project with her, inhaling her rose perfume, stroking her smooth pink cheek with the side of his hand.

"Your honor, we would like to call our next witness. Miss Norma Belcher."

Who the hell, Riley thought, is Norma Belcher?

Up the aisle of the courtroom came a tiny girl, dressed well, no more than five feet tall who weighed no more than ninety-five pounds. She wore no make-up and look like she could be no more than thirteen or fourteen years old. Riley didn't recognize her until she reached the witness stand and was sworn in.

Norma Belcher was better known by her stage name, Shyla Bright.

"Miss Belcher, would you state your age and profession for the court."

"I am a twenty-two year old adult entertainment professional."

"You're a stripper?"

"I am an exotic dancer who performs at a number of gentlemen's clubs. I don't like the term stripper."

"How do you know the defendant, Riley Lynch?"

"Riley picked me up one day and flew me and a couple of other girls to Las Vegas for a gig at a new club on the Vegas strip. It was a real big deal."

"What did Mr. Lynch ask you to do when you got there?"

"I was supposed to dance as a featured performer, which I did. But he also asked me to be available for a special client of his he was trying to impress."

"Could you explain what you mean by, 'be available?' Was he asking you to become a prostitute for him?"

"No, not at all. It's an all nude club. Riley just wanted me to drop by and give his VIP friend a little private show."

"So did you give his client this show?"

"Yes I did. I came to his table, took off my robe and sat in the man's lap."

"What was the nature of the conversation that Mr. Lynch and his client were having?"

"There was some sort of contract that the man didn't want to sign. They were going back and forth about it. Then Riley got very upset when the man said he wouldn't sign the papers until he talked to his boss."

"Did the man say who his boss was?"

"Marcellino."

"And what happened next?"

"Then Riley got mad and jumped up. When he did, I fell bare-assed on the floor, then I saw Riley press a gun into the man's back."

"Mr. Lynch, the defendant, had a gun?"

"Yes he did. And with the gun pressed to the man's back, I saw him sign the papers."

"Do you believe Mr. Lynch is a violent man?"

"I don't know, but I know he scared me."

"No further questions."

Malcolm stepped up to address the witness next.

"Miss Belcher, you said you saw a gun, is that correct?"

"Yes, I did."

"Could you describe it?"

"I don't know anything about guns."

"That's OK. Just tell the court what color it was. Black? Brown? Silver?"

"Oh, I couldn't tell. It was in a bag."

"The gun was in a bag?"

"Yes, and it was in Riley's pocket."

"You are testifying that what you think was a gun was in a bag and in the defendant's pocket. So you really couldn't see it, could you?"

"I guess not. But I am sure it had to be a gun by the way he pointed it."

That night back in prison, the correctional facilities air conditioning failed and the room full of angry men were hot, bored and uncomfortable. Riley's fame made it difficult for him to maintain his anonymity any longer, as man after man would approach him trying to gain his trust and forge an ally. He was offered all sorts of gifts that he declined, including a cookie smuggled from the dining hall, marijuana, and even a homemade shank fashioned from a bolt from a cot. He elected to maintain himself as quiet and aloof, but knew that if he was to lose his trial and be in prison for the remainder of his life, he would need to change.

The two men who had argued about the pillow before were arguing again, no doubt fueled by the steamy air and array of foul odors that displaced the clean air of the room. This time, the argument took a violent turn when one of the men found himself on the receiving end of a flailing fist, and grabbed his adversary around the neck. Guards jogged in from all angles, and the prisoners, including Riley, stood as spectators to the evening's entertainment. The guards wrestled the assailants and pinned them to the floor, and as some of them hooted and jeered, Riley felt someone very large standing against his back. Riley spun around in terror.

"You think you are tough, eh?" The man said, deliberately exhaling into Riley's face, causing him to gag and wince. "They all think you are tough, but you don't look so tough to me. Why don't you show me how tough you are, huh, little boy?"

Riley had been told earlier the man was some sort of gang leader from the inner city of Philadelphia who had been arrested for armed robbery during a recent visit to Boston. His body was wallpapered in tattoos that included a dagger centered from his forehead down the bridge of his nose. The man, Riley surmised, didn't watch much TV news.

"I'm not tough and I don't want any trouble." Riley raised his hands in defeat before the battle was engaged, hoping the brute would back away. He didn't.

The man placed both hands on Riley's shoulders and shoved him down onto his cot and laughed. One of the prisoners who was watching and enjoying the guards subdue the other fight turned and saw the brutish man standing over Riley. Without invitation or instruction, a wall of orange-clad alleged thieves, robbers, murderers, dealers and cons formed between Riley and his attacker. Riley scooted across his cot and stood behind them in relative safety.

"You don't mess with him, man. Not him. You just don't," one of them said.

"He's the man. He's Lynch. You don't fuck with Lynch," said another.

Riley's assailant surveyed the situation, and accepting that he was outnumbered, backed away snickering. A message had been sent not only to any future would-be attacker, but to Riley as well.

Behind them all on the television, a cable news program was broadcasting a special report on the trial, and as special guest that evening, live via satellite from Boston, sat brilliant mob attorney and white suit-clad Malcolm Ward. The volume had been turned off so no one could hear what they were talking about. Riley approached a guard and offered him a smuggled dining hall cookie to change the channel back to the cartoons.

At ten a.m. the next morning, in the sweltering August heat and humidity of the waning New England summer, Attorney Malcolm Ward began the arduous task of defending Riley Lynch and repairing the damage done to his reputation from the prosecutor's fervent attack. The circumstantial evidence presented by Attorney Birdwell was impressive, and her delivery enchanting. He knew the jury was following the story like a weekday afternoon soap opera and feared that they would choose to side with the great story rather than vote with the facts of the case. It was a challenge for any attorney to present credible witnesses to prove, beyond a shadow of a doubt, that something did not happen.

Malcolm took his position and fired salvo after salvo in his counterattack, attempting to blow holes in the prosecution's fairy tale. Malcolm called several witnesses to the accident, produced document after document of evidence, but it would be the last few witnesses that would attest to Riley's honor that he hoped would score with the jury the most.

"Your honor, the defense would now like to call Professor Julius Friedman."

Professor Friedman gave Riley a reassuring nod as he walked up and took his seat on the witness stand. Riley felt guilty as he had done nothing but ignore the man's efforts to help him since the day he enrolled, even disregarding his persistent calls, and now the man was aiding in his defense.

"Please state your name and occupation for the court."

"I am Julius Friedman, professor of finance and economics at Columbia University in New York."

"And how do you know the defendant, Riley Lynch?"

"He has been a student of mine since his admission to the university four years ago."

"Would you describe Riley Lynch's academic performance for us?"

"It would be my pleasure. Riley is a delight to have in class. He has become one of the brightest students I have met in my fifteen years in the department. His ideas and opinions on international financial matters are insightful and his contribution to classroom discussions is inspired."

"The prosecution has painted a portrait of Mr. Lynch as a distracted, obsessed and violent young man. Have you seen any of those tendencies in Mr. Lynch's behavior?"

"I would say he is distracted. But no more so than any other young man in an international city such as New York. But obsessed? Violent? Hardly. In fact, the department fosters a relationship with an impressive list of companies looking for new talent, and after presenting some of Riley's academic work to them, we had several inquiries about his availability after his successful graduation."

"But isn't his status at the university on hold?"

"Yes, pending a favorable outcome of this trial, I would expect Columbia to re-admit him so he can complete his degree."

Riley was thrilled to hear that if by some miracle he could extricate his loathsome carcass from this mess, he could still go back to school. Maybe there was still a chance to become that invisible undergraduate he longed to be. He wanted to hop up and kiss the top of Professor Friedman's bald, spectacled head.

"Professor Friedman, "Birdwell began, circling the witness stand like a low flying turkey vulture. Riley became concerned. She looked too confident. "We have heard you describe Mr. Lynch's impressive academic performance. Did he have any behavioral problems that concerned you or your department?"

"No. Nothing unusual."

"Nothing unusual. Hmmm. If there was nothing unusual, then I must assume there must be something... usual?"

"Riley did have a few attendance problems. But I have seen worse."

"I hold in my hand a term paper written by Mr. Lynch last year. Do you recognize it?"

"How the hell did they get their hands on that paper?" Riley asked Malcolm, whispering into his ear.

"They obtained it with the search warrant they executed on your dorm room." Malcolm answered.

Professor Friedman was looking confused and anxious, but gave Birdwell an honest answer.

"Umm, yes I do. It was for a project on business ethics."

"Mr. Lynch received an F."

"Yes.., yes he did. It was a good paper, but my grade was overruled and was re-assigned by our finance department chairperson."

"Would you explain to the court why the grade was so poor?"

"Riley, quite by accident, submitted a nude photo of a porn star in the body of the paper."

"Professor, do you have other students at Columbia who submit pornography with their coursework?"

"No, ma'am. I am not aware of that happening before."

"Do you think he may have been distracted by something?"

"I couldn't say. I don't know"

"A moment ago, you testified that Mr. Lynch's behavioral problems were not unusual. In your years teaching at the university, do you consider this incident usual or unusual?"

"Unusual, I suppose, but..."

"Thank you, professor. I have no further questions."

Riley was devastated as he watched his professor's testimony become shredded in the hands of a superior trial attorney. Malcolm had been his champion from day one, but signs of concern were visible in his expression and demeanor. Malcolm may have been a brilliant legal mind, superior negotiator and reliable resource, but he was overmatched at trial -- it was becoming evident he had all the flash, but lacked the substance. But that didn't mean he was planning to roll over or stop fighting.

"Your honor, as our next witness, I call Mr. Alvin Foster."

Riley had begged Malcolm not to call Alvin. Alvin was a wildcard and Riley considered him an intellectual nitwit. And though he had elected to tolerate his womanizing and lack of common sense, he did value his peculiar friendship. Malcolm believed he needed to portray Riley as a normal college student in the eyes of the jury, flaws included, therefore, the existence of a quasi-normal friend was what the doctor ordered. And for a loner like Riley who had accumulated few friends, Alvin would have to do. There weren't many options.

Malcolm smiled at Alvin as if he was a long-lost friend. "Please state your name and occupation for the court."

"I'm Alvin Foster. I'm a recent graduate in political science from Columbia University, on the Dean's List!" Alvin mugged a toothy grin and gave the thumbs up sign to the jury. The gallery giggled and Judge Hoffman lectured the witness about proper decorum. "And I don't have a job yet."

"What is your relationship to the defendant, Riley Lynch."

"Riley was my roommate. We had a lot of fun. He's a great dude."

"What were some of the things he enjoyed doing while he was a student."

"He liked to study a lot. It was hard to get him to loosen up sometimes. He'd go to the library when I had a date over. Oh... he liked to hang out at a cafe on Amsterdam Avenue. The food sucked, but the view was great."

"Did Riley have a lot of friends?"

"Yea, he had a few."

"What were they like?"

"There was this chick Magnolia he had a thing for. She was a little weird, you know, but not in a bad way, and she was always in the mood and willing to..."

Malcolm had Alvin on a short leash and cut him off before he said anything too damaging. "Was there anything else?"

"He liked to read books, and he liked to cook sometimes. He'd make this Irish stuff his mother used to make -- some of it was even good. And we watched a lot of TV. We would watch all kinds of movies, and we never missed the news. I'd keep my eye out for news about a murder in New Jersey..."

Malcolm interrupted him again. Riley sat upright and held his breath. If Alvin revealed information about the Hanratty murder at the carwash, the game was over. Even Malcolm wasn't aware of Riley's involvement in that mess and the interruption was timed well by accident, or maybe even divine intervention. Riley glanced at Birdwell and Calderwood who were in deep discussion, ignoring Alvin's testimony. They had not caught the remark. It was obvious they didn't think much of Alvin as a defense witness, and chose to not even pay attention. It was the first bit of good luck Riley had in the trial.

"You have known Riley Lynch for four years, and you have seen him almost every day. Have you seen anything, or would you know of anything, that would tell you he was capable of committing murder?"

"Riley? Murder? No way, dude. No way."

Riley's brother Ryan appeared next for the defense. Ryan had requested and received a leave from the diocese in Nicaragua to attend to a family emergency. He even was able to convince the church to pay for the flight. Outside of a Christmas card, Riley and Ryan had not had any contact since he left on the overseas assignment. Despite the awkward feeling Ryan's presence afforded Riley, he and Malcolm agreed that having that little white collar on the witness stand in such a predominantly Catholic neighborhood could only enhance the cause.

"My name is Father Ryan Lynch. I am Riley's brother."

"It has been implied by the prosecution that your brother Riley, the defendant, grew up in a home under difficult circumstances that may have driven him to a life of crime. Was your home life difficult?"

"Not at all. In fact, I would describe it as inspiring. My father disappeared when I was very small, and Riley had yet to be born. My mother, Sarah, worked her fingers to the bone to provide for us and make sure we never went without."

"Was your home life violent?"

"No. My mother was a very religious and pious individual. She would pray every day and the Church was a big part of our family life. In fact, it was her devotion to God that inspired me to become a priest."

"But with six brothers and sisters besides yourself living in one apartment, things must have been chaotic."

"At times it was chaotic, sure, but my mother had a lot of support. Those of us who were older tried to care for the younger kids, and neighbors like Mark Murphy who ran a bookshop downstairs always made sure we got home from school safe and did our homework. It was a rich and collaborative community upbringing."

"What kind of child was Riley?"

"Although he was the youngest in the family, as he grew older, he became the most responsible, and always had an eye for helping the rest of us whenever he could. We all knew we could rely on Riley."

Malcolm continued the line of questioning for some time, attempting to hammer the jury with stories of his childhood and to get them to accept Riley's compassion for his loved ones and profound sense of personal responsibility. Ms. Birdwell listened to the testimony with both her arms and legs crossed as if it pained her to hear such nice things. She released a heavy sigh when Malcolm finished his questioning and turned Ryan over to her.

"I have just one question for the witness, your honor," Birdwell said.

"Please proceed."

"Father Lynch, you grew up in a home with no father and six siblings, in a neighborhood most would consider low income, and you have had at least three of your siblings arrested for a variety of charges from drug possession to murder. My question to you is, when you chose to serve your calling so far away from this experience you loved, which of these delightful incidents in your life were you running away from?"

"Objection!" Malcolm shouted, slapping at the table.

"Sustained. That was inappropriate counselor," Judge Hoffman ruled.

I am sorry. I will withdraw it."

It was an inappropriate question – a calculated low blow – but not a question that hadn't crossed even Riley's mind. Father O'Connell adored Ryan, and he had the connections to serve anywhere he wanted within the Diocese of Boston, or anywhere in New England, for that matter. Riley always felt Ryan's emotions were disconnected somehow from the day-to-day drama his family produced, and he acted as if he hadn't been called to the priesthood as much as he was chased. Knowing now what he did from Marcellino about his mother's sordid past, he could only wonder if his older brothers and sisters played any part in the crime. Perhaps Ryan was in on the con. Perhaps he was part of the conspiracy to suppress the truth.

Riley knew Malcolm's witness list, and it was running short while time was running out. Malcolm hadn't proven anything and there was only one remaining witness the defense intended to call other than himself. And Riley was not happy about it.

"The defense calls Ms. Michelina Mantano."

Mici walked into the chamber with her head down and arms folded and marched with haste to the witness stand. When she looked up to give her oath for the bailiff, Riley could see the trepidation that had sunk deep into her dark eyes. She was still as stunning and as beautiful as any woman Riley had ever known. But the loss of her grandfather must have extracted its toll on her spirit. When she glanced over at Riley seated at the defense table, Riley expected they might both start crying.

Mici's very presence was a calculated risk. Malcolm expected Birdwell to interrogate her about Mr. Mantano's old mob lifestyle and connections, but he believed that if Birdwell stayed consistent and grilled Mici without mercy when she got her chance, the jury would side with the sweet, pretty lonely girl and demonize the prosecutor. Mici could out charm anyone. Malcolm began his questioning.

"Miss Mantano, would you describe for the court your relationship with the defendant."

"Riley was a waiter for my grandfather at my family's restaurant, called Americo's, in New York. And he was also my dear friend."

"Was?" Riley repeated in a whisper to himself. Even she didn't believe he had any chance for acquittal.

"I know this may be painful, Miss Mantano, but could you please tell the court what happened to your grandfather?"

"Last December, there was a horrible, awful fire at the restaurant. He died. There was so much smoke, it was hard to see. He went inside the smoke and flames to make sure all his customers got out. No one else was hurt. He was a hero."

"I am so, so sorry Miss Mantano. I know how hard this is for you. Could you tell us what your grandfather thought of Riley?"

"Oh, *Nonno* loved him. Riley worked very hard for my grandfather and did such a wonderful job. He would often make jokes that he wanted to adopt him."

"Was Riley a dependable employee?"

"Riley saved our restaurant. He saved our business and our way of life. My grandfather assigned him to work in the office, and Riley was so smart, he found ways to save us all kinds of money.

"Miss Mantano, did you have a romantic relationship with the defendant?"

Riley blushed and tried not to move. He would have crawled under the table if he could have. But Malcolm knew it was on the minds of the jury and had to be asked.

"Oh my goodness, no. Riley was my best friend in the world. I could tell him anything. He is the sweetest boy on earth."

"Your witness."

Birdwell waltzed up to the witness stand and circled like a hyena going in to finish off an injured wildebeest. Riley swore to himself that if she did anything to harm Mici, he would jump the table and launch himself at her.

"Miss Mantano, I am sorry to hear about your grandfather. It is tragic."

"Thank you."

"Would you tell the court about him for me? How did he purchase the restaurant?"

"It was before I was born. He bought it from a former business partner."

"Was that business partner a member of any of the New York crime families?"

"I do not know."

"OK then, was your grandfather?'"

"I could tell you that I do not know, but that would be a lie. Yes.., yes he was a member of an organized crime family, and he bought his restaurant when he was still involved in that evil world. He was allowed to open in the Irish West End as a thank you for his years of service to the Family. But years ago after he opened, he gave up that life. He hated everything about it with every breath he took. He devoted his life to raising me and running his business. He was a very special man. I miss him so much." Mici's eyes moistened, but she maintained her composure.

"When your grandfather died, did he leave his estate to you?"

"Yes he did."

"Did your inheritance include the half million dollar insurance settlement from the restaurant fire?"

It was an underhanded and tasteless insinuation, and Mici did not answer, but instead, she fired a look at Birdwell so chilling that Riley swore he saw fire shoot from her eyes. Riley could see Birdwell stagger and take a half step backwards; she had been intimidated. It was a fierce and angry side of Mici Riley did not know existed. Good for her, Riley thought. Good for Mici.

Riley knew the moment was approaching when he would have to take the stand in his own defense. Too much of his hope for acquittal would hinge on his persona and attitude and there was no other way to present it than to answer questions himself. Riley spent a whole day fielding softball questions from Malcolm and doing his best to remain charming and positive, even after spending multiple sleepless hot nights in the Boston jail. He and Malcolm chatted about how much he enjoyed his childhood, the pride he felt for his brothers and sisters, and the admiration he felt for his poor dead mother. He talked about his longing for the pizza at Theodora's and how much he loved going to school in South Boston with all the kids he knew since he was born. He talked about his Christmas stroll up East Broadway in the snow and although the specter of the Irish mob hung over the neighborhood, he and his family made the effort to ignore and shun it and spiritually thrive in spite of it. Riley talked about his life at school, about how proud his family was that he was accepted to Columbia. He talked about his friendship with Alvin and his romance with Magnolia, and believed he was no different than any other wide-eyed kid at the university. He explained how his upbringing forged in him a work ethic that drove him to perform well at school, help America's Restaurant and run important errands for Mr. Fabrizi. By the time Malcolm was wrapping up his questioning, Riley was hoping half the jury might want to adopt him.

"Mr. Lynch," Malcolm continued, "let's talk about the day of the car accident. Why were you asked to pick up Mr. Marcellino at the airport?"

"I volunteered to do it. I wanted to fix a mistake I made during a negotiation with one of Mr. Marcellino's employees in Las Vegas."

"And Mr. Fabrizi trusted you to do this?"

"No, not at first. He was angry, but I convinced him I needed to redeem myself."

"A flight attendant testified you were acting strange and that you threw your cell phone in the airport. Is this true?"

"Yes. I did. I was still upset that Mr. Mantano had died in that fire, and that I couldn't get in touch with Mici. Then, someone called and upset me even more. I guess I over reacted. I didn't mean to disturb anybody."

"When you met Mr. Marcellino, did you lie and say you were Edward Fabrizi's son?"

"To be more accurate, he mistook me for his son. And I didn't correct him. I thought I could smooth things over better if he trusted me a little more."

"And then you took him to your old neighborhood?"

"Yes, he wanted to inspect two properties he was purchasing before he and I went off to dinner to discuss business. That's when the accident happened."

"Riley, did you kill Giovanni Marcellino?"

"No!"

"But several witnesses have testified you were laughing at the accident scene. Is this true?"

"Yes it is. I was so upset, so stressed about school, so depressed about the fire at America's, and with fresh adrenaline pumping through my veins from the accident, I think I lost control of my emotions for a moment. I am embarrassed by that.

Birdwell and Calderwood scribbled notes and hung on Riley's every word, and when she stood to begin her cross examination, Riley felt his heart pump and his hands go cold.

Mr. Lynch," Birdwell began massaging her own hands as if sharpening her talons, "do you consider yourself a violent person?"

"No ma'am."

"So when you threw your cell phone and smashed it, that was an aberration?"

"It was a mistake. I'm not usually like that."

"I see. So when you laughed, uncontrollably, while Mr. Marcellino's broken body lay at your feet, that too was an aberration?"

"I was upset. I over reacted."

"Did you over react once again when you pulled a gun on Mr. Marcellino's associate at the Queen of Diamonds Cabaret in Las Vegas?"

"I did not threaten that man with a gun. I swear to God. It was a roll of antacids I bought at a gift shop in the hotel."

"Do you even own a gun?"

"Absolutely not! I hate them. I have never owned a gun in my life."

"Mr. Lynch, do you recognize this?" Calderwood held up a transparent bag containing one pistol and a box full of bullets. Riley's heart stopped and he felt flush.

"Oh no," Riley muttered loud enough for a few jurors to hear him.

"This gun was stored in the same kitchen in which your roommate testified you enjoyed whipping-up those old Irish dishes of yours. It was found by the police during a search of your room. Can you tell the court where you got it?"

"It's not mine. It belongs to my roommate Alvin."

"Your honor, please accept this into evidence as item 27B. Mr. Lynch, could you explain to the court why then if it belongs to your roommate, your finger prints are all over it?"

The closing arguments were postponed until the next day and Calderwood and Birdwell had all but brought their Champagne into the courtroom to celebrate. As Attorney General, Calderwood had stayed in the background for most of the trial, allowing his brash, aggressive attorney to do the dirty work. But now with the conviction all but a certainty, he pulled rank on the impetuous Birdwell and elected to deliver the closing remarks himself, to benefit his legacy and re-election bid. Birdwell had exposed Riley's throat; Calderwood would now lean over and rip it out.

Calderwood stood and adjusted the vest of his thousand dollar suit, tightened his silk tie and cleared his throat. He was tall and thin and youthful, with a manicured goatee, a look more akin to a movie set than a courtroom. When he sashayed across the room to the jury box to begin his comments, he flashed a cool white smile and the women on the jury couldn't help but swoon a bit. He even appeared to pose for a moment in front of the courtroom artist as he made his way to the jury.

"I can't help but be a little jealous of this jury today. You have been offered a tremendous opportunity to extend a public service to your community that will save lives and make the world a better place. Behind me sits a hardened, loathsome and evil individual. If you look at him, you may be fooled by his meek demeanor and believe that he is a victim of circumstance. He isn't and it's an insult to my and your intelligence. Rather, he is the epitome of evil. He is the element that our police and public servants worked so hard to clean out of our community. Listen to what the evidence tells you. Riley Lynch is a man who has grown up in a family atmosphere of crime, used his intelligence and God-given abilities to forge alliances with the great mob leaders of yesteryear, and used that influence to seek out and destroy an adversary he considered a threat to his way of life. And he chose to make that hit in public, in the middle of the day, in front of innocent men, women and children like a 21st Century Al Capone. What more proof could we present? Don't expect the modern mob capos to have their affiliation tattooed on their forehead..."

Calderwood performed for some time. As the last syllable of Calderwood's address left his lips, Malcolm hopped and with aggressiveness he hadn't shown at any point in the trial so far. Malcolm charged past Calderwood so fast he rushed into his arm spinning him around. Malcolm pointed his index finger at the jury box as if they were under arrest themselves and spoke fast. It was Malcolm's moment of great theater.

"When you go to the store to buy a jigsaw puzzle, you expect to open the box and find hundreds of pieces that all fit together to create a nice picture. But what if... what if instead you took one piece from a hundred different jigsaw puzzles and tried to assemble them?

You'd find that most of the pieces wouldn't fit. But you would also find that some of these random puzzle pieces, through nothing but coincidence, did in fact fit together. And if you had enough pieces from enough puzzles, you would eventually create a completed puzzle. But what would the picture on the puzzle show you? The picture wouldn't make sense, and you might struggle to find some pattern among the different colors. And then along comes someone like Ms. Birdwell, or Mr. Calderwood, who says, 'Hey, that's a picture of a devil! Don't you see it?" And though you struggle and squint so hard, you just can't seem to make it out. But they are confident and very persuasive, and you also fear and hate devils, and they explain that if you don't see this devil something bad will happen. You want to see the devil so badly it pains you. You want to be helpful and agreeable because you are a good person and you don't want bad things to happen. After several days of listening to them badger and explain all the unrelated pieces, you concede and believe you can really see the devil, content in your mind that it is best for everyone if you do.

Riley Lynch did not murder Giovanni Marcellino. But the unrelated puzzle pieces the prosecution has assembled might make you think he did, and might even make you want to believe it even when the pieces don't begin to show it. They are prosecutors who make their reputation from convictions, not truth. There is a wonderful comfort when things fit together in a recognizable pattern for us – the way Hollywood or convention tells us they should. But real life is not like that. Do not allow yourselves to be led by fear or how you would prefer the pieces fit together. Trust your eyes and your intellect, and take refuge within the facts from this raging storm of deception and coincidence."

TWENTY-THREE

The ceiling inside each cell of the Souza-Baranowski Correctional Center is high, a dull gray and hard to see. Yet enterprising former prisoners found ways to etch their initials and other bits of graffiti into the ceiling tiles for posterity, immortalizing the time they spent in the ten by twelve foot cell. Riley lay on his cot each afternoon and stared up at the artwork, forever etching the designs into his permanent memory, wondering how the former tenants of his cell managed to get themselves all the way up there. A prisoner with an unlimited amount of time on his hands can be enterprising.

Each day, as he lay there fully awake yet with his eyes closed, he would replay the moments from the surreal end of his trial over and over again in his mind. It would start with the jury foreman declaring him guilty of first degree murder, then follow with a shriek from the gallery behind him from his sister Erin who he didn't even know was there. That moment was followed by the joyful and creepy embrace between Calderwood and Birdwell as if they were long lost lovers on a Parisian holiday. He remembered the handcuffs tearing into his flesh as they were reaffixed to his wrists, Malcolm's despair, and the deep and painful frown displayed on Tammy's face as he was led past her and out the door. He remembered seeing the press conference being set up on the courthouse steps in a driving summer thunderstorm, lightning flashing and torrents of water creating impromptu rapids flowing into the street. He remembered people with umbrellas shouting his name from behind a barricade like he was a rock star. He remembered being cold, sweaty, wet and sick to his stomach all at once. As miserable as it was, he wanted to remember that moment forever as his last moment in the outside world – a world that had insulted and discarded him, relegating him to a human trash heap.

Inside prison he was a celebrity, though most of the other inmates showed him a wide berth. He meditated on the old conversations he had with Mr. Mantano and Mr. Fabrizi when they would share their disdain for mob wannabes – those feeble-minded tagalongs who enjoyed all the sexiness and prestige of being a member of the mob, and played the part to a tee without ever having proven their muster. Riley was no mobster, but he had been exposed to the lifestyle, and it was a persona he could easily adopt and use to his advantage in prison. If society wanted to label him a criminal, he would oblige and act the part the way the world expected it to be portrayed.

He learned a lot in his first year behind bars. One thing that surprised him was the unwillingness of other prisoners to be assigned to his cell. It wasn't that they were afraid to be hurt or murdered, it was that Riley's reputation had taken on a life of its own, and they didn't want to be caught or associated within his sphere of influence. After months of complaining and disruptions, prison officials acquiesced and provided Riley a private cell of his own. It was a shocking move that Riley not only appreciated, but showed further evidence of his alleged power. Prisoners were convinced his aura must reach into the office of the warden himself. Riley's new persona had become so believable – his walk, manner of talking, unemotional responses to violence – that even an occasional prison guard would be fooled and visit to ask for certain favors on the outside.

"Mr. Lynch, do you think you could find a job for my brother-in-law?"

"Mr. Lynch, I think my wife is screwing around with some guy. I want to put a scare into him..."

"Mr. Lynch, my son was arrested. He was set-up. Do you know a lawyer who..?"

Riley accepted a prison job in the kitchen, and preferred the early morning shift to gain access to the better quality food before it was pilfered and stolen by the staff. It was here Riley befriended Mikeé Evans – a colossus of a man who was serving a five year sentence for his participation in an illegal gambling operation but was hopeful of parole soon. Riley's friendship with Mikeé was instant, and the two became inseparable. Inmates trying to make a name for themselves by harassing Riley not only had to put up with his army of loyal, ragtag cohorts, but they also had to go through his three-hundred fifty pound sidekick to boot.

Riley's meetings and correspondence with his attorney Malcolm Ward became less and less frequent as the months rolled by. After the conviction, Malcolm had fired off a serious of motions and appeals to the court that had all been denied. He was still working angles and trying to negotiate with Attorney General Calderwood, who had been re-elected and was more cooperative, but the time for serious negotiation had long passed. Malcolm swore to Riley that he had a team of good people working on the case almost around the clock, but as time wore on, Riley believed him less. Riley also learned Malcolm had taken on a few new cases, likely clients who could pay their bills, which funded his frequent junkets out of the country. Malcolm had also become a celebrity on his own, popular on the college lecture circuit, and television talking head whenever another first-class mob story popped up. Malcolm contributed to his own image as much as he could by keeping the legend alive. It was great for business.

The only feature of prison life Riley enjoyed was the mail. His brothers and sisters wrote often, and he was able to rekindle closeness to them that he hadn't felt since he was in high school. He believed he had mended all fences with Erin and Meghan, who both wrote him once a week and he enjoyed following their life stories like a television serial, anticipating the next episode in every arriving envelope. Erin had married herself off to a doctor from New Hampshire who she met at an AA meeting. She said they were very much in love and looking forward to starting a family, and she wanted to name her first born Riley after him, in his honor. After all, he had become a Southie legend. Meghan had worked her way up to not only manage her restaurant, but several others and was now making decent enough money to rent her own house in the more affluent Boston suburb of Natick, and was scrimping to save enough money to buy it outright. Siobhan didn't write as often but stayed in touch with her sisters, and Riley learned she had been able to regain custody of little Brian – who was now much older and going to school at the same elementary school he had. They said Brian was very smart and had a bright future ahead of him, maybe even college someday like his smart and famous uncle. Siobhan had forged a warm friendship with Malcolm, and stayed involved with Riley's appeals and legal proceedings. She limited her writing about it for fear she was raising Riley's hopes and then dashing them, again and again. Riley's good spirits were tantamount in her mind, as she knew from personal experience what he was feeling. She knew the depression ahead of him was inevitable. Sean wrote least of all, and would reveal nothing about his personal life, but would update Riley on how the Sox or Pats were doing once in a great while. Ryan, however, wrote long missives from his parish in San Carlos, Nicaragua every week. The letters which rambled on for pages were impersonal, and read more like revelations of his soul than a letter to an incarcerated brother. It was evident the criticism levied at Ryan at trial stung him, and his letters reeked of guilt and a search for atonement. Maybe he was hiding something after all.

Riley never heard a word from Magnolia or Mici.

But the letters that surprised Riley the most were from fans. His crime and its coverage, coupled with Malcolm's continual, shameless self-promotion, had made him a cult star of sorts. Countless websites had been created either to profess his innocence or celebrate Marcellino's elimination with Riley portrayed as the savior of the masses. A week didn't go by where he wouldn't receive at least one marriage proposal. Riley saved the more entertaining fan letters for laughs, and his good buddy Mikeé – who had no family and never received letters – enjoyed them more than anyone. His loud, guttural laughs would echo and bounce down the cell block, annoying guards and causing even the most hardened and violent criminal to turn his head to the wall and snicker.

Mikeé brought one particular steamy letter out to the recreation yard one day, reading it aloud, to the entertainment of a handful of prisoners. Mikeé's laugh was infectious and as he read each sentence, the laughing escalated. Throughout, Riley stayed within his cool, dour character and wouldn't flinch. Mikeé took it as a personal challenge to get Riley to crack before the recreation hour ended. The battle raged on for some time.

"Riley, you are the goddamn devil." Mikeé declared. "I know you have a sense of humor in there someplace. I am taking you down, man."

Riley didn't respond, but shot him his best Fabrizi imitation of disgust and boredom, and stared off into the yard with his arms crossed as if in thought about something important.

"He's a fraud. A fucking fraud!" A voice pierced the air from behind. Riley refused to turn around, and acted aloof, knowing that he couldn't show any outward sign of emotion. The affront was not the first attack on his status, there had been many who wanted to prove their strength and establish their creds by taking a shot at him. He came to expect it almost as part of the daily routine. He also accepted that his act might someday get him killed.

"Man, you need to calm down," Mikeé told the stranger, pumping out his chest as he spoke. The rest of Riley's impromptu gang stood ready to assist.

"Oh, I'm calm alright," he said. "You know who you got here? A fraud. A waiter. A pussy Ivy League mob wannabe. You're all a bunch of fools following this loser."

The stranger was asking for serious trouble, and Riley turned with his head held high and looked down his nose at the man. Riley recognized him instantly. It was Armand. But Armand's face had been disfigured, he was missing an eye and his face displayed a thick, deep purple scar that ran from his forehead to the corner of his mouth. He was a wretched sight, and even the most hardened among them found it difficult to look at him for more than a moment. Armand and Riley had never enjoyed much of a relationship back at Americo's. In fact, Riley couldn't recall any more than a handful of conversations he ever had with the guy. Armand always seemed content to stand in Lorenzo's shadow and let Lorenzo do the talking and complaining. But now there was no one to protect Armand, and his defiance against the new order of things was about to get him in serious trouble.

"Why don't we take Quasimodo here for a little walk?" Mikeé offered with an ear to ear smile. "We'll set him straight on how things run around here."

"Wait a minute." Riley interrupted. "I used to know this guy."

"I'm not as pretty as I used to be." Armand answered, defiance still clear in his tone. "Should I bend down now and kiss your rings, or your skinny Irish ass, your highness?"

"Armand, what the fuck is your problem? I haven't seen you in a couple of years, and you show up and disrespect me like this." Riley struggled to stay in character.

"Don't give me that tough guy mafia bullshit, I know you and I know better. I was sent here to find you, to bring you a warning.

There are a lot of people from Marcellino's organization looking to bring you and your friends here down a peg. They might even have a full contract on you by now. They're still pissed off that you killed him. If I wasn't stuck in this hell hole for the next thirty years, I might slit your throat myself for the fun of it. Did you think you could kill a top guy like Marcellino and there would be no repercussions? There are friends of ours all over this prison system, and they're gunning for you."

"So you want me to believe you are part of Marcellino's organization, huh?"

"You can believe whatever the hell you want to believe. My proof is this scar, if you have the balls to look at it. I fucked-up the hit on Marcus Etruscan and the bosses were pissed when the police found the body. This is how I paid for my mistake. This is what real organized crime looks like and does to people. See it? Take a good hard look, you coward. Let it sink in to that big brain of yours. If you hadn't killed Marcellino, I might never have been arrested for that murder either. A lot of shit went down that day."

Riley looked at Armand and remembered hiding at the carwash in Hoboken watching Armand and Lorenzo run away after Hanratty was killed. All this time Riley had questioned Lorenzo's outside connections and loyalty to Mr. Mantano, and it turned out that Armand was the real traitor all along. Riley remembered what Lorenzo told him about Armand not coming to work the night of the fire at Americo's, and he thought about holding Mici in his arms the night she was attacked by Marcus and his thugs. It was now clear that Armand had been the facilitator.

"Well Armand, things are different now." Riley answered, still cool and aloof. "Mikeé, I think it's time you had that chat with our new friend here."

Armand's one good eye widened and the group circled around. Riley held his head high, turned and walked in the other direction of the yard. He heard Armand scream and swear in fear of his life, but knew that this time at least, the punishment would be only verbal as none of the men wanted to risk committing an assault in broad daylight. But after Mikeé and his friends were done with their threats, and he knew how persuasive they could be, Armand would never be able to relax again. If violent physical encouragement was needed, it would be handled inside at a carefully selected moment out of the sight of guards. And if Armand became too much trouble, Riley could just order the hit himself and be rid of him. He would think about it.

Back in his cell, Riley paced back and forth and considered Armand's threat. He wasn't surprised to hear Marcellino's organization was looking for retribution. Though he was surprised it had taken them this long to reorganize after his demise. To a prisoner, the biggest threat to one's psyche and existence is time. Seconds feel like minutes, and minutes feel like hours. When a prisoner is worried about something, like impending violence, his internal timepiece slows down even more. Riley looked back up at the initials carved into the ceiling once again. He needed a plan to get himself immortalized on those tiles very soon. He feared his time on this Earth was running out.

TWENTY-FOUR

Riley rolled over and attempted to right himself in the back seat of the Town Car as it raced away from St. Peter's Center. From the passenger's seat, Agent Manning spun around and grabbed him by the back of the neck, pressing him down against the leather seat so he would not be seen.

"Keep your head down, Lynch! I'll tell you when it's safe to get up."

Riley looked up and out the window, and he could see the sun beginning to emerge from behind a dark cloud. It was becoming a sunny day after all, and the sky was a crisp, clean blue beneath the menacing overcast. He could just see the car's rear view mirror from where he laid, and he was able to catch brief glimpses of the other two black Town Cars following them, also moving at a high rate of speed attempting to keep up. The three cars stayed together until Agent Manning shouted an order into his two-way radio, and then the two cars behind them sped off in different directions. The gaggle of news vehicles followed them, allowing Riley's car to escape onto a course all its own. The agents smiled and sighed in relief.

"Son of a bitch. I think that maneuver worked." Wills said.

"Keep your eye out for any stragglers," Manning added. "We have to make certain we don't pick up a tail."

"Is anybody going to tell me what the fuck is going on?" The nervousness and shock within Riley was wearing off, and was being replaced by anger and belligerence. Manning allowed Riley to sit up now and his clothing was twisted and wrinkled. Riley struggled to adjust himself.

"No, we can't tell you anything. You will be meeting with your attorney in a little while. We have been instructed to let him answer your questions." Manning said.

"Can you at least tell me where we are going?" Riley was persistent, and had no reason to trust either of them.

"There is a campground about a half hour from here in Concord. Our instructions are to deliver you there. That's all we are authorized to say. Now shut up and stop asking us questions." Neither Wills nor Manning showed any indication they would crack.

One of the agents flipped on the radio, and Riley looked through the window and watched the world ramble by. As angry and confused as he was, the bright vivid colors of the outside world were an uplifting sight for his repressed eyes, and the brightening sun produced a dull ache in the back of his skull. But he didn't mind. Riley felt like a puppy who wanted to stick his head out the window to experience every sight, sound and smell all at once. He noticed the air even smelled fresh and clean as they approached more rural communities, and the fragrances tickled his lungs. Feelings of joy and pleasure were creeping back into his character, and it became more of a challenge to wrestle them down so he could remain cold blooded and evil.

The car weaved up a paved one-lane road through the compound of the Walden Acres Campground. The car passed a white, A-framed camp store, a fish pond, a large in-ground swimming pool, several one room cabins, and even an occasional gray squirrel. The camp was closed and deserted as November was not peak season for New England camping, and most everything was locked up and in hibernation in preparation for the forthcoming winter. Riley marveled at how thick and tall the pine trees were and how the brown carpet of spongy needles appeared to have been placed by design, offering a softness and peace to the rolling landscape. It reminded him of the woods behind the park near South Boston where he would lose himself and play as a child. The car pulled forward and stopped in front of one of the interchangeable cabins. Riley could see steady puffs of black smoke rising from the field stone chimney, and waiting at the front door stood his old friend and attorney Malcolm Ward.

Riley jumped from the car and jogged over to meet Malcolm, and the two embraced. The two agents had also exited the car and stood on either side of the vehicle with their doors hinged open. Both of them placed one hand on their holsters and scanned the horizon of the compound as if expecting an unwelcome intrusion.

"How are you Riley? I can't tell you how excited I am to see you!" Malcolm was almost jubilant, an uncharacteristic smile was cut through his white beard and moustache, and he couldn't seem to stand still.

"Malcolm, what the hell is going on?" Riley looked toward the cabin window and he could see two eyes peering out at them from between the curtains. Riley tensed and jumped back. Marcellino's organization had deep influence. He started to worry this could be a set-up, and as loyal as Malcolm had been to him and his family, he respected no one was immune to influence. Riley feared he was about to be hit, and Malcolm sensed Riley's increasing anxiety. Riley's head spun around from side to side looking for signs of trouble and he prepared to flee. He felt naked without Mikeé or his posse standing guard.

"Relax, Riley, you look like a wreck. Everything is good. In fact, everything is great. I have worked out a deal with the district attorney for your immediate release. You are free, Riley. It's over. It's all over." Malcolm was downright bubbling, but Riley wasn't buying it.

"What do you mean a deal?" Riley knew the DA wouldn't just acquiesce and let a convicted mob murderer walk away, especially after the public bludgeoning he endured. There had to be a catch. "And who is in that cabin?" Riley remained on his toes, alert and suspicious.

"We're going to go inside in just a moment and I'll explain everything, I promise. But first, I want you to promise me you will relax. I understand your emotions must be out of control and all over the map right now, and you must be confused. That's understandable. Everything will make sense in a few minutes. But before we go inside, I wanted to give you a chance to catch your breath and compose yourself. You have been through quite a lot."

Malcolm reached forward with a bottle of water, "Do you want a drink of water?"

"Malcolm! I do not want a drink of goddamn water! I want to know what is going on and who is in that cabin?" Riley could feel his blood pressure rising and wanted to lash out.

"Ok then, fine. Suit yourself."

Malcolm opened the door but the room was dark. Riley placed one wary foot inside the entryway and was snatched and tackled in an instant by three young women -- Siobhan, Magnolia and Mici. The

303

four of them collapsed as one to the soft carpet of needles on the floor of the pine grove at the front of the cabin, and all three girls shrieked, cried, laughed and carried on, their voices merging and winding together as each tried to out-squeeze the other two.

"Girls, girls! Don't kill him now!" Malcolm laughed. "It was way too much work to get him out!"

All Malcolm could see of Riley were his two big round eyes and the top of his head. Despite Malcolm's begging, the girls wouldn't let go. Instead, they squeezed harder, crying, sobbing, laughing, rambling and carrying on even more than before.

"OK, OK that's enough," Malcolm pleaded. "Tammy, please come here and help me."

From inside the doorway, Tammy appeared from the shadows. Her eyes were as moist and face just as flushed as the others, and she and Malcolm untangled all the arms and legs and helped everyone get back onto their feet. The group giggled and dusted themselves off while they walked together into the warm cabin and Malcolm latched the door behind them.

"So Riley, what do you think of your all-star legal team?"

Riley's shock was clear on his face and he had stopped breathing while his eyes darted back and forth among the faces of the four giddy girls. They were all in different stages of smiling, crying and sobbing, and Riley felt his own sinuses begin to throb, and then he noticed he could no longer see. His eyes filled up with fluid and he too was now crying, bawling like an infant. Years of frustrated, pent up emotion had found a fissure in his resilient soul and was erupting to the surface. He couldn't make it stop -- didn't want to. It felt wonderful. Riley fell back onto a sofa and buried his face in his hands and laughed through the tears. Magnolia latched onto his right arm, and Mici onto his left. Siobhan scooted up behind him and wrapped her arms around his neck like she used to do when they were kids and kissed the top of his head still adorned with a few stray pine needles. Tammy sobbed and smiled from the large table in the middle of the room. Another round of howling ensued. Even the stoic Malcolm brushed his eyes with his handkerchief and had to clear his throat more than once.

When everyone seemed to be calming down and breathing again, Malcolm spoke to Riley first.

"Riley, your friends here have been hard at work since the end of your trial to find a way to secure your release. You owe them everything. I would say you owe them your life."

"I don't know what to say, Malcolm. I am in shock. But why didn't you tell me all this was going on? Why was this such a big secret?"

"That was my fault," Siobhan confessed. "We didn't know if it was going to work. I didn't think it was a good idea to get your hopes up if our deal fell apart. As a matter of fact, this was our third attempt at executing a plan. The first two didn't work out so well."

"And I have to apologize for the lack of personal notice to you about today," Malcolm conceded. "I got word through one of my other clients that your life was in danger. Marcellino's organization put a contract out on you. We had to act fast. We didn't have the luxury of time, and we only had a few days to react and get you out of there."

"There's a hit ordered on me? What's the difference then if I'm in there or out here? They will find me somehow."

"Maybe not, let me explain." Malcolm walked about the cabin with his hands clenched behind his back like he was in a courtroom at trial. "The district attorney has agreed to enter you into the federal witness protection program right away, today in fact, in exchange for certain key information to help them close several other open cases."

"But I don't know anything about any crimes," Riley insisted.

"First, you need to tell them everything you know about the Hanratty murder in Hoboken. They are under a ton of political pressure to solve that crime."

"So I will become an informant?"

"Yes. And shame on you for not telling me about Hanratty before the trial. It might have made a difference." Malcolm wagged his index finger in his direction, scolding him like a parent reprimands his naughty child.

"How did you even find out that I knew anything about Hanratty getting shot at that car wash?"

"Alvin told me," Magnolia bragged. "He told me everything. You know I have my ways of finding out things when I need to."

"And," Malcolm continued, "you will also be delivering the details to the district attorney's office on three other unsolved mob related murders as well."

"How can I do that? I don't know anything about any other murders."

"I would expect not, Riley. However, Carmine Mantano did."

Riley spun around and looked at Mici. Her smile was unrelenting, and pride and joy continued to sparkle in her eyes.

"Mici? You know something about these murders?" Riley was astonished. Mr. Mantano had worked so hard to shield her from all the wickedness in the world. It was unlike him to involve her in his affairs from the old days.

"*Nonno* told me everything. Tammy here has all the information you need." Tammy reached between them and handed Riley a blue folder full of papers. Mici continued. "You will have to read all this information in detail and know everything about each case. I know how smart you are, and what a good mobster you have been in the prison this last year. I think you will convince them of everything."

Riley shuffled through the folder, scanning the papers.

"Wait a minute, oh no! No," Riley declared, hopping up from the sofa. "I won't do this! You want me to accuse Mr. Mantano of being involved in these other murders? I can't pin this all on him. I know he didn't do this, and I won't tarnish his memory and insult Mici with these lies. He was a great man -- a wonderful man. I loved him as much as I would have liked to have loved my own father!"

"It's alright, Riley." Mici stood to console him. *Nonno* doesn't mind."

Riley paused and looked into Mici's eyes. His suspicious mood had returned, and he placed each of his hands on her shoulders.

"You said he doesn't mind? Do you mean to say he is still alive? He didn't die in that fire?"

"Oh Riley, don't ask me such things," Mici blushed as she answered, looking away. "If he were here right now, you know he would want you to do this. Please Riley, please, you can trust me on this."

Riley shuffled and scanned through the papers again. The detail on each of the incidents he was to study was thorough and impressive, and he recognized the handwriting from the paperwork in the office of Americo's. He knew only Mr. Mantano could have put all this together. He looked at Mici once more who had still not stopped smiling at him. He decided he didn't want or need to know the details at that moment. Besides, if he believed Mr. Mantano was alive it would implicate Mici. He tried to convince himself that it didn't matter.

"So what you expect me to do is meet with the district attorney and reveal all this information to him in exchange for a new identity and a new life. Is that correct?" Riley asked, trying to re-focus.

"That is correct. It's all set in motion. Calderwood got a lot of mileage from your conviction, and he needs more." Malcolm answered, a little surprised by Riley's resistance.

"But I'm not a murderer, nor am I a member of any organized crime family. I never have been and I never will be. The Riley Lynch that just got out of prison was all an act -- you know that Malcolm, in fact you all know that. Now you're asking me to lie, deny my heritage, renounce who I am and forget everything I have ever stood for? Why?"

Malcolm was blunt. "For your freedom."

Siobhan leaned over and spoke next. "Riley, you know who I am, but the courts think I am someone else. We are the people who matter to you. We here know the truth. We don't care who the rest of the world thinks you are."

"And what if I refuse?"

"Then the agents outside will put you back in the car and take you back to prison. I would guess you will survive two, maybe three more days at best before one of Marcellino's thugs finds you." Malcolm smiled, the irony of the blackmail not lost on him.

Riley pondered the offer and smiled. There wasn't much to think about.

"OK, so you've got me. So where the hell am I going to live?"

"My mom and dad had an idea about that," Magnolia chimed in. "You loved the garlic farm so much they suggested California, near San Francisco. They provided a list to Malcolm of all the farms and friends they have in and around Sonoma and the Napa Valley -- they know a lot of people out there. You have plenty of business experience running the restaurant and LSE's finances, so we decided it would be a good fit with all the vineyards, stores and cafes out there. You will get a new name and a new job. It's all being arranged as we speak."

"Magnolia, did I hear you just say your parents were involved in all this?" Riley asked.

"You betcha. They couldn't help it. They loved having you around that Spring you came to visit me. Mici stayed with us for a couple of weeks last summer, and my mom and dad heard us talking about your case. We thought California was a wicked cool idea."

"Mici stayed with you at the farm in Ticonderoga... for a couple of weeks?" Riley was dumbfounded. He hoped no one saw his jaw hit the floor.

"Oh, the countryside was soooo beautiful, and Mr. and Mrs. Fair are very nice people. We had so much fun!" Mici explained. "I am going back to visit them after Christmas and Magnolia is going to teach me how to ski." Mici then stood and gave Magnolia a hug. "We have become such good friends. Magnolia is so sweet!"

Of all the odd things that had happened to Riley in the last few hours, this was, by far, the oddest.

"You'll have to let me know when that happens," Riley kidded. "I think I would pay good money to watch that ski lesson."

"I'm sorry, Riley." Malcolm interrupted. "Once you accept this deal and admission into this program, you will be prohibited from having any contact with your family, friends or old business associates ever again. Riley Lynch will disappear and cease to exist. It's part of the deal."

Riley had spent the last half hour feeling his heart expand and re-inflate from its sad, decrepit, wilted state. And with one sentence, Malcolm had shot a cannon ball through it.

"No! That's not fair! I thought I lost you all forever, then I get you all back, and now I have to lose you all over again?"

"That's why I arranged this meeting here today." Malcolm explained. "I didn't think it was fair that these girls worked so hard on your release and never get to see you again -- you mean a lot to them. You are supposed to be under constant guard and confinement right now. We are not allowed to stay here long. This brief little meeting is their celebration, too. And I am sorry, but it's also their final goodbye."

Riley felt the tears welling up all over again, and wanted to reach out to hug someone, but couldn't decide who. Siobhan solved the problem for him by hugging him first.

"I have to go now, Riley. I have to get back to Brian and his babysitter. I wish you could see him and play with him. Sean says he acts just like you when you were little. We are all going to miss you. I can't wait to tell Erin and Meghan I saw you and that you'll be safe and everything worked out so well. I love you, Riley." Siobhan ran through the door with her hand over her mouth and out of sight. Before he had time to say anything or call for Siobhan to come back, he noticed Mici and Magnolia stand together on a cue from Malcolm and gather up their coats and belongings.

"I can't believe you made me care about something this much," Magnolia told him, placing her head on Riley's chest one last time. "I promise to hate you the rest of my life for making me love something so much again." Magnolia looked up and winked at him as they held each other.

"And I will miss you, too." Mici gave him a warm, sweet kiss on his cheek, and she stroked his hair. "I don't know how I will get by without my best friend in the world. You will be in my thoughts and memories every day. And please don't ever forget me. Goodbye, Riley." The two girls left together, arm in arm, sobbing.

Riley strolled over to the fireplace and tried to gain his composure, feeling the white hot flames singe his arms even as he stood a few feet away. He tried to catch his breath. His heart, though broken, had never beat faster. Then Tammy rose and stood next to Malcolm.

"Tammy here," Malcolm explained, "has been the quarterback of this operation right from the beginning. You need to know how hard she has been working on this case right from the first day of your arrest, and pushing me to get the deal done for your release. She has been an inspiration."

"My God, thank you, Tammy. You have no idea how much I appreciate what you all have done... what you have done." Riley looked into her face and eyes. He was transported like magic back years to their childhood when he would gaze at her from across the classroom. In her pretty, honest eyes he still saw the angelic round face that he fell for at age thirteen. She looked back at him now as a beautiful and confident adult, except his loving affectionate gaze was now being returned.

"I think I'll go outside for a cigarette," Malcolm said.

"I didn't know you took up smoking." Riley responded.

"I haven't."

Riley walked to Tammy and took both her hands in his. Tammy's head tipped to one side, letting her dark hair fall off her shoulders, and she smiled.

"Tammy, thank you. You have no idea how many times over the years I thought about you. I would wonder where you were, what you were doing, and even what you looked like. I had the biggest crush on you when we were kids."

"Yes, I know. I had the biggest crush on you, too. Did you know that?"

"I had no idea. I assumed you didn't know I was alive. Until that day we met by accident on the train, I wasn't sure you even knew my name."

"Oh, Riley, I'm sorry. That was no accident. I had been looking for you for months. My father would send me into New York on courier errands for his clients. I had heard through the neighborhood that you were accepted to Columbia. After I took care of my errands, I would walk around the Columbia campus hoping to bump into you, making it look like a coincidence. I was always thrilled when my father would send me to the city. And I enjoyed New York. I thought you were brave to live there alone. I was so proud of you."

"You came to Columbia? To see me?"

"Yes. And then one day I got lucky and I saw you come out of the library, and I followed you to that cafe on Amsterdam Avenue. You would sit in the corner by yourself and just watch people. You looked so lonely, I wanted to run over to you but I couldn't work up the nerve. And then one day I followed you all the way to your calculus class and walked right up to your seat in the lecture hall. Just as you looked up, I chickened out and ran away. I had no idea what to say. And then on that day we talked on the train, I had been waiting outside your dorm room for an hour and followed you to Penn Station. I was terrified to approach you so when I saw you fall asleep, I just took the seat next to you and waited."

"Oh Tammy! I saw you at Columbia! I saw you at the cafe and in the study hall. I thought I was going crazy."

"No, I'm the crazy one. I was the one out there stalking you." Tammy lowered her head and placed her hands over her face. "I am so humiliated!"

"Oh, no... don't be embarrassed. I'm thrilled. I always wanted to get to know you. I would think about you all the time, and how you were getting along. I am guessing I would have stalked you right back if I had thought of it. So then I guess you heard I was arrested and volunteered to help with my legal defense?"

310

"No, not exactly. After the train ride, I kept my eye on you. You always seemed to get in so much trouble. I wanted to help you, I wanted to be your guardian angel."

"What do you mean?"

"For example, when your mother died...."

"You notified Columbia! You told my professors! Didn't you! You're the one!"

"I'm sorry, don't be upset." Tammy stepped back and crossed her arms.

"No, I'm not upset. I am so grateful to have someone looking out for me. I never knew."

"And then when the police were looking for you over that stolen rental car...."

"It was you! You paid that bill."

"The one time I sucked up the nerve to knock on your dorm room door, you weren't home. Your roommate Alvin seemed very nice and he invited me in. He was hitting on me when the police came by looking for you that day. He was supposed to tell you I dropped by. He told me at the trial that he forgot."

"Goddamn that Alvin!"

"And then a few weeks later, I contacted Malcolm and asked to be his legal intern while I was at Northeastern..."

"Then it was you who sent me those tax documents for Mr. Fabrizi! And I'll bet you had something to do with getting Siobhan out of jail, too."

"I worked on Siobhan's case for a long time. It was complicated. But I found a social service non-profit that helped with her legal fees so you didn't have to pay anymore."

"My God, Tammy. I don't know what to say. But why me? I'm not that important. I'm not that good looking. I'm stupid, I'm lazy and I'm neurotic. I'm even a convicted murderer. I am worthless. And look at you, you are so beautiful, so smart and so successful. Why me?"

"It's because of this."

Tammy reached into her pocket and pulled out a piece of old, gray wrinkled paper. She handed it to Riley. He opened it with care so as not to tear the frayed edges any more than they already were.

Hi Tammy, how ya doin? I love you...

It was the love note he started writing years ago and never finished or delivered. It was to be his offer to take Tammy to the South Boston Middle School dance, but he chickened out and destroyed it, or so he thought.

"Oh my God. I remember this. Where did you get it?"

"It was on the floor in front of my middle school locker all those years ago. I knew it was from you because I saw you drop it, and it was in your handwriting."

"I did write it. And you saved this all these years? I was writing to invite you to be my date at the middle school dance and I was afraid to give it to you."

"Riley, you know what kind of loser I was when I was a kid. No one liked me and no one wanted to be my friend. My loneliness ran deep, to my core, and just the simple act of going to school every day filled me with a terror I can't describe. I would throw up every morning in the bushes near my house when I walked to school. Then I would get in fights and get beat up all the time. The scratches and bruises never hurt that much, but the pain I had in my soul was excruciating. And you were the only one who ever looked out for me. You were always trying to distract that crazy, mean Yvonne girl and all the other troublemakers to keep me safe. You cared. And then when we went our separate ways to different high schools, my depression reached rock bottom. I wanted to kill myself, and decided I would. I would get out my dad's razor blades and sit in the warm water in the bathtub and think about slitting my wrists. I would also look into the medicine cabinet at my mom's prescriptions. I hated myself. And I would always bring this note with me. If it didn't cheer me up, I told myself, I would end it all that night, right then and there. But the note always did manage to cheer me up. It told me there was someone out there who loved me, who cared about me, who believed I was important. Someone cute and handsome who liked me just because I was me. Riley, you don't know this but you saved my life -- many, many times during those years. Compared to that, sending you a few tax documents or making a few phone calls on your behalf didn't seem to me to be such a big deal."

Riley started to reach out to hold her. He wanted to kiss her and feel her soft, red lips against his. But he stopped cold.

"Oh no, oh no!"

"What's wrong?"

"I am standing here falling in love with you just like I am thirteen all over again. Look at me. I'm sweating and my hands are shaking. But in a few minutes, you will be walking out that door like the others and I will never see you again. I can't do this. Like Malcolm said, this is our last goodbye!"

"No, no Riley. It's not. I have my law degree now. I was admitted to the bar. Malcolm has appointed me to coordinate your relocation with the attorney general's office. I will be the one person from your old world who will be required to stay in touch with you."

Riley paused to let it sink in.

"Then you will be allowed to see me again?"

"Yes."

"But will you be allowed to come to California?"

"As often as I want to."

Riley exhaled. He then walked over to an old radio sitting on the window ledge and switched it on. The small cabin filled with soft music which joined the sweet smell of the burning pine logs. He took a deep breath and guided Tammy's hands into his own once again.

"Tammy, there is something I owe you. Something I should have asked you years ago."

"What is it?"

"You were too special and beautiful to sit home the night of that dance. Of all the things I have been accused of doing, that was my one true crime, and we have both been paying the price ever since. Imagine what different paths our lives may have taken, how different they would have been, had I found the courage within me to ask you that day? I need to make it up to you right now, before it's too late. I will not make the same mistake twice. Tammy... will you dance with me? Now?"

Riley held out his hands, Tammy nodded, and they embraced. He held her as tight as she held him. They rocked back and forth together and became one with the gentle music. Riley lifted her chin to gaze into her eyes, and he kissed her. He had dreamed of that very moment since he was thirteen, and it felt so much better than he had imagined it would. For Riley, he sensed something at that moment shift in the cosmos, and for the first time in his life, despite the trouble and serious problems that stretched ahead of him, he felt content that all was right with the world. Tammy reached down and grasped the old crumpled note that was now lying on the table. To

Riley, the note represented an adolescent expression of love and a lifelong want of acceptance. To Tammy, it was the tender beacon that guided her through her darkest hours, and represented a hope for her future. Tammy opened the note and read it one last time.

"I don't think either of us need this anymore." And Tammy tossed it into the flickering fire.

As the note burned and its smoke and ash spiraled and fluttered up the chimney, Malcolm stood outside in the crisp November sunshine and cracked jokes with two FBI agents. At the St. Peter's Center, Mikeé had tricked the local pizza joint into sending over ten pepperoni pizzas for all the ex-cons, and Mrs. C was furious. In South Boston, little Brian was looking out the window anticipating the return of his mom, hopping up and down each time a different red car rounded the corner. In New York, Mr. Edward Fabrizi was chewing out his new financial advisor while consuming a meatball sub, and considering leaving big business for good. In Los Angeles, a young college graduate named Alvin was at an important job interview, asking the pretty receptionist in the waiting room for a date.

And in a cabin at a deserted campground, under the canopy of an old emerald-green pine grove, witnessed only by the orange flames of a crackling fire, two young lovers misplaced long ago rediscovered each other. And then Tammy asked Riley for a second dance.

###

AUTHOR'S NOTE

Confessions of the Meek and the Valiant is a work of fiction. All characters are figments from my own imagination and are not portrayals of any one person living or dead. If you believe you are, or know of a person I am attempting to portray, then I am confident in my assertion that you are wrong. In addition, many of the ideas, concepts and themes present in the book have been languishing in my mind for decades and are guaranteed to be one hundred percent original.

If you have read this far, I want to thank you for the investment of time you gave to my first novel. I hope you enjoyed it. Writing a book has been both a dream and a goal for twenty-five years. Part of me wishes I had written it long ago, but once it was complete, I realized why I had waited so long -- I had simply not lived enough. To steal from Abbie Hoffman (who I once picked up at the airport for a personal appearance in 1984) don't trust any novelist under thirty.

Steven R. Porter
Spring 2011
Harmony, Rhode Island

ABOUT THE AUTHOR

Steven R. Porter is a self-employed writer, marketing consultant and former Director of Advertising and Public Relations for Lauriat's Bookstores, Inc. Steven is also a frequent speaker and lecturer on Internet job search technologies in his role as a consultant for www.JobsinRI.com. He and his wife Dawn are active volunteers in their local community and reside in the village of Harmony, Rhode Island with their two children Thomas and Susannah.

Confessions of the Meek and the Valiant

Available Summer 2011
Confessions of the Meek & the Valiant
(a novel)

Coming Late Summer 2011
The Kanc
(a short story)
A bitter elderly couple are caught in a violent winter storm while driving along New Hampshire's Kancamagus Highway.

Coming Fall 2012
Manisses
(a novel)
The fictional history of an unassuming rock on a small, New England island and the natives, explorers, pirates and charlatans who rely on it.

For updates and information about forthcoming and new releases, visit:
Website: http://www.StevenPorter.com
Blog: http://AlongtheVillageGreen.wordpress.com/
LinkedIn: http://www.linkedin.com/in/stevenporter
FaceBook: http://www.facebook.com/people/Steven-R-Porter/554283413
Twitter -- http://twitter.com/stevenrporter
Email: Steve@StevenPorter.com

Made in the USA
Charleston, SC
23 July 2011